Beneath the Surface

Published by BookLocker.com, Inc., Bradenton, Florida.

Printed in the United States of America.

BookLocker.com, Inc.
2014

First Edition

Dedication

To the words and wisdom and spirit of Bill W. This book would simply not be possible without that inspiration.

Acknowledgements

I would like to thank a number of people for helping me on this journey. It takes a village to write a book. My village includes beta readers and advisers: Mike MacDonald, Andy Redmond, Barb Stewart, Robert Way, John Baglow, Lynne Tyler and Denise Zendel. And Evan Cathcart for his copy editing at the end.

Special thanks to my partner, Joan. Thank you for putting up with me thinking and talking about Windflower long enough so that I could get it out of my head and onto the page. Thank you for sharing this journey with me.

Also by Mike Martin

The Walker on the Cape

The Body on the T

Chapter One

Sgt. Winston Windflower froze when he saw the big bold letters on the front of the newspaper… "Champion Rower Found Dead" and below that the bright, beautiful face of a young woman smiling back at him.

Amy Parsons, the story said, had come to St. John's from Grand Bank, Newfoundland to attend university. And not two weeks ago, she had been a member of the rowing crew that captured the Women's Championship Race at the St. John's Regatta.

That was just a month ago, thought Windflower, who had missed the annual rowing competition and general St. John's celebration, but had seen the crews practising on Quidi Vidi Lake since spring for the big event. He had smiled and waved at many of them as he ran the Quidi Vidi loop every morning when he was in St. John's.

That happened to be a lot since Sheila, his girlfriend, had been undergoing rehab at the Miller Centre in the city after a serious car accident last year. He made the trek from his temporary post in Marystown every second week, and had lots of opportunities to watch the rowing crews take their practice spins on the lake in the east end of St. John's.

He wondered if he had waved to Amy Parsons during his morning runs. Probably, he thought. The best crews were regulars on the 'pond' as the lake was known. But he didn't think he had ever met her.

Mike Martin

The newspaper had few details on the death, other than the blanket statement that the police were treating this death as suspicious. Windflower phoned someone who would certainly have more information, his former second-in-command, Corporal Eddie Tizzard, who was now heading up the Grand Bank RCMP Detachment.

"Tizzard," answered the other RCMP officer.

"Good Morning, Corporal," said Windflower.

"Sarge," said Tizzard, "Good to hear from you. Are you in St. John's?"

"I am," said Windflower. "I'm heading back to Marystown this afternoon. Did you hear the news about the Parsons girl?"

"We had a call from the Constabulary last night," said Tizzard. "They're sending someone over from St. John's tomorrow to talk to the family, and asked for our help in setting up some interviews."

"Did they tell you anything?" asked Windflower.

"Not much," said Tizzard. "They seemed to have more questions than answers. They did say that they're conducting a murder investigation, and that's about it."

"That's more than what I read in the paper," said Windflower. "Do you know her family?"

"I went to school with her brother, but we were on different paths, if you know what I mean. He smashed up a couple of cars in high school and then went on to motorcycles. The last I heard about him he was in

Toronto, causing more trouble. The girl's father is dead; must be 10 years ago at least. Died of cancer, I think. The mother is still alive and lives in a cottage out near the L'Anse Au Loup T. I'm going to drop out and pay my respects before the locals arrive," said Tizzard.

"Keep me posted if you hear anything else. Okay, Eddie?" said Windflower.

"Will do, boss," said Tizzard.

Windflower tucked his cell phone back in its holder and left the RCMP dormitory. He gazed across Quidi Vidi Lake towards the boathouse where there were still crews coming and going from their excursions on the pond. Like many mornings there was an apron of fog encircling the lake making it hard to see exactly what they were doing, above or below the water. But Windflower was sure that many of them, especially the female rowers, were wondering what had happened. He imagined them thinking that it just as easily might have been one of them lying dead on the stone cold examination table in the coroner's office.

He shivered and pulled his jacket tight as he began his own tour of the fog-shrouded lake. Windflower ran the Quidi Vidi Loop every morning when he was in St. John's. He could catch the trail at the bottom of the hill below the RCMP dorm and for 20 minutes or so he could follow the pathway around the lake.

At the bottom where the water drained into the ocean through the 'gut', he could look back over the area called Pleasantville. It had once been an American Air Force Base, Fort Pepperell, but now like most of St.

John's, it was being rebuilt and modified to meet the housing needs of a growing population.

As soon as the weather warmed enough, sometimes in April, but more often May, you could watch the rowing crews move onto the water from their dry land training to get ready for "The Races", as the St. John's Regatta was commonly known.

"The Royal St. John's Regatta", its official title, was the oldest organized sporting event in North America, dating back to the early 1800's. Windflower knew this because his friend, Ron Quigley, a self-described expert on all things St. John's, had told him all about the Regatta.

According to Quigley there had been a history of various kinds of boat races in St. John's Harbour for many years before the actual Regatta was established. These races featured rowing and sailing competitions between the crews that crowded St. John's from May to September each year for the cod fishery. In the Regatta's early days, the races took place in the harbour and sometimes were spread over two or three days. At some point the event was moved to Quidi Vidi Lake. Then one day, the first Wednesday in August was officially declared as Regatta Day in St. John's.

Today the Regatta was still about "The Races", but it was also a public holiday and a time for great merriment in a city that was renowned for its ability and stamina to party. Fifty thousand people or more would gather around Quidi Vidi Lake each year not only to watch the rowing competition, but to play games of chance and to eat, drink and generally be merry, especially at the giant beer tent. Windflower had no great desire to partake in this celebration, and hadn't even been in town when the event was held this year.

He was back in Marystown, where he was serving as a special assistant to Inspector Kevin Arsenault. He'd been doing this job for just about a year now, and while he liked both Arsenault and his work, he was thinking that it was about time for him to move back home, at least the home he had adopted in Grand Bank.

As he circled the lake, he made a mental note to talk to the Inspector when he got to Marystown later that day. That reminded him as well to go and see how Sheila was doing before he headed back. He sped up his pace and was back at the RCMP house in what seemed like a flash. Fifteen minutes later he was showered, dressed and in his car on the way to the Miller Centre.

The Miller Centre, originally built as a military hospital in 1851, was named after an influential Newfoundland doctor, Dr. Leonard A. Miller. It later became the General Hospital in St. John's and in 1978 it was transformed into a special care health facility providing continuing care and rehabilitation services. It still had some of the external vestiges of an old-time hospital, but it had been renovated and updated in recent years to become the leading vocational and occupational rehabilitation facility in the province.

Windflower's girlfriend and the love of his life, Sheila Hillier, was an in-patient at the Miller Centre. Since a dark night almost a year ago she had been actively engaged in putting her mind and her body back together after a brain injury, an aneurism and a stroke. Her life had completely changed from a confident and independent businesswoman, to a nearly dependent and partially paralysed wreck. The process of recovery had been long, tedious and painful, but Sheila was almost ready to start her life all over again. So was Windflower.

Sheila had regained the use of all her faculties and facilities and, apart from a slight limp in her left leg, she felt nearly as good as new. The problem was that she wasn't sure that she wanted to just pick up her old life where she had left off.

As she gazed out the window of her room on the fifth floor of the Miller Centre, she saw Windflower's RCMP cruiser pull up and head towards the visitor parking lot. She smiled as she saw him reappear walking towards the front entrance. He cut a fine figure, as her Grand Bank friends would say, in his tall brown boots and scarlet tunic. She was glad he was here because she had some very big news to share.

Windflower bounded into Sheila's room with a broad smile and Sheila laughed easily at the sight of her happy Mountie. He started to speak, but she covered his mouth with her hand.

"I'm going home," she said.

"Wow! That's great," said Windflower. "When did you get the good news?"

"Dr. Francis told me this morning. He's developed a second stage plan that I can do on my own, and I only have to come back here every three months so that he can measure my progress," said Sheila. "I am so happy."

"Me, too," said Windflower. "You've worked so hard for so long."

"I couldn't have done it without you, Winston," said Sheila. "You have been my rock."

"Happy to help, ma'am," said Windflower. "So, when do you leave?"

"I can pack up and leave Friday," said Sheila. "Will you be able to come back and get me?"

"Absolutely," said Windflower. "I'm going back to Marystown this afternoon and it shouldn't be a problem to swing back around on Friday."

"Great," said Sheila. "I'm going to get Marie to go over and clean up my house in Grand Bank this week so it will be all ready for me when I get back."

"By the way, there's a bit of bad news in the paper today. A young woman from Grand Bank, Amy Parsons, was found dead in St. John's," said Windflower.

"Oh my God," said Sheila. "Amy used to help out in the café a few years ago when she was in high school. Her mother must be out of her mind. Do they know what happened yet?"

"There's nothing in the paper, but I've got Tizzard checking it out in Grand Bank," said Windflower. "The Constabulary from St. John's are on their way out there to talk to the locals today."

"Poor Amy," said Sheila. "She was a hard worker and pretty determined to make something out of her life. She had so much to offer the world, and now it's over."

"It is pretty bad news all around," said Windflower. "If I hear any more I'll let you know."

Sheila nodded and Windflower wrapped his arms around her and held her tightly. "I'm glad you're coming home," he said.

"Me, too," said Sheila and she kissed him gently on the cheek as he left the room. "Call me later," she shouted at his back, and with a wave he was gone.

Sheila watched him retrace his steps to the car from her window and then sat at her desk to review her list of things she had to do before she left the Miller Centre on Friday. She scribbled a new item at the top of her list. Send flowers to Peggy Parsons in memory of her beautiful daughter, Amy, now lost forever.

Chapter Two

As Windflower drove across St. John's he kept his wits about him. The city had some of the country's worst drivers; not because they sped or drove recklessly, but because they just didn't pay attention. He knew that you always had to watch out for the children on bicycles, but the real challenge was the older drivers who were 'dodging along', code for driving too slow in busy traffic. Or else they would be 'edging out'. This practice which wasn't limited by age or gender involved playing a game of chicken at intersections when you clearly didn't have the right of way, but you kept 'edging out' the nose of your vehicle to try and get the other driver to stop and give you a 'break', by letting you go first.

Windflower didn't think they would play these games while he was driving his RCMP cruiser, but he was wrong. And once, when he failed to slow down suitably to meet the needs of one irate female driver, he felt her wrath rain down upon him with several long, sharp blasts of her horn. He wasn't completely sure, but he thought he got a glimpse of an upraised middle finger as well as he passed his disgruntled fellow driver. He just shook his head and kept going, happy to get out of the crazy St. John's traffic.

When he hit the overpass outside of St. John's that designated the beginning of the rest of Newfoundland, at least according to the city-dwellers, he issued a sigh of relief.

There wasn't a whole lot to see on the highway outside of 'town', but the open country helped him relax and almost always improved his mood. It was interesting, he thought, that this stretch of windswept rock reminded him so much of home; interesting, because it looked nothing like back home.

The Cree community where Windflower came from was set among the mountains and mighty rivers of Northern Alberta, but here there was just a little grass and a few hills. While there might be a little mist in the mornings in Alberta, there was nothing to compare with the constant walls of fog that rolled in from the ocean. Yet, he somehow felt at home here, and for now that was good enough.

His reverie was broken just outside St. John's as he entered one of the new moose monitoring zones.

Wildlife detection systems (using sensory technology to detect the presence of a moose in the vicinity and then triggering a system of flashing warning lights to get drivers to slow down) were brought in a year ago by the provincial government in an effort to reduce the number of moose versus car accidents on the province's highways; contests that the moose almost always won. Windflower wasn't sure about the effectiveness of these new 'moose zones'. But anything that would get motorists to slow down, especially at night and when the light was poor, was always a good idea.

He managed to get through the detection system without any signals or signs of any moose in the vicinity.

Before long he was nearing Goobies and the turn off to the road to the Burin Peninsula. It was the halfway point, and his usual stop to gas up and have lunch at the restaurant.

He was feeling particularly hungry, so he ordered a bowl of pea soup and the pan-fried cod, with mashed potatoes and vegetables.

The pea soup came first. It was the traditional creamy Newfoundland split pea soup with tiny flecks of salt meat and a rather doughy looking dumpling in the middle. Windflower didn't want to fill up on flour so he ladled out the dumpling, applied a heavy dose of black pepper and dug in. The soup was good, if not great, and just as Windflower was enjoying his last spoonful, the rest of his meal arrived.

This portion of his meal was not as tasty as the soup, but the fish was relatively fresh, although a little underdone for his liking. He remembered why he didn't usually order fish at a restaurant, except for fish and chips; he could do it better himself at home. Nonetheless, he ate up all the fish, a few forkfuls of potato and just one stab at the frozen peas and carrots that made up the entire vegetable selection in the eatery. He was at least full when he paid his bill on the way out.

As luck would have it, the bakery lady was just bringing out a fresh batch of homemade molasses raisin bread, so he added two loaves to his bill. One he would offer to Eddie Tizzard as thanks for letting him pick his brain on the Parsons investigation, and one he would keep for himself that would go great with some fresh blueberry jam when he got back to Grand Bank.

But first he had to go to Marystown and check in with Inspector Arsenault. He had been planning to talk to Arsenault about going back to Grand Bank on a permanent basis, and now that Sheila was going to be there, he was even more determined. With that in mind, he drove the next hour and a half to Marystown practising his speech and thinking about the Inspector's inevitable objections.

When he got to the Marystown RCMP, all his planning and thinking went for nothing when he found out that the Inspector had been called to St. John's, and wouldn't be back until Wednesday. He left a message with Louise, Arsenault's admin person that he was going to Grand Bank and would be there until Wednesday, unless the Inspector needed him for anything.

Windflower left the RCMP building, picked up a large double-double at the Tim Hortons drive-thru and pointed his car down the highway towards Grand Bank. As he drove, he could see the fog circling the coastline, almost waiting for an invitation to come ashore.

No, it didn't need an invitation, thought Windflower, and before he got halfway home he and his car and the highway were completely immersed in its damp blanket. Ah, it still feels good to be back, he thought.

Windflower pulled into the first exit lane off the highway and passed the welcome from the Town Council, the replica lighthouse, and the Tidy Town sign. He drove directly to check on his little house in the middle of town. He hadn't spent more than a handful of nights there since Sheila's accident and his assignment in

Marystown, so he wanted to make sure that everything was still okay, especially if he was returning full-time to Grand Bank. He was very surprised when he turned into his driveway to see a window open and his kitchen curtains blowing in the breeze.

He was even more surprised to open his door, smell bacon frying and hear the sounds of someone gently singing in his kitchen. He walked into the kitchen expecting almost anything but the sight of his Uncle Frank wearing a pair of what appeared to be Windflower's long johns and an apron. He was holding what looked like a rum and coke, and a cigarette was burning in the ashtray next to him.

"Winston, you're home," said the other man. "I was just cooking up a late day breakfast or an early dinner. Care to join me?"

Windflower just looked at the scene in his neat little house, frozen, unable to speak. Finally, a few words leaked out.

"Uncle Frank, what are you doing here?"

"I told you already," the other man replied. "I'm cooking up some grub. Do you want any or not?"

Windflower just shook his head.

"No, Uncle, I don't want any food. I meant, why are you here in my house in Grand Bank?"

"Oh that," said Frank. "I sent you a letter telling you I was coming for a visit. Here it is right here," he said, holding up an envelope with Windflower's name and address on it. "I picked up your mail from the Post Office. The lady there was very nice to me."

"What!" exclaimed Windflower, "They let you into my personal post office box?"

"I told them I was your uncle," said Frank. "That is the truth, isn't it?"

"Yes," said Windflower, "But…."

His next few words were drowned out by footsteps from the outside and people yelling hello to his uncle.

"Come on in," said the older man. "The bacon's almost done and I'm putting on the eggs. Grab yourself a drink," he said pointing to a bottle of dark rum on the kitchen counter. "I want you to meet my nephew that I've been telling you about."

Windflower shook hands glumly with the new arrivals, scowled at his uncle, and left his house quickly with steam almost visibly rising from his head. As he left, he could hear voices behind him.

"Is he all right?" asked one of the men. "Should we leave?"

"No, no," said Windflower's uncle. "Don't worry about my nephew. He'll be fine."

Fine, thought Windflower. That's not the adjective I was thinking about.

Still steamed, he drove his car over to the Grand Bank Detachment and pulled up in front. Cooling himself down, he went inside. The first person he saw was the receptionist, Betsy Molloy, who greeted him warmly and moved towards him as if to give him a hug.

Windflower warded off this awkward intimacy by putting out his hand for the woman to shake.

"Betsy, it's so nice to see you. Have you been well?"

"I have, thank you very much and it's great to see you too, Sergeant," said Betsy. "Are you here for a visit or are you coming back for good?"

"Just a visit right now," said Windflower, "But hopefully I'll be back on a permanent basis soon."

"That would be great," said Betsy. "Not that Corporal Tizzard is a bad boss or anything," she said slightly blushing at her mild disloyalty.

"Speaking of the Corporal, is he around?" asked Windflower.

"He is, but he's with somebody right now, a detective from the Constabulary in St. John's," said Betsy.

Just then an inner door opened and Corporal Eddie Tizzard came out. He was in the company of a taller man, athletic build, dressed in a dark blue suit, white shirt, and darker blue tie, which Windflower recognized immediately as the universal uniform of criminal investigators everywhere. Tizzard smiled broadly when he saw Windflower and guided his companion over to meet him.

"Good afternoon, Sergeant," said Tizzard formally. "Let me introduce Detective Sergeant Carl Langmead, from the C.I.D. in St. John's. Here's Sergeant Winston Windflower, head of the Grand Bank Detachment, now on temporary assignment in Marystown."

Both men shook hands and said hello.

"I was going to take Carl for a coffee and a piece of cheesecake at the Mug-Up, if you'd like to join us, Sarge. I hear they might have your favourite," said Tizzard.

"You don't have to ask me twice," said Windflower. "I'm in."

The three men jumped into Tizzard's car and were at the café in a flash.

"Haven't slowed down any, have you Corporal?" asked Windflower.

"This is real police business," said Tizzard with a laugh and held the café door open for the other two men to enter.

Windflower pointed to a quiet table in the corner and soon all three men were enjoying large mugs of hot coffee and slices of the Mug-Up's speciality cheesecakes. Langmead had plain baked cheesecake with fresh blueberry jam; Tizzard had the same cheesecake with his favourite, partridgeberry jam. And Windflower had his dream dessert, peanut butter cheesecake.

When they finished their snack, Windflower told them about the encounter with his uncle at his house earlier. Both Tizzard and Langmead somehow found the spectacle that Windflower described as hilarious and even Windflower was soon laughing at the crazy situation.

Since this was clearly a social part of the day, Windflower didn't ask any questions about the investigation of the visiting detective. But as soon as Langmead had left, Windflower began probing Tizzard for the inside scoop.

Chapter Three

"So what's going on, Corporal?" asked Windflower

"You mean with Langmead?" Tizzard asked.

"That, and why didn't anybody tell me that my uncle was here?" said Windflower.

"Well, your uncle is a character isn't he?" Tizzard laughed, but when he saw that his mirth wasn't shared with Windflower he added, "He told us all that you knew. I think he said you invited him."

"I might have said that he was welcome to drop in if he ever got out this way, but that's not really an invite," said Windflower.

"He took it as one, apparently," said Tizzard. "Anyway, he fits right in with the locals. They even accepted him as part of the crew on the wharf. He loves telling stories and sharing yarns. I even heard him telling stories about you when you were about half as high as the corn, I think he said."

"Oh, great," said Windflower, "I have a crazy uncle going around telling stories about me and my so-called friends think it's great."

"He's been no trouble so far," said Tizzard. "Well, almost no trouble. We had him as a guest one night in the back when he fell asleep in the graveyard on the way home. It seemed safer for the boys to bring him back to the lock-up than to take him home in that state."

Windflower just stared incredulously at Tizzard's nonchalant recounting of these recent events.

"In any case he won't be here long. Not when my Auntie Marie finds out where he is," said Windflower.

"Oh, she already knows, at least according to Uncle Frank. He told me that she might be coming for a visit too," said Tizzard.

"What?" said Windflower, "And did I hear you call him Uncle Frank?"

"He tells everybody to call him Uncle Frank, says he's proud to be related to the best Mountie on the Force," said Tizzard.

"Oh my god," said Windflower. "Save me from my relatives, and my friends!"

Finally, Windflower joined his Corporal friend in having a good laugh about his uncle's unexpected visit. He would deal with that situation later, he thought.

"Do you want to hear about the Parsons case?" asked Tizzard.

"What did Langmead tell you?" asked Windflower eagerly.

"Langmead just got here this afternoon so it was more him grilling me than providing any detailed information," said Tizzard. "Plus, there's always a little tension between us and the Royal Newfoundland Constabulary."

Mike Martin

"Yeah, I've seen some of that whenever there are joint operations in St. John's," said Windflower. "But the people I've worked with have been first rate. It must be because they think we're looking over their shoulders. They don't realize we're usually too busy to notice what they're doing."

"I agree," said Tizzard. "We're all on the same side and Carl Langmead is a great guy, at least to talk to. He told me that they're waiting for the autopsy, but that it looks like murder. He said he saw the body in the morgue, and it had ligature marks around the neck that were consistent with strangulation. She was clothed when they found her and there were no other signs of violence. But he didn't know yet if there was any evidence of sexual assault. She was found near the waterfront in a parking lot on a street called Bishop's Cove. Do you know where it is?"

"Not exactly," said Windflower, "But I think it's not too far from Water Street. As I recall all the 'coves' in St. John's have access to the harbour front from Water Street. Quigley told me that years ago these were places the fishing ships docked to offload their cargo into the merchants' warehouses. What do you think Langmead is hoping to find out by visiting Grand Bank?"

"I'm not really sure," said Tizzard. "I think he's just trying to get a sense of who Amy Parsons was and if there was any reason for anybody to kill her. Even though she hadn't lived here for the last three years while she was in university, there might be some information that he didn't want to miss. I don't think they have much to go on in St. John's, by the look of it."

"Hmmm," murmured Windflower. "Sheila said that the girl worked at the Mug-Up when she was going to high school. Did you know her?"

"No, she was a lot younger than me," said Tizzard. "We didn't have a lot of contact. She was just Shawn Parson's younger sister to me. I would say hi, and she'd blush and run away."

"A real charmer, even back then, eh Tizzard?" teased Windflower. "Have you been out to see the mother yet?"

"I dropped by out there this morning for a minute. The mother's still in shock. I spoke to one of the aunts and told her if they needed anything from us I'd be happy to help. They just want to get the body back so they can have the wake and the funeral. I told them I'd try and facilitate that with St. John's. But other than that there's not much anybody can really do, is there?" asked Tizzard.

"I guess not," said Windflower. "Oh, I've got something for you back in my car," he said.

"What are we waiting for?" asked Tizzard who was almost out the door of the café before Windflower had his hat on.

After giving Tizzard his still-warm loaf of molasses raisin bread from Goobies, Windflower promised to meet up for breakfast in the morning.

It was still light when Windflower walked down the short hill from the RCMP offices to Herb Stoodley's house near the water. As he walked around the back he could see that his friend was still at work. A retired Crown Attorney, Stoodley now spent his "working" hours engaged in painting seascapes, and as Windflower noticed from his work today he was getting quite good at it.

"Afternoon, Herb," said Windflower. "Hope I'm not disturbing you."

"I am quite content to be disturbed," said Stoodley, "And even happier to see you. Sit down, my son, while I put the kettle on."

Herb Stoodley had been Windflower's friend almost from the first time they met, and even though they were generations apart in age, they shared a kindred spirit and a love of the law.

It didn't hurt either, that over the years their partners, Stoodley's wife Moira, and Sheila Hillier, had also become close friends. Moira, in fact, was running the Mug-Up café while Sheila was in St. John's. Windflower had learned to listen to and trust Herb Stoodley. In turn, Stoodley was grateful to have an intelligent police officer that he could mentor in the myriad twists and turns of law enforcement.

"So what's new, Winston?" he asked as he poured boiling water into two cups and added a tea bag to both, Newfoundland style.

There was nothing better for many Newfoundlanders than a strong cup of black tea, the blacker and stronger, the better. Most took it without sugar, as did Stoodley and Windflower, but some, like Herb Stoodley, also added Carnation condensed milk. It was almost like white syrup that you poured liberally into your tea, and it was an acquired taste, one that Windflower had never acquired.

"Well, Sheila is getting out of the Miller Centre, which is good news," said Windflower.

"That's great news," said Stoodley. "She has certainly come a long ways since the accident: almost as good as new from the sound of it."

"Better, I think," said Windflower. "Her mind is certainly sharper than ever. I'm not sure that she'll be willing to settle for living in little Grand Bank after this. She keeps talking about wanting to travel and see the world. She even spoke about going back to school and finishing her degree. That got postponed when her parents got sick and she had to stay home to look after them."

"Sounds pretty exciting," said Stoodley. "I know that she's talked to Moira about continuing as manager of the Mug-Up, and you know Moira, she's just delighted. She really loves being active again. I just have to do more walking to keep off the calories from those desserts she's always bringing home."

"And of course there's my house guest to deal with," said Windflower. "I assume you've met my uncle."

"Oh, yes, Uncle Frank," said Stoodley with a smile. "He's a real character. Except for the lack of a Newfie accent, you'd swear he was born here."

"You could call him that, a character," said Windflower. "Fortunately it appears that he has been on his best behaviour so far, which you may have noticed is still not very good."

"Well, he likes to sing," said Stoodley laughing. "I can tell when he gets out of Tuckers Lounge at night because he serenades the whole neighbourhood. He particularly likes sea shanties, but I think I heard the first verse of 'The Ode to Newfoundland' the other night."

"I'm glad that everyone is being entertained by my relative," said Windflower. "But I still wish at least one of my friends had told me he was here."

"What, and spoil all our fun?" said Stoodley, laughing again. "It's fair game to make fun of the Mounties here in Newfoundland. Haven't you ever heard about Aunt Martha's sheep?"

Windflower just smiled weakly at his friend's joke. He had heard that story, which was turned into a song about a group of hungry locals in Carmanville who stole a sheep from one Aunt Martha and were in the process of cooking it up in a stew when a Mountie arrived at their door. The locals pretended they were eating moose stew and invited the RCMP officer to join them. The joke was that the Mountie joined in the feast and believed it was moose stew. The punch line of the song was that in fact "the Mountie ate the most."

"I think that Uncle Frank will be singing a different tune once my Auntie Marie finds out what he's been up to," said Windflower.

"Didn't you hear?" asked Stoodley, again smiling, "She's on her way here too. At least that's what Uncle Frank says."

Windflower just shook his head, thanked Stoodley for his cup of tea and started off for home.

When he arrived, the house was peacefully quiet, but a table load of dirty dishes and glasses, an empty rum bottle and a full ashtray stood between Windflower and his bed. His bed, he thought, I hope I still have a bed. He rushed into his bedroom to find Uncle Frank's belongings strewn everywhere, his dressers and closets open and a large pile of dirty laundry lying on the bed, another on the floor.

"Shoot", Windflower whispered under his breath, holding back the other stream of vile oaths that lingered at the back of his throat.

In a silent rage he went back to the kitchen where he worked off his mass of negative energy by washing all the dishes, cleaning up the glasses and dumping the contents of the ashtray down the toilet. He then opened all the windows in the kitchen and the living room and swept and scrubbed the kitchen floor. After he had vacuumed, he went back into his bedroom and threw all the dirty clothes into two duffle bags for laundry tomorrow, and opened the windows wide. Then he closed the door to his bedroom and went into the small storage room, where he spread his sleeping bag on the floor.

Sleep did not come easy, but eventually Windflower did drift off. His last conscious act was a prayer to Creator whom he asked for the patience and strength not to kill one of his last remaining uncles.

Chapter Four

When Windflower awoke he was surprised that it was light, and that he had slept through the night. He expected to be woken by some version of a sea shanty or old country western song, his Uncle Frank's favourites when he was in his cups. He went to the bathroom and noticed that his bedroom door was closed, but a loud snoring noise was almost shaking that side of the house. Luckily, he had a change of clothing in his overnight bag, so he didn't have to wake the snoring giant in the bedroom.

He had a quick shower and shave. He also did a brief prayer and smudge, a morning ritual that involved burning some of his sacred and medicinal herbs. This was part of his traditional Cree culture, and it helped to remind him who he was in the world. Soon he was on his way out the door to meet Tizzard for breakfast at the Mug-Up.

The morning air was beginning to hold on longer to the coolness of the night, although the fog that had followed Windflower home was now being burnt off by the sun. A beautiful late summer day in paradise, Windflower thought to himself, as he strolled the short walk to the café.

Tizzard was already there, wide awake and joking with the few early morning locals who made the Mug-Up their first coffee pit stop. Windflower was surprised to see Herb Stoodley with an apron on at the cash, and waved good morning. Soon Stoodley was by with his own personal greeting: a steaming hot cup of coffee.

Tizzard joined the two men and both ordered the breakfast special of fried eggs, bacon and homemade toast with fresh jam. He and Windflower also decided to share an order of toutons, dough fried in fatback pork to a golden brown, and then smothered in molasses.

"So how's Uncle Frank this morning?" asked Tizzard with a mischievous twinkle in his eye.

Windflower forced a smile and said, "He's sleeping it off. I'll deal with him later. Let's just enjoy our breakfast, okay?"

Tizzard took the hint and sat quietly drinking his coffee until his breakfast arrived. Then both men were happily engaged in devouring the plates of food in front of them, each saving the best part of their breakfast, the toutons, until last.

"I know I shouldn't eat this, but it is so good," said Windflower as he mopped up the last drop of molasses with his remaining sliver of the toutons.

"Don't worry about it," said Tizzard. "As my old man would say, a man's gotta' eat."

"Yeah, but just remember we are what we eat," said Windflower. "And right now I feel like I've eaten a hot air balloon. I guess that makes me a blimp."

"So I hear that Sheila is coming back," said Tizzard. "Does that mean you are coming back here too?"

"I was going to talk to you about that," said Windflower. "I would like to, but I have to convince Arsenault to let me go. I don't want to upset the applecart here either."

"Well, don't worry about me," said Tizzard. "I'm grateful for the opportunity but I could do without the headaches and the paperwork. And the Mayor is driving me crazy with his ideas."

Windflower laughed.

"I miss being here too," he said. "It's been fun doing some different work in Marystown, and it made it easier to get back and forth to St. John's, but I'd rather be in Grand Bank on my old patch again."

"That's good," said Tizzard. "So all you got to do is convince the Inspector."

"Yeah, wish me luck with that. He's pretty fixed in his thinking and he likes getting his own way. I think he was happy to have me there to off-load some of the work that he didn't like to do. Anyway, I don't have to worry about that until tomorrow. Today I'm taking the day off," said Windflower.

"That's a luxury," said Tizzard. "If you get bored, drop by and say hello to everybody. They'd be happy to see you."

"Thank you, Corporal," said Windflower. "I'm going to say hello to Herb, our new waitress, and then it might be an earlier morning than planned for my hung-over uncle."

Tizzard smiled and waved goodbye as Windflower went up to the cash register to pay.

"Easy on the insults," said Stoodley. "I get a lot of points from the boss in back for this early morning shift."

With that, Stoodley's wife Moira peeked her head around the corner from the stove and waved good morning as well.

"Morning, Moira," said Windflower. "The food is great, but the beauty of your serving staff has gone down quite a bit since my last visit."

Both husband and wife laughed, and Windflower was soon on his way back home to his little house just up the road.

When he got there, the noise from the bedroom hadn't dissipated, so he pushed open his bedroom door. His uncle was still solidly asleep and rather than wake him, Windflower just took the two duffle bags of laundry from the room, found his spare roll of quarters, and walked the short distance to the laundromat.

Windflower actually liked doing the laundry. It gave him time to think and to read, and luckily he had brought his new book with him.

It was *The Golden Egg*, by one of his favourite mystery writers, Donna Leon, and featured Commissario Guido Brunetti. It was set in Venice like all of the Brunetti mysteries, and one of Windflower's joys was reading about the Italian meals that were a staple of Leon's books. He savoured over the mouth-watering descriptions of risotto, scampi, calamari, lamb and thick, rich Italian pastries for breakfast. Windflower was in heaven just reading about it. Maybe he should take Sheila on a holiday. They could go to Italy, even to Venice, and try some of this food that he drooled over whenever he read Donna Leon's books. Now, thought Windflower that is an appetizing idea.

A few hours later, with his laundry dried and folded, he was feeling relaxed both from his time reading, and listening to the gentle hum of the dryers. He was also getting a little bit hungry from reading about Brunetti's lunch of carpaccio and involtini of chicken breast and thinking about what to have for his own lunch.

He lugged his duffle bags back to his house where his uncle was up, but barely, and moving about even less.

"Good morning, Uncle," said Windflower in his RCMP voice, the one he used when he wanted someone making a disturbance to both realize that resistance was futile, and to go gently into the back of his cruiser. Or else.

"Morning, Winston," said his uncle, much quieter than his antics of yesterday.

His head hung down to his chin as he slouched in his long johns, Windflower's long johns, looking every bit of his 63 years.

A good sign, thought Windflower. He must be really hung over.

"Uncle, I am glad you came to visit but I need you do a few things for me. First of all, no smoking in the house; it stinks and it's dangerous, especially if you are drinking. Secondly, no drinking when I'm not here, and you can't have your friends over drinking either. I trust you, but I don't want strangers here when I'm not," said Windflower.

"They're not strangers, they're my friends," said his uncle. "I can see that I'm not wanted here. I'm leaving. I'm going to St. John's as soon as I can get a taxi out of here."

And with that he retreated back into his bedroom, actually Windflower's bedroom.

Windflower pleaded with him from outside the bedroom to come out and discuss the matter as adults, but there was no sound from the other side. Finally, he gave up, at least for now, and decided to make the most of his day off on a nice September day in Newfoundland.

He found a few plastic containers and a bucket, and made himself a thermos of tea and a thick cheese and lettuce sandwich with plenty of hot mustard on his molasses raisin bread. Then he was off for a spate of blueberry picking.

He had heard that one of the best places to pick berries was up on a place called "Farmer's Hill", where the old radio and television tower had been built. Years ago, it had been an area where some of the locals had grown root vegetables and oats for their animals. Now it had been supplanted by Sobeys, where everybody went to get their fresh fruit and vegetables. Maybe, because the land had been cleared before, it was now a prime place for blueberries. Windflower didn't really care why. He just hoped there was enough for him to give a few cups to Herb Stoodley so that he could make him some jam to get through the winter. And enough for Sheila to make him a blueberry buckle.

There was now a new nature trail in Grand Bank. It started at the back of the Grand Bank Health Centre and meandered its way up and around the brook and past the dam. The dam kept the brook from overflowing its banks further down, and there was a side path leading up to the transmission tower. Along the way, there were benches to rest on, a myriad of settings and views, and an opportunity sometimes to see hares, an occasional moose or even a black bear.

One sighting of a young black bear had already been reported in the area. The local man who saw it said that 'it was bout 250 pounds and I probly coulda rassled it but e probly coulda given an ard slap up the ead.'

Windflower wasn't interested in the wildlife today. He was focused on the berries, and along the trail found a few small patches and got to work filling his bucket. But he was still looking for the mother lode of berry patches. He was sure it was up the hill and further away from the lazy pickers at the bottom.

So he left the trail and headed up towards the tower. There, near the top and just inches away from the trail he found what he was looking for, the Holy Grail of berries. There were so many blueberries that Windflower didn't know where to begin. Finally, he just spread out his picking materials and sat and relaxed for a minute. He gazed back down the hill at the little town of Grand Bank where people and cars scurried like ants. He also remembered that he had not even said thank you to Creator this morning.

He didn't have his smudge kit with him, but he could still do his prayers. So there, in the abundance of nature's beauty he thanked Creator for his many blessings and prayed for Sheila and his relatives, especially his Uncle Frank, that they may find a good path to travel. He also thanked his ancestors, his mother, father and grandfather, who were no longer with him, that they would guide him on his journey. His final prayer was for Mother Earth who was nurturing him today with blueberries; that people would learn again to love and respect her for the gifts that she gave them every day.

After his prayers were finished Windflower spent the next hour in the quiet and reflective task of berry picking. Once he was halfway through his goal of a full bucket, he took a break and had his cheese sandwich and tea.

There's nothing better, he thought, than having what the Newfoundlanders called a "boil up", in the woods. Refreshed from his meal Windflower returned to his task, and was soon back walking down the hill with his brimming bucket of fat, ripe blueberries.

At the bottom he cleaned the berries, removing stalks and stems and the occasional misfit berry and divvied them up into portions. Half a bucket would go to Herb Stoodley for jam-making and the other half would be split between a portion for Sheila's blueberry buckle, and some to just sprinkle on top of cereal or toast or even just as a snack. Feeling particularly pleased and proud of his efforts, Windflower returned home, just in time to see Foote's Taxi speed away from his house with his Uncle Frank sitting in the back, already engaged in telling a story to his fellow passengers. I just hope it's not about me, thought Windflower, but knowing his Uncle Frank, he was pretty sure it was.

Chapter Five

Windflower stepped inside and stripped the bedding from what was once again his bedroom. He put on fresh sheets and pillowcases and opened the windows wide.

Next he went over to Herb Stoodley's to drop off the blueberries destined for his friend's jam-making operation, but there was no one home.

Probably helping Moira at the café or getting supplies, thought Windflower.

He placed the half bucket of freshly-picked blueberries in the unlocked back porch. That was another reason to like Grand Bank. No one locked their doors here because they didn't have to. That task completed, he went back home where he was quite happy to settle in for a few more hours of reading his Donna Leon book.

As he read he began to get hungry, so he started scrounging about his refrigerator looking for some suitable supper materials. There wasn't a lot there. Just some left over bacon and a half-green package of cooked ham that he threw into the garbage. Trying the freezer, he was more successful. There were a number of frozen entrees and soups that he had salvaged from previous meals or scrounged from neighbours. Taking out a large tub marked "Sheila's turkey soup", he knew his problem was solved.

He put the soup on the counter to start the thawing-out process and then he remembered that he hadn't called Sheila. He picked up his phone in the living room and knew from the beeping noise that he had unheard messages; six in fact. Three were telemarketers offering him a variety of products, even a free vacation if he could just call back with his credit card number. The other three were from his Auntie Marie calling him about his Uncle Frank. The first was warning him that his uncle was on the way, the second was wondering if he got there, and the third was a strong suggestion to send him home. Windflower laughed at the final message and made up his mind to phone his Auntie later. First, he had to talk to Sheila.

"I was wondering what happened to you," said Sheila when she answered the phone and realized that it was Windflower.

He explained that the surprise arrival and equally surprising departure of his uncle were his main excuse for not calling.

"Have you heard any more about Amy Parsons?" asked Sheila once she was satisfied with Windflower's explanation and that he was okay.

"Just that an investigator is here from St. John's," said Windflower. "Eddie Tizzard went over to the house to see the mother and I guess everybody there is pretty upset."

"Oh my God, the poor mother," said Sheila. "I don't know how you cope with the loss of a child, no matter how old they are. Do you know when the funeral is?"

"Not yet," said Windflower, "but I'll ask Eddie when I'm talking to him again. Is everything still okay for Friday?"

"Everything is good on my end. I met with the therapist this morning and I've got my three-month plan. I am so excited about coming home. Did you talk to the Inspector about moving back to Grand Bank yet?" asked Sheila.

"Arsenault was away when I went to Marystown, but I'll talk to him tomorrow when he's back. Tonight I'm looking forward to sleeping in my own bed for a change. The house in Marystown is fine, but there's nothing like home for a good sleep," said Windflower.

"Tell me about it," said Sheila. "I can't wait. So, I'll see you on Friday, about four?"

"I'll be there," said Windflower. "Have a good night. I love you."

"Love you too," said Sheila as she hung up the phone.

Windflower put his bowl of turkey soup in the microwave to heat it up and cut himself a thick slab of molasses raisin bread. Enjoying these few moments of solitude, he casually spooned out the turkey soup from the container and washed it down with his bread, butter and a bottle of iced tea from the fridge.

Ah, the bachelor life, he thought, no need to even dirty a bowl.

His supper complete, he ran himself a hot bath and finished off his Brunetti book for dessert. Then he climbed into his clean bed and waited for the sleep angels to carry him off.

But that night was not going to be the sleep of angels. Windflower had two dreams, both unsettling. And both of which gave him reason to think about the strange things that might be going on in his subconscious. Something was definitely going on in there.

The first dream which woke him was terrifying. He found himself wandering in a graveyard shrouded in fog. At least he thought it must be a graveyard, even though there were no headstones. It wasn't a Christian graveyard he finally figured out, but an Indian one.

Then he saw her. Her hair was long and stringy. Her eyes and face were hollowed out, and her body was wracked with sores. She was crying, wailing at Windflower. She held out her hands to him.

"Help me," she said. "I am the last of my people. And I am dying."

And as she faded into the mist Windflower awoke, shaking.

He got up and went to the bathroom. By the time he got back to bed he had calmed himself down.

"It was only a dream," he reminded himself.

Even though he knew he was tricking himself and knew that all dreams meant something, it was enough to get him back to sleep. And he did sleep well for almost all of the rest of the night.

The second dream that woke him was even more startling than the first. In this dream he was lying in a hotel bed. There were no lights on, but the moon was shining in through the window so he could see all around him. He was naked and hot, steamy even. And lying next to him was a woman with her back to him, also naked. But when he reached over to touch her, she was cold, and stiff, and very dead. As he reached over to pull her towards him to see her face, he woke up.

That dream was enough to end his sleep for the rest of the night. Even though it was barely light he got out of bed. He had to. He showered and shaved as the sun rose in the East. Yesterday's fog had blown back out into the Atlantic. The morning was cool but was slowly giving way to a little warmth from the sun.

Windflower decided to walk down to the beach and up to the Cape overlooking Grand Bank where he could offer his morning prayers and smudge. There was nobody up in town yet, except for a few yard dogs that seemed to know Windflower needed quiet this morning, and saved their yapping for later prey. Windflower arrived at the beach just as the sun peeked a pink eye over the Cape, also known as the Grand Bank Head.

He walked along the beach with its multi-coloured rocks in every imaginable shape and size. He passed through the mossy barrens until he came to the path at the foot of the Cape, a path that would lead you all the way to Fortune, like the boys used to do years ago to get to the Saturday night dance at the church hall. A few hundred yards up the hill was a large rock that had rolled down from the top in another millennium. It looked as if it was a planned stop on the way to the summit. This was where Windflower stopped this morning to carry out his daily rituals.

He paused and took a couple of deep breaths as he looked down over the still-sleeping town of Grand Bank. He took his smudge bowl and eagle feather out of his knapsack and laid them on the ground. Then he carefully measured out a portion of his smudging herbs: wild tobacco, a little sage, an even smaller portion of sweet grass that he guarded closely because he had yet to find a source for more on the island, and a heap of moss that he had heard called reindeer or caribou moss. He liked the latter because it fired up quickly and generated a quick smoke from his medicine.

When his bowl was lit and smoking Windflower began his smudge by thanking his ancestors who he hoped would travel with him and give him advice on his journey. In particular he honoured his grandfather who had been a chief of his nation and had given him the eagle feather when he first left home. He also remembered his mother and father who were no longer with him. Then he took the eagle feather and directed the smoke over his head to clear his mind and give him wisdom, over his heart to give him strength and courage, and under the soles of his feet to help him stay on a good path.

Windflower then allowed the smoke from his smudge bowl to burn freely and offered it as medicine to Mother Earth who was supporting all creatures to walk in this world, and to Grandfather Sun who held up the sky and who, along with Grandmother Moon, was the caretaker of hopes and dreams.

After he was finished he packed up his supplies in his knapsack, pausing before he left to place a little tobacco on the ground for his uncle who was now alone in St. John's. Then he laid down a little more for the spirit of the dead girl and her family, to bring them all peace in this difficult time.

His morning practice complete, Windflower walked in silence back to his house, not passing a soul and grateful not to have to speak to anybody. He made himself a quick breakfast of scrambled eggs and toast with a cup of fresh blueberries as his morning treat. He was still bothered by last night's dream adventures but at least he had quieted his mind, his spirit, and now his stomach. He packed an overnight bag to take with him to Marystown and was soon on the highway heading to work and his meeting with Inspector Arsenault.

It was a quiet morning on the highway as well, and the only other car he saw until he came to Garnish was another RCMP cruiser. It was zipping along when Windflower spied it coming over an approaching rise in the road. Judging by the speed he thought it might be 'Fast Eddie' Tizzard but when it got closer, he realized that it was a female officer. He waved and smiled, and the other officer waved back.

That's interesting, thought Windflower: Tizzard didn't say anything about having a new, and female, officer on staff. He also wondered how the officer was being received, not only in the Grand Bank detachment, but also in the community.

Windflower made great time on the highway and was early enough in Marystown to be able to stop and get a large double-double at Tim Hortons. There were already a few other Mounties in the coffee shop when he arrived and he said a brief hello before he sat down to enjoy his first coffee of the morning. He found a two-seat table in the window and sipped his coffee as the real morning rush began in Marystown, at the Tim Hortons drive-through window.

Chapter Six

Windflower finished his coffee, drove his cruiser over to the RCMP building, and parked in the back. He walked up the stairs to Inspector Arsenault's office. The Inspector's administrative assistant, Louise, was on the phone and waved good morning to Windflower, indicating that he should sit down. When she finished her call, she told Windflower that Inspector Arsenault wanted to see him at 9 a.m. Windflower nodded his agreement and went down the hall to his office.

RCMP Inspector Kevin Arsenault was Windflower's boss, and had been his supervisor for about two years. Arsenault was initially responsible for the southeast coast of Newfoundland, which included Windflower's Grand Bank detachment, but his area of responsibility had grown in recent years to include almost all of the island portion of the province where the RCMP had jurisdiction; that meant all of the Trans-Canada highway and all communities except for St. John's and Corner Brook, which had their own police. It also meant that he was a very busy man.

The sign on the door to Windflower's office said Staff Sgt. William Ford. Windflower just hadn't bothered to replace it. Bill Ford had been Windflower's first friend in Marystown, and while he had gone to a new posting on the west coast of the province, it had not yet been decided who would replace him on a permanent basis.

Inspector Arsenault had indicated, hinting strongly, that he would like Windflower to take over the job on a permanent basis, but there was too much office work, too many meetings, for Windflower's liking. He liked police work in the community, and wanted to be back on the beat in Grand Bank, especially if Sheila was going to be there.

At 9 a.m. Windflower strolled past Louise and was greeted warmly by Inspector Arsenault.

"Good morning Winston, how are you this morning?"

"I'm fine, thank you sir," said Windflower. "You wanted to see me," he said, letting the Inspector go first with whatever he wanted to discuss.

"Yes," said Arsenault. "I was at a meeting in Halifax the last couple of days, and one of the big issues emerging in our region is human trafficking. Are you familiar with the issue?"

"Just what I've read in the memos and seen on T.V.," said Windflower. "I knew it was a big issue in British Columbia and Toronto, but I didn't realize it was a problem in this area."

"It isn't a big issue yet," said Arsenault. "But as the other routes get tighter and get more scrutiny, the human smugglers are looking for different ways to get in. In the last six months there have been two major incidents in Halifax. The first involved a boatload of Chinese migrants who arrived from Europe. The plan was to have them land illegally in Halifax and then ship them in specially equipped trucks across Canada to Markham, north of Toronto, where there's a large Asian population, and they could blend in easily."

"The second case involved a dozen young Romanian girls who arrived at the Halifax airport, claiming they were here on holiday. The immigration officer thought it was strange that so many beautiful young women, accompanied by an older man, who spoke only Russian, would come all the way to Halifax for a vacation. He let them in because he had no reason to stop them, but he raised a red flag to keep an eye on them. Three weeks later, six of them were found in a raid on a massage parlour in Dartmouth," said Arsenault.

"Wow," said Windflower. "But that stuff is not happening here, is it?"

"Well, we don't really know," said Arsenault. "They've tightened the screws in Halifax so they might try something here. And with the increased economic activity in St. John's, there's been a major spike in street prostitution and escort services."

"Wouldn't that be a local matter?" asked Windflower, thinking that it would be on the Constabulary's turf in St. John's.

"It would be if it were all local activity," said Arsenault. "But if it involves bringing women in from other countries then it's human trafficking, and that's our baby. Plus, we've picked up a rumour from our friends in Europe there might be more people heading our way, both as illegal immigrants and as workers for the sex trade."

"To Newfoundland?" asked Windflower, with a note of surprise.

"Why not?" asked Arsenault. "Think about it. We have hundreds of miles of unprotected coastline and dozens of likely landing points where there are no police to monitor, and certainly no immigration officers to check their papers."

"I am getting the feeling that you're leading up to something," said Windflower. "And that something involves me."

"You are bright, Windflower, that's why I like you," said Arsenault with a laugh. "I want you to be our point person on this issue. You can start by getting up to speed on the file, make the necessary contacts, and then come up with a plan to help us deal with it here in this province. You'll be part of a bigger group that includes a few more people from the region including Ron Quigley, whom I think you already know."

"I do know Ron," said Windflower. "And I'm honoured that you thought of me, sir, but I was hoping to go back to Grand Bank soon. I've been here a year, and while I really enjoy working with you, I think my place is back there, sir; with all due respect."

Arsenault just smiled. "I'm not surprised at your request, Winston, although I hoped you'd want to stay. You've earned the right to be where you want right now in your career, and I won't stand in your way of going back. But I do want you to take on this human trafficking file. You can do it from Grand Bank if you want. How does that sound?"

"That sounds great, sir, and thank you," said Windflower. "I'd be happy to take on that project. If it's okay with you, I'll clear out my stuff at the end of the week and be back in Grand Bank, starting on Monday."

"Agreed," said Arsenault and he rose to indicate the meeting was over.

"Thank you again, sir," said Windflower, but by this time Arsenault was already back on the phone.

Now to phone Sheila with the good news, Windflower thought. And I guess I'd better phone Tizzard to tell him to get out of my office!!

Sheila was excited to hear about the news that Windflower was going to be moving back to Grand Bank. She wasn't as keen about his special assignment, but she had long ago accepted the fact that sometimes he would have to be away.

Windflower spent the rest of the day going through the briefing materials and getting up to speed on the world of human traffickers. He was particularly interested in an RCMP special report on the issue, 'Project Seclusion'. This report studied human trafficking activities in Canada from 2005 to 2009 and gave some baseline data on the issue in Canada.

One of the key findings of this report was that organized crime networks with Eastern European links had been involved in the illegal entry of women into Canada for employment in escort services in Toronto and Montreal. It also pointed out that the majority of these sex workers came into Canada as tourists, visitors or students, and simply outstayed their visa.

The report also highlighted the fact that many victims believed that if they did not comply, their employers would have been capable of inflicting harm on family members in Canada or overseas. Those who were forced into sex work also feared that their overseers would let their families know that they were engaged in prostitution in Canada.

They tricked them to come here, thought Windflower, and then threatened to tell their families if they tried to get out. He also noted that human traffickers were just like pimps in Canada. They got the girls hooked on drugs to control them, often using them as mules to smuggle drugs in and out of the country for them.

The final piece that Windflower saw as he ran through the materials was that these Eastern European and Russian operators were tightly connected to gangs all over the world. That meant the Mafia in Montreal and biker gangs and their affiliates in Toronto, and throughout the east coast as well. There was some biker gang activity in Halifax when Windflower was there a few years back, but he wasn't sure what was going on there now. That was something else to check out later.

Before he knew it, Windflower's stomach told him it was lunch time, and as he was leaving the office he had a pleasant surprise.

"Hello, Winston, how's she goin' b'y?" came from a familiar face in the hallway.

It was Staff Sgt. Bill Ford.

"Hello, Bill," said Windflower. "What are you doing here?"

"I came to put my house on the market," said Ford. "I've decided to make my move on the west coast permanent, and I want to put down some roots out in Deer Lake."

"Well, that's good news," said Windflower. "I've got some news too. Are you free for lunch? I was just going to go over to Timmy's for a bite. Want to join me?"

"Great," said Ford. "I was just in to see Arsenault for a sec. Let's go."

The two men happily walked over together to the nearby coffee shop where they ordered the soup and sandwich deal. They talked as they waited for their order and continued to chat as they ate their lunch.

Windflower told Ford about moving back to Grand Bank and the good news about Sheila. Ford gave an update about his activities in the western part of the province. That wasn't so much about police work, as it was on the rivers and streams where Ford had found the best salmon and trout fishing. He also invited Windflower to come out later in the fall for some moose hunting.

"I'd like that Bill, but I think I'll have my hands full with this human trafficking project and helping Sheila get re-established. Those are kinda' my priorities for the fall. But if I can see an opening I'd be happy to come," said Windflower.

"I'd like that too," said Ford. "Being the boss makes it a little more difficult to make friends with the other officers. I miss our little chats after dinner when you were staying over at my house last summer."

"I do miss your barbecuing," said Windflower with a laugh. "Do you still make those pork chops? My mouth is watering just thinking about them."

"You'll just have to come out and find out," said Ford. "Actually there is something I wanted to talk to you about," he said. "We have a female Member in one of our detachments who has approached me confidentially. She says that the guys treat her like a second class citizen, and she feels like they're making fun of her. She says that they leave magazines around the lunch room, you know, inappropriate magazines, and there have been some practical jokes at her expense. She doesn't want to file a complaint; she just wants it to stop. I've never had to deal with anything like this before," said Ford.

"Me, either," said Windflower. "So what have you done about it so far?"

"I've talked to the local supervisor, and he says there's no problem. I even talked to Arsenault this morning who said something like 'boys will be boys'," said Ford. "I don't think he gets it. I have a feeling that if I don't nip this in the bud, that it will get worse."

"I agree with you," said Windflower. "These types of situations don't get better on their own. Is there anything in the supervisory manual about this?"

"Only a blanket statement about treating fellow officers with respect," said Ford. "It's not worth even sending that out to people. I think I'm going to have to bite the bullet and send something out that directs everybody to behave better, and professionally, with all members of the opposite sex," said Ford. "Will you have a look at the memo before I send it?"

"Sure," said Windflower. "I have to head back. Are you staying at your house tonight?"

"I am, if you have a room for me," said Ford.

"How about the pink room?" joked Windflower, referring to Ford's daughter's room that had been Windflower's home away from home when he first arrived in Marystown.

"That will do me just fine," said Ford. "I even brought supper with me. A friend of mine dropped over a brace of rabbits just before I left. I thought we could cook them up for supper if you'd like."

"Absolutely, Bill," said Windflower. "I'll see you there around six."

The two men parted with Ford heading to his lawyer's office and Windflower back to digging into the human trafficking files again.

Around 4 p.m. when Windflower was just getting up to yawn and stretch his legs, his cell phone rang.

"Windflower," he answered.

"I hear you're coming back, Boss," said Eddie Tizzard. "Were you going to make it a surprise return?"

Windflower laughed. "Is there anything you don't know, Corporal? Yes, I'm coming back next week, but only if that's okay with you," he said.

"No problem here, Sarge," said Tizzard. "The doors are always open in Grand Bank for a good old Alberta boy."

Chapter Seven

"Thank you, Corporal. So why don't we start my re-orientation program by telling me about the new staff member?"

"She's Miriam Evanchuk, from downtown Estevan, Saskatchewan, sir," said Tizzard. "She's an expert marksman, I guess that should be markswoman, and is fresh out of the academy in Saskatchewan. This is her first assignment, so I've been showing her the ropes."

"I bet you have, Tizzard," said Windflower. "That's one of the responsibilities I'll be assuming when I get back."

"Great," said Tizzard. "I've been looking forward to taking a few days off. My dad wants to take a boat ride back to Ramea. I told him I'd go along, if that's okay."

"Sure," said Windflower. "When are you going?"

"Probably next weekend," said Tizzard.

"Okay," said Windflower, "Any news on the Parsons girl?"

"They released the body last night and it just arrived this afternoon. They're setting up the wake at the funeral home to start tonight, and the funeral service is on Saturday morning," said Tizzard.

"That's good timing for Sheila," said Windflower. "She wanted to attend the funeral. I'm picking her up in St. John's on Friday and bringing her home."

Beneath the Surface

"She must be looking forward to that," said Tizzard. "By the way, I heard you kicked your uncle out."

"I didn't kick him out," said Windflower indignantly. "He chose not to follow my rules and left of his own accord."

"I believe you Boss, but that's not the word on the street," said Tizzard.

"Thank you, Eddie," said Windflower. "I'll see you on the weekend."

Well, I guess I shouldn't be surprised, thought Windflower. Somehow I always get a bad rap from my family.

Windflower figured that he'd probably done enough for one day, so he turned off his computer and closed the door to his office. He walked by Arsenault's office and said good night to Louise, who was also packing up for the day. Then he remembered that his friend Bill Ford was cooking supper, and his mouth started to water in anticipation.

"I'm going back home and my lady is coming home, too. And I have a great meal and probably a good conversation to look forward to. It doesn't get much better than this," he thought.

Windflower's car almost knew the way to Bill Ford's house on Smallwood Drive by instinct, so it was like he was teleported home. He had enjoyed his time living in Ford's house while he was in Marystown. It was pleasant and comfortable. Windflower loved sitting out on the deck on a fine evening to watch the sun set into

63

the water. He was ready for supper and when he opened the door the aroma from the kitchen only whetted his appetite even more.

"What is that smell?" Windflower asked Bill Ford, who was busy chopping vegetables in the kitchen.

"Oh, that's my secret rabbit sauce," said Ford. "Normally I've got the rabbit cut up and stewing in it by now but I didn't have enough time today. So I sautéed some onions and garlic, and then put the rabbits in the sauce long enough to braise them. Then I added a little sage, thyme and oregano and some water and let the rabbit soak in its own juices for a couple of hours. It should be ready by six as planned. I'm just cutting up a few carrots and celery, and when we throw in some canned tomatoes and cook up a little rice we should have ourselves a fine scoff," said Ford.

"Anything I can do?" asked Windflower.

"Just make yourself comfortable," said Ford.

"Thanks, Bill," said Windflower. "I think I'll grab a quick shower."

Windflower showered and put on his civvies in no time, and was back in the kitchen with his mouth watering again before long.

"Why don't you cut us up a few chunks of that crusty bread on the counter?" said Ford. "It will be great for soaking up the rabbit sauce. And then I think we're ready."

Ford had taken the cooked rabbits out of the sauce, deboned them and returned the meat that was now swimming in a thick brown sauce. He scooped a heavy ladle of rice on each of their plates and covered the rice with pieces of rabbit and vegetables.

The smells now held Windflower completely in their grasp, and he greedily grabbed his plate and the basket of bread and went out to the deck. Ford followed with the butter and his plate, and the two men set about enjoying their supper.

They both had seconds and were completely stuffed when Windflower took the opportunity to tell Ford, for probably the twelfth time, how delicious the rabbits were.

"I've never had rabbits like that before," said Windflower as he wiped the last of the sauce from his plate with the remaining piece of bread.

"They're good, aren't they?" said Ford. "I'm still learning the knack of cooking them, and I still can't do the stew with the pastry that the locals use, but it's coming."

"I thought it was great," said Windflower, "Another super Bill Ford meal in the books. You sit there and relax; I'll clean up and put the kettle on."

After the dishes were done, Windflower brought the teapot and two mugs out to the deck. They had their tea along with a slice of blueberry cake with vanilla sauce that Windflower found in the freezer and heated up in the microwave. That put the finishing touches on their dinner, and Windflower nearly fell asleep a short while later while trying to watch the Blue Jays game with Bill Ford. He finally pulled himself off the couch, brushed his teeth and went to bed. He just hoped that he wouldn't have those dreams again.

Windflower quickly fell fast asleep, but a couple of hours later found himself bathed in sweat and gasping for air.

He realized he'd had one of the same dreams as the previous night. But this time the lady was chasing him along with what looked like skeletons, maybe ghosts, calling his name, and asking him to help them. Just as one of the skeletons reached him and touched him with a bony finger, he woke up.

Windflower got up and went to the bathroom and put a cold facecloth on his head to try and cool down. He also had to spend a little effort just getting his breathing back to normal.

Whatever that was, it was scary, he thought. Not wanting to revisit that dream anytime soon, he went out to the living room and turned on one of the all-night movie channels. He found an old musical, *High Society*, with Bing Crosby, Grace Kelly and Frank Sinatra that he had seen many times before. Based on the play, *The Philadelphia Story*, it was one of his all-time favourites. It was fun and campy and was notable for being the last film appearance of Grace Kelly before she became Princess of Monaco.

For Windflower, it was a great relief from the terror of his dream and by the time the movie ended, he was feeling relaxed and peaceful again.

With some trepidation he went back to bed, but his fears proved groundless and he managed to sleep all the way into the morning when he heard the front door close and Bill Ford's truck pull out of the driveway.

He must be heading back to Deer Lake today and wants to get an early start, thought Windflower, as he rose and began his day.

He was still a bit bothered by his dream as he went about his morning routines of cleaning and prayer and smudging, done quickly because it wasn't just raining this morning, it was a torrential downpour.

Maybe he should talk to somebody about his dreams, he thought, but to whom? Since he couldn't think of anyone, he decided to try and forget about it as he scrounged around for breakfast in the kitchen.

He made himself a boiled egg with toast and jam and a banana for dessert. And as he was putting away the jam he noticed the leftover rabbit meal from last night sitting on a shelf in the fridge.

That looks like lunch, he thought, so he scooped out a generous portion of meat and vegetables along with a couple of ladles of rice into a Tupperware container. Voila, Lapin de Ford for lunch!!

Windflower drove the short distance to work with his wipers on full blast. This was a good day to be indoors, and he was grateful to have lots of paperwork to finish off before he left tomorrow, and more human trafficking research to do.

He worked his way diligently through his in-box all morning and by the time lunch came he had whittled it down to a manageable size. He dropped off his completed paperwork to Louise, and waved hello to Arsenault whose door was open, but of course he was on the phone.

Then he went to the lunchroom where he warmed up his leftover rabbit in the microwave. Everyone who came by the lunchroom in the next two minutes stopped to ask him what smelled so delicious. He was happy to tell them that it was Bill Ford's special rabbit dish, but even happier when he had his first bite of the tender meat and vegetables.

He was still smiling long after his lunch was gone and just back at work when his cell phone rang.

"Windflower," he answered.

"Winston, I'm so worried. I haven't heard from Frank in a week. Is he still with you?" asked a woman's voice at the end of the line.

"Auntie Marie, Uncle Frank is not at my house anymore. He went to St. John's earlier in the week," said Windflower, deciding not to give full disclosure yet on the reasons for his uncle's departure.

"The last I heard he was at your house in Grand Bank," said his aunt. "He sounded so happy when I talked to him. I know he was drinking again, but I was hoping that would stop when you got home."

Windflower decided to come clean.

"I guess that's maybe the reason he went to St. John's, Auntie. I talked to him about his smoking and drinking in the house. He got a bit huffy about it and the next thing I knew he was in a taxi on the way to town."

"Oh, it's not your fault, Winston," said his aunt. "Frank is a nice man when he's not drinking, but he gets real stubborn when he starts in again. I just hope he's okay. It's not like him not to call after a few days, even when he's on the booze."

"Let me see what I can find out, Auntie," said Windflower. "I can make some calls and I'll be in St. John's tomorrow to pick up Sheila."

"Oh, so she's coming home," said his aunt. "Both of you must be pleased about that."

"We are, Auntie," said Windflower, and he almost asked his aunt, who was known for her dream interpretations about his dreams, but he thought she was too worried about Uncle Frank to bother her.

So he just said goodbye and promised to call her as soon as he had some news to report. Windflower thought that his Uncle Frank was probably too hung over to call, but if his aunt was worried, he'd make a few inquiries to see if he could find out anything about his uncle's wanderings in the big city of St. John's.

Chapter Eight

He might not be able to find his Uncle Frank easily in St. John's, but if something bad had happened, lots of people would know. Windflower decided to enlist some help in this venture, and he phoned the Grand Bank detachment to see if Betsy Molloy could help.

"Hi, Betsy," he said as she answered the phone.

"Sergeant Windflower," gushed Betsy. "I'm so glad you're coming back. I mean Corporal Tizzard is fine, but ... I like working with you, Sergeant. You're so professional, not that Corporal Tizzard isn't..."

Windflower cut her off, "Thank you, Betsy. I was wondering if you could do me a favour."

He explained that he wanted her to call St. John's and check police reports, and then the Health Sciences Complex, the major hospital in St. John's, to see if his uncle had shown up at the emergency department. Then he asked for Tizzard.

"Hey, Sarge," said Tizzard. "What's up?"

"Eddie, do you have a number for that Constabulary guy, Langforth or something, the guy who was in Grand Bank? I'm trying to track down my uncle in St. John's," said Windflower.

"Sure," said Tizzard, and Windflower could hear papers being shuffled around in the background.

"Here it is, Carl Langmead, 709-762-0000, extension 232. Is there something wrong?" he asked.

"I don't think so, but my aunt is worried so I'm checking around. I've got Betsy doing the hospital and the police. I'll call Langmead after that if nothing shows up. Thanks, Eddie. I'll talk to you later."

Now, as happens so often with police work, we wait, thought Windflower.

Windflower burrowed back into the human trafficking files, and started going through the newspaper clippings on cases in recent years. He was shocked at the number that had become public from Vancouver to Hamilton to the Maritimes, because that meant at least 10 times as many cases were likely unreported. He was also shocked at the leniency of the courts when it came to prosecuting and sentencing the perpetrators of these crimes.

In Ontario a man who earned about half a million dollars from marketing a girl for sex got three years in federal prison. A Montreal man got a total of one week in jail, and another man got a sentence of one day plus his time served while waiting for trial.

Sadly, but not surprisingly, Windflower also read about the growing number of Aboriginal girls who were being tricked or forced into the sex trade. He had seen some of this first-hand when he worked in Winnipeg, but now it was an epidemic throughout Edmonton, Vancouver and urban Saskatchewan as well. And just like the Asian and Eastern European girls who were brought in from outside the country, the young Indian, Inuit and

Metis girls were beaten and sometimes killed if they tried to break away.

It was sombre reading, but it helped Windflower get a grasp of the extent of the problem, and made him more determined to do something about it.

His office phone rang to break up his grim reading time; it was Betsy from Grand Bank.

"Your uncle was in Emergency last night," said Betsy. "He was brought in by the police and treated for cuts and bruises and held overnight for monitoring. He was released this morning. He gave his address as somewhere in Alberta."

"Thanks, Betsy. That's great," said Windflower as he hung up.

Well, at least he's not dead, thought Windflower, but I guess I should try and find out how much trouble he's managed to get himself into.

Windflower called the number that Tizzard had provided.

"RNC, Langmead speaking," came the voice at the end of the line, using the acronym for the Royal Newfoundland Constabulary.

"Carl, it's Winston Windflower, from the RCMP. We met in Grand Bank the other day."

"Windflower, oh yeah, I remember you. What can I do for you?"

"My uncle is in St. John's and he's in a bit of trouble. I don't think it's serious, but he ended up in Emerg last night with cuts and bruises and he was brought in by your guys," said Windflower.

"Just gimme' a sec here while I pull up the reports from last night. Yeah, I see it. Francis Pendleton. The report says he was found bleeding on the sidewalk in a laneway off Duckworth Street, taken to the Health Science Complex at 11:50 p.m. He had no recollection of what had happened, but according to the reporting officers it looked like he was jumped. He claimed to have lost his wallet, his watch and a couple of hundred dollars. The officers took his statement and left him at the HSC overnight," said Langmead.

'Thanks," said Windflower. "Unfortunately, it's not the first time that my uncle has been in this situation. I'm just trying to track him down for my aunt. I'd like nothing better than to put him back on the plane to Alberta."

"We all have relatives like that," said Langmead with a laugh. "If you know where he's staying I can take a run by and check in on him if you'd like."

"That would be great," said Windflower. "I'll find out and let you know. I am going to be in St. John's tomorrow, and I need him to be okay at least until then."

"Okay, let me know," said Langmead.

"How's the case going by the way?" asked Windflower.

"It's still early, but so far I can't find a person who had a bad word to say about the late Amy Parsons. But there are some things that don't just add up," said Langmead.

"Like what?" asked Windflower.

"Like the fact that we found $5,000 cash in her apartment, and her bank accounts have another $17,000. Plus, she lives in a luxury suite at Elizabeth Towers and supports her mother back home," said Langmead.

"I guess she had a good job," said Windflower.

"That's what's interesting," said Langmead. "She's a full-time student, with no student debt after three years in, and no apparent job that we can yet identify. And oh yeah, the one person who may know something about this, her roommate, is missing."

"Missing?" asked Windflower.

"Yeah, we found her name on the lease, Mercedes Dowson, but all of her stuff, luggage, everything is gone. We are trying to track her down but so far no luck. I was hoping that someone in Grand Bank might have some information for me, but no one there knows too much about her," said Langmead.

"She could be anywhere, even out of the province by now," said Windflower.

"True," said Langmead. "We're trying to track her down through the airlines but no success so far."

"You know, maybe we could help with that," said Windflower. "I've got a crackerjack person in Grand Bank who can find almost anything. I could get her to plug the name into our system and see what shows up."

"Sure, that would be great. Our system here is new and top of the line but quite frankly most of us don't know how to use it, me included," said Langmead, chuckling.

"Me too," said Windflower. "But I'll get Betsy to have a look for you. Right after I find out where my Uncle Frank is hiding out."

"Okay," said Langmead.

Windflower hung up from Langmead and called Betsy back with a new mission: to find his Uncle Frank's hotel in St. John's. He also asked her to plug in the Dowson woman's name, and to see if she could find a way through Informatics in HQ to check the airlines, and even the Marine Atlantic ferry to see if the mysterious roommate had left the island.

This has been one interesting day, thought Windflower.

He had hoped to be getting out of the office early, but now he had to wait to hear from Betsy about Uncle Frank. He decided to phone Sheila to check in.

"Hello, dear," said Windflower after she answered.

"Oh, Winston, how are you? Moira Stoodley just called to tell me the funeral for Amy Parsons will be on Saturday," said Sheila.

"I was just calling to tell you that," said Windflower. "How come everybody has the news before I get it?"

"You should know that our women's network is much faster than yours," joked Sheila. "Anyway I'm glad I can be there for it, and for her poor mother. It really is tragic. A young girl from Grand Bank, murdered. I still can't believe it."

"So I guess the network has decided it's murder as well," said Windflower. "The RNC will be pleased to know their suspicions have been upheld."

"Who have you been talking to, Winston? And is there anything you are allowed to tell me, off the record of course?" asked Sheila.

"Well, I haven't been sworn to secrecy, but I would appreciate your usual discretion in not informing the network, assuming they don't already know some of this," said Windflower.

"Spill the beans, Sergeant," said Sheila laughing.

"It looks like a murder but they're just beginning the investigation," said Windflower. "They're also trying to figure out how she came to have a sizable amount of money on her and in her bank account. And ..." Windflower paused for effect.

"And what?" asked Sheila, playing along.

"And they're looking for a roommate, a woman by the name of Mercedes Dowson. Does that name ring a bell with you?" asked Windflower.

"Not really," said Sheila. "There was a family of Dowsons over in Red Bay, but I don't know any of the children's names. Do you want me to check and see what I can find out?"

"All on the Q.T., okay, Sheila?" asked Windflower. "Don't say anything about the case or the RNC may hunt you down and hold you prisoner in St. John's."

"Anything but that," said Sheila.

Windflower's office intercom was blinking, so he said a quick goodbye to Sheila.

Shoot, he thought, I didn't even get a chance to tell her about Uncle Frank.

"Hello, Betsy, what did you find out?" asked Windflower.

"Your uncle is a guest at the Crosbie Hotel on Prescott Street in St. John's, sir. He has a room pre-paid until tomorrow," said Betsy.

"Thank you, Betsy, that's great. Anything on the other file?" said Windflower.

"Nothing yet, sir but I expect to have an answer by the morning," said Betsy.

"Thank you, Betsy. Have a great evening. I'll call in the morning," said Windflower as he replaced the receiver.

Uncle Frank, he thought, high class as usual.

Windflower phoned Langmead back with his uncle's location, and the latter agreed to stop in and pay him a brief visit. Windflower also told him that Betsy had put her inquiry into HQ and that he would get back to Langmead if and when he heard anything. Langmead sounded grateful for the help, and Windflower felt good that somebody would be looking after his somewhat crazy uncle in the big city of St. John's.

His final phone call of the day was to his Auntie Marie to tell her both of Frank's adventures, which she wasn't really surprised about, and that his police friend was going to visit him, which left her relieved. When Windflower told her that he planned to take Uncle Frank home with him to Grand Bank, she was very appreciative.

"I'm glad that you're there to look after him," said his aunt.

"I'm not sure how well I can do that," said Windflower. "But I will try and keep him safe, Auntie."

"That is all we can do," said Auntie Marie. "We have to look after each other."

"True, Auntie," said Windflower. "I have a favour to ask of you, too, Auntie. I have been having some disturbing dreams lately, and I want to talk to somebody about them, to understand their meaning. I know that you've helped many people interpret their dreams from our teachings," he said.

"That is true, Winston," said his aunt. "But you know I actually learned all of my dream interpretation in the women's circle and while I can give you the perspective from Mother Earth, you'll also need to understand what messages Grandfather Sun is sending you, since he rules the sky world along with Grandmother Moon. You have someone walking with you that understands that world, Winston."

"Who?" asked Windflower.

"Your Uncle Frank is a dream weaver," said Auntie Marie. "It was a gift of teaching to him from your grandfather when he was our chief. He studied with Grandfather for many years until he too mastered the craft. He can still do it, if he chooses to. But his power is limited if he's drinking alcohol. It blurs his mind and he cannot see into the dream world. He has told me that himself. So you will need to help him abstain from alcohol for at least three days before he can help you. But that would be a great gift for him and for you. And I think, Winston, that he would be pleased and honoured if you'd ask him."

"Thank you, Auntie," said Windflower. "As usual your words are wise and powerful. Meegwich."

"Get some rest, Winston, said his aunt. "You sound weary. You are carrying many burdens on this journey. You need rest too. Tonight before you go to bed place some of your medicine, a little sage, in the window of your bedroom to protect you from the spirits of the night. You can then have pleasant dreams. Like when you were a boy running through the forest here at home."

"Thank you, Auntie. Good night."

Windflower closed up his office and headed home. He picked up a Subway sandwich for supper, and while it wasn't the healthiest meal, it wasn't bad. At least it had a few vegetables, kind of like a salad, he chuckled to himself.

Windflower ate his sandwich out on the deck along with a cold iced tea from the fridge. Before he settled down for the night he took his usual long walk down to the shipyard where the presence of men and vehicles signalled another overnight shift.

Good work and a shift premium too, thought Windflower. At least that was some protection against the winter and the up-coming slowdown of work.

The rain held off long enough for Windflower to complete his nocturnal route, but as he turned the corner for home the wind picked up a few big drops and deposited them on his cheek. He slipped inside just before the clouds opened wide to release their full force.

After a nice warm bath and the top of the news, he was snuggled safe and warm in his bed. He had remembered to place a few crumbs of sage in his open window just to be on the safe side. Whether that worked or whether it was the gentle rhythm of the steady rain, he was soon asleep, and slept all the way until his alarm clock sounded its loud good morning at 7 a.m.

Chapter Nine

Windflower reached over and gave his alarm clock a healthy knock to turn it off. But it had done its job, and he was wide awake, and well rested. There was nothing like a good night's sleep to refresh the body and calm the mind too, as he realized that he had not been interrupted by his recurring dreams. Windflower made a mental note to thank his aunt, and a second note to himself to remember always to listen to her advice.

It was garbage day in Marystown and Windflower went through the house to empty the waste paper baskets into a large green garbage bag. It was also moving day, so he took all of his personal stuff out to his car.

After his shower he took all the towels and sheets off the beds in the house and laid them in a pile in the kitchen. The cleaning lady, Mrs. Moriarity, would put them in the wash later.

Windflower also cleaned out the fridge of the perishables, some of which went into his cooler for back home, but most went into the garbage bag. He managed to salvage a fair sized chunk of bologna, a small container of homemade beans from the freezer, and enough odds and ends of fruit to make a fruit salad. Along with the last of his Goobies bread and two cups of strong black coffee, he had a perfect breakfast.

He locked up Bill Ford's little house on Smallwood Drive after his breakfast and did his morning smudge. He made sure to say a special prayer of thanks for his aunt, and even for his uncle, who he hoped was going to help him with the dreams.

He dropped off his green garbage bag on the curb at the edge of his driveway and put his netting over it to keep the seagulls from carrying it off for their breakfast. Then he waved goodbye to the house and headed up the road to work.

A heavy rain was still pelting down this morning, and Windflower by-passed Tim Hortons rather than add to the traffic problems. He could get a cup of coffee at work. He was hurrying his office when his phone rang.

"Good morning, Sergeant," said Betsy. "I hope you slept well."

How did she know I was having trouble sleeping? thought Windflower, but he resisted the urge to ask.

He simply said, "Good morning, Betsy. I'm fine and how are you this rainy morning?"

"I'm well," said Betsy. "A little wet, but none the worse for wear. I have some news on that woman you asked me about. Marine Atlantic has a record of a Ms. M. Dowson on the Argentia ferry last Sunday, arriving in North Sydney at 11 a.m. on Monday morning. She showed up at the last minute and booked a ticket and a cabin just for herself. Oh, and she was driving a black Honda CRV with Newfoundland and Labrador license plates. Do you want me to put a tracer on the car, sir?" she asked

The tracer referred to the Trace Identification System. It allowed any RCMP officer or detachment anywhere in the country to enter a vehicle license plate number into the system. If that number appeared in any police identification in the country, not just the RCMP, an automatic message was sent back to the originator, showing where the vehicle was located, and which police force had found it.

"Yes, that would be great," said Windflower. "And thank you, Betsy. You are very helpful, as usual," said Windflower.

Windflower could feel her beam right through the phone line as she replied, "No problem, sir, just doing my job."

After hanging up from Betsy, Windflower called Langmead with his news, only to get his answering machine. He left a message with the details Betsy had provided and went to get his coffee. Along the way he was sidetracked first by Louise, who wanted his signature on a myriad of forms that facilitated his transfer back to Grand Bank, and then by Arsenault, who just wanted a chat. By the time he was finished with Arsenault, he had forgotten about his coffee and was back in his office when the phone rang again.

This time it was Langmead who thanked Windflower for the info, but also told him that they had already figured out that Mercedes Dowson had left the province. They were just a little bit slower than the RCMP apparently. Langmead also said that they had posted a photo on their website and put out a nation-wide notice on Dowson as a person of interest in the Parsons case.

"I saw your uncle, last night," said Langmead, "He's quite a character."

"So people keep telling me," said Windflower, with a touch of weariness in his voice.

"He told me, he's off the booze, maybe for good," said Langmead. "He also said that the whole family is very proud of you, Windflower. He said you were a credit to his people."

"Well, it's good to hear positive comments, even if they're few and far between," said Windflower.

"I told him that you were coming in today to pick him up. He said he'd have his bag ready," said Langmead. "I think he behaved himself last night so he should be in pretty good shape."

"Thanks, Carl. I owe you one," said Windflower.

"It's always good to have the RCMP owe you a favour," said Langmead. "Enjoy your weekend."

After his call with Langmead Windflower realized that he had yet to have his coffee, and though it was just past 11 a.m., he decided to head over to Timmy's for an early lunch.

After chicken noodle soup and a grilled cheese sandwich, along with a large coffee, Windflower felt ready to deal with the rest of the day. That included calling the Crosbie Hotel and leaving a message for his Uncle Frank to stay put around the hotel until he could pick him up later. He also phoned Sheila to check in, and to tell her about the drama involving his uncle, and that he would be coming back to Grand Bank with them.

About 2 p.m., he starting packing up his office and went to see Louise to drop off the last of his paperwork. He was hoping to say a quick goodbye to Arsenault, but his office door was shut, so he told Louise he would call the Inspector early next week.

With that, Windflower strolled out of the RCMP detachment building in Marystown and into his car for the 90-minute drive to St. John's. He didn't have time to stop in at Goobies along the way, but made up his mind to definitely stop by on the way back. He had eaten the last of his bread supply that morning and his stock needed replenishing.

The day was dark and gloomy, but Windflower's spirits were high as he drove through the barren stretch of land between the Burin Peninsula and the highway. There was a rugged magnificence to this drive that was quiet and unbroken until you came into the community of Swift Current. There the ocean breached through the rock and crept up towards the highway.

It was one of Windflower's favourite drives. The road narrowed and crawled around the curves, and the ocean was always a treat as it glimmered on poor days and sparkled gloriously on sunny ones. Small fishing and leisure boats dotted the shoreline, and tiny islands poked their heads out of the water to peer at the visiting traffic. Every time Windflower saw this scene unfold he smiled at its peace and beauty. This was a place where he knew there was no reason not to be happy.

The highway was less scenic on the last leg into St. John's but it didn't bother Windflower a bit. He was going into town to pick up his lady and bring her home. And he had the weekend off. He couldn't remember the last weekend he was completely away from work.

When you worked for Inspector Arsenault, whose mind never stopped, you were always on call. Well, not this weekend, he thought.

In no time at all he was driving on the arterial road on the south side of St. John's and heading into the city. He decided to get off on the Gower Street exit. He used to go along the waterfront, but now that they had put up the security fence on the wharf it made Windflower feel uncomfortable. He could see the old guys wandering the harbour front, as they had been doing for years just to watch the comings and goings. Surely they were no great threat to security, he thought.

He drove past City Hall and the Mile One Stadium where the Maple Leafs farm team hung its shingle. He could also see the building cranes from this vantage point, two, no three, new buildings going up.

More ways to block the view of the harbour, he thought. Sometimes he wondered if the city and its residents really knew what natural beauty they had here, especially near the water. He knew that progress was inevitable, but he just wished that they could hold on to the old, especially the most valuable parts of it, in their rush to the new and better future.

Windflower turned up by the Hotel Newfoundland, and travelled down Kings Bridge Road to the turnoff to the Miller Centre on Forest Road.

When he arrived at Sheila's room, she was packed and ready to go. She'd been ready to go for hours, she told Windflower, as they rode the elevator to the ground floor. Sheila breathed a loud sigh of relief as they left the building and walked towards the parking lot.

"Thank goodness, I'm done with that place," she said, getting into Windflower's car.

"Thank goodness, you are so much better," said Windflower. "I can still remember the days before we brought you here. Those were scary days for me. And now look at you. Good as new, maybe even better."

"Oh, Winston, you are a card," said Sheila. "A wild card sometimes, but you are my card anyway."

Windflower swung back down Kings Bridge Road and turned left when he came back to the Hotel. He turned down Prescott Street, one of the long steep hills in St. John's that led downtown towards the waterfront. There had been a hotel on Prescott Street for years, although the one remaining was getting far too long in the tooth.

It had much of the mustiness of the past and few creature comforts. But it probably suited his Uncle Frank just fine, he thought, as he pulled up next to the hotel to see his uncle sitting on his bag, smoking a cigarette.

"Hello, Winston," said Uncle Frank. "And this must be your beautiful lady," as he held out his hand to shake

Sheila's. "I'll just jump in the back, shall I Winston? Just remember to let me out later, okay?"

Windflower got out and opened the door for his uncle. "I'm glad you're okay, Uncle," he said, surveying the scattering of cuts and bruises on his face, head and hands.

"You can't really hurt an old guy like me," said Uncle Frank. "It was a good thing that there was a gang of them or they'd be sorry today."

Windflower thought about the saying that God looks after drunks and fools but decided to keep that one to himself.

"Is anybody hungry?" he asked.

"I could eat a bite," said Uncle Frank.

"I'm a little peckish too," said Sheila. 'We might as well eat something in town before we hit the road. What were you thinking, Winston?'

"I was thinking about going to Leo's," said Windflower.

He had been introduced to that little fish and chips shop in the Higher Levels area of St. John's by Dan Quigley who had grown up in the neighbourhood.

Quigley told him that at one time there were half a dozen fish and chip shops in this area catering to the never decreasing demand. The fries were hand cut each morning just as the fresh cod was being dropped off from the local fishermen. Now sadly, there were just two or three such establishments remaining.

The patriarch, Leo himself, was long gone, but his family carried on the business without him. They had made few changes since the early days, and it was still a place where deep fried fish and chips were king. You could get it small, medium or large. And you could get it with gravy, and, if you wanted, with dressing.

When asked to describe the dressing, the best Windflower could do was to say it consisted of breadcrumbs and spices, especially local Newfoundland savoury. It had the consistency of sawdust, and it tasted great when covered with thick, homemade gravy.

Windflower ordered a medium, which was two pieces of deep fried cod with dressing and gravy, while both Sheila and Uncle Frank had a one-piece order. There was no alcohol served at Leo's. They didn't want to deal with it, nor with late-night drunks. That's why they shut the place down tight at 7 p.m. every night except Saturday, when they went home at 6.

They did have the most interesting soft drinks. There were three kinds of root beer including low-cal and caffeine-free, and in addition to Orange Crush they had Lime Crush, Cream Soda Crush, and Birch Beer Crush, which had a unique flavour that Windflower could only place as vaguely woodsy.

After supper they drove over to the nearby Tim Hortons and picked up a coffee for the road. This coffee shop had a marvellous view out through the Narrows in St. John's and perhaps not surprisingly was located right next to the HQ of the local police.

"Let's drive out through downtown," said Sheila. "For all the time we've been in St. John's this year, I haven't been on Water Street once."

"No problem, ma'am," said Windflower. "I'm just the taxi driver."

Everyone laughed at that little joke, even Uncle Frank in the back, who was starting to nod off. By the time they got to the east end of Water Street he was fast asleep.

"We used to come to St. John's at least twice a year," said Sheila. "Once in the spring to shop for our summer clothes, and again in the fall for our back to school wear. A few times I came in with my Mom in the taxi, because she wanted to pick up a few things for Christmas. Those were the best trips of all because all the store windows would be decorated, and there used to be a raffle for the Mount Cashel Orphanage with a real live turkey in the window."

"That sounds like fun," said Windflower.

"It was so much fun. This is where all the shopping was in St. John's, before they built the Avalon Mall," said Sheila. "I loved the London, New York and Paris Department Store. It was on the corner across from the courthouse, that three story building right there," she said pointing across the street. "We called it 'The London' and it had one of those old metal tube coin exchanges. You went to the cash and gave them your money. They put your money in with your bill, put it in a metal cylinder and it whisked up to the office, where they made the change and whisked it back. I always wanted to buy something at 'The London' so we could see them do that magic trick."

Windflower laughed at that story and continued to drive up Water Street, which was getting busy with both pedestrians and vehicles.

Maybe getting ready for an early night on George Street, St. John's party central, he thought.

Sheila had grown quiet and Windflower reached his hand over to touch hers. They held hands for a minute as Windflower took the ramp to the arterial road that would take them high above St. John's, out to the highway and home.

Chapter Ten

By the time Windflower's car made the turn onto the Trans-Canada Highway towards Clarenville, Sheila was fast asleep, and Uncle Frank was snoring peacefully in the back.

I guess they both needed a rest, thought Windflower.

He put his car on cruise control at 110 and sat back to enjoy the ride. The sun was just beginning to fall into the western sky, and the day had cleared up just enough to enjoy it. Windflower decided to do just that, and there was little noise or movement inside the car, until Windflower pulled up at the gas pumps in Goobies.

"Pit stop, anybody?" he asked, and Sheila gently woke and smiled at him.

"Goobies?" she asked.

"Yes, ma'am," said Windflower. "I thought we could gas and go if it's okay with you. Plus a washroom break," he added.

"Perfect," said Sheila as she got out of the car and walked towards the convenience store and restroom entrance.

"Uncle Frank, do you need to go?" asked Windflower to his sleeping uncle in the back.

"What? Oh yeah," said his uncle. "I gotta' go pee."

"Now's your chance," said Windflower as he got out to pump his gas.

After filling up, he moved his car and parked it at the side to make room for the people waiting behind. Then he went inside where there was a long line-up at the cash, so he went directly to the men's room.

He passed Sheila along the way and gave her the car keys with directions to where the car was parked. He almost bumped into his uncle as he opened the door to the Men's and told him where the car was as well.

After doing his business, he walked back out and got into the line-up to pay. Then he remembered the bread. But when he glanced over at the bread rack it was empty.

Too bad, he thought.

Just as he was leaving after paying for his gas, he caught sight of a woman in a white coat rolling a tray on wheels out to the bread area. He could tell right away that this was the bread lady, and made a beeline back to the bread shelf. But his way was blocked by a fairly large lady who grabbed the last two loaves of freshly baked brown bread, still steaming inside its plastic bag. He was sure that her smile was pure spite, and he thought about offering her twenty bucks for one of the loaves, but he didn't want to give her any satisfaction. So he just smiled back.

But he was as hot inside as the bread in the package, and he didn't cool down until the calming curves of Swift Current. By then it was almost dark and he needed to pay attention for moose on the highway. There had been multiple reports of moose wandering in the next stretch of road, right up to the Terrenceville turn-off, and Windflower didn't want to take any chances, especially with his precious cargo aboard.

He didn't have to worry about either of them. They had both fallen fast asleep almost as soon as the car hit the highway, and neither woke until they reached Windflower's house in Grand Bank.

"I'll be right back," said Windflower to Sheila who stirred beside him.

"Okay, Uncle Frank. This is your stop," said Windflower and he got out to unlock his uncle's door and to help him in with his luggage. "You can have my bed tonight, Uncle Frank. It's all made up clean and fresh. And no smoking in the house, okay?"

"Okay, Winston," came the reply from his uncle who walked into the house after him. "I think I'll just have a cup of tea and go to bed."

"Good night, Uncle, I'll see you in the morning," said Windflower as he went back out to his car.

"Is everything okay?" asked Sheila.

"It will be," answered Windflower as he drove to Sheila's house in the middle of Grand Bank.

The lights were on and there was a large "Welcome home, Sheila" banner on the front porch. Sheila beamed when she saw this, and was even happier when she went inside and saw a beautiful bouquet of flowers and her spic and span clean house.

"You have great friends," said Windflower.

"I have great friends and a super housecleaner," said Sheila as she inspected her surroundings. "I'm so glad to finally be home," she said as she sat down on the couch to survey her house again.

"How about a cup of tea and a nice hot bath?" asked Windflower.

"You, Sergeant, are the absolute best," said Sheila. "Both would be great."

Windflower turned on the kettle and started running the water for her bath.

I'm really glad she's finally home too, he thought.

After their baths and a pleasant couple of hours watching an old Bette Davis movie on television, Windflower turned out the lights and went to bed. Sheila was already peacefully asleep. He reached over to hold her and was soon out like a light.

A few hours later he was sitting up and wide-awake. His dream of the woman and her ghostly friends chasing him through the forest had returned, and Windflower was both sweaty and shaken. He got up, went to the bathroom, and doused himself with water to cool and calm himself down. He opened the fridge and had a long drink of cold water straight from the jug that Shelia kept there.

Finally, after all of that, he felt cleansed enough to go back to bed and within minutes he was fast asleep. But again, in the early morning hours, he woke to the horror of the dead woman sleeping ice-cold next to him. This time it woke Sheila as well.

"Winston, what's wrong?" she asked. "You're shaking. Are you okay?"

"Just a bad dream," said Windflower, once again reaching over to hold her in the dark.

Sheila snuggled back in and Windflower's heart slowed back to normal, as he felt her calmness next to him. But he was still shaken, and he knew that peaceful sleep would be elusive for him again that night.

He drifted in and out of a fitful sleep, and finally got up so as not to wake Sheila again. He sat on her back porch in the rain and fog and watched as the light, if not the sun, rose gently over the ocean. He went back inside and made some coffee. He was on his second cup and the last of the left over magazines that had accumulated in Sheila's absence when she got up.

"I didn't know you enjoyed 'Oprah'," said Sheila mischievously.

"I usually just look at the pictures," said Windflower. "I want to know if my colours are right for the season. I wouldn't want to make a fashion faux pas. Are you ready for breakfast, my dear?"

"I could kill for a cup of that coffee, first," said Sheila. "And anything with fresh fruit would be great."

Windflower went to the kitchen and returned with a steaming hot cup of coffee for Sheila and passed it over to her.

"Hmm, that's good java," said Sheila. "I think I'll keep you. Being able to brew a good cup of coffee ranks pretty high on my lists of must-haves," she said with a smile.

"I'm glad you approve," said Windflower and seeing the 'look' on her face decided to talk first before she started asking questions about his new sleep patterns.

"So, I've had a little trouble sleeping, lately," he began. "Actually it's not the sleeping part that I have trouble with, it's more the waking-up part."

"And you are waking up, because...?" asked Sheila.

"Because I guess I'm having bad dreams," said Windflower. Then he told her about the dreams, and that he had talked to his Auntie Marie about them.

"And what did she say?" asked Sheila.

"She said that I should talk to Uncle Frank about them. I didn't realize it, but Uncle Frank is what they call a dream master or dream weaver. He studied the traditional teachings about dreams with my grandfather," said Windflower.

"Your grandfather who was an elder and Chief?" asked Sheila. "Wow."

"Exactly," said Windflower. "So I am going to take some time to talk to Uncle Frank this weekend and see if he can help me make sense of this. They say in my culture that until you hear the messages your dreams are conveying and act upon them, that the dreams will remain. But if you listen carefully and follow the directions from the spirit world, you will gain great knowledge and live, and sleep, in peace."

"Double wow," said Sheila. "Well, on Sunday I'm going to Marystown for a spa day, at least a spa afternoon, with Moira and some of my friends. That might be a good time to get together with Frank if you want."

"Maybe," said Windflower. "I'll talk to him later today after the funeral to see if he's interested. First, breakfast, m'dear."

Windflower went back to the kitchen and found the fixings for a small fruit bowl each and then cracked a few eggs, mixed them with a little salt and pepper and threw in a shredded slice of Nova Scotia smoked salmon for flavour. A few slices of toast later, they were sitting at the kitchen table enjoying their breakfast and Saturday morning together.

After breakfast Windflower went over to check on his uncle while Sheila got ready for the funeral. He drove by the funeral home along the way and saw a number of cars already there.

The family, he thought, come to pay their last respects.

When he got to his house there was no sign of Uncle Frank. No sign except that his bed had been neatly made, and his breakfast dishes washed and left in the rack to dry.

This might just work out, thought Windflower.

Having a few minutes to spare before Sheila would be ready, he swung his car around and headed down to the wharf.

There was Uncle Frank with a tin mug of tea in his hand, holding court with the other old-timers. Windflower drove by and waved good morning but didn't get the feeling that his uncle wanted him to stop and talk.

He's probably telling them how he fought off the first dozen of his attackers until the next wave took him down, thought Windflower. Oh, well, let him have his fun. There's probably no harm in embellishing the truth, and judging by the audience with him on the wharf, Windflower suspected that they'd all told a few whoppers in their day.

Chapter Eleven

Windflower arrived back at Sheila's just as she was putting on her coat to go to the funeral. He held her umbrella for her as she walked to the car, and then drove right up to the front door of the Anglican Church on Main Street.

The parking lot was full, and people were milling around the front door, waiting for the service to begin. Just as Sheila was getting out, the long black car from the funeral home with the casket arrived. Right behind was the family car, and Windflower and Sheila could see a woman in black hunched over in the back seat.

"Poor Peggy," said Sheila quietly as they waited for the funeral procession and the family to go into the church. "I'll save you a place," said Sheila as she went inside.

Windflower nodded and went to park the car. When he came back into the church the service was just beginning, and he spotted Sheila a few pews from the back. The church was filled to overflowing with the mourners and the curious, all paying their last respects to a young woman that many of them had seen grow up.

The Anglican priest was an older gentleman who stumbled a little in his delivery, but was sincere in his intentions of trying to help the family find some solace in their faith after such a tragic loss.

There was a large delegation of young women from St. John's there too, many of them wearing their rowing club colours, six of them serving as pallbearers as the casket was rolled out of the church at the end of the service.

The mother was clearly distraught and almost inconsolable as she wept into her handkerchief all the way out. She was held up, if not entirely comforted, by a man at her side who must be her son, thought Windflower.

So that's Shawn Parsons, he said to himself as he watched the pair move slowly down through the church, followed by other relatives and close family friends.

The man, as if he heard Windflower's thinking out loud, paused and glanced briefly in his direction, but made no attempt to acknowledge him.

Once the family had left, the rest of the church emptied onto the steps and huddled in small clumps under the overhang to stay somewhat out of the rain. Sheila went to say a few quiet words to the mother before she left to go to the cemetery, and then spied some of her friends and went over to talk to them.

Windflower saw Tizzard and Detective Langmead from St. John's at the back of the crowd.

"Good morning, gentlemen," said Windflower.

"Sarge," said Tizzard.

"Good morning, Winston," said Langmead. "How did your uncle make out?"

"Frank is good. So good in fact that he's down on the wharf right now telling his buddies how he beat off the gangs of thugs in St. John's," said Windflower, and all three men laughed.

"We're just going for an early lunch at the Mug-Up," said Tizzard, "I want to get this townie a good feed of por' cakes. Why don't you join us?"

"Let me check with Sheila, and I'll catch up with you there," said Windflower.

The other two men walked off to Tizzard's car while Windflower scanned the crowd for his lady friend. He spotted her talking to Madge Molloy. They were old buddies and Madge had been in the car with Sheila when she had that terrible accident last year. Windflower caught her eye and she came over to him.

"I'm going to catch a ride with Madge over to the Parsons' house after they get back from the cemetery. Peggy is a wreck and there may not be much I can do, but I want to at least offer to help. By the way, I found out a bit more about that Dowson girl. She's from Red Bay, at least her family is. What's more interesting is that Madge says that she once went out with young Shawn Parsons. I'm not sure if anything came of it, but that's my report from the network," said Sheila with a wink.

"Thank you to the prettiest informant in Grand Bank," said Windflower. "'I'm going to meet up with Tizzard and the guy from St. John's at the café. Give me a call later and we'll make a plan for this evening."

"I'm thinking a cold plate and a warm fire," said Sheila.

"That would be great, Mrs. Hillier," said Windflower as he pecked her cheek and took his leave.

That is one great lady, he thought. Now, I've got to see another lady about some of those por' cakes.

Por' cakes (or pork cakes) were a Grand Bank staple and had been for as long as anyone around there could remember. They were cheap and easy to make, with the only basic ingredients being minced fat back pork and potatoes, along with a little baking powder and flour to bind them together. Baked in the oven and served hot with molasses and a bowl of pea soup, this was the traditional Saturday morning lunch in Grand Bank. And this is what Windflower hoped was awaiting him at the Mug-Up.

But as he joined his fellow officers there, Windflower only achieved half of his culinary dream. They were sold out of pea soup for the day, but the waitress, Marie, kindly offered him homemade beans and a fresh roll to go along with his por' cakes, an offer that Windflower graciously accepted.

"So what did you think of the por' cakes?" Tizzard asked the detective from St. John's.

"They were delicious," said Langmead. "I especially liked them with the molasses. I've had potato cakes before but never with pork like this. The pork really adds flavour."

"So, how's the investigation going?" asked Windflower.

"It's slow," said Langmead. "Based on what we've seen so far it looks like the girl was likely killed somewhere else, and her body was dumped in the alleyway. I don't want to sound too melodramatic, but it almost looks like a professional hit. We don't get much of that in St. John's."

"Professional?" said Tizzard as he rose up in his seat, his eyes growing very large.

Windflower just glared at him until he eased back down in his chair.

"What makes you say that?" asked Windflower.

"Well, there are no prints anywhere on the body, or near the scene; aside from the person who found the body. And while the victim was choked to death, her neck was also cleanly broken. And we found enough barbiturates in her body to knock out a horse," said Langmead.

"Wow," said Tizzard, unable to hold back any longer. "Did you talk to her brother yet?"

"I got a chance to talk to the brother last night," said Langmead. "He wasn't much help. He says he hadn't talked to his sister in months. And of course all of the girl's rowing friends are shocked. None of them really socialized much with her except for the practice and races, and a couple of keg parties where she'd show up for a few minutes and then duck out. At school she had a few classmates that she went to class with, and had lunch with sometimes, but none of them really knew her either. It was like she was living a completely separate life from the rest of the young people her age."

"Shawn Parsons has always been on the wrong side of the law," said Tizzard. "As long as I knew him, which would have been right up until about Grade 11, he was in and out of trouble. It wasn't serious enough to go to jail for, but lots of drinking and some drugs that I know about. That wasn't really my scene, and we travelled in very different circles. This is the first time I've seen him since those days, and by the looks of him I'd say he's still up to no good. I'm going to run a check on him when I get back."

Then looking at Windflower, who was now staring directly at him, Tizzard said, "If that's okay with you, Boss?"

"Very good, Corporal," said Windflower. "It's good to acknowledge the big dog is back in town." He smiled at Tizzard and winked at Langmead, who was also enjoying the joke.

"I have a bit more information on the Dowson girl that you might find interesting," Windflower said to Langmead. "My sources tell me that she's actually from around here. Her family is from Red Bay. I don't know how long it's been since she's been there, but at one point she had a boyfriend from this area."

"Who was it?" asked Tizzard and Langmead together.

"Shawn Parsons," said Windflower. "Now isn't that interesting?"

"That is very interesting," said Langmead. "I think I better have another chat with Mr. Parsons to see if there's anything else he neglected to mention. And I wouldn't mind having a look at anything you find out about him in your search, if you don't mind Tizzard. Or maybe I should be asking your boss?"

Tizzard gave Langmead a ride back to his car and went back to the RCMP detachment to do his research on Shawn Parsons.

Windflower mopped up the last of the molasses on his plate with a remaining morsel of por' cakes and pronounced himself well satisfied. His contentment grew when he went to the cash, and was told by Marie that the lovely man from "Sin John's" had paid for his lunch.

He drove past Sheila's house but there were no lights on, and no signs of anyone home.

Perfect, he thought. This is a great opportunity for an afternoon nap, and if the gods were with him, his uncle would be holed up somewhere else this rainy afternoon, telling stories and hopefully not getting into any more trouble.

Windflower's prayers were answered when he arrived to find the house warm and empty, a perfect combination. He went into his bedroom and lay on top of the bed, pulling a homemade quilt up over his shoulders. For the next two hours he was oblivious to the world.

He woke around 4 p.m. and saw that the sun had finally decided to make an appearance. So too had his Uncle Frank, who was sitting in the living room watching wrestling on television.

"You know that stuff's not real, don't you, Uncle Frank?" teased Windflower.

"It's as real as those fake hockey games everybody watches. Everyone knows that Montreal pays the refs to beat the Leafs every year," was Uncle Frank's retort.

"Have you eaten today?" asked Windflower. "I could make you a snack if you're hungry."

"No, thanks," said his uncle. "I had por' cakes and pea soup for lunch and I'm invited over to Jarge's for supper. I think he's got moose stew."

"Okay," said Windflower. "I'm going over to Sheila's again tonight. But I was hoping maybe you and I could have some time together tomorrow. The weather looks like it's clearing off and it would be good to take a walk in the woods."

"Sure," said his uncle. "Is there something going on that you want to talk to me about?"

"No. Well, yes, actually," said Windflower finally owning up. "I've been having some strange dreams and I was hoping that you could help me to understand them."

"Dreams, eh?" said Uncle Frank. "I haven't done any dream work for years. I better get out my stuff if we are going to do some dream work," and off he went to rummage around in his duffle bag. He came out later with a large pouch and his smudge bowl.

Windflower left the older man poking around in his pouch, and walked through the now sunny day to Sheila's. She was home by the look of the light in her kitchen that wasn't on before. Windflower went in through the back door, and called out his greeting to Sheila to let her know that he was home.

Chapter Twelve

Sheila was relaxing in the living room catching up on her magazines and called back hello to Windflower.

"And put the kettle on, will you?" said Sheila.

Windflower filled the kettle, placed it on the stove to boil, and went out to see Sheila in the living room.

"Well, somebody is happy with me," he said.

"And who would that be, besides me?" asked Sheila.

"Why, thank you, dear," said Windflower. "But my Uncle Frank appears to be excited that I have decided to talk to him about my dreams. He's home right now getting everything ready for tomorrow."

"What's he getting ready?" asked Sheila.

"I don't know exactly," said Windflower, "But he's got his medicine pouch out and he said something about having to get it prepared before it gets dark."

"I guess people take dreams pretty seriously in your culture," said Sheila.

"We were taught to never ignore our dreams," said Windflower. "In the old days some people believed that dreams gave messages and guidance about all matters of their life, even whom to marry. That's why dream catchers are so important. They were thought to protect our children from nightmares, and catch the bad dreams in the webs before they came to reality."

"Today we've lost many of those beliefs and even our teachings are getting lost. So much of our traditional knowledge isn't even written down," Windflower continued. "It may not all be completely true but what religion can claim any monopoly on the truth? It is all just what we remember and what we believe. I think I hear the kettle boiling."

Windflower came back into the living room with the tea and two cups. He poured one for Sheila and found her curled up asleep. He placed a blanket over her and picked up the 'Good Housekeeping' magazine she had been reading.

Maybe I'll find some new recipes, he thought.

When Sheila awoke she made them a light dinner of sliced cold cuts along with a couple of salads she'd picked up from the Mug-Up, where she had stopped by earlier. Along with a couple of Parker House rolls, also from the café, and a big piece of blueberry pie for dessert, both of them were quite satisfied.

Windflower suggested a post-dinner walk to which Sheila happily agreed. He needed to walk off some of the mass of calories he had consumed that day, and Sheila wanted to get some exercise to continue strengthening her legs.

They walked all over town, and it seemed like the whole of Grand Bank had decided to join them on this late summer evening stroll. Sheila particularly enjoyed seeing her neighbours and friends again, many of them for the first time since she'd been in St. John's.

The happy couple continued their walk down by the brook that was heavily swollen from the recent rains. They stopped to watch several families with young children feed a flock of ducks that had gathered for what looked like their regular evening snack.

The two continued along the wharf, and watched as the newly painted and refurbished lighthouse blinked out its beacon to the ocean and all the ships at sea.

"I'm so glad that the Council got that grant to fix up the lighthouse," said Sheila.

"Yeah, it's hard to imagine Grand Bank without that beauty," said Windflower. "And I heard Herb Stoodley led the local fundraising drive to put in the town's share."

"Let's drop by and see if the Stoodleys are home on the way back," said Sheila. "I've seen Moira a few times already, but I'd love to say hello to Herb."

"Perfect," said Windflower. "I'll race you up the hill," and he pretended to run up the short slope towards the Stoodley house.

"I'm happy just to be able to walk up the hill," said Sheila with a laugh.

The Stoodleys were sitting on a picnic bench in back of their house enjoying the late summer evening while waiting for the sunset. They were happy to see Sheila and Windflower, and Moira stepped inside to put on a fresh batch of tea. She came back with both tea and a sweater for Sheila.

"Stay and watch the sunset with us," said Moira. "We won't get too many more evenings where we can sit out here this year, and the view is spectacular when we have a clear night."

And as the couples sat and drank their tea the view was extraordinary. The sun out over the ocean started to dip slowly, and it filled the sky with a light so bright red that it looked like the sky was on fire. Then it fell, dropping like a rock into the ocean, leaving in its wake a range of colours that blended blue and red, and turned the green aqua of the ocean into mauves and purples.

After a time the sky turned into pure black until the moon appeared over their shoulders to create an endless shimmering wave on the horizon.

The four friends shared a few moments of reverent silence and awe. Then they moved back inside, where Moira insisted on serving Windflower a piece of her fresh peach pie, which of course, he accepted. They spent a few more minutes in small talk until Sheila suggested to Windflower with a smile that it was time to go.

"Thank you very much," said Windflower, "Especially for my peach pie."

"You're very welcome, Winston," said Moira.

"Why don't you guys come back tomorrow night for dinner?" asked Herb Stoodley. "Moira's got a night off and I was going to try a beer can chicken on the barbeque."

"Don't burn the place down, Herb," said Moira. "I remember some of your other experiments with fire and cooking."

"I got it covered, m'dear," said Herb. "Besides, you don't have to cook or clean."

"In that case, go for it," said Moira with a laugh.

"I think we'll go for it too," said Sheila, "Unless you have plans to cook me something else, Winston?"

"No ma'am," said Windflower. "We accept your kind offer Herb. See you tomorrow night."

The pair walked hand in hand home to Sheila's and by the time they arrived both were tired and ready to wind down.

Sheila had a hot bath while Windflower looked around for some new reading material, but was just as happy when Sheila announced that she was heading to bed and invited him to join her. He didn't need to be asked twice.

Windflower awoke in the morning to the delicious smell of fresh coffee. He followed his nose to the kitchen where Sheila was cooking, humming to herself, and listening to the *Weekend Arts Magazine* on CBC Radio. Windflower crept up behind her and clasped her in a friendly bear hug.

"Good morning, beautiful," he whispered in her ear.

"Good morning Winston," said Sheila. "I appreciate the warm embrace but unless you want to spoil your surprise, I suggest you grab a cup of coffee and go have your shower."

"Yes, ma'am," said Windflower happily, as he went off to clean up with his fresh cup of coffee in hand.

After his shower and shave he pulled on his cords and a sweatshirt that had a picture of a moose and a car on the front with the caption "Rule #1 The Moose Always Wins, Rule # 2 See Rule #1".

When he came back out to the kitchen, Sheila directed him to his seat and loaded his plate with fresh, hot blueberry pancakes. Along with local pork sausages, this was Windflower's ideal breakfast. At first he just stared and then quickly dove in. With a mouthful of blueberry pancake smothered in maple syrup, he managed to mumble a "Thank you, Sheila," before continuing on his breakfast adventure.

He didn't look up again until his first plate of pancakes was gone, and then, as Sheila suspected, held out his plate for more. Sheila just watched in amazement as he worked his way through plate two of pancakes and sausages.

"You sure can eat, Sergeant," she said as he finally put down his fork long enough to pay attention to something other than food.

"Sheila, you are the absolute best," said Windflower. "I was hoping you'd find the blueberries I left in the fridge."

"Well, you had better get some more if you want me to make that blueberry buckle you like so much," she replied.

"We'll get some more today when I go out with Uncle Frank," said Windflower. "Now, my lady, is there anything special I can do for you this morning?"

Sheila just smiled and said, "If you really mean that, I have an extra-large load of laundry that needs doing. If you take it up to the laundromat and get it washed I can hang it on the line while I'm in Marystown this afternoon."

That wasn't exactly what Windflower had in mind when he made his offer, but minutes later he was sitting in the laundromat watching the suds fly round and round.

At least he had found another good book to read, *The Orenda,* the latest by Joseph Boyden. It was about the 17th-century clashes involving Jesuit missionaries, the Huron and the Iroquois nations in pre-Confederation Canada. Fascinated, he didn't realize where the time went until a little old lady came into the laundromat and asked him if he knew that his "machine 'ad done finished?"

He thanked her, bundled the wash back into his bag, and left as quickly as possible. She just shook her head and had another story to tell her neighbours "bout dat strange Mountie feller from away."

Windflower dropped off his basket of chores and got a peck on the cheek from Sheila for his efforts. Waving goodbye, he set off back towards his house to see if Uncle Frank was up and ready to go.

Frank was more than ready. He had been up early and had even made them a thermos of tea and found a package of raisin tea biscuits in the freezer that he had thawed, buttered and packed in his large pouch.

"I'm ready to go," he announced when his nephew came through the door.

"Great," said Windflower. "Let's grab a few containers. If we get a few more berries, Sheila promised to make me a blueberry buckle. And I'll share it with you."

"That's a deal," said Uncle Frank as he took his stuff out to the car with Windflower who had his Tupperware and a bucket for the berries.

They drove to the back of the Health Centre where Windflower noticed a lot more cars since his last visit.

More competition for the berries, he thought.

He led his uncle up through the trail to the narrow path that led up to the transmission tower. They found an unoccupied berry patch about three-quarters of the way up the hill, and both settled in for an hour of solid picking.

After filling his plastic container, Uncle Frank found a little hillock where he could see back over the town of Grand Bank. He sat down and rolled himself a cigarette. When Windflower had filled his Tupperware bowl he went over and sat beside him. They rested quietly for a few moments, admiring the view which included scattered pockets of berry pickers all the way down the hill, their backs bent and intent on completing their mission.

"Well, I think we have enough blueberries for Sheila," said Windflower.

"Do you want to talk now?" asked Uncle Frank.

When Windflower nodded he took the smudge bowl out of his pouch along with a baggie of what he called his special medicine.

"It's what your grandfather taught me to use before I start my dream work," he said to Windflower.

Uncle Frank poured some of the herbs from his baggie into the smudge bowl and struck a match to light it. He cupped the bowl in his hands and blew gently into the bottom to make it smoke without burning too quickly. Then he took a long brown and white feather from his bag and started to wave it over the smudge bowl.

"This is a hawk feather," he said. "A hawk can see forever; even inside our dreams."

He passed the smoke over his head and body using the feather. Then he handed both to Windflower who repeated the actions for himself. Uncle Frank then spoke in the Cree language, saying his prayers and asking for guidance.

Windflower, like many of his generation, only knew a few Cree words but recognized the actions and intent from other ceremonies that he had witnessed in the past.

"I am asking your grandfather, and Grandfather Sun and Grandmother Moon to help us see into the dream world," said Uncle Frank. "They will help to guide me and to guide you on this journey. You may begin now," he said to Windflower.

Windflower told him his first dream about the lady and the skeletons chasing him and asking for his help. He was very sombre in the telling of this dream and was quite surprised when Uncle Frank began to laugh.

Windflower felt a little hurt by this and said to his uncle, "Why are you laughing at me, Uncle?"

Frank stopped laughing and said with a smile, "I am not laughing at you, son. I am laughing because I have had the same dream."

And then he proceeded to tell Windflower about his dream in exact detail.

"What does that mean, Uncle?" he asked.

"I do not know for sure, but I believe that it is a message from those who came here before. The ones who once lived here but are no more," said Uncle Frank. "I believe they are asking us to honour them, to remember them. They feel that they have been forgotten. It is only those who share the same pain and hold the same memories in their hearts who can hear their cries. That is why we hear their voices and see their faces in our dreams. The fact that you have had the same dream must mean that your generation is the one who must act and speak on their behalf, since I am old and my generation is growing weak."

"You will need to find out more information about these people who were here before us, Winston. Then I can help you understand what to do. Now, didn't you have a second dream?" asked Uncle Frank.

Windflower nodded and then proceeded to tell his uncle about the dream of waking up in bed with a dead woman. His Uncle Frank listened closely but this time did not laugh at the end of Windflower's story. Instead he closed his eyes, sat still and concentrated for what seemed like an eternity.

"Ah," he finally said. "This dream is a warning dream. Someone whom you know, a woman, is in danger. Do you know who this woman is?"

"No," said Windflower. 'I could not see her face in the dream. I always wake up first."

"You must see her face," said Uncle Frank. "She is in great danger and you have to warn her. The next time you have this dream you will have to force yourself to stay in the dream long enough to see who it is. You must do this so that you can tell her that she is in danger. She must have an ally in the spirit world who is trying to protect her, but she will not listen. You have to tell her. You have been chosen," he said.

Windflower looked in amazement at his uncle who had already moved past the dream interpretation to opening his pouch and pouring himself a cup of tea from the thermos.

"Care for a tea biscuit?" he asked Windflower calmly.

Windflower certainly didn't feel like eating but gladly took a cup of tea from his uncle.

Seeing his obvious distress Uncle Frank reached over and touched Windflower on the shoulder.

"It's in your family to help others," he said. "We just don't know yet what we will be asked to do. Don't worry. You will find a way to do this. You would not have been chosen otherwise."

Windflower wasn't so sure, but after their tea he walked silently behind his uncle down the hill until they reached the car. He dropped his uncle off at the wharf to see his buddies and then drove out to the best place he knew for some quiet time alone. He needed time to think, and there was no better place to do that than out on the L'Anse Au Loup T.

Chapter Thirteen

Windflower drove his car out of Grand Bank until he reached the L'Anse Au Loup T sign, where he turned off the highway onto a rutted gravel road that led to his destination.

The T is a body of land that reaches out into the ocean from two sides and comes together in the form of a T. At this time of day the T was deserted, and you could stroll along the beach or just find a quiet rock to sit on and watch the seals at play.

Windflower decided to walk because he did his best thinking then. And he needed to think about what his uncle had told him. As he strolled he thought about his options.

He could do nothing and hope that the dreams would go away, but that appeared unlikely to happen. So he had to do something. That was his first decision. Deciding exactly what that would be would involve a lot more time and much more walking.

Forty-five minutes later Windflower's head felt clear at last. He would honour his uncle's advice.

First, he would have to do some research. If what his uncle had said was true, then the images in his dreams were memories of this island and the people, First Nations who had lived here before the Europeans had arrived. Windflower had heard a little about them. The Beothuks, they were called. He knew that they had been wiped out, apparently from diseases brought by the settlers to Newfoundland. He would have to find out more, much more.

Secondly, he made up his mind to try and see the woman's face in his dream; that was of course, if he ever had that dream again. With any luck that wouldn't happen. But given his luck lately, Windflower wouldn't bank on it. So he steeled himself to the possibility and probability that when it happened, he would find the courage to take the necessary action.

Maybe Uncle Frank could give me some special medicine to help me, he thought.

With that reassuring plan in his mind, he remembered that he had dinner to look forward to at the Stoodley's. Both images cheered him greatly.

Sheila had barely returned from Marystown when Windflower got back from the T.

She looked relaxed and refreshed with the freshly scrubbed red face of a woman who had recently submitted to the rejuvenating charms of a facial. She was sitting on the couch with her long legs tucked up beneath her and her dark red hair tied up on top of her head, the way Windflower loved it. She lifted her head from her book to smile at Windflower, and as usual he fell more in love with her. It wasn't just her natural beauty, he thought, but that inner goodness that shone when she smiled.

"Hello, gorgeous," he said. "How was your afternoon at the spa?"

"It was sooooooo nice," cooed Sheila. "I had a massage that was to die for and a facial. Although it feels like I left half my face back there. How was your time with Uncle Frank?"

"It was productive," said Windflower. "I put a couple of cups of blueberries in the fridge. Enough for my buckle, I hope?"

"You'll get your blueberry buckle, don't worry," said Sheila. "How did your chat go?"

"Well, I'm still processing what he said," Windflower replied, "But a piece of what's going on has to do with old memories of this place."

"Grand Bank?" asked Sheila.

"No, Newfoundland," said Windflower. "I think I'm having dreams about the Beothuks. And Uncle Frank said he had the same exact dream. What do you know about the Beothuks?" he asked Sheila.

"Only what we learned in school," said Sheila. "That wasn't very much, to tell you the truth. I'm not sure why, but it just wasn't talked about a lot; it still isn't."

"We heard that they were the native people who were living here when the English first came and that they eventually became extinct. There were a few cultural artifacts at the old Newfoundland Museum and they are probably at 'The Rooms' complex in St. John's now. The last known Beothuk was Shanawdithit, a young woman who died of tuberculosis in 1829. After she died no more Beothuk people were ever seen in Newfoundland."

Windflower sat silently while Sheila spoke and he remained wordless as she came over and gave him a hug.

"I'm going to go get ready for supper," she said.

Half an hour later the two of them were walking hand in hand over to their friends' house where they were greeted with warm smiles and a cool glass of sparkling white wine each. Sheila stayed in the kitchen to help Moira with the salad while Windflower went outside to see how Herb Stoodley was making out with the barbeque.

"Man, that smells good," said Windflower. "So, how's your chicken in a beer can coming along?"

"It's going great," said Stoodley. "It's actually quite easy. I just rub a few spices on the chicken and plunk its butt onto a half empty beer can. Then you cook it on the cool side of the barbeque for an hour, basting it occasionally with any sauce you like. I use a base barbeque sauce and then add some jalapeños and a heavy dose of Frank's Red Hot. The beer steams the chicken and keeps the inside moist while the heat crisps up the outside."

"We're on the last 15 minutes now. I've tested the inside temperature to make sure it's done. I don't want to poison us. You can't be too careful with chicken or other poultry in the summertime. I don't know how they managed not to get food poisoning in the olden days," said Stoodley as he applied another thick basting of sauce to the chicken on the barbeque.

"Speaking of the past, what do you know about the Beothuks?" asked Windflower.

"I was wondering when you'd start asking about that sordid part of our Newfoundland history," said Stoodley.

"The Beothuk people were here hundreds of years before any Europeans set sight on Newfoundland. What little we know about them is mostly anecdotal, and of course you have heard that they were wiped out. I don't use that term with any relish, but I believe it to be true."

"The common belief is that they died from the 'white man's diseases' which is factually true," continued Stoodley. "But they were also driven away from the ocean by both the English and French, who wanted the access for themselves. That meant they had no way to feed themselves, and had to live in the interior of the country where they still had to compete with the Europeans for food. That was a game they couldn't win. There are also stories of bounties placed on their heads and other horrors, but I don't know how much of that is true."

"I do know that we killed them off. And it's part of our history that we do not often speak about; at least not until recently. The newer generation has a more open mind about what many people call genocide. They want to know about the Beothuks and what happened to them. There are even songs about them. The band, Great Big Sea, has a song called 'Demasduit Dream'. It's about a Beothuk woman, Demasduit, who was known by her English name as Mary March," said Stoodley.

"I've heard about Shanawdithit," said Windflower.

"Mary March, 'Demasduit' in Beothuk, was her aunt," said Stoodley. "Both died in the 1820's and were some of the last Beothuks ever seen. There's also a book by Michael Crummy, a Newfoundland writer, called *River Thieves that* tells some of the Beothuk story in Newfoundland. I have a copy if you want to borrow it."

"I would very much like that," said Windflower. "I've been wondering a bit about what happened to the Beothuks."

"Well, this will help give you some of the background, at least from the European's perspective. And there are also a lot of artifacts at 'The Rooms' in St. John's, and more at the Mary March Museum in Grand Falls. You should check some of it out," he said.

"I will," said Windflower.

"Let me go get that book for you. Why don't you put another basting of sauce on the bird while I'm gone?" said Stoodley.

Before he got back Windflower had applied another layer of sauce to the brown and crackling chicken on the barbeque. When Stoodley came back, he handed Windflower the book and checked on the meat.

"I think our work is done out here," said Stoodley. "The best part of cooking like this is that you just throw away the beer can and eat the chicken. Which is what we're going to do right now," he said as he moved the chicken from atop the beer can onto a waiting platter and led Windflower inside.

Moira had made a terrific salad featuring three kinds of lettuce along with slices of Granny Smith apples, dried cranberries, and diced carrots and cucumbers with a homemade strawberry vinaigrette dressing. Along with baked potatoes with fresh sour cream and steamed green beans, they made the perfect accompaniments to Herb's moist and crispy chicken.

The couples ate and chattered their way through supper and dessert, an apple-peach cobbler from the Mug-Up. Then they took their Irish coffees outside on the deck and waited, stuffed and satisfied, for the sunset.

"That was a marvellous meal, you guys," said Windflower.

"Yes, thank you very much," said Sheila. "Now that I'm back, we'll be happy to return the favour any time you're free, although I know how busy you are at the café, Moira."

"How about me?" said Herb, "She's got me run off my feet."

Everyone laughed and Windflower patted him on the back in solidarity.

"I've really enjoyed being back in the business," said Moira, "Although I'm happy to see the end of the tourist season. You get run off your feet. Why just a few weeks ago we had a whole crew of Chinese tourists. I think they were coming back from St. Pierre. The guide was a Russian fellow. He seemed to be in charge and made all the arrangements. They had a whole day planned right here in Grand Bank."

"Chinese?" asked Windflower. "Wasn't that a little strange?"

"It's the second time we've had them, not the same ones, but the same tour group," said Moira. "They come into town in the morning, usually two or three small buses, 50 or 60 people. They go to the swimming pool in the morning, and then come here for an early lunch. We set them up at the Theatre next door and feed them. Then we make up a whack of sandwiches and juice packs and they're on their way."

"Do you know where they were headed?" asked Windflower.

"Across the island, as far as I know," said Moira. "I have the tour guy's card somewhere, let me find it."

As she went to look for it, both Sheila and Stoodley were staring at Windflower.

"Are you planning to take a tour of the island?" asked Herb Stoodley mischievously.

"Yes, is there something you want to tell us, Winston?" asked Sheila.

Windflower was saved from answering by Moira Stoodley who returned with a tattered business card with Gorky's Tours, Sergei Fetisov, and an address and phone number in Halifax written on it.

"Here it is," she said.

Everyone kept staring at Windflower but he simply said, "Do you mind if I borrow this? I need to check something out."

"Sure," said Moira and further questioning was postponed as Windflower pointed to the sky that was beginning its magical night-time transformation.

After another beautiful sunset, he and Sheila said goodnight and headed for home. Sheila and Windflower held hands on the way and she moved closer as the night grew chilly.

"I think that summer is over," said Sheila.

"I think you're right," said Windflower.

Chapter Fourteen

When they arrived home Sheila went off to have her bath and Windflower settled in on the couch with his new book.

River Thieves captured his attention right from the beginning, as he read the story of how the then British Governor of Newfoundland sent out an expedition of sailors to determine if they couldn't make a fresh start with the local "Red Indians", the Beothuks. To the sailors, "Red Indians" seemed to be an obvious name for this eerily mysterious people who painted their bodies with a pigment made from red ochre.

There was a great deal of unease and mistrust between the natives and the settlers, as each other's customs and cultures were so very different.

The Beothuks would from time to time "borrow" utensils and supplies from the settlers without any real intention of returning them. They saw it as a down payment on the rent they were owed since the Europeans had taken over their prime fishing and trapping areas.

The settlers took these acts as threats to their survival in a hostile climate and responded with regular raids on the Beothuks, sometimes destroying entire encampments and killing anyone they found there.

Windflower liked that the book tried to capture the idea that this was not a fair fight in any regard. Any of the Beothuks that were not killed off by diseases like smallpox and tuberculosis were at risk of being wiped out by either hunger or the settlers' guns.

Even though the Beothuks were often described by the settlers as savage, the author had managed to portray them as normal human beings, with a culture and civilization of their own. They were described as people who were just carving out an existence, like the settlers who feared and hated them.

By the time Windflower put the book down he noticed that the light had gone off in the bedroom, and as quietly as he could he washed and undressed for bed.

He fell asleep quickly next to the gentle snoring of Sheila. As he drifted off to sleep he realized he had begun the work that his uncle had been suggesting: to find out more about the people in his dreams. And he knew, somehow, that he would not have any more of those dreams tonight.

Windflower was right, and did not remember anything else until he woke with the sunlight streaming into his room. That was good, because the sun was still rising early, and he would have plenty of time to get ready for work before 8.

He washed and shaved quickly, and grabbed a banana from the counter for an instant breakfast. He could get something later on in the morning at the café if he was hungry.

He went out on Sheila's back porch to do his morning smudge and today he added his thanks for a good night sleep with his usual request for guidance. He also added an extra prayer this morning for the spirits of the Beothuk people who had come before him on this land. He honoured their greatness and their ability to survive for so long in such a harsh climate, and he prayed that they would find peace in the other world.

Sheila was still sleeping, so he kissed her gently on the cheek and left the house quietly. He decided to leave his car at Sheila's and because it was a Marystown RCMP car, he could call them to come pick it up later. He would use one of the cruisers at Grand Bank.

Maybe he could talk Tizzard into giving up his RCMP jeep. He could order him to do it, but he really didn't want to spoil his return to Grand Bank by being that petty. Plus, he thought, Tizzard had been a good soldier all through the time that he spent on assignment in Marystown, and going back and forth with Sheila in St. John's.

He made the decision to take whatever car was available, and when it came time to order a new one for the detachment, he could have his pick of vehicles. That matter resolved, Windflower started thinking about all the ideas rolling around in his head. He was just starting to make his priority list when the RCMP jeep came roaring around the corner.

"Morning, Boss," said Tizzard, as he rolled down the window to say hello. "Need a ride?"

Windflower was going to say something to remind Tizzard to slow down, but instead smiled and said, "Hope you're going for a cup of coffee, Corporal."

"Yes, indeed," said Tizzard. "Hop in."

As usual, Tizzard got them to the Mug-Up much faster than Windflower would have preferred. They got out and went into the café where Herb Stoodley was guarding the cash and the coffee pot. He was busily engaged in deep conversation with one of the locals, so Tizzard simply held up two fingers to order their coffees, while Windflower found them their regular corner table. Soon Herb was by with two mugs of freshly brewed coffee, and after morning pleasantries, took their order for two raisin tea biscuits to go with their coffee.

"So what's new around here, besides our new fresh-faced female constable?" asked Windflower.

"Well, it's been a fairly quiet summer," said Tizzard. "We've had a few impaired, and a couple of moose/car incidents, but luckily no fatalities, not even a moose, so far this year. The fall is usually the worst though. I think the bulls are out looking for a cow while the cows are running from the hunters, and everyone is driving like they're crazy. It makes for a dangerous time of year, that's for sure. What did you think of those moose sensors on the highway outside of St. John's?"

"I'm not sure if anyone knows if they work or not yet," said Windflower. "But it seems to me that a whole of lot of money is being put into a pilot program that this province could never afford to implement all the way across the Trans-Canada. And that's not the only road that the moose travel on. It doesn't even include the highway down here."

"Personally, I don't think it's the answer, nor is the plan for moose fences, or even a mass moose cull. Sooner or later, we'll just have to learn to live together as man and moose."

"And slow down," said Tizzard.

Windflower was just about to remind Tizzard of his own shortcomings in this area when Herb Stoodley brought them their tea biscuits.

"Right out of the oven," he said.

Tizzard and Windflower laughed and almost simultaneously broke open their tea biscuits and watched as the steam escaped. Then they smothered both sides in butter and for a few brief moments were completely silent, as they savoured their morning treat.

"That was good," said Tizzard, wiping his mouth with a napkin.

"Agreed," said Windflower. "What about the increase in tourists this year?" asked Windflower, "Any problems with that?"

"What do you mean?" asked Tizzard.

"The Chinese visitors," said Windflower.

"Oh them," said Tizzard. "They weren't any trouble at all. They arrived one morning, went to the swimming pool, and then came back for lunch at the Theatre. They were gone by 2 p.m. The Mayor was happy to see them, even came over to say hello. I didn't think much of the tour guide though, Russian I think. He didn't speak very good English, and seemed a bit nervous when the Mayor came over and wanted to shake hands with the visitors."

"Didn't you think it was strange to have two large groups of Chinese tourists with a Russian tour guide come to visit Grand Bank?" asked Windflower.

"Yeah, I thought it was strange. But there's nothing illegal about it that I could see. Although I did think it was odd when one of the guys who was over at the swimming pool said that all the Chinese had their soap and shampoo in the pool with them. But I thought that maybe that was the way they always went swimming," said Tizzard.

Windflower just shook his head and went up to the cash to pay.

"Thanks, Herb, and say thanks to Moira for the delicious tea biscuits," he said. "See you soon."

Tizzard had the Jeep going and was revving the engine when Windflower came out.

"You go ahead, Corporal. I think it's safer to walk the rest of the way," said Windflower.

Windflower was happy to walk back into the Grand Bank detachment as the officer in charge. He was even happier when he got to his office and saw that both Tizzard and Betsy had cleaned the place up for him in advance.

Betsy arrived soon after and dropped in to see him and to bring him a cup of coffee in his old mug. This seemed like a dream come true but it probably wouldn't last, thought Windflower. As usual, he was right.

The first sign of trouble was the large pile of correspondence and reading materials that Betsy deposited in his once-empty in-basket.

"Sorry, sir," said Betsy sympathetically. "Corporal Tizzard never really caught on to the paperwork."

The second sign was when Windflower looked out of his window to see two male officers giggling as they hid behind a cruiser. Then he saw Constable Evanchuk bending over to pick up something on the ground behind her car. As she reached over to pick it up, one of the other officers took out his cell phone and snapped her photo from behind. They then resumed their hiding place until Constable Evanchuk got in her car and drove away.

Windflower watched in a combination of shock and outrage as the two officers laughed and slapped each other on the way into the detachment.

Windflower called Betsy on the intercom.

"Is Tizzard around?" he asked gruffly.

"No, Sergeant," said Betsy formally. "He said he'd be back around 11. He had to take his car in for maintenance."

"When he comes in, tell him I want to see him," said Windflower, this time a little more softly.

"Yes, sir," said Betsy. "Oh, and I have some information for you. Our tracer came back with a hit. The car was found abandoned by the side of the road in Cape Breton, in a small community called Meat Cove."

"Do you know where Meat Cove is?" asked Windflower.

"I looked it up, sir," said Betsy, who was sounding very proud of herself. "It's at the tip of Cape Breton Island just off the Cabot Trail. It's apparently very popular with campers."

"Good work, Betsy," said Windflower. "Can you call our guys down there and see if you can find out anything else?"

"Yes, sir," said Betsy. "I'll get right on it."

I bet she will, thought Windflower as he hung up and then looked in his cell phone for Detective Langmead's number in St. John's.

"Langmead, RNC," came the familiar voice over the phone line.

"Carl, it's Windflower in Grand Bank," said the RCMP Sergeant. "We got a bite on our tracer. They found the Dowson girl's car in Cape Breton. I'm just following up to hear what else I can find out from our guys down there."

"Thanks," said Langmead. "You guys are fast. I'll get on them today too. I was going to call you this morning anyway. Apparently, the brother has taken a runner. He wasn't there when I went back yesterday, and some of his relatives reported that he was gone, even though his rental car is still there."

"What do you make of it, Carl?" asked Windflower.

"I'm not sure but I don't like the feel of this. Now there are two people missing who might know something that can help out in this case. I wonder if you can spring Tizzard to help me find out where Shawn Parsons might be, and if anybody might be helping him out in Grand Bank," said Langmead. "I'd do it myself but I've got the Chief and the media beating down on me here so I really can't get away."

"Not a problem," said Windflower. "I'll talk to Tizzard about it later this morning."

"Thanks a lot," said Langmead, "Another one we'll owe you."

"Good luck," said Windflower. "I'll have Tizzard get in touch."

Windflower spent the next couple of hours sorting his in-basket into manageable piles. He had barely completed that task when Tizzard arrived in his office just past 11.

"You wanted to see me, Boss?" asked Tizzard.

"Sit down, Corporal. This is going to take some time," said Windflower.

Chapter Fifteen

"I know we have different styles Corporal, but I think things have gotten a little slack in my absence," said Windflower.

"What do you mean?'" asked Tizzard, getting the very real feeling that this was not going to be a pleasant conversation.

"First of all, what exactly is acceptable behaviour around here when it comes to dealing with members of the opposite sex? Because what I saw this morning from Fortier and Lewis doesn't come anywhere close to my standard," said Windflower.

"I still don't understand," said Tizzard.

"Well, let me make it clearer for you," said Windflower. "To have two male officers taking pictures of a female officer's butt when she is bending over and laughing like schoolboys about their trick, is despicable behaviour," said Windflower, his voice rising despite his attempts to remain cool. "And it says to me that there is a serious discipline problem and a lack of respect for authority.

"I know that the boys kid around a bit and I've warned them about their stupid behaviour, but they don't seem to take it serious, at least not from me," said Tizzard.

"Well, they will take it seriously from me," said Windflower. "And you will too, Corporal. This is a slippery slope we're on here and I intend to stop the slide right now. I want both of them in here to see me, and we're going to have a chat about what's acceptable and what the consequences are if anyone's behaviour is not up to my standards, and the standards of the Force. Set it up for this afternoon and I want you here too. Understood?"

"Yes, sir," said Tizzard meekly.

"And another thing, Tizzard I didn't expect to come back here and have to clean up your lousy paperwork. I'm not your mother, Corporal. I'm not your baby sitter. If you want to be a leader in this Force then you better start acting like one. Understood?" said Windflower, blowing full steam by now.

"Sorry, sir," said Tizzard, in a strained whisper.

"I don't want you to be sorry, Tizzard. I want you to be professional. And if you're not you can lose that stripe faster than you ever thought possible," said Windflower. "Understood, Corporal?"

'Understood, sir," said Tizzard, ready to melt into the floor.

"Good," said Windflower. "So set that meeting up and don't breathe a word about what it's about to them, okay? And Corporal, I want you to help Detective Langmead with his search for Shawn Parsons. Call him and get the details. But I want to be kept in the loop, okay?"

"Yes, sir," said Tizzard.

"Dismissed, Corporal," said Windflower with a wave of his hand and Tizzard backed slowly out of his office, sweating but relieved that his penalty had been verbal, at least so far.

Windflower was also relieved that task was over. He hated the discipline part of this job, but recognized it as completely necessary to maintain good order amongst the troops. And he wanted to send a strong message to Tizzard, that when Windflower was away, he expected him to follow up on his orders and provide direction to the other officers. After all, that's why Tizzard was a Corporal. He may be young but he had the stripe and he had to learn to use it wisely.

He was diving deeply into his in-basket again when the intercom buzzed and Betsy said, "Inspector Arsenault wants you to call him, sir."

"Thanks, Betsy," said Windflower, and he punched Arsenault's speed dial number on his phone.

"Good morning, Louise. How are you this morning?" said Windflower as he spoke to Inspector Arsenault's assistant and gatekeeper. "Thank you," he said as she passed him through.

"Windflower, how are you?" said Inspector Kevin Arsenault.

"I'm fine, sir," said Windflower. "And you?"

"I'm well, thank you," said Arsenault. "I hope you've been getting up to speed on the human trafficking file. There's a meeting set up for tomorrow with some of the other team members in the region. Apparently there have been some developments on the other side of the pond that Immigration wants to let us in on. You can participate by teleconference. I'll get Louise to send you the information later this morning. Anything else going on over there?"

"Not too much," said Windflower, choosing to omit offering up details about the earlier encounter with his errant constables. "I'm just getting back up to speed on things around here. The principle matter of interest is that we've been helping out the RNC with the murder investigation of the Parsons girl. Other than that it's pretty quiet, and I'm hoping it stays that way."

"Good stuff, Winston. Let me know how the call goes tomorrow," said Arsenault as he hung up.

After a few more minutes of struggling with his paperwork, Windflower was relieved to hear his cell phone ring, and to see it was Sheila.

"Good morning, Sergeant," said Sheila. "How's my favourite RCMP officer on the South Coast?"

"Only the South Coast?" joked Windflower, "I thought I'd at least get most of the island, maybe Labrador too."

"Can I make it up to you with a bowl of pea soup for lunch?" asked Sheila.

"Now that's more like it," said Windflower. "I'll be over in fifteen minutes."

Windflower checked himself out on the board and waved goodbye to Betsy who was busy on the phone. He took a look out the window to see what the weather was like, and to his disappointment it was dark and foggy, and he could feel the dampness in the air. He thought of asking Betsy for the keys to the pool car, but noticed that Tizzard's RCMP jeep was parked right in front of the door.

He walked to the back where Tizzard was making himself a cup of tea and simply said, "I want your keys."

In semi-shock, Tizzard didn't say a word, but reached into his jacket for the keys to his car, and handed them over to his Sergeant.

Windflower took them in hand and walked away without saying a word. Tizzard silently watched as his boss and his car disappeared out of the parking lot.

Windflower didn't have any intention of keeping Tizzard's jeep. He just wanted to shake him up a little. Judging by the look on Tizzard's face, he had succeeded. It wasn't very nice perhaps, but Windflower had a wide smile on his face when he arrived back at Sheila's.

Windflower called out a hearty hello, and hung his coat up in the hallway. Sheila was busy in the kitchen, but when he came in she stopped what she was doing and went over to give him a tight squeeze.

"What's that for?" asked Windflower, "Although I'm not complaining."

"I'm just glad to see you, Winston," said Sheila. "Sit down and I'll get you some soup."

Windflower didn't need to be asked twice and was soon fully engaged with his thick pea soup and homemade dumplings. It was nicely spiced too. Sheila used a very liberal sprinkling of hot black pepper. Both she and Windflower liked the hot stuff. After Windflower had finished his second bowl, his attention turned from his lunch to his girlfriend.

Sheila was used to coming second place to Windflower's appetite and waited for him to finish before trying to engage his brain.

"So, how does it feel to be back on the job in Grand Bank?" she asked him.

"It's good," said Windflower. "Betsy seems happy to have me back, mostly because Tizzard couldn't keep up with the paperwork to her liking. But there's something happening over there that's bothering me."

He then told Sheila about the incident he had witnessed that morning.

"It sounds rather unprofessional," said Sheila. "But you really can't expect the other guys to just follow what Tizzard has to say. Some of them are years older than him and he doesn't have the experience."

"Don't go sticking up for Tizzard just because he's young. He knows better than to allow that type of behaviour, and if he doesn't then he shouldn't be Corporal. He's in the chain of command and has to play his role," said Windflower.

"Don't get mad at me because Tizzard screwed up," said Sheila. "I'm sure not defending his behaviour."

"I know. I'm sorry if I was cross with you, Sheila," said Windflower. "I guess the truth is I'm more than a little disappointed with Tizzard, and I worry that if I don't stop this kind of thing in its tracks, then it just gets worse in a hurry. The Mounties haven't done a good job with this issue in the past, and it's coming back to bite us everywhere. I just want a positive and respectful workplace. And if I've got to knock a few heads to make that happen, so be it."

"Bravo," said Sheila. "We need a few more men like you taking action on sexual harassment, instead of just talking about it. I'm proud of you, Sergeant."

"Thanks, Sheila. How's your day been going?"

"It's going good, Winston," said Sheila. "I thought I'd really miss work, but you know I'm starting to realize that there's more to life than just trying to make a buck. I'm not rich by any means, but I've still got a few dollars and my share of the Mug-Up is paying most of my bills. I'm going to enjoy this little bit of time off while I figure out what I want to do with the rest of my life."

"As long as that includes me I am in full support of whatever you decide to do," said Windflower.

"I know," said Sheila. "I'll let you in on more of my thinking once I sort it out inside my own head. And I've got lots to do here, what with making desserts for you and visiting my old buddies."

"Did you say dessert for me?" asked Windflower.

"I thought that would get your attention," Sheila said. "Yes, I'm making your blueberry buckle this afternoon. But you'll have to wait until later to get a piece. I'm going with Myrna and Edie over to the United Church Women's supper in Fortune this evening. So you're on your own for supper."

"That's great," said Windflower. "I'll scrounge up something for me and Uncle Frank for tonight's supper and then come over here for dessert."

"You're the best, Sheila," he said, as he gave Sheila a hug before heading back to work.

"I know," said Sheila smiling.

When Windflower got to the office he parked the jeep in the same place as it was before lunch. He wasn't sure, but he could have sworn that he saw Tizzard peeking out from behind the blinds in another office.

Maybe he was worried that I wasn't going to bring "his" car back, thought Windflower.

When he got inside Tizzard was nowhere to be seen. But he magically reappeared when Windflower was safely inside his office.

"Here are your keys," said Windflower by way of greeting, and threw the jeep's keys back to Tizzard.

"Thanks," said Tizzard, relieved but not quite sure he was out of the woods yet. "I talked to Langmead, sir and I'm going to check around the local bars and with our informants to find out if anyone has seen Shawn

Parsons. I've got Fortier and Lewis coming in at 2 p.m. if that's okay, sir?" he asked gingerly.

"That would be fine," said Windflower coolly, deliberately letting Tizzard hang out a little while longer, at least until he saw how the meeting went.

Tizzard went away and Windflower decided to make a phone call to someone he knew in Halifax to check out the Russian tour guy. Staff Sergeant Guy Simard was a crusty old Francophone whom Windflower had worked with at the Halifax Airport years ago. Simard had fallen in love with the Atlantic Ocean and a woman he met at the Legion in Dartmouth, and had managed to swing a permanent assignment on the security detail at the airport.

Guy Simard knew everybody and everything that was happening in the port city. He had taken Windflower under his wing and taught him the inside tricks of the police trade; like how to spot when someone was holding dope, or trying so hard to look inconspicuous that they stood out like a sore thumb in a line-up at the airport. Windflower soaked up everything Simard gave him like a sponge, and the older cop made him his protégé. Windflower knew he could ask the old man for anything, and would never be refused.

"Hello Staff Sergeant, it's Windflower. How's it going?"

"Winston, mon gars, good to hear from you," boomed a loud voice on the phone. "Are you back in Grand Bank yet?"

Simard had encouraged Windflower to go back to Grand Bank where he could run his own show versus being what he called 'Arsenault's bum boy' in Marystown.

"Yes, sir," said Windflower. "I just got back this weekend. Sheila's back too, so we're looking to settle in here for a while more," he said.

"Good for you," said Simard. "You'll have to bring that lady of yours over to meet my Louisa," he said. "We'll have a night out at the Legion."

"That sounds like a plan," said Windflower. "But listen Guy, I've got something I need you to check out for me."

Windflower gave his friend the information about Gorky's Tours and the Fetisov name, along with the address on Spring Garden Road in Halifax.

"I need to know if this is a legit tour company, and if you wouldn't mind running Fetisov's name by the locals I'd much appreciate it."

"No problem, Winston. I'll get back to you when I have something. And stay in touch, okay?" said Simard.

"Okay, Guy, I'll do that. Bye."

When Windflower hung up the phone he could see shadows moving outside his door. He walked outside and saw the three male officers waiting to see him.

Chapter Sixteen

"Let's go in here," said Windflower. "There's room enough for all of us." As the men proceeded to the interview room in the back of the detachment, Windflower stopped at the receptionist's desk and said to Betsy, "No interruptions, okay?"

Betsy nodded her agreement, knowing from the mood in the air that something bad was likely to happen. If possible, she did not want any association with whatever that might be. She preferred to keep her head low.

Windflower sat on one side of the table and directed Tizzard, Fortier and Lewis to sit on the other.

Looking first at Fortier, and then at Lewis he said, "So who wants to go first?"

When neither volunteered, he spoke again.

"Okay, then I have something to say."

Windflower then proceeded to tell the two men what he had seen them do earlier that morning and what he thought of such behaviour in clear, loud, and very colourful language.

At the end of his initial comments he asked the two men, "What exactly were you doing, and what were you going to do with the photographs?"

This time Windflower didn't give them any options about who would or could go first but instead pointed at Fortier and said, "What was so funny, Constable?"

When no answer was offered he turned on Lewis and asked, "What were you going to do with the pictures? Post them on the bulletin board? Post them on Facebook? What in Hell were you guys thinking?"

Fortier started to speak but Windflower simply held up one hand and turned to Tizzard who was not expecting any questions to be asked of him, and said, "Corporal, could you please educate these officers as to why their behaviour is unacceptable and what standard of behaviour we expect in this detachment and throughout the Royal Canadian Mounted Police?"

Without another word Windflower got up, walked out of the interview room, and closed the door behind him.

He could hear Tizzard yelling at the two constables all the way down the hall. It went on for quite some time, and Windflower got a glimpse of Fortier and Lewis slinking out of the office shortly after things quieted down.

I think we may have dealt with that little problem for a while, thought Windflower. Now let's get the rest of this place back in shape.

Betsy came into Windflower's office shortly afterwards.

"I've got more news from Cape Breton, sir," she said. "A woman's body was found in the woods near the campgrounds in Meat Cove. And Detective Sergeant Langmead wants you to call him."

"Thank you, Betsy," said Windflower, as he picked up the phone to call St. John's.

"Langmead," the voice answered.

"Carl, it's Windflower. I guess you heard about the body?" said Windflower.

"Yeah, it looks like the Dowson girl, but I'm waiting for a positive identification from Cape Breton. I know that your team over there will want to deal with it, but I'm pretty sure that our cases are connected. We should be working together on this," said Langmead.

"Agreed," said Windflower. "I'll talk to my boss in Marystown, Inspector Arsenault, and see if he can smooth the waters on this one. Plus, I can get any inside info you need from Cape Breton. Just let me know what you want."

"Thanks, Winston, I appreciate it. Any news from Tizzard on the Parsons brother?" Langmead asked.

"Not yet, but he's on it," said Windflower. "If anybody around here knows anything, Tizzard will ferret it out."

"Great," said Langmead, "Let me know if he hears anything."

"Will do," said Windflower.

Windflower called Arsenault's office after hanging up from Langmead but only managed to reach Louise, so he left a message for the Inspector requesting him to call back.

Back to the grindstone, thought Windflower, and he spent the next couple of hours signing off on forms and documents that Tizzard had left behind for him. He was not particularly happy with his Corporal when Tizzard showed up at his door.

"I've got a lead on Shawn Parsons," said Tizzard, happy as a puppy to show his master that he wasn't really a bad dog after all. "My sources tell me that he's hooked up with Frankie Fallon."

"Who's Frankie Fallon?" asked Windflower.

"Frankie is the closest thing we have in this area to an outlaw biker," said Tizzard. "You likely haven't heard about him because he has been in the Renous Institution in New Brunswick for the last seven years after he knifed a guy in a fight in St. John's. He had contact with the Angels a few years ago through one of their puppet gangs in Halifax, but I don't think he was ever part of that organization. I think he was just a hang-around."

"Is he from here?" asked Windflower.

"His family was, but they moved to St. John's when he was still in high school. He stayed here and spent all of his time getting into trouble," said Tizzard.

"And one of his pals was Shawn Parsons?" asked Windflower.

"You got it, Boss. I think I heard they hooked up for a while in Toronto, but I don't really have much info on that. In any case, Fallon is back and someone saw him talking to Shawn Parsons. Fallon's folks still have a cabin up in Molliers, a shack really, but I'm going to take a run up there to see if there's anybody around. That's if you don't need the car, sir," said Tizzard.

"I'm not going to take your jeep, Tizzard," said Windflower with a laugh. "Go on, get out of here."

Windflower tried to get his head back into the pile on his desk, but really didn't have the head or the heart for it, especially when he looked up he saw it was 5 o'clock.

Time to get going anyway, he thought. So he turned off his lights and went out to walk home.

Pulling his collar up against the wind and digging his head into his shoulders, he walked through the light rain, drizzle and fog to his little house.

Summer is really over now, he thought. Two months of rain, drizzle and fog, and then winter.

When he arrived, his Uncle Frank was sitting on the couch watching *Judge Judy,* and chortling at some of the show's defendants.

"That one is lying for sure," he said to nobody in particular, and laughed out loud when the Judge ordered the obvious liar to pay up, and apologize for his misdeeds as well.

"Oh, hi Winston," he said when he saw his nephew come into the living room. "I love Judge Judy. There's no bull. She just tells it like it is."

"I'm glad you're enjoying the show," said Windflower. "What do you feel like having for supper? I could just throw a couple of those salmon steaks on the barbeque if you'd like."

"That would be good," said Uncle Frank.

"I'm going to get changed and then I'll get moving on it," said Windflower, his uncle once again fully immersed in his courtroom drama.

Windflower could hear him chuckling from his bedroom as he slipped off his uniform and put on his jeans. He went back to the kitchen, took the salmon steaks out of the freezer, and put them in the microwave to defrost. Then he got two large baking potatoes and scrubbed them clean.

He didn't have time to marinate the salmon which he would have preferred, but instead whipped up his own instant barbeque sauce with a little ketchup, soy sauce, ginger, Worcestershire sauce, cayenne pepper, and salt.

He placed a little olive oil on the grill and fired up the barbeque, placing the baking potatoes into the microwave. Next, the salmon steaks went directly on the hot grill with a light basting of the sauce. While they were cooking on one side, he removed a bowl of frozen vegetables from the freezer and put them in a little water to boil.

By the time he returned to the barbeque, the salmon was ready to be flipped, and he added a little more sauce.

Time to give the potatoes one more turn in the microwave and set the table for dinner, he thought to himself.

The vegetables were boiling when he went out to flip the salmon one more time, turn off the barbeque and pour the rest of the sauce over the fish. Back inside, he put a piping hot potato on each plate, cutting them open to add a large dollop of butter and salt and pepper. The vegetables were slid into a clean bowl on the table and as he retrieved the salmon, he called out to tell his uncle that supper was ready.

The two men sat down and both aahed appreciatively as they tasted the grilled salmon; pink, moist and tender on the Inside with a tangy, crispy texture on the outside. They enjoyed their meal silently but with great delight, and at the end, when Uncle Frank shuffled outside to have a smoke, Windflower put the kettle on for tea and washed up the dishes. When he was done, Uncle Frank was back in the living room with his feet up as Windflower was bringing the teapot and two cups in with him.

"So, I've been doing a little thinking about what you said about my dreams. And I think you're right. And I've started to do a little research," said Windflower said.

"Research is good," said Uncle Frank. "Researching means that you're searching for something again. That means you may already know where it is. Just remember that action is always better than just looking for something."

"Okay, Uncle. I get it. It's just that I know so little about the people who came before us here, other than what I've seen in my dreams. I thought I could get to know them better by reading about them," said Windflower.

"That might work," said Uncle Frank. "But it would be better if you could talk to them."

"But they are all dead. All we have is some history," said Windflower.

"And who wrote the history?" asked Uncle Frank. "It was likely not the First Peoples."

"That is true," said Windflower. "I'm reading a book about them but it's written by a white person. He's sympathetic but couldn't really know what the Beothuks were thinking."

"Ah," said Uncle Frank. "Now you're beginning to understand. You cannot talk to dead people using someone else's language or culture. It must come from in here," he said, pointing to his heart. "Not from here," he said, then pointing to his head. "Trust your instincts and stop thinking and researching. Follow your heart. Now if you will please excuse me, it's time for "Jeopardy"."

With that, Windflower was once again left speechless by his uncle's words and finished his tea in silence. He said goodnight to Uncle Frank who simply waved a goodbye to his nephew's back.

Chapter Seventeen

Windflower walked over to Sheila's house to find she wasn't home yet.

Sheila must still be out at supper in Fortune, he thought.

She had left behind a note saying that the blueberry buckle was on top of the fridge, and to cut himself a piece and warm it up in the oven. She had added that there was ice cream in the freezer to top it off.

Windflower easily found the blueberry buckle and it looked fabulous. It was golden brown on top, and when he sliced off a large chunk he could see that the rich cake batter had enveloped the blueberries in the middle. He knew that Sheila made her buckle from an old Newfoundland recipe that had been in her family for years. She told him that she divided the cake batter in half, and poured it into the bottom of the cake pan. Then she mixed up the batter with the blueberries and added the topping, which was kind of like a streusel. Once it started to bake, the batter would rise up around the fruit, causing the topping to start to buckle. That's where the blueberry buckle got its name.

Windflower called it 'delicious', and after about 10 minutes of warming in the oven his chunk of buckle was ready to be topped with rich vanilla ice cream.

This must be ten thousand calories, he thought.

He tried to savour this treat as slowly as he could to make it last as long as possible. In any case it wasn't very long before he had finished, and was licking the spoon with delight.

Tomorrow, I start running again, he said to himself, as the blueberry buckle settled into his stomach. Tonight though, I'm just going to relax.

He turned the television on, but was hardly paying attention as his full stomach lulled him to sleep. He woke as Sheila rustled into the living room.

"I see you found the blueberry buckle," said Sheila.

"It was wonderful," said Windflower groggily. "How was supper with the church ladies?"

"They're not exactly church ladies," said Sheila. "But supper was good. Just a cold plate but you should have seen the desserts, Winston."

"I'm glad I didn't," said Windflower. "I'm turning into a fat pig already. But I've made up my mind. Tomorrow I start running again."

"That's good, Winston. The way you eat you better do something if you don't want to lose your girlish figure," joked Sheila.

"Well, I do like to eat, and I can't see giving that up any time soon," he said. "So it's back on the road for me."

"I'm starting my training tomorrow, too," said Sheila. "I have to walk two kilometres in the morning and another two in the afternoon, with stretching sessions in between. That's my goal for the next three months. At least three times a week. I'm not really looking forward to braving the rain and fog, but that comes with the territory I'm afraid."

"It does indeed, my dear," said Windflower. "It does indeed."

That night Windflower had trouble falling to sleep. He thought it might have something to do with the size of the piece of blueberry buckle that he had recently consumed. Whatever the reason, he finally settled down and by snuggling in close to Sheila was soon fast asleep.

Near dawn, Windflower found himself in the familiar dream with the cold woman next to him. He knew he was supposed to reach over to see her face but couldn't bring himself to do it. He awoke wondering why he didn't just do it, and ended up more perturbed than usual with himself. Oh well, he thought, I guess I need to do some more research.

Windflower got up and dressed in the dark, and was back home before the sun rose dimly on the horizon. There was still more dark than light when he put on his track pants, nylon jacket and running shoes to head out for his newly regimented run. He started slowly and went around his usual loop up near Sobeys and down behind the Health Centre. Followed by a trip through town, and finishing up at the wharf.

Arriving at the wharf, he noticed another runner coming the other way. As they got close he saw that it was a woman, Constable Evanchuk. Windflower waved good morning, and was greeted with some surprise and a wave back from the young constable.

So that's how she stays in such good shape, he thought.

After a quick breakfast of a boiled egg and toast and a bowl of blueberries, Windflower was on his way to the RCMP detachment.

The villagers of Grand Bank were just rising slowly for the day, and it seemed that even the tied-up dogs on every corner were having a lazy morning, since none barked at Windflower on his travels. He arrived at the building just as Constable Evanchuk was coming in, so he waited to say a more formal good morning, and to see if she wanted to share a cup of coffee.

"Here you go, Constable," said Windflower as he poured her the first cup of coffee from the freshly brewed pot.

"Thank you, Sergeant," said Evanchuk. "I also want to thank you for what you did yesterday."

"I see word travels as fast as usual in Grand Bank," said Windflower.

"That would be true, sir. But you know sir, with all due respect, I don't need anyone to fight my battles for me," said Evanchuk.

"I figured as much," said Windflower. "The fact that you survived training means that you likely have what it takes to be a Member," he said. "But I didn't intervene yesterday just for you. We have to fix a few things that are broken in our system," he continued. "I did it yesterday as much for the men as for you. They're going to have to learn to be role models in the community, and it starts with how they behave when they're in uniform. Just like you are the model for the young women and girls in this place, so too are they. We just need to get them pointed in the right direction."

Evanchuk just nodded and sipped her coffee but Windflower could see that she was thinking about what he said.

She's smart too, he thought.

Before either of them could add anything else, Tizzard came into the back room and poured himself a cup of coffee.

"Good Mornin, Sarge," said Tizzard. "Mornin, Evanchuk".

"Good morning, Corporal," said Evanchuk. "If you'll excuse me sir, I have to relieve Fortier on the highway," she said to Windflower.

Windflower and Tizzard nodded to Evanchuk as she left the office and went out to the parking lot.

"She's got a lot going for her," said Windflower.

"I know," said Tizzard. "She picks up on stuff real quick, is the first to volunteer for the crap assignments, and I've never heard her complain once. I was thinking that when I'm away next week she might be able to assist you if you have any special assignments," he said.

"That's a good idea, Tizzard. I just might do that," said Windflower. "Was anything going on in Molliers last night?" he asked. "Any sign of our buddy, Parsons?"

"It looked to me like someone had been around the cabin, but there was nobody there when I went over," said Tizzard. "I put a note on the board to have the patrol do a quick check every time they're in the area. I also have a source over there keeping a look-out for me. If either Fallon or Parsons shows up, we'll know soon enough."

"That's good. Give Langmead a call and let him know what you're up to. Did you hear they found the body of the Dowson girl?"

"Yeah," said Tizzard. "If they're connected then it's starting to be a big deal, isn't it?"

"I think it's already a big deal," said Windflower. "I just hope it doesn't get any bigger."

Windflower left Tizzard to finish his coffee and went back into his office. Betsy came by a few minutes later and was happy to see how much progress he had made on the piles of paper on his desk. But he was not as happy in return when she came back with an equally large stack to dump into his in-basket.

Oh well, he thought, that's why they pay me the big bucks!

Betsy had also dropped off the teleconference info, and Windflower called in just before the meeting began. He was pleasantly surprised that his old buddy Ron Quigley was on the call from Halifax, but he didn't recognize any of the other participants.

A Superintendent Morgan from RCMP HQ chaired the call, and he was both brusque and professional. Windflower didn't mind that at all. It meant the call wouldn't drag on the way they did when Arsenault chaired them. Sometimes the Inspector just wanted to tell old war stories. Morgan was all business.

He introduced an Inspector-General from Interpol. Windflower didn't catch his name, but he spoke fairly good English under a thick German accent. The Interpol officer explained that they had been dealing with a range of human traffickers, mostly centred out of the former Soviet Union in places like Belarus and Georgia.

They had two main streams, he explained. One was used to ship young women and girls to Western Europe, Canada and the United States for use in the sex trade. The other, which was fairly new, was to help Chinese migrants who had managed to get to Europe, make the shift to Canada where there were significant Chinese communities. Both were very lucrative, but the Chinese angle was the better of the two, he explained, because the risk and penalties were low. And the payoff was high and immediate, about $25,000 per person.

The sex trade was the most problematic because these young women were being forced into escort agencies, massage parlours, and street prostitution when they arrived in the West. The European Union had managed to stem the flow into Western Europe somewhat, and the Americans had tightened up their borders through their Homeland Security initiatives.

But Canada, the Interpol agent went on to say, was still pretty lax and that was where most of the human smuggling activities were happening now, and likely to continue in the future.

Superintendent Morgan jumped in to add that the large Chinese population centres in Ontario, especially in the Toronto area, were like magnets for Chinese migrants who had slipped out of China through the back door into Europe. Now they were trying to get into the middle class dream in Canada. Most of them had money from the recent economic boom in China, and were willing to pay a high price to get to a safe haven in Canada.

The Interpol officer came back on to say that their intelligence showed a remarkable uptick in human smuggling activity headed for Canada, and that Immigration had been put on alert in Toronto and Montreal. This likely meant that the human traffickers would look more closely at the East Coast.

"What about the West Coast?" asked Ron Quigley.

Good question, thought Windflower.

An Immigration official, Dick Turris, a senior coordinator of the project at HQ piped in and said, "Ever since we had the Tamils trying to land in Vancouver, we have been on high alert there. That's been going on for the last six or seven years. There's still lots of smuggling going on out there, but very little of human trafficking."

"That's why we brought you gentlemen together," said Superintendent Morgan. "These activities may be happening right under our noses and unless we're looking for them, they might continue under our radar. I want each of you regional guys to develop a mini-plan to inform all RCMP and local police forces to be on the lookout for groups of Chinese migrants, and also start digging into your strip clubs and the like to find out where the girls are from. This situation is going to get a whole lot worse before it gets better."

"Questions?" he asked.

Windflower was about to speak up about his information, but wanted to be sure of his intel first so decided to hold his tongue, for now. Hearing no questions, the Superintendent gave the last word to the man from Interpol.

"They are coming your way," said the Interpol officer. "Our intelligence suggests that these gangs have hundreds of girls waiting to come over. They're just looking for a way in."

Chapter Eighteen

When the conference call was over, Windflower went to the back to get another cup of coffee. He bumped into Tizzard who was just on his way out.

"Tizzard," said Windflower. "Where did those Chinese tourists come from? Moira said that she thought they were coming back from St. Pierre? Can you check the dates and see if there are any records of them crossing over on the ferry?"

"You don't think they did, Boss?" asked Tizzard.

"No, I have a feeling that they actually did not," said Windflower. "So it's easy enough to find out, right? If they were on the ferry, there would be a record. If not, Corporal, find out where they did come from. Okay?"

With that Windflower walked away and got his fresh cup of coffee.

He could see Tizzard shaking his head, and heard the sound of squealing tires as the other officer left the RCMP parking lot.

He doesn't know what happened, thought Windflower. It was like the Superintendent said on the call, if you didn't know any better you'd think it was normal. Maybe that's exactly what Tizzard and Moira, and perhaps even the Mayor of Grand Bank thought.

Windflower decided to wade through his e-mail backlog and there were a number of new messages to deal with. They included general notifications from HQ on the ever-changing priorities of the RCMP and new policy directives on a range of issues that Windflower simply sent to Betsy, who would circulate them to all the officers. There was also a private and confidential e-mail from Bill Ford in Deer Lake.

Ford's problem had gone from bad to worse, and he now had a complaint from a civilian employee in Barachois Brook.

That would be somebody like Betsy, Windflower thought.

The woman had sent Ford an e-mail asking him to intervene because one of the officers kept making rude comments and asking her out. Ford had the guy in and reamed him out, but the woman had recently filed another complaint claiming that the same officer was now taking it out on her. And he was still making rude comments. Ford knew that he would have to take more action, but wanted Windflower's advice first.

Windflower thought about it for a while and then suggested that he would suspend the officer, and ask him to apologize. If he refused, then Windflower recommended to take him off the duty roster and put him on full report. Windflower added that he was dealing with a similar situation in Grand Bank, and explained what he did to try to resolve it. He told Ford to call him if he wanted to talk more about it.

Windflower didn't understand what was up with these guys who were acting more like cavemen than police officers. He guessed that like lots of other male-dominated professions, the RCMP was going through a few growing pains as more women came into the service, but this seemed so simple to him.

Treat all people with respect. How could they enforce the law if they didn't follow all of it, including respect for individual and human rights? He just didn't get it.

Betsy beeped in on the intercom to break his reverie, "Inspector Arsenault is on the phone, sir,"

"Thank you, Betsy," said Windflower and he pressed the blinking button on the phone.

"Good morning, Inspector," he said.

"Winston," said Arsenault. "How did the call go this morning?"

"It was interesting, sir," said Windflower. "It looks like there are two different angles to this, one focusing on the sex trade, and the other on Chinese migrants coming from Europe. I think there might have been some Chinese transients who came through this area the past summer," he said.

"Why didn't we pick that up?" asked Arsenault.

"I guess because we weren't looking for it, sir," said Windflower. "I'm still trying to track down what happened. Once I do that, I can give you a better report. Plus, I am trying to trace a person of interest in Halifax who might know something about all of this. Guy Simard is helping me out."

"Simard is a good guy," said Arsenault, who sounded to Windflower like he was getting warmed up to tell one of his stories.

"And I've got to put together a plan for our region to get us ready for what HQ thinks will be a bigger wave coming our way soon," said Windflower.

"Yeah, send me over a draft by the end of the week on that," said Arsenault.

"Will do," said Windflower. "I need you to run some interference for me on something else if you can, sir," said Windflower. "If you can talk to Cape Breton and ask them to cooperate with the Constabulary on a possible murder, Mercedes Dowson; that would really help. Langmead is the RNC guy. He's looking into the murder of the Parsons girl."

"She's the one from Grand Bank, right?" asked Arsenault.

"Yes, sir, a few words from you in the right direction would help," said Windflower.

"No problem. I'll call Roundtree in Sydney. He's an old buddy of mine from back in the days when we were chasing rum runners on the South Shore," said Arsenault.

"Thank you, Inspector," said Windflower, still trying to cut him off at the pass. "There is one more thing I'd like to talk to you about, if you have a minute."

"Sure, fire away," said Arsenault.

"It's about Bill Ford, sir," said Windflower. "I think he's headed for a serious situation with some of the sexual harassment complaints on the west coast. I've talked to him a few times about it, and I think he could use your support."

"He has my support," said Arsenault, "But I think he's making too big a deal about this stuff. It'll blow over. It's just boys being boys."

"I don't think so," said Windflower. "I hear there's a formal complaint from a civilian member, and with respect sir, I don't think you want a case like this finding its way into the media. That has happened in some other areas."

"That won't happen here," said Arsenault. "Listen, Winston, I know that Ford is your buddy, but these things always look big at the beginning, and then they're gone. Trust me. I've had lots of experience with these issues."

"Okay, sir," said Windflower, even though he knew it wasn't.

"Good," said Arsenault. "Send me that report by Friday." The phone line went dead.

Well, at least I tried, thought Windflower.

Then he remembered to call Carl Langmead. When Langmead answered the phone, Windflower told him about his conversation with Arsenault.

"Thanks for that," said Langmead. "Sometimes these things get royally screwed up. I'm flying to Sydney this afternoon to have a look at the car and the evidence, so the intro from your man will help."

"No problem," said Windflower. "Did Tizzard tell you what he was looking into about the brother?"

"Yeah, he called earlier. I had a look at Fallon's file. He looks like one of the real bad guys. We had a look at him years ago for some drug dealing activities, but he ended up in prison for his bar fight before we could get anywhere. Oh, and I wanted to tell you that I've got another lead I'm following up on," said Langmead.

"One of the other girls from the rowing team called me. She said that she saw Amy Parsons downtown a few times with Mercedes Dowson and an older guy, once in a wine bar, and another time at The Keg on the waterfront. She said the guy was older, maybe in his forties, and spoke with an accent, possibly Russian, but she wasn't sure. She thought his name was Yashing or something like that. I'm trying to get her to help do a composite sketch so that we can get an idea what the fellow looks like, and with a little luck, maybe his picture will show up somewhere," said Langmead.

"That's interesting," said Windflower. "Maybe he was a boyfriend, the one who was paying her bills."

"That's a possibility," said Langmead. "Anyway I gotta' run. Thanks again for your help, and tell Tizzard to call if anything turns up on the brother."

"Bye," said Windflower whose stomach was giving him direction that it was past time for lunch.

Heeding the call, Windflower walked over to the café to see what Moira Stoodley had going for lunch. He was thinking a turkey sandwich with dressing or a nice bowl of soup.

He was thinking so hard that he was almost knocked over as he was going into the Mug-Up. As they both recovered from the shock, and Windflower his near knock-over, he realized that it was the Mayor of Grand Bank, Bill Sinnott.

Mayor Sinnott was a large man, a very large man. He had been a long distance trucker in his younger years, and had both the weight and the gait that a sedentary life often gives a person. In other words, he walked slowly and had a big belly. And as Windflower had found out, he was a solid wall of a man, at least six foot four and an inestimable number of pounds. He also spoke as loudly as he looked.

"Hello, Sergeant, I heard you were back. Lemme' help you up there b'y," said the Mayor.

"Thank you, Mr. Mayor. How are you today?" asked Windflower.

"Well if I wuz any better I'd be dead," said Mayor Sinnott so loudly that it almost knocked Windflower over again. "I'm just on my way over to meet with the tourism board. They want to know what plans we have in Grand Bank to boost tourism. It's easy, I sez. Just give us the money and we'll look after it. Eh, b'y?"

And with that last comment he clapped Windflower on the back and Windflower stumbled and nearly fell again.

"Having trouble with your balance, Sergeant?" asked the Mayor. "I take cod liver oil every morning, and my balance and my digestion are both fine," said the Mayor. "Anyways, I gotsa go see these guys. I'll be over one of these mornings for a chat. Okay, b'y?"

And with that the Mayor was gratefully gone, waddling over at full speed to give the tourism board his pearls of wisdom.

Windflower smiled to himself as he stepped into the warmth of the Mug-Up. His smile grew when he spied Sheila sitting in the corner nursing a large mug and making notes in her agenda book.

Chapter Nineteen

"Planning a big getaway?" asked Windflower as he took the seat beside her.

"Actually, I have a fair number of things scheduled for someone who isn't working," said Sheila. "How do people with jobs manage to get anything done?"

Windflower gave her a peck on the cheek and smiled.

"This is a pleasant treat. I was just coming in for a quick bite. Care to join me?"

"I just ordered a turkey with dressing sandwich," said Sheila. "But if you're buying it'll taste even better."

Marie came over with Sheila's sandwich and Windflower ordered the same with a cup of hot tea. Throughout their meal, people kept dropping over to say hello to Sheila, which she didn't seem to mind at all.

Windflower thought it was nice too that so many people liked her. She really was great person, he thought.

After lunch, Sheila shared her umbrella with Windflower as he walked her home. The rain was going to come and go all day, apparently, and right now it had decided to stay a while. When they arrived at her house the rain let up a bit, and Windflower assured Sheila that he was fine to walk back to work without the use of her red polka dot umbrella.

People in town already thought him weird enough, Windflower thought to himself.

With a delicious turkey sandwich in his stomach, and a promise from Sheila of home-baked beans for supper, and of course another piece of blueberry buckle for dessert, he was quite content to head back to work for the remainder of the day.

The afternoon was going along quite nicely and quietly until a few hours later when Windflower heard a commotion in the front area of the detachment near the receptionist's desk. Betsy was hiding underneath the desk, and Constable Evanchuk was sitting on top of a large bearded man putting cuffs on him. Tizzard was standing to the side, seemingly enjoying the show.

"Sergeant Windflower, I'd like you to meet Frankie Fallon. Constable Evanchuk is bringing Mr. Fallon in for questioning about some possibly stolen goods that were discovered in plain sight near his cabin."

"They're not mine, you scumbag," said the bearded man. "And get this broad off of me."

"Now, it's that kind of talk that got you in that position in the first place, Mr. Fallon."

"It was going along well, Sergeant, until young Frankie here got lippy with the Constable and she had to show him who's boss, sir," said Tizzard, clearly having a good time.

"Put him in back," said Windflower, "And then come see me, Tizzard."

Frankie Fallon was pulled back onto his feet by Evanchuk and propelled towards the back cell, continuing to mutter, but at least somewhat subdued. Tizzard went along to supervise, but it looked to him that Evanchuk had things well in hand.

"So what's going on?" asked Windflower when Tizzard came back into his office.

"Evanchuk did the tour this morning and she noticed an old ATV at the back of the cabin," said Tizzard. "She checked the registration number and it matched one that was reported stolen a while back. I came over with her and we tried talking to Fallon about it, but he basically told us to screw off. That's when I figured we should bring him in and talk to him here. He got more upset on the way over, and Evanchuk had to subdue him."

"He probably didn't have anything to do with stealing the ATV," said Windflower.

"Maybe not," said Tizzard. "He was likely a guest of the federal government when it happened. But it is stolen, and it is on his property. That wouldn't look very good to his parole officer."

"Okay, hold him for a few hours and see if you can squeeze anything out of him. But as soon as he asks for a lawyer, let him go. Okay, Corporal?"

"Yes, sir," said Tizzard, pleased as punch to have a chance to interrogate Frankie Fallon.

"And Tizzard, take Evanchuk with you when you talk to Fallon. It will be good experience for her."

"Okay, Boss," said Tizzard.

Windflower went back to work and back to thinking about his beans and blueberry crumble until just after 5 p.m., when he saw Evanchuk walking Frankie Fallon out the front door. He looked up to see Tizzard in his doorway smiling.

"It all worked out, Sarge," said Tizzard. "Under threat of reporting him to his P.O., Fallon finally started talking."

"He told me that he drove Shawn Parsons to St. John's a few nights ago and dropped him off there. He doesn't know where he's staying but at least we know where Mr. Parsons went from here. Whether he's still there or not, is anybody's guess."

"I wouldn't be surprised to find he's still there," said Windflower. "The RNC would have the airport monitored as well as the ferry, and I bet that Parsons has a place to lay low in St. John's. Call Langmead and let him know. He's gone to Cape Breton to check out the Dowson woman, but he'll want to know that Parsons might still be in town."

"Will do," said Tizzard. "And we get to return the ATV to the rightful owner. Another property theft resolved."

"Good job, Corporal," said Windflower.

"Thank you, sir," said Tizzard, happy to finally be back in his superior's good books. "I'll pass it along to Evanchuk too."

Now Windflower could finally go home, and while he might have been embarrassed, he kind of wished he had Sheila's polka dot umbrella for the walk.

It was spilling buckets when he ventured outside, and the rain didn't let up all the way to Sheila's. He was drenched to the bone by the time he reached his destination. But had a change of clothes there, and was starting to warm up once he smelled dinner cooking in Sheila's bean pot.

"Just go right in and jump in the shower," said Sheila. "Supper will be ready whenever you are."

Windflower followed her directions and felt much better after he had towelled off and dressed in his civvies. When he came out, Sheila had the dining room set up for the two of them. There were even candles, and in the flickering light Sheila's dark red hair glowed a golden bronze.

"It's not a very fancy supper, but we might as well enjoy ourselves," said Sheila. "Being sick has made me more aware and grateful for the little things in life, and since I've been given a second chance I think I, and we, should make the most of it."

She raised her water glass to Windflower and proposed a toast.

"To the future," she said.

And Windflower replied, clinking her glass, "To the future."

Sheila served Windflower a heaping bowl of beans, and passed him the mixed salad while she cut up some of the crunchy Italian bread she'd picked up at Sobeys. She gave him a chunk of the bread and a thick slice of the Huntsman cheese, the one with double Gloucester on the outside, and a ribbon of Stilton running up the middle.

"I love that cheese," said Windflower. "It's the perfect combination to go with the bread and the beans. And these beans are so good. What's your secret?"

"My secret is that this is an old family recipe and if I tell you I'd have to kill you. And I kind of like having you around, but if you promise not to tell, I double the molasses it calls for. That makes the beans extra sweet," said Sheila.

"Just like you," said Windflower, holding out his bowl for more, "But only half this time. I have to get serious about my diet before I just blimp up and blow away in the wind. Plus, I've got to save room for my blueberry buckle."

After dinner and his scrumptious dessert, Sheila lent Windflower her car so that he could head back over to his house to drop off a small pot of beans for Uncle Frank, and to pick up a clean and dry uniform for the morning.

Uncle Frank was busy watching television again and was pleasantly surprised when he saw both Windflower and the pot of beans.

"Thank you, Winston," said his uncle. "And pass my thanks along to Sheila. I was about to open a tin of soup for myself but this is great."

"There's a few pieces of bread in there too, Uncle," said Windflower, as his uncle dug through the bag.

The older man pulled a large spoon out of the drawer and began eating the beans right out of the pot. Windflower laughed and thought that he would do the same if he were here alone. He put some Good Luck margarine on the bread and brought it out to his uncle, who was now back sitting in front of the TV.

"I am thinking about heading back home," said his uncle, in between bites of bread and beans. "I think Marie misses me and I've been dry for a few days so that'll make the transition smoother."

"I guess you were in a bit of trouble with her when you left, Uncle," said Windflower.

"Ah, that's just the ups and downs of married life," said his uncle. "She'll be happy to see me."

"So how's your dream research going?" he said with a twinkle in his eye.

Windflower just smiled. "It's going well, Uncle. I haven't had any of the dreams since I started working on them", he fibbed, and "Maybe they're gone away."

"Maybe," said his uncle, who seemed to know that they had not. "But I'll be here for a few more days if you want to talk more about them. Or if you have them again."

"Okay, Uncle, but I think I'll be fine now," said Windflower and he bid his uncle a good night.

Upon his return to Sheila's the lights were off in the dining room. In fact they were off all over the house, except for a twinkling in the back, near Sheila's bedroom.

"I'm in here, Winston," came Sheila's voice from the back. "I thought we could have an early night."

"That sounds perfectly good to me," said Windflower. "I'll be right in."

Chapter Twenty

Hours later, Windflower was peacefully asleep when he began to dream again. It was the dream in the forest with the aboriginal woman.

This time when the woman was calling to him and the others were chasing him, Windflower did not run. Instead, he stopped, and one by one the ghost-like creatures passed by or through him, all except the one woman. Windflower forced himself to stand there as the woman came closer to him. She reached out and touched his face and hair, and then in a language he did not recognize, she spoke to him.

Windflower still did not move, so the woman took his hand in hers and pulled him back towards the area where the others had just come from. Windflower resisted a little, and then a lot, but it made no difference. Her grip on him was secure, and she simply pulled him along with her, until they came to a clearing in the forest. When they got to the opening, Windflower could first hear, and then see, a mighty river.

It reminded him of the Athabasca River back home, but he knew somehow that this wasn't his river. It was another one, closer to where he was living now.

The woman pulled him into the river, which at first was icy cold, and then almost warm and inviting. She started dancing and singing in the water, and invited Windflower to join in, beckoning him to move further into the water.

Windflower kept venturing further and deeper into the fast moving river until suddenly he could not feel his feet below him. He was fine up until that point, but now he grew afraid as he began to sink into the river.

The woman continued dancing and was oblivious to Windflower's dilemma. He fell deeper into the river, passing other people as he fell until suddenly, and with a jolt, he hit the bottom.

That's when he woke up, drenched in sweat and panting, and trying to figure out exactly what had just happened.

Windflower crept out of the bedroom and went to the bathroom to rinse himself off and try to calm down. He fumbled for a pen and paper and started to write down his dream so that he wouldn't forget it. Once that was done he tried to think about what the dream meant.

 Obviously, the big difference in this dream and the others was that he decided to participate. He thought that his Uncle Frank would be proud of him for that.

Another interesting part of this dream was that it involved water. Windflower knew that water was an important element in all forms of indigenous cultures. Water also played a role in many formal religions, from water rites in Hinduism, to baptism in Christianity. He had been taught to respect water as a gift from the Creator. And to acknowledge that respect by trying to keep all water, as well as the earth and the air, pure and clean.

Mike Martin

Many other aboriginal nations considered the places next to water to be sacred or holy places. They built settlements and communities near the mouths of rivers and at the forks where rivers came together. Windflower suspected that the Beothuks would have had a great respect for the ocean as something that nourished and sustained them. It was no surprise then that they felt diminished and were weakened when they were forced away from it by the white settlers in Newfoundland.

But even with that information, Windflower really didn't understand this particular dream, nor what the relevance of the river was in it. That would be another job for his Uncle Frank.

Windflower was glad that he was not going home right away. I've got a few more questions for him, he thought. He also thought his dreaming was over for the night when he crept back into the warm bed with Sheila. He thought wrong.

After a few minutes of restless tossing and turning, Windflower got comfortable and finally fell back asleep. He remembered later dreaming of many things; a series of vignettes rolling through his mind, unconnected passages with various people in his life. He remembered Tizzard bugging him about something, Arsenault yelling at him, and even being in the Mug-Up watching other people eating, and wondering why he couldn't get served.

The other dream returned as well. Windflower was lying naked in bed. It was a hot night and he had thrown the sheets off. A ceiling fan whirred above him. Lying next to him with her back to him was a woman, also naked,

184

with long black hair down almost to her waist. Windflower reached out to touch her and to pull her to him, but her body was cold, deathly cold. He wanted to get up and run from the bed. He was afraid and didn't want to know see any more.

But he forced himself to follow his Uncle Frank's advice and he began to pull the dead woman's body closer to him. He reached to turn her over towards him. He remembered holding his breath as he looked into her face. He gasped as he realized that it was Anne-Marie Littlechild, his old girlfriend.

The next thing he remembered was Sheila holding him, telling him it was all right, as he kept muttering, "No, no, it can't be."

It took Windflower quite a while to settle down, and when he finally did, Sheila went out to the kitchen to put the kettle on for tea. It was just getting light when Windflower came out of the bedroom and sat in the kitchen across from Sheila.

"You look like you've seen a ghost," said Sheila, noticing that most of the colour had drained from Windflower's face.

"It was just a bad dream," said Windflower, trying to reassure Sheila, and himself.

Sheila shook her head.

"Whatever is going on with you is more than just a dream," she said. "Look at the effect it's having on you. And it's affecting your beauty sleep," she said, trying to lighten the mood a little. "Talk to your Uncle Frank again about this. You obviously have something you need to sort out and maybe he can help. Now I'm going back to bed; make yourself something to eat before you head out," she said as she kissed him on the forehead and returned to her warm nest.

Windflower still couldn't believe that was Anne-Marie's face he saw in the dream. He hadn't seen her in years. The last he had heard from her was a message she left him saying she wanted to talk to him. That was almost a year ago.

Anne-Marie and Windflower had once been engaged, and everyone in their home community was sure they would be married. But somehow they had drifted apart, he to pursue his career in the RCMP, and she as an art therapist and First Nations activist.

Windflower hadn't returned her call because he was preoccupied with helping Sheila to get better from her horrific accident. And he was a little afraid of re-opening old wounds after the difficult break-up. He knew that Anne-Marie had been working with her art and healing workshops in aboriginal communities all over North America. Recently he heard that she had been working in Labrador with the Inuit in Nunatsiavut. She might even still be there.

One person who would know for sure was his Auntie Marie. If he wanted to reach Anne-Marie, he could call her for the number. That was, if he wanted to talk to her.

The first person he wanted to talk to was his Uncle Frank. Fortunately, his uncle was an early riser, and perhaps, if Windflower went over and made him breakfast, they could have a chat before work. Windflower whispered a hushed goodbye to Sheila who was fast asleep, and walked over to his house to determine if Uncle Frank was moving about yet.

It was barely light, as Windflower covered the short distance home from Sheila's house. The fog had descended like a heavy woollen comforter, and hung around his shoulders like a ten-ton weight. The wind whipped at his back, as he scrunched as low as possible to try and stay out of its path.

This will be a beauty, walking into this weather on the way back, he thought. He would put off his running regime for another time.

He saw the light on in the kitchen of his house, and the shadow of what he assumed and hoped was his Uncle Frank moving around.

"Good morning, Uncle," he called out from the porch as he hung up his windbreaker. "Hope you got the coffee on."

"Grab a cup," said his uncle. "I am just making up some fish and brewis, if you'd like some."

"I wasn't aware that you knew how to make fish and brewis," said Windflower. "You are a man of many talents."

"Flattery will get you everything, including breakfast this morning," said Uncle Frank. "Could you put the rest of those beans in the microwave to heat them up? We might as well finish them off too."

Windflower spooned the remainder of last night's beans into a plastic bowl and put them into the microwave while his uncle dished up helpings of fish and brewis for each of them. When the microwave beeped, Windflower took the beans out and divvied them up in two small bowls each and placed them on the table.

"This is an unexpected treat," said Windflower as he tucked into his breakfast. "Where did you learn to cook this?"

"My friends showed me," said the other man, forking a generous heap of the salt fish and brewis into his mouth. "It's easy enough if you've got some salt fish and hard tack. Although I had to ask them what 'ard tack' was. Who would have thought that it was these rock hard Purity Biscuits? And who could've imagined they would taste so good fried up with a bit of fat back pork and salt fish?"

"I guess this used to be a staple breakfast for fishermen before they headed out on the water," said Windflower. "I think it's the scrunchions that make it so tasty."

"It is good," said his uncle.

After breakfast Windflower volunteered to clean up while his uncle had a smoke.

When his uncle came back in Windflower decided to talk to him about his dreams. He told him first about the dream with the woman and the river. His uncle listened carefully and asked Windflower a few questions along the way. When Windflower was done his uncle sat quietly thinking for several minutes. Finally he spoke up.

"You are right when you speak about the water as being very important in this dream. Water is one of the sacred elements. When it is present in our dream world it is a vehicle that our ancestors and the spirits who live in the dream world use to get around, and to send messages from one world to another."

The older man paused and closed his eyes.

Then he continued, "The presence of the river in this dream is also important. Rivers are a symbol of our journeys through life, both physical and spiritual. And being underwater often means that you are going deep inside the spirit world, and deep within yourself. There is a message waiting for you at the bottom of the river," he said. "You must go back to this dream and when you hit the bottom you must dig your hand into the sand. There is something there for you."

Windflower just listened quietly and at the end said, "Meegwich, Uncle. Thank you for your help and guidance."

Then he told him about the other dream, about seeing Anne-Marie's face.

Uncle Frank grew more animated when he heard about this dream.

"You must warn her," said his uncle. "She is in great danger. You cannot wait. Contact her as soon as you can."

"What will I tell her, Uncle?" asked Windflower.

"Tell her about your dream, and that I said for you to warn her. She may not choose to listen but it is your responsibility to give her the message," said Uncle Frank. And then seeing the hesitation on Windflower's face he said, "And don't delay. She is in grave danger. You do not have the luxury to research this matter."

Windflower simply nodded to his uncle in reply.

"Now I'm going to go down to the wharf. I only have a few more days here with my friends, and I want to enjoy them."

"Thank you again, Uncle," said Windflower but the older man was already halfway out the door.

Windflower sat for a few minutes to digest what he had been told, and then had his shower and shave.

He spent a little extra time with his smudging and prayers this morning, asking for guidance and strength and being grateful for his blessings. As he left he laid down some tobacco in honour of his Uncle Frank, to give him continued wisdom in this world.

His meditations complete, Windflower was ready to start his work day, and fifteen minutes later was sitting in the lunchroom at the detachment talking to Corporal Eddie Tizzard.

Chapter Twenty-One

"Mornin', Boss," said Tizzard, "Another damp one by the looks of it."

"Yeah," said Windflower, sipping his coffee and waiting for the caffeine to kick in. "Have you talked to Langmead yet?"

"Left a message for him last night," said Tizzard as he stuffed his mouth full of a second blueberry muffin. "I expect he'll call back this morning."

"How can you eat all that stuff and not put a pound on?" Windflower asked as he watched Tizzard reach into the plastic container for muffin number three.

"Good living," said Tizzard. "And I never slow down. You can't hit a moving target. That's my motto."

"I believe the not slowing down part, but that good living thing is a bit sketchy," said Windflower.

"By the way, I've also got Betsy checking the ferry manifests to and from St. Pierre," said Tizzard. "If there was a boatload of Chinese, it should be pretty easy to identify when they came over."

"And if not?" asked Windflower.

"If not, then I was thinking that they must have come from somewhere, and maybe somebody along the shore saw something this summer," said Tizzard.

"Well, I'm glad you're thinking at last," said Windflower. "I'm trying to get some more information about the tour operator. I have my sources too, you know."

Windflower left Tizzard to ponder his last remark, and strolled out to the main office to say good morning to Betsy. Despite the damp and miserable weather, Betsy was in fine spirits, and greeted him with a cheery hello.

I must be keeping up to her standards on the paperwork, Windflower thought.

He was burrowing deeply into that very same paper when Sheila called.

"Hi, Winston, I just wanted to check in on you," she said. "You were pretty upset this morning."

"I'm much better now," said Windflower. "I had a good chat with Uncle Frank and he made some helpful suggestions that I'm going to try out. What's your day like today?"

"I've actually got a busy day," said Sheila. "I have my therapy, and then I have a meeting with Moira Stoodley to talk about the café. I think I'm ready to make some decisions about moving forward. Let's talk about it tonight, okay?"

"Sure," said Windflower. "Let's go out to dinner tonight, my treat," he said. "The B&B is still running that dinner special. It's only $20 apiece, and I hear it's really good."

"That sounds like fun, Winston. I can get a bit dressed up too," said Sheila. "Okay, I've got to run. I'm glad you're feeling better. You sound better too. Love you."

"Love you too," said Windflower as he placed the phone back on the receiver. The intercom buzzed as soon as the phone hit the hook. "Can you call Guy Simard in Halifax, sir?" said Betsy.

Windflower dialed Simard's number.

"Good morning, Guy, what have you got for me?" asked Windflower.

"Well, I went down to that address you gave me but there's nobody home. Nobody alive anyway," said Simard.

"What do you mean?" asked Windflower.

"That address on Spring Garden Road is a cemetery," said Simard, laughing. "Somebody is pulling your leg, my boy."

"What about the phone number?" asked Windflower.

"That one is real," said Simard. "It's registered to Gorky Park Tours, but the name on the phone is Peter Yashin."

"Does that name mean anything to you?" asked Windflower.

"Yashin, who also uses at least three other aliases, is well-known in Halifax," said Simard. "He's part of a group that some people call the Russian Mafia. I think they're just thugs who happened to find a way to get into Canada. The group Yashin pals around with is into the escort business in a big way around the Dartmouth area. They've even been trying to cut the bikers out of the downtown drug business. And you know there aren't too many people crazy enough to mess around with the bikers."

"Where is he now?" asked Windflower. "Is he still in the area?"

"Our guys haven't seen him for a few months. We think his group is bringing in girls to work in the business. Yashin might be setting some things up or helping with a recruitment drive right now. He's not in Halifax, but if he shows up, I'll let you know. In the meantime I'll e-mail you Yashin's photo," said Simard.

"And what the hell does the Grand Bank detachment want with a guy like this?" asked Simard. "We believe Yashin's crew is responsible for at least three 'business-related' murders in the past year. They're ruthless and don't screw around," he added.

"I'm doing a project for Arsenault on human trafficking and this guy, Yashin or Fetisov, or whatever his name is, was likely in Grand Bank this summer with a load of Chinese visitors, probably illegal migrants," said Windflower.

"Winston, be careful with this guy. They are meaner than even the Angels we used to deal with at the airport. They really do shoot first and ask questions later. Okay?"

"Okay, Guy, and thanks for your help," said Windflower.

Windflower wrote Peter Yashin's name down on a piece of paper so he wouldn't forget it. He wanted to get Betsy to have a look in the database, and see what she came up with.

Then he remembered what Langmead had told him about the guy that Amy Parsons had been seen with in St. John's. Wasn't it Yashing? It might be the same guy, he thought.

Windflower called Langmead's cell phone number and after it rang a few times he answered, "Langmead here."

"Carl, it's Winston. Listen, what was the name of the guy that the other girl saw with Amy Parsons? I've got a Russian on my radar by the name of Peter Yashin and he might be the same person. He's based in Halifax but he was in Newfoundland this summer. I'm getting a photo e-mailed to me and you can check with the girl. Are you still in Cape Breton?" asked Windflower.

"I am," said Langmead, "And thanks for this. If we can put a face to this man we can start looking around for other people who may have seen him. I've also got my team scouring the streets of St. John's looking for Shawn Parsons. It's good to have a few more leads on this case."

"What did you find out over there?" asked Windflower.

"It looks like the Dowson girl was murdered as well," said Langmead. "Same M.O.; strangled and neck broken by the looks of it. Given the isolated area where she was found, it also looks like it was a pre-arranged meeting. There's no other reason for her to be all the way up in Meat Cove. Only a few hardy campers are left this time of year, and it doesn't seem like she had any connections to the area."

"I hope our guys were helpful," said Windflower. "I asked my Inspector to make a call."

"They've been great," said Langmead. "I'm just waiting to go through the evidence box they took from the car and then I'm heading back this afternoon. Thanks again for your help."

When Windflower finished his last call he looked up at the clock and couldn't believe it when he saw it was 11:30 a.m.

Time for lunch, he thought, as he went to the back to look for Tizzard. The corporal was out, but Constable Evanchuk was putting her coat on to go out when he arrived at the lunchroom.

"Grabbing a bite to eat, Constable?" he asked.

"Yes, sir, I was just going to go over to the café. Did you want me for something?" she asked.

"Only if you wanted company for lunch," replied Windflower, "And if you have a car. I'm tired of getting wet."

"No problem, sir," said Evanchuk. "You're welcome to join me."

A few heads turned when Windflower walked into the Mug-Up with the female RCMP constable, and Windflower smiled at every one of them. Evanchuk let him lead and he chose his familiar table in the corner.

Herb Stoodley was on waitress duty today and came over to take their orders.

"Don't say anything, Windflower," said Stoodley. "Molra is at a meeting with Sheila and I'm filling in for the lunchtime rush."

"As long as you bring us lunch I'm sure we'll have nothing but good things to say," said Windflower as Evanchuk smiled beside him. "I'll have the macaroni and cheese and a cup of tea," said Windflower.

"I'll take the turkey and dressing sandwich on whole wheat, please," said Evanchuk, "And a glass of water."

"Coming right up," said Stoodley as he went to put in their order.

"I didn't see you out this morning, Sergeant," said Evanchuk.

"Too wet for me today," said Windflower. "I suppose I'm not as committed as you to the morning regimen yet. It takes me a while to get it going on a regular basis."

"So, you're from Saskatchewan," he said. "I'm from Northern Alberta myself."

"Yes, sir," said Evanchuk. "I'm from Estevan, the eighth-largest city in Saskatchewan. It's close to the border with North Dakota, and it's going through a boom time right now with the oil and gas, and a big power development."

"Like a lot of the West," said Windflower. "How did you get involved with law enforcement?"

"It's in my blood, sir," said Evanchuk. "I'm third generation on the Force and two of my older brothers are Members as well. I never really wanted to do anything else."

"Here's our lunch, Constable," he said as Herb Stoodley came by balancing their food and drinks.

Chapter Twenty-Two

After lunch Windflower caught a ride back to the detachment with Evanchuk and resumed working at reducing his boring stack of paper. There on top, neatly typed, obviously by Betsy, was the duty roster for the next two weeks.

Maybe Tizzard is getting the message, he thought, as he scanned the sheet for his name and shifts, before initialling it and putting it back in his out-basket for posting.

Early into his afternoon schedule Windflower was surprised to see Mayor Bill Sinnott pull his massive frame into the RCMP detachment. He went out to greet him.

"Mr. Mayor," said Windflower, "Nice of you to stop by."

"Good afternoon, Sergeant. And to you too, Ms. Molloy," said Sinnott. "I hope you can spare me a few minutes, Sergeant. I have a few things to talk to you about."

"Absolutely," said Windflower. "Why don't we go into my office?"

Mayor Sinnott barely squeezed himself into the chair in front of Windflower's desk. Windflower closed the door behind him and sat down to face the Mayor.

"We are likely going to have a little bit of trouble, Sergeant, and I want to know where the RCMP is goin' to stand on it," said Sinnott. "I think we are going to have us a labour dispute at the fish plant. It's been building up for 'bout six months now and it's starting to boil over. Some of the local fishermen and plant workers don't agree with the plant's decision to take and process some of their catch from the Frenchmen," said the Mayor.

"You mean from St. Pierre and Miquelon?" asked Windflower.

"Exactly," said the Mayor. "They have a quota for redfish that is being cleaned and sent out of here without processing," he said. "There's a deal like this in Fortune as well, but at least they are using local fishermen to get their product, and not the forinners."

"What do you want us to do about all of this?" asked Windflower. "Shouldn't you be talking to the Fisheries people?"

"We are," said the Mayor. "But they're as tick' as a board on this; might as well be talking to ourselves. So, some of the local people are going to start dealing with this on their own. They are plannin' to put a picket line up at the fish plant to stop the forinners from unloading."

"So, what exactly do you want us to do?" asked Windflower.

"Nutting," said the Mayor. "We want you to do nutting so we can put pressure on the fish plant. Now I know you are gonna' tell me that you have the law to uphold, but we're asking you to let tings ride themselves out, if you know what I mean."

With that Mayor Bill Sinnott drew his large frame up and moved slowly towards the door.

"We'll be seein' ya, Sergeant," he said to Windflower who was still trying to figure out exactly what was going to happen and when.

The Mayor was at least giving him a heads up, and that would be an improvement over his past relationships with municipal officials. Another thing to worry about, he thought, but at least, not today.

The next thing Windflower heard was the squealing of tires coming into the parking lot, and that could only mean that Tizzard was back. Windflower peeked out the window and saw the Corporal running into the detachment with his jacket over his head in a futile attempt to stay dry in the pelting rain.

Tizzard rushed into his office still dripping wet.

"Hey, Boss, got a minute?" he asked.

"Let's get a cup of tea in the back," said Windflower, and the two walked into the lunchroom where Windflower plugged the kettle in to boil.

"What's up, Corporal?" he asked.

"You were right. There's no record of any groups of Chinese departing from St. Pierre or Fortune this summer. The biggest groups were about 20 people, and they were both cycling groups from Quebec," said Tizzard. "But it appears that there was a lot of activity down near the bottom of the peninsula this summer."

"When was this?" asked Windflower.

"There were a number of mini-buses parked in Lord's Cove one night in June, and in the morning they were gone," said Tizzard. "And there was a similar event in the Lawn area later on in July. The mini-buses rolled into town, empty according to my sources, and simply parked near the beach without the drivers talking to anybody. There were no signs or markings on the vans and somebody said they looked like rentals."

"I am assuming that nobody took down license plates," said Windflower.

"No, but at least we know they were local plates. That probably means they're from St. John's and since we know the rough dates from the lunches at the Mug-Up, we can likely trace the rentals," said Tizzard.

"That's good," said Windflower. "What about the drivers? Did any of your sources recognize any of them?"

"They weren't local, Boss," said Tizzard. "Nobody knew them and they didn't get out of the vans, even for a smoke, until it got dark. And some people watch everything. The only thing they knew for sure was that they were males. Even when they came to Grand Bank, they just dropped the people off and went somewhere quiet until the time came to pick them up again."

"That's all very interesting, don't you think, Tizzard? Can you tell me again why you didn't think this was very strange when it was happening?" asked Windflower.

"You know, I think that we were all so happy to have visitors or tourists that were spending money in the community, that we didn't question it," said Tizzard. "Plus, it's not like the people who do the smuggling out of some of the small communities on the shore are going to call up the Mounties to give us a tip. They're quite happy to have us leave them alone altogether. It's changing, but not very quickly," he said.

"I guess so," said Windflower. "Anyway, we do our best now with what we got, right Corporal?"

"Right, Sergeant," said Tizzard looking unusually thoughtful while sipping his tea.

Windflower took his tea back to his office and uninterrupted, spent the last couple of hours in peaceful solitude until it was time to return home.

As he headed out the door he pulled an RCMP umbrella out of a stand near the door. He clutched It tightly to keep it and him from being blown far out into the Atlantic and managed to get home fairly quickly and relatively dry.

Windflower yelled a brief hello to his Uncle Frank, and went in for a quick soak in the tub before his big dinner date with Sheila.

Towelling off, Windflower got out of the tub and found his grey trousers and blue blazer in the closet. Along with a crisp white shirt still in the plastic wrap from the dry cleaners, he was ready to go.

Rather than risk getting wet yet again, he phoned Sheila to ask for a ride. In a few minutes she pulled up in his driveway, and they were soon sitting in the dining room of the B&B waiting for supper.

It was a quiet night at the historic B&B, and the only other couple was a pair from Rimouski, in Quebec, who spoke as much English as Windflower spoke French – hardly any.

The Quebec pair was travelling in a large motorhome, and had just returned from a week in St. Pierre. That was as much information that they could convey in their limited English, and that was okay with Windflower, who really wanted to spend time with his girl.

The B&B was warm and cozy on this wet night, and Windflower and Sheila enjoyed their complimentary glass of wine while admiring the antiques and the inspired restoration that the old house had undergone in recent years. It had once belonged to a famous merchant and sea captain in the town, and had been brought back to life by a succession of innkeepers over the last twenty years.

The menu for dinner included a Matane Shrimp Salad with field greens, Coq au Vin as the main course, and Chocolate Lava Cake for dessert.

The salad featured a dozen or so small tasty shrimps from the Gulf of St. Lawrence with small pieces of celery and avocado in a dressing that had a taste of lemon and a bite of horseradish. It was presented on a bed of mixed green lettuce, and along with fresh, hot rolls from the kitchen, was absolutely delicious.

Windflower and Sheila shared a little small talk while they waited for the main course, happy to be out and enjoying each other's company.

The main course was another delectable treat, Coq au Vin with a Newfoundland twist. According to the menu, the chicken pieces had been marinated in a red wine that came from a winery near Whitbourne. Then the chicken was sautéed in fat back pork and served with tiny mushrooms, pearl onions, and baby carrots on a bed of egg noodles. It was hearty and filling, and both Sheila and Windflower sent compliments to the chef along with their empty plates.

They opted to take their coffee and dessert in the living room, or parlour as they called it here. The other couple from Quebec ate their dessert in the dining room so Windflower and Sheila were alone in the beautiful parlour to finish off their meal.

The Chocolate Lava Cake had a strong taste of both bittersweet and dark chocolate. When you dug your fork into the moist cake, the liquid chocolate oozed out. Of course, the best part of the dessert for Windflower was the blueberry ice-cream, creamy and cool. And good as he often would say "to the very last drop."

"That was perfect," said Windflower.

"I agree," said Sheila. "It's so nice just to get out on a date night. It seems like forever since we've done this."

"It has been forever," said Windflower. "We have to do it more often and we can now that you're going to be home again."

"That's one of the things I wanted to talk to you about, Winston," said Sheila. "I've made a few decisions about my future."

Windflower looked a little startled, and Sheila continued. "I don't mean about you and me," she said. "I'm very happy with you, Winston. You're a fine man."

"Well, that's good to hear," said Windflower, his mood clearly brightening.

"But my accident has got me thinking that I want to do more with my life. I want to be an active participant in my life, instead of waiting for things to happen outside of me. I am also tired of being in the service business. I've cooked too many meals and made too many cups of tea for other people. I want to serve in another way now," said Sheila.

"So, the first decision I've made is that I'm selling the Mug-Up. Moira has agreed to take it over completely and buy me out. And I'm happy to sell it to her."

"But what will you do?" asked Windflower. "Everybody in Grand Bank thinks of you and the café as being inseparable."

"That's it exactly," said Sheila. "And you know after Bart's death that was great. I put my heart and soul into my work and that little café. And it gave me back a lot. I'm grateful, but now it's time to move on. That brings me to my second decision. I'm going back to school," she said.

"What are you going to take?" asked Windflower.

"I'm going back into nursing," said Sheila. "That's a part of my life that I feel is unfinished. I had to leave university and come home when my parents got sick, and I'm going to go back and get my R.N. designation."

"Congratulations, Sheila. You should have the opportunity to fulfil your dreams and why not go back to school? You're still a young woman," he said.

"Thank you, Winston. I'm not that young. But neither is anybody else around here, and when I look around the community I see all the old people with nobody to look after them. I'm going to specialize in geriatric nursing so I can be more useful to these seniors who've done so much for our community," she said.

"When will you start?" asked Windflower.

"I've been talking to Memorial, and they'll give me a half-year credit for the work I've done before. If I'm accepted I can pick up the second term in January. I've applied as a mature student so I think I can get in. I'll know by the end of September," said Sheila.

"I support you fully in this, Sheila," said Windflower. "But I have to ask, where do you and I fit into all of this?"

"I think we need to talk about that," said Sheila, "But not tonight. Let's just enjoy our time together."

Chapter Twenty-Three

Windflower paid the bill and joined Sheila in the car for the short ride home.

The rain had stopped and even the wind had subsided. At Sheila's suggestion, they drove down to the wharf where they could see the moon shimmering low over the ocean. The lighthouse blinked its bright red beacon to Grand Bank and all the ships at sea. For once everything was peaceful and quiet.

Sheila and Windflower talked a little more about food and possible vacation destinations, but it was clear that they were both in a pensive mood. And there was a lot to think about now.

Windflower asked Sheila to drop him off at his house. That wasn't unusual. They often spent nights apart. Windflower knew that he needed time alone to go through the news that Sheila had unexpectedly sprung on him. They had a long kiss, and an even longer hug before Windflower was standing in his doorway, waving goodnight to Sheila.

The lights were out at Windflower's, which meant that his uncle wasn't in, or had gone to bed. That suited Windflower just fine. He had a few things he had to do tonight anyway.

First on his list was to phone his Auntie Marie. He needed to check in with her about Uncle Frank, but he also wanted to find out where Anne-Marie might be these days. In case he made the decision to call her.

"Auntie Marie, it's Winston," he said when he heard her voice on the phone.

"How are you, my little rabbit?" asked his aunt, using her favourite childhood name for him.

"I am well, Auntie," said Winston. "How are you? Is your arthritis bothering you these days?"

"It's not too bad, Winston. I have my medication and it's a small price to pay for the privilege of growing old," she said. "I have made arrangements for Frank to come back on Saturday, Winston. Do you think you can take him to the airport? I worry about him in St. John's after what happened the last time."

"Yes, Auntie, I can do that. You'll be pleased to know that he's not been drinking since his experiences in town," said Windflower.

"That is good news," said his aunt. "Did you talk to him about your dreams?"

"Yes, Auntie, and he was very helpful," said Windflower. "I think one of the dreams may have something to do with Anne-Marie. Do you know where she is now?"

"Anne-Marie is such a lovely girl, Winston. You know that my dreams were always to see you and her with a dozen beautiful children. Do you miss her?" asked his aunt.

"That part of my life is over, long ago," said Windflower. "You know that, Auntie. I have a new woman now, Sheila. I've talked to you about her before."

"Yes, but Anne-Marie must be on your mind or somewhere in your mind, or else you wouldn't be dreaming about her," said Auntie Marie. "Uncle Frank may know a lot about dreams, but he does not have a woman's intuition."

"Do you know where she is now?" asked Windflower, trying to shift the conversation back to more comfortable territory.

"Anne-Marie was here for the pow-wow this summer, just as she has been every year," said his aunt. "I thought I heard her say that she was going to be in New York for some big conference, and then was heading down your way, to Labrador to do some of her healing work. I can ask her mother for her cell phone number if you'd like," said Auntie Marie.

"I would like that, but please don't say it's for me, Auntie. I don't want people to get the wrong idea," said Windflower.

"I'll do that and call you back," said Auntie Marie. "Be safe, my little rabbit."

"Good night, Auntie," said Windflower.

Windflower took *The Orenda* with him to bed, but could not read very much. His mind was too occupied with so many things and he found some of the novel's vivid descriptions of torture between the Huron and Iroquois a little hard to take, especially late at night.

Instead, he picked up his Brunetti book again. Even though he had read it already, it was still fun to read about another cop who loved food.

He fell asleep while Brunetti was eating his risotto with shrimp, and trying to mediate between his environmentally aware daughter and his carnivore son.

 Ah, domestic bliss, he thought, as he drifted off to the dream world.

This night the dream world was blissful too, at least for Windflower, and he didn't wake until his very loud country music alarm pierced the peace and quiet of the morning.

He could hear his Uncle Frank's loud snoring in the other room. Only for two more days, he thought. As Windflower looked out the window he could see the sun, a rare and welcome sight.

He made himself a banana-strawberry smoothie in the blender, and put on his shorts and running shoes. He felt rested from a good night's sleep, and clear-headed despite the many things swirling in his head. A run will help with that, he thought, and he set out on his usual downtown swing through Grand Bank.

He passed Evanchuk on the way and exchanged a quick greeting, mostly about how nice it was to not have to run in the rain. Then he made his way back home where he finished the rest of the smoothie in the blender, and made a fried egg sandwich to take to work with him. He wanted to get there early today. He had a lot of loose ends to tie up and not much time to do it.

The weather held up for Windflower's walk to work, which was an unexpected bonus. Even the town dogs were in a pleasant mood this morning, and almost every one of them barked good morning to Windflower. At least he took it as good morning.

He was the first one in for the day's shift and put on a large pot of coffee. While he was waiting for it to brew, he took the time to read the latest issue of Law Enforcement Review, which had been sitting on the corner of his desk since he got back. He was deep within a story on the pros and cons of stun guns, Tasers, as force deterrent, when he heard Tizzard and Evanchuk come in.

He went out to the lunchroom to say good morning and to get a cup of coffee to go along with his fried egg sandwich. Luckily he escaped back to his office where he could enjoy it in peace for a few moments.

Betsy popped her head in to say good morning, and Windflower gave her the Yashin name and the request to see what the system popped up about him.

"Can you also tap into any on-going investigations? If there is a problem getting access you can talk to Guy Simard in Halifax Ops. Okay?" he added.

"No problem, sir," said Betsy. "I'll get on it right away."

Soon afterwards Windflower's cell phone rang.

"Windflower," he answered.

"Winston, it's Bill Ford."

"Hi Bill, how's she goin' b'y?"

Ford laughed at Windflower's attempt to speak the local dialect. "Not too bad, b'y," said Ford, playing along. "But you have to drop the h in how to be more believable," he said.

"I'll try that," said Windflower.

"So, thanks for your advice," said Ford. "But Arsenault wouldn't go for the suspension. He told me that he would overturn it if it came across his desk. He said that I was making too much out of this, and that he had dealt with similar situations in the past. His words to me were that this would all blow over."

"That's what he told me, too," said Windflower. "But I don't think that's the right way to handle these situations. I believe we have to put a stop to it before it gets worse. I think that it's pretty weak of him not to back you up on this."

"Arsenault is not a bad guy, but I think he's got blinders on when it comes to how we should deal with these issues. I'm with you on this, and besides I have a daughter and would not want to see her treated badly in any workplace, let alone the RCMP," said Ford.

"So what are you going to do?" asked Windflower.

"Well, I've already talked to the guy and put him on notice. If anything else happens I'm going to suspend him anyway, and take my chance with Arsenault later," said Ford.

"Good for you," said Windflower. "I'll back you up if you need me. I suspect that somewhere along the way I'll need you too."

"That's a deal then," said Ford. "I'll let you know if anything else happens."

"Okay, Bill. And good luck," said Windflower.

Betsy came into his office shortly after the call.

"Here's the printout on Peter Yashin," she said, passing Windflower the paper. "There is no Canadian criminal record but a notation talks about an Interpol file. And there are currently three separate investigations; one by Halifax Ops, one by Metro Halifax Major Crimes, and a deportation process that is almost finalized by the looks of it. I have the information on the Immigration file, but I've had to call Staff Sergeant Simard to get his assistance on the other cases. I've left a message for him."

"Thank you, Betsy," said Windflower, but when he looked up from the sheet Betsy had already returned to her workstation at the front.

According to the file, Peter Yashin, aka Sergei Fetisov, and three other aliases, was born in Minsk, Belarus, and was 42 years old. He had first officially entered Canada six years ago on a refugee claim that had been rejected on several occasions.

Yashin had been deported and returned to Belarus, but had since returned to Canada a number of times, as a registered visitor for three month periods at a time.

Apparently, his new scam was to seek permanent status as an entrepreneur in both tourism and the import/export business.

Now that was rich, thought Windflower.

Windflower's intercom buzzed again.

"There's someone here to see you, sir," said Betsy.

"I'll be right out," said Windflower.

He walked to the front and was very surprised to see that his visitor was Sheila. She smiled at him and said, "Can I buy you a cup of coffee, Sergeant?" she asked with a smile.

"Absolutely," said Windflower. "Thank you, Betsy," he said to the receptionist. "I have an appointment. Be back in half an hour."

"Yes, sir," said Betsy, looking very pleased to be part of this pleasant encounter.

Chapter Twenty-Four

"To what do I owe the pleasure of your company this morning?" asked Windflower.

"I feel like there's a bit of space between us after last night," said Sheila. "I know we can't figure everything out right now, but I'd like to at least have a common understanding between us. And I needed a cup of coffee," she added. "Let's go to the Mug-Up."

"Yes, ma'am," said Windflower as he grabbed his coat and headed for the door after Sheila.

"What a grand day," said Sheila, "A good day to be alive."

"Indeed," said Windflower as he struggled to keep pace with Sheila, who was clearly getting very proficient at her power-walking technique.

When they arrived at the café, Sheila went behind the counter to say good morning to the girls in the kitchen, and came out with two cups of coffee and two hot tea biscuits. "I thought you might like one," said Sheila.

"Thank you," said Windflower as he buttered the hot treat and popped a piece into his mouth.

"This is so good."

After he had finished his tea biscuit, he looked up to see Sheila staring at him.

"You know, I still love to watch a man eat," said Sheila with a smile as she sipped her hot coffee. "I'm looking forward to cooking for you more, at least for a little while."

"What does a little while mean?" asked Windflower.

"Well, since you asked, I think we should break things down into manageable pieces, the short, medium and long term," said Sheila. "How does that sound?" she asked.

"Okay, keep going," said Windflower.

"In the short term, let's say 'til January when I go to school, nothing should change, right?" Sheila asked. "We will both still be here and I hope to see a lot of you, Sergeant," she said with a twinkle in her eye.

"I like that," said Windflower, "Especially the part about you cooking for me more."

"I thought you would," said Sheila. "After that I'll be going to university in St. John's. But I have no idea yet about where I might live, or even if I'll come back on weekends."

"Well, for me, I think I can stay in Grand Bank, at least for a couple of more years, and we've already figured out how to do the back and forth to St. John's routine. It's not great but it's doable," said Windflower, "But what about the long term?"

"I don't know," said Sheila. "I have some ideas about it, but I bet you do too. I'll want to work in my new career but I'm not sure where that might lead."

"I guess I'm kinda' in the same boat," said Windflower. "My career with the RCMP is going along pretty well. But I have no idea where I'll be or what I'll be doing. I'm not even sure what type of work I want be involved in. But where does that leave us, Sheila?"

"We're in the same place we've always been," said Sheila. "We love and care about each other, and want to spend time together. My suggestion is that we acknowledge that, and then figure out what we want to do, at least for the medium, if not the long term, over the next couple of months."

"Ah," said Windflower, "Now I get it. It's a deal, ma'am." And Windflower put out his hand to shake Sheila's.

Sheila took his hand and said, "Agreed, Sergeant. But don't you think there would be a better way to cement this relationship than just shaking hands?"

This time Windflower had the twinkle in his eye when he replied, "I might be able to think of something."

On the way home they made plans for supper. Windflower would cook some fish, and Sheila would make a salad and bring dessert. They would eat at Windflower's so they could have one last evening together with Uncle Frank before he went back to Alberta.

The sun disappeared from Grand Bank after Windflower had walked Sheila back home. It went missing somewhere in a giant bank of fog out towards the French islands. The wind had returned though, and he felt it creep up his back and underneath his collar. And just as he opened the door to the RCMP detachment, he felt the first of many drops of rain.

Betsy smiled a knowing and satisfied smile at him on the way in, and Tizzard arrived at his office at almost the same time.

"What's up, Corporal?" asked Windflower as he hung up his coat and sat down at his desk.

"Well, I've found where the vans came from this summer," Tizzard said, holding up faxed copies of rental agreements. "They were rented from George G.R. Parsons in St. John's and were under the name of Gorky Park Tours. The signature on the bottom and the credit card used belonged to one Peter Yashin."

"That's good, but do we know where the vehicles came from or where they went?" asked Windflower, "Or where they picked up or dropped off the passengers?"

"That's the next step," said Tizzard. "I had Evanchuk calculate the mileage on the vans from when they were picked up to their return. And making a few estimations, we think that the vans drove to this area, and then back to St. John's, with very little additional mileage."

"If you are right, then the passengers would have been dropped off in St. John's then?" asked Windflower.

"That's what I thought, except that Evanchuk suggested that maybe the passengers and the vans could have taken the ferry at Argentia," said Tizzard.

"Did they?" asked Windflower.

"Evanchuk checked the passenger lists for Argentia to North Sydney, Nova Scotia for around both of these dates and, voilà," said Tizzard, pulling more paper out from behind his back. "Both the vans and the passengers travelled to Nova Scotia, which of course the odometers wouldn't pick up because the vans were travelling on the ferry. Pretty good, eh?"

"That is pretty good," said Windflower. "Now we need a way to follow the trail into Nova Scotia. I think I'll give Quigley a call in Halifax to check in, and see if they picked up anything on their end."

Tizzard went off happy with himself and Windflower felt pretty good too.

At least they were beginning to unravel one mystery, he thought. Maybe Quigley could shed some more light on things from the mainland.

Ron Quigley answered Windflower's call on the first ring.

"Winston, how the hell are ya, b'y?" he asked. "I was thinking about calling you to touch base on this human smuggling file."

"I'm well, thanks, Ron," said Windflower, "That's what I was calling you about. We've had some strange stuff happening over here involving possible Chinese migrants, and also maybe even some Russian gang activity."

"That is interesting," said Quigley. "I know a little bit about some of the Russians operating up here. The king pin is a guy by the name of Igor Gregorinsky, also known as Iggy or Big Iggy. They're involved in lots of nasty stuff including prostitution and drugs. I think there's an active investigation on those guys."

"Yeah, I've been talking to Guy Simard," said Windflower. "You ever heard of a fellow named Peter Yashin?"

"Nope," said Quigley, "But Simard definitely would. They've got their hands in pretty deep there. Tell me about the Chinese angle."

Windflower ran through what he knew about the Chinese visitors to Grand Bank including the fact that they were off-loaded in Nova Scotia earlier this summer. Quigley said he hadn't heard anything about that from his end, but would do some rooting around to see what he could come up with.

"And I'm going to be over in Newfoundland this weekend," said Quigley. "I've got a wedding in St. John's on Saturday."

"I'm going to be in St. John's too this weekend," said Windflower. "I'm dropping my uncle off at the airport. If you have time we can grab a coffee."

"Good enough," said Quigley. "Talk to you later."

Windflower didn't need to look at the clock to know it was lunchtime, but he found it hard to justify to himself, or Betsy for that matter, going out for lunch. So he went to the back and found a can of soup, which, along with a few of Tizzard's Purity Cream Crackers, hit the spot and carried him through to mid-afternoon.

Then it was time for more java to get through the rest of the day. Windflower made a fresh pot and was just sitting down to enjoy a cup when Tizzard flew into the lunchroom.

"Slow down, Corporal," said Windflower. "Do you have any speeds besides Formula One?"

"Sorry, Sarge, but I'm in a hurry. And I'm glad I caught you. You'll never guess who I got a call from," said Tizzard. "Frankie Fallon."

"And what did young Frankie want?" asked Windflower, blowing on his coffee to cool it down.

"He wanted to tell me that he heard from Shawn Parsons," said Tizzard. "Parsons wants to talk to me. According to Fallon he's scared to death."

Chapter Twenty-Five

"What should I do?" asked Tizzard.

"I guess you should talk to Parsons and see what he wants," said Windflower, "And tell him that the RNC is looking for him, and if he knew what was good for him he'd turn himself in to Langmead."

"Okay," said Tizzard. "That's what I thought, but I wanted to run it by you."

"Thank you, Corporal. Let me know what happens next, okay?" said Windflower.

"Okay," said Tizzard and he went away to make his call.

When Windflower got back to his office, Betsy was busy dropping a pile of printouts from her computer onto his desk.

"Investigation updates courtesy of Staff Sergeant Simard," said Betsy. "He said to read and shred, if I can quote him directly. And he wants to talk to you after you've had a chance to go through them."

"Thanks, Betsy," said Windflower.

For the next hour he pored through the information that Simard had provided. It was clear from reading these files that Gregorinsky was the ringleader for the operations described in much detail in the reports. Yashin was there too, along with several others, but he was playing second or third fiddle to the man they called Big Iggy. Windflower got so wrapped up in this interesting reading material that he lost track of time, and when he looked up it was already half-past five.

Dinner, he thought. I'm supposed to be making it.

He closed up his office, turned out the lights, and then ran for home. Which was probably a good idea, because the few drops of earlier rain had now turned into a torrent.

When he arrived home, soaking and out of breath, his uncle and Sheila were both tuned into Judge Judy on the television.

"Don't worry about me," he said rather wistfully, but neither of them moved.

Sheila did at least wave and called hello. Windflower had a nice hot shower and changed into clean, dry clothes.

He took a plastic-wrapped bundle of cod out of the freezer and put it into the microwave to thaw. Then he cleaned and scrubbed three large baking potatoes. He thawed the fish halfway to keep its firmness. When it was done, he took it out and replaced it in the microwave with the potatoes.

Normally, he would dip the codfish in flour and fry it up in hot fat from scraps of pork fat called "scrunchions" that were cut up small and sprinkled over the fried fish. But he saved that method for special occasions. Tonight, he would spice it up as usual with salt, black pepper and a heavy shot of cayenne pepper and flash fry it in extra virgin olive oil so the fish would be cooked crispy on the outside, remaining moist inside. And, as they would say in those health food claims on TV, "with only half the fat and calories."

The fish was done by the time the potatoes were ready, and Windflower called Sheila and Uncle Frank to supper. Sheila got her mixed vegetable salad with carrots, broccoli and cauliflower sprouts and put it on the table. Windflower gave everyone a baked potato and put the fish platter on the table for all to serve themselves. Sheila and Uncle Frank talked about Judge Judy until Windflower gave them both a stiff glare and the rest of supper was concluded in a welcome peaceful silence.

After dinner, Sheila and Windflower did the dishes while his uncle had a smoke. One of his friends came by while he was outside, and Uncle Frank invited him in for a cup of tea and dessert. This was to be the last of the blueberry buckle, and while Windflower would have preferred saving the rest for later, Sheila dished it all up between the three men who happily devoured everything, including the crumbs. Then the visitor was persuaded to join in a game of cards that rounded out the evening.

Once the card game was over, Sheila and Windflower headed back over to her house and had a special and quiet evening together.

That night Windflower had one of his best sleeps ever too, except for the dream that came as it often did nearer the early morning hours. This dream was with the woman, the Beothuk lady, Windflower had decided to call her.

Again she beckoned Windflower, and again he followed her through the woods and back to the river.

This time he could see that the river was no mere forest stream but a full-fledged river that stretched as wide as he could see. It had a powerful roiling current. Nonetheless, he stepped into the moving river behind the Beothuk lady and as she sank beneath the water, he lost sight of her.

He tried to find her again but only succeeded in sinking farther into the river. Down and down he dropped, until he felt his feet finally hit bottom. When that happened his whole body wanted to run, to get out of there, and he heard a voice calling him to wake up. But he forced himself to stay there, and to reach his hand down into the silky sand beneath his feet.

At first he felt nothing and was ready to give in to the urge to return to the surface, but then he felt it. It was something hard and oblong shaped, about the length of his hand. It was stuck, but he pulled it hard out of the sand, and brought it up to his face to look.

It was murky underneath the water, and Windflower couldn't really see enough to know exactly what it was. It was made of some kind of wood and when he looked closer he could see that it had the shape of a mouth and two eyes carved into it. It still had a few strings of straggling rope hanging from its top. It was a doll, a child's doll, he realized. That was my gift, he thought, a doll? Why would I receive a doll? That's when he woke up.

Windflower lay in the dark of the early morning for a few minutes to try and process what had just happened in his dream, but he couldn't quite connect the dots.

I'll need more time to process this, he thought, as he felt Sheila stirring gently beside him.

He crept out of the bedroom and put on his running gear. It would be good to have a run to wake up his body and clear his mind.

Windflower glanced outside, and could see that while it was damp and drizzling, the monsoons seemed to be over for now. He pulled on his running shoes and thin nylon jacket and sneaked out the door into the gray morning.

The streets were quiet and slick, and the only sound he could hear was his own breathing. As he approached the road down to the beach, he could see the pink just starting to fill the sky behind the Cape. It was pleasant and calming to be running in such beauty, thought Windflower, and it filled him with gratitude.

As he turned the corner and headed back towards downtown and the wharf area, he could hear noises, at first faintly and then growing louder as he got closer. When he finally arrived at the water's edge he could see the reason why. Two large tractor-trailer trucks were idling on the wharf, and in front of them was a crowd of about fifty people, and almost as many pick-up trucks. The pick-ups and the people looked like they were blocking the entrance to and from the fish plant, preventing the trucks from leaving.

Windflower was approaching the scene from the west, and he could see Constable Evanchuk at the end of her morning run coming in from the east. They met in the middle just as Constable Fortier was pulling up in his RCMP cruiser. Fortier got out of his car and all three RCMP officers walked together to the head of the scene.

"What's going on here?" asked Windflower.

"It's a picket line," said one of the men standing between the trucks and the exit. "It's a picket line and like our sign sez, no fish for forinners."

"Who's the leader here?" asked Windflower to no one in particular.

And no one answered.

Windflower pulled his officers aside and said to Evanchuk, "Go and get changed and then come back here right away."

To Fortier he said, "I want you to stay here and monitor the situation." And seeing the growing number of gawkers stopping to have a look at the action, he added, "And keep the traffic moving on the road."

"What are we going to do about that?" asked Fortier, pointing to the growing picket line.

"We are going to keep everyone calm until we find out what's happening," said Windflower.

Windflower then went to Fortier's car and turned on the exterior microphone.

"Good morning ladies and gentlemen," he started. "I am Sergeant Winston Windflower of the Royal Canadian Mounted Police. Our job is to keep everyone safe this morning. To help us do that we would ask you to remain calm and respect all of the property on this site. We will not tolerate any violence or violent behaviour of any kind. Thank you for your cooperation."

"Is that it?" asked Fortier.

"It is for now," said Windflower. "Call Tizzard and get him down here to help you," said Windflower. "I'm going for a shower. Don't do anything or let them do anything until I get back, okay?"

"Okay," said Fortier.

By the time Windflower had his shower and was preparing to change into his uniform, his cell phone was ringing.

"You better get down here, Boss," said Tizzard. "I think she's about ready to blow."

"Pick me up," said Windflower, grabbing his fresh uniform from the closet.

By the time he was dressed, Tizzard was out front waiting for him.

Sometimes it's good that he's fast, Windflower thought.

Chapter Twenty-Six

Soon they were both standing near the wharf entrance surveying the scene. There were now over a hundred people actively engaged in the protest, including a couple of dozen fish plant workers who didn't look too happy about losing a day's pay. Forty or more on-lookers hoping for more excitement shuffled about nearby. To add to the carnival atmosphere, Windflower saw a VOCM radio vehicle and a CBC television van pull up.

"Let's go," said Windflower as he led Tizzard up to the front of the picket line where Fortier and Evanchuk were doing their best to keep the peace.

Then a man in a dark suit walked out from the area where the trucks were parked and strode directly up to Windflower. When the men on the protest line saw this man they began to shout some very disturbing and choice words at him. Windflower thought he heard the word traitor, but he couldn't really be sure in the commotion. He walked over to the man and pulled him to one side.

"I'm George Whiteway, and I'm the manager of the fish plant. I demand that you clear the road to let me get my trucks out of here. There are thousands of pounds of fish on board those trucks and they need to get to market. This action here," he said, pointing to the picket line, "is illegal and they are impeding my right of way. Move them out of the way. That's your job."

"My job is to protect the peace," said Windflower, "And to ensure the safety of everyone here today; that includes my officers and your truck drivers, by the way. How safe do you think it would be for them if we just cleared the road? That's if we could," he said pointing to the even highly agitated crowd that continued to yell at the fish plant manager from the sidelines.

"I'm not doing anything until we can get everything settled down here."

The plant manager looked like he was about to explode, but after hyperventilating for a moment, went away in a huff, shouting at Windflower as he left, "If you won't fix this I'll get someone who will."

"That went well," said Tizzard.

Windflower shot Tizzard a death glare and walked back to the picket line.

"So who's in charge here?" he asked.

When no one replied he continued, "Unless I have someone to talk to in the next five minutes I'm going to ask my officers to clear this line, and arrest anyone who gets in the way."

He then turned and went to stand by Evanchuk and Fortier. After a couple of minutes a small, older man came up to Windflower.

"I guess you might as well talk to me as anybody," he said. "I'm no leader but I am a fisherman who's got a stake in this. So if you want I can talk to ya. I'm Fonse Tessier from Grand Bank."

"I'm Sergeant Winston Windflower," said the RCMP officer. "So what are you doing here and what do you want?

"Well, I tinks the signs speak for themselves, but we want a share of the red fish quota for us and not just the forinners. And some of the plant workers want more fish to be processed here," said the fisherman.

"What does the company say about this?" asked Windflower.

"Ah, they don't care 'bout us," said Tessier. "They're makin' lots of money and just shippin' that fish right outta here as fast as they can. They said that they got an agreement with the government, and they don't care what we want or need."

"How long do you plan to stay here?" asked Windflower.

"As long as it takes," said the fisherman.

Or as long as we'll let you, thought Windflower.

"Well, thank you, Mr. Tessier," said Windflower, holding out his hand for the fisherman to shake. "You've been very helpful. You realize that you can't stay here indefinitely, though."

"Oh, we know that," said Tessier. "But the ways that tings are goin' we figured we'd do what we could." Tessier then went back to confer with his fellow protestors.

"Are we going to do anything, Boss?" asked Tizzard.

"Haven't you been watching, Corporal?" replied Windflower. "We have been doing something. We're preserving the peace and good order of Grand Bank. I thought that was our job. Fixing this problem will require more skills than you and I have. That's why they're bringing in the heavy artillery," he said, pointing to a mini-media scrum that the radio and TV people were having with the newly arrived Mayor Bill Sinnott.

"Good morning, Mr. Mayor," said Windflower when the Mayor had extricated himself from the media. "Somehow, I am not surprised to see you here this morning."

"A Mayor's job is to keep on top of tings," said Mayor Sinnott. "Have you seen the plant manager yet?"

"Mr. Whiteway was here earlier," said Windflower. "He didn't like my advice and went off to seek a second opinion."

"So you'll probably get a call from your boss soon," said Sinnott. "All I want is to try and have a meetin' with all the parties before you do anyting, okay?" he asked.

"We'll see what we can do," said Windflower as the Mayor went off to pay his respects to the protestors.

"Corporal," said Windflower to Tizzard after the Mayor had left, "Can you get us all some coffee and maybe a few grilled cheese sandwiches too? And let Betsy know where we all are this morning? Tell her if anybody needs me, I'll likely be here 'til after lunch."

Windflower thought he felt a drop of rain, which, considering the situation, might actually be helpful. Luckily, Fortier had an extra yellow slicker for him to put on when it started to pour. Windflower's hopes of the rain diminishing the protest were a little fanciful though. Most of the people here were well used to being outside, and soon the whole area was covered in a sea of raincoats that people had retrieved from the cabs of their pick-ups.

So much for that strategy, thought Windflower.

Tizzard was back sooner than expected with coffees and sandwiches wrapped in tin foil packets for the officers on duty. Windflower had gone over to Tizzard's jeep to eat when his cell phone rang.

"Windflower," he answered.

"What the hell is going on over there this morning?" said an obviously agitated Inspector Arsenault. "I've got the plant manager and the CEO of the company screaming at me, and telling me that you and the RCMP are supporting a protest in Grand Bank."

"Well, we're not really supporting anybody," said Windflower. "We're trying to prevent a riot and to keep anyone from getting hurt. I don't know what the fish plant manager expects us to do, sir."

"He expects, and I expect, you to stop allowing a group of hooligans to take matters into their own hands by impeding traffic or business operations. Your job, Sergeant, is to uphold the law and not assist them to break it. I want that illegal protest gone and I want it gone now," said Arsenault. "Do I make myself clear, Sergeant?"

"I understand sir," said Windflower, "But there's over a hundred people involved in the protest and only four officers on the scene. I don't feel it would be prudent to try and move these protestors with such a small force. And I'm not sure that they would cooperate, with all due respect, sir."

"I am giving you one more hour to fix this on your own, Windflower. If not, I will be coming over there myself to deal with it. And neither you nor I will be happy if that happens." said Arsenault as the phone went dead.

"I'm guessing that didn't go well either," said Tizzard who had been sitting beside Windflower during this call.

"We have an hour," said Windflower, "After that the cavalry is coming from Marystown. Can you see if you can find the Mayor and bring him over here to have a little chat, Corporal?"

Tizzard returned soon after, and deposited a dripping Mayor Sinnott into the RCMP jeep with Windflower.

"You and I have an hour to fix this mess, or Inspector Arsenault will be coming over with a crew from Marystown to fix it for us," said Windflower.

"Okay," said the Mayor. "I've got a meeting lined up in half an hour with all the players. You're welcome to attend," said Sinnott.

The meeting was at the town offices, and the Mayor welcomed each participant individually. There was

Whiteway from the fish plant, Tessier from the picket line, a fish plant worker whom Windflower recognized by face if not by name. Also in attendance was a business rep from the fish plant workers' union, and surprisingly, the local Fisheries guy, Billy Roche, whom Windflower knew well from previous work. This crew, plus the Mayor and Windflower, made up the quorum for the meeting.

Windflower watched with not a little admiration as the Mayor coaxed all of the various factions, none of which were close to agreement with the other, into putting out their concerns, and then trying to get everybody to move a little bit. The hardest part was trying to get any commitment from Roche and the Fisheries department. But in the end, even Bill Roche had agreed to take the matter back to the department for further consultation.

There was no resolution of the issues that day, but Tessier did agree to ask his fellow protestors to stop holding up the traffic for now, and consider a two week cooling off period while discussions continued with Fisheries.

The fish plant manager agreed to allow the workers who had lost time to make it up by working later on their shift, and agreed to support the local fishermen's request for a small share of the red fish quota. And Mayor Sinnott would be talking to the Mayor of Fortune, to see if they couldn't process the fish from French fisherman at their plant to avoid another confrontation in Grand Bank.

As discussions wound down, the Mayor made a small speech about cooperation and working together, and everybody went away to confer with their allies or superiors.

After a heated meeting on the wharf, the protesters agreed to support the plan for more dialogue and the picket line was withdrawn. Windflower called Arsenault to tell him the good news, but the Inspector remained resentful from the previous conversation.

"I guess we should just be glad it's over," said Arsenault. "I don't understand why people won't follow my directions around here anymore without challenging my authority."

Windflower decided to let that one go by.

"First Ford and now you," Arsenault continued.

Windflower let that one go too.

"In my day, the men of the RCMP had balls and weren't afraid of women or protests," said Arsenault.

Strike three, thought Windflower, now you've gone too far.

"I think we're trying to use common sense and good judgement to resolve some difficult situations, sir. And when it comes to women," Windflower paused, and then realized that the phone line had gone dead.

Oh well, he thought, we've done our good work today. Work that allowed the peace to prevail and maybe even some good will come out of this morning.

Windflower looked for the Mayor to congratulate him, but he was already surrounded by well-wishers.

"Fortier and Evanchuk, you mop up here and then go get warmed up. Tizzard, let's you and me go get a hot cup of tea."

Chapter Twenty-Seven

Tizzard swung by the Mug-Up, but the café was still busy and buzzing from the morning adventures on the wharf. Windflower directed Tizzard to head back to the RCMP offices.

Once safe and dry inside, they went to the back room and Tizzard put the kettle on to boil. He also took out a large plate of crackers and a slab of old cheddar cheese and put them on the table.

"Having a light snack, Tizzard?" asked Windflower.

"Oh, you can have some too," said Tizzard.

Both men smeared butter on a couple of crackers, and topped them with a chunk of cheese while they waited for their tea.

"I guess it must have been a lot different around here when the inshore fishery was going well," said Windflower.

"Not just here, but all over the coast," said Tizzard, "All over the island." He paused to finish off a last bite of cracker and to put a tea bag in the teapot now that the water had boiled. "There were fishermen and fish plants everywhere. There was a plant in Grand Bank, one in Fortune, one in Burin, and two big ones in Marystown and St. Lawrence. They were all processing cod and ground fish that the locals were bringing in, along with some side catches from the draggers and the trawlers."

"That was a lot of activity, a lot of money involved, I guess" said Windflower.

"And good money too," said Tizzard. "For many families there were two or three incomes with the father and sons working in the fishery, and the women working a few shifts at the plant, but those days are long gone now. There are still a handful of fishermen working with their long liners, and a few of the plants like Grand Bank might have a hundred employees all together. But the days of King Cod are gone, likely forever," said Tizzard, a little sadly.

"But there's still people fishing," said Windflower. "What are they fishing for?" he asked.

"There's still a bit of cod in some areas," said Tizzard. "In fact some people say that the cod is coming back, but most of the fishermen have diversified their catch now. They try and get a license or a quota to fish for cod, but also may do a bit of lobster or shrimp fishing as well. Right now, everybody is trying to get a quota for halibut, which is a very good cash catch, but you have to compete with everybody all over the island for a quota."

"And you have to compete with Nova Scotia fishermen, and even the French," added Windflower.

"Yeah," said Tizzard. "Somewhere in Europe they're still sitting down to decide who is going to be able to fish off Newfoundland," he said, "Just like when we first started out here."

"Well, Corporal, it's back to the paper pile for me," said Windflower as he stood to leave.

"Oh, I guess I should give you these," said Tizzard as he passed over the keys to the RCMP jeep to Windflower. "I won't be around next week."

"Why thank you, Corporal. I'll make sure to take good care of your baby," said Windflower as he left the lunchroom.

Betsy flagged him down on the way back and said, "Staff Sergeant Simard called again, sir. He's waiting for your call. I didn't want to bother you this morning with all the activity going on."

"Thank you, Betsy. I'll give him a call right now," said Windflower.

"Guy, how are you, my friend?" asked Windflower when he heard the other officer answer the phone.

"Winston, I am so happy that I could burst. I got a great lady, and only two years to go to a full pension. We're thinking about moving down Lunenburg way when I retire. Sit on my boat and watch the world go by. So, you got my stuff?"

"I did, thank you very much," said Windflower. "Is this the latest intel or is there an update?"

"There's a big update," said Simard. "That's why I wanted to talk to you. You didn't get this from me, but I think the guys in major crime are close to turning Big Iggy," he said.

"Wow," said Windflower. "Do they really think they can get him to talk?" he asked.

"Apparently, the deal is that they have him cold on two of the murders involving the bikers, but will go for deportation if his stuff is good enough. That's why it's so hush-hush. Nobody else, especially the local cops, are going to be happy about him walking on a murder charge," said Simard.

"My guess is that Interpol wouldn't be too pleased either," said Windflower, "Any news on my guy, Yashin?"

"No sign of him over here," said Simard. "I asked my source at Majors about him and they said he was a bit player in the big scheme of things. The other interesting thing is that they hadn't heard anything about this Chinese migrant idea; neither had Iggy, apparently."

"That's interesting too," said Windflower. "Is it possible that Yashin was running this thing on his own?"

"It might be," said Simard. "I'll keep you posted if anything else pops up."

"Thanks, Guy, have a good weekend," said Windflower before hanging up.

More information, but nowhere closer to any answers, he thought.

The next few hours were tedious slogging but almost carefree, as Windflower did his best to keep both the paper and e-mail systems moving. Before he left for the night, Tizzard popped his head into Windflower's office.

"Fallon called again and says that Parsons wants to meet. I told him I was going away for a week but that maybe Parsons would talk to you. He's going to go back to Parsons to see what he thinks," said Tizzard. "I gave him your cell phone number. I hope that's okay."

"That's fine," said Windflower. "I'd be happy to talk to Mr. Parsons, preferably when he is on the other side of a set of bars."

"Okay, well I guess that's it for me. You got my number if you need to reach me," said Tizzard.

"Enjoy your time off with your Dad," said Windflower. "We'll see you in a week."

Tizzard left, and Windflower started to leave as well. Then he remembered that he had Tizzard's jeep, and went back and got the keys. He turned the ignition and the music from the radio just about blew him away; some kind of heavy metal and very, very loud. Windflower found the classical music station and just let the soothing sounds wash over him. It was Beethoven's Moonlight Sonata, a piece that Sheila had introduced him to.

Within minutes he was relaxed, happy and off for the weekend. He arrived home as Uncle Frank was leaving.

"I'm going over to Jarge's," said his uncle. "What time are we leavin' in the morning?"

"About 10 o'clock," said Windflower.

"Okay, I'll be ready to go," said Uncle Frank as he pulled his woollen cap's flaps down over his ears and bent low into the wind, which was considerable by this time.

Windflower waved goodbye, and after a quick shower was on his way over to Sheila's for their dinner with the Stoodleys.

"Hi Sheila," said Windflower. "What is that wonderful aroma?"

That is my baked salmon à la maison," said Sheila. "The dill really brings out the flavour of the salmon," she said, as she opened the oven door to take a peek at the fish inside the tin foil.

"How long 'til supper?" asked Windflower.

"The salmon's been in for about two hours at 250 degrees so I guess another half hour will be perfect," said Sheila. "And I picked up some asparagus from the supermarket. I don't know where they get it this time of year, but that will go well with those red potatoes you like so much," said Sheila. "I'll get the veggies ready if you'll make us up a salad."

"No problem," said Windflower, and he got the leafy green lettuce out of the fridge along with a red pepper, the better half of a cucumber, and a Honey Crisp apple.

He washed and tossed the greens in a light vinegar and oil mixture, and cut the vegetables and apple to throw in on top. He then found a handful of left over blueberries and sprinkled them on top too, along with a shot of fresh pepper, and a few tiny chunks of parmesan cheese that he found at the last minute.

The Stoodleys arrived just as Sheila was finishing setting the table, and they came bearing gifts, one of which was a chilled bottle of champagne to celebrate the transfer of the Mug-Up from Sheila to Moira Stoodley. Windflower opened the champagne and the foursome toasted both women's continued success in their new endeavours.

The Stoodleys also came with a box that Windflower knew must be for him. It went into the fridge as soon as they arrived, but Windflower's nose told him that it just might contain his favourite, peanut butter cheesecake.

Chapter Twenty-Eight

Sheila had artfully arranged the salmon on a fish shaped platter with slices of cucumber and cherry tomatoes as garnishes. She topped it off with fresh parsley and rosemary flakes, and when she placed it on the table it filled the air with the aroma of dill and lemon juice and fresh baked fish. The salmon was done to perfection, and it melted off the diners' forks smoother than the butter on the asparagus. Windflower's salad was a great delight as well, and he basked in both the compliments and the companionship of good friends.

They finished off their meal by enjoying the "surprise" cheesecake and coffee with a splash of Bailey's Irish Cream. The men did the dishes while the ladies relaxed and chatted in the living room. A friendly game of cards rounded out a perfect evening. It was about half past ten when the Stoodleys finally headed for home.

Sheila had her bath while Windflower brushed his teeth and headed off to bed to read until she joined him. But when Sheila arrived, Windflower was fast asleep after his long day at work. Sheila gently nudged him over so she could slip in beside him, and snuggled in tightly for the night.

When Windflower woke he was happy to find Sheila still close beside him, and to realize that he had gone through the night without any of those persistent dreams.

He got up and put on the coffee. Then he went out to check out the morning and to do his prayers. It was a continuation of yesterday, more rain, drizzle and fog. He hoped it would clear a little bit for the drive to St. John's, but he could live with the RDF. He had to, since it was likely going to linger, on and off, mostly on, until Christmas.

He pulled his hoodie up over his head and carried out his daily meditations. He smudged and said his prayers and was back inside just as the coffee was ready to serve. He poured himself a cup and thought he heard stirring in the bedroom, so he brought that cup into the bedroom with him. Sheila was already awake, and propped up on her pillows reading one of her magazines. She gratefully accepted the cup of coffee from Windflower and he went back out to get his own.

He poured and sipped his coffee and then cut up the last remaining Honey Crisp apple which, along with some strawberries, a sliced banana and the few remaining blueberries was just enough for a healthy start to the day. He carried one bowl in to Sheila and then went back to the kitchen to look out at the morning and enjoy his fresh fruit concoction. He scrambled a few eggs and put some of the leftover salmon in for flavour. A couple of toasted and buttered bagels on top made a delicious breakfast tray, at least he hoped Sheila would think so. He was very happy when she did.

A long kiss and a promise of more were his thanks from Sheila and he headed over to pick up his uncle for the trip to St. John's.

It was another great day to be alive, thought Windflower. When he pulled up to his little house in Grand Bank. Uncle Frank was standing in his driveway

talking to a few of the buddies he had made during his
time with Windflower. He waved to Windflower to
indicate he was ready, and shook hands with his
friends. His uncle threw his luggage and kit bag in the
back of the jeep and jumped in with Windflower.

"I'll miss those old guys," he said to Windflower.
"They're good people."

"It looks like you made a lot of friends in Grand Bank,"
said Windflower.

"They're easy to get along with," said Uncle Frank. "But
I'll be glad to get home and sleep in my own bunk
again. Oh, by the way, Marie gave me a phone number
to give to you. It's for Anne-Marie Littlechild. I left it on
the coffee table in the living room- if you are ever
looking for it," he added.

"Thank you, Uncle," said Windflower. "I'll look for that
when I get back. That reminds me. I had another dream
that I wanted to talk to you about."

"Oh," said Uncle Frank. "That's interesting. So tell me
about it."

Windflower told his uncle about following the woman
back to the river, which he noted was bigger and more
powerful than he'd noticed before.

Once again they went into the river and again he fell
beneath the surface until he felt his feet hit bottom. This
time however, he told his uncle he forced himself to stay
there and to reach his hand down beneath his feet. At

first he felt nothing, but then he pulled the object out of the river bottom.

"It was a doll," said Windflower, "A child's doll."

His uncle listened attentively and nodded as Windflower related his dream. When the younger man was finished he stayed quiet for a few moments and then said, 'What do you think it means?"

"I don't know," said Windflower. "I didn't feel bad or anything. I just didn't understand, still don't."

"Well, dreams about dolls or toys are usually about one or more things. They often relate to our childhood and finding a lost doll might be that you are looking for something that you may have lost or never had as a child. I know your mother died young and her spirit may have left the doll for you," said Uncle Frank.

"But, because there was a woman guide in tho dream it may be leading you in another direction," he continued.

"I still don't understand," said Windflower.

"Dreams are not easily understood," said Uncle Frank. "They are cloaked in mystery, in riddles, and are often symbolic. But I'd think that the message of receiving a doll as a gift in your dream may be about your desire to have children of your own," he said.

"I've never even thought about it," said Windflower.

"Your spirit has," said Uncle Frank.

"Deep inside you have these thoughts, even if they haven't manifested on the surface. When you dive deep beneath the surface you often discover the truth. Lucky for you, the truth is a blessing, or it can be, if you choose to act upon it."

Windflower grew silent and was thinking about this intently when Uncle Frank added, "I guess you better start looking for a partner to make your dreams come true."

And, chuckling to himself he said, "Wake me up when we get to Goobies."

Windflower now had a lot to think about.

Between watching for moose and processing the ideas that his uncle had just put into his head, the time flew until the RCMP jeep pulled up at the Goobies gas pumps. His uncle went for a smoke while Windflower filled the car with gas. He went inside to pay, and picked up a coffee and muffin for both of them to tide them over on the last leg of the journey.

Just after noon, Windflower dropped his Uncle Frank at the departures entrance and went to park the car. When he came in Uncle Frank was talking to a woman from Air Canada who took his ticket and bags and got him his boarding pass.

"Still the charmer," said Windflower to his uncle as they sat in the Tim Hortons in the terminal waiting for the pre-boarding announcements.

"Once you get it, you never lose it," said Uncle Frank, winking at Windflower.

"There's your flight," said Windflower, as he heard the announcement over the public address system.

"Have a safe journey and thank you for your help."

"Thank you for your hospitality," said Uncle Frank. "I really enjoyed my time here."

"Come back again," said Windflower without really thinking about it. "And bring Auntie Marie with you next time," he added.

Windflower waited until he saw his uncle walk through security, and then went back out to pick up his car in the parking lot. On the way he picked up his phone to call Sheila and noticed that there was a missed call. It was Tizzard's number.

"Hey, Corporal, I thought you were on vacation," said Windflower when Tizzard answered the phone.

"We're getting on the boat right now," said Tizzard. "I wanted to let you know that I talked to Shawn Parsons last night. He called around 11:30 p.m., pissed out of his mind, bawling and crying that he needed help. He said that someone was going to kill him."

"Who's going to kill him?" asked Windflower.

"He didn't say, Boss," said Tizzard. "He was too drunk to make a lot of sense, but I gave him your number. I also have the phone number he called from if that's of any help. Here it is," said Tizzard.

Windflower grabbed a pen out of his pocket and scribbled the number down in his notebook.

"That's great," he said. "I'll follow up with Langmead. Maybe they can find Parsons through this number."

"Okay," said Tizzard, "I'm off; see you next week."

Windflower found his jeep and scrolled through his phone until he found Carl Langmead's cell phone number.

"Hi Carl," he said when the voice mail came on. "It's Windflower, I'm in St. John's and I've got some information about Shawn Parsons. Give me a call if you get a chance. Thanks."

His work and responsibilities looked after, Windflower decided to go for a little drive, despite the poor weather. He loved the road that went down past the airport into Portugal Cove and right up to the little ferry to Bell Island. Ron Quigley had told him about a great fish and chips place along the way. How perfect was that?

As Windflower exited the airport he turned right and headed down towards Portugal Cove. Along the way he passed a number of newly developed areas where housing had been built to meet the growing needs of bursting-at-the-seams St. John's.

He continued past Windsor Lake, which still served as part of the water supply system for the St. John's area, and into the small community of Portugal Cove. He stopped right next to the dock where the ferry shuttled across to Bell Island and back twice a day.

There had once been a thriving mining industry on Bell Island dating back to the early nineteen hundreds. Windflower had seen an article about the mines in the area of Bell Island called Wabana, which became the one and only incorporated community on the small island. He also learned that Wabana was an old Beothuk name for "place where the light shines first."

The community of Wabana was home to 14,000 people at the peak of its iron ore production, but declined dramatically after the mines closed in the 1960's. Another claim to fame of Wabana was that during the Second World War, German U-boats would often patrol the waters, and they sank four cargo ships carrying iron ore to the steel mill in Sydney, Nova Scotia.

Today it was a much smaller community, although Windflower had heard it was growing again. People seemed to like the idea of living in a small town, and didn't mind the daily commute by ferry to their jobs in St. John's.

The ferry was loading up to head over to the island when Windflower arrived, so he parked and stood to watch the boat make its short trip to the island.

Chapter Twenty-Nine

After the ferry left port Windflower continued on into St. Phillips where he found the restaurant he was looking for down by the beach.

It looked like an old cottage that had been converted into a restaurant, and judging by the number of cars in the parking lot, it was very popular as well. There was a line up for a table but Windflower was happy to take his order to go. He ordered his fish and chips and stood by the side, waiting for his number to come up.

It took a while, but when it came he was not disappointed. There were two large pieces of crisply browned fish and a heaping order of homemade French fries. Windflower doused his food in salt and malt vinegar. He found a seat out on the deck to enjoy both his fish and chips and the sun, which had decided to make at least a brief appearance. The fish was coated in a thin flour batter, which gave it a crispy flaky texture that was both light and tasty. The fries were double deep-fried and soaked up the malt vinegar like a sponge.

Windflower had a delightful lunch, and as he was putting his now empty cardboard container into the garbage can, the rain started up again.

Oh, well, thought Windflower, maybe it will keep the moose off the road on the way home.

Windflower was turning onto the ring road to go back to the highway when his cell phone rang. He pulled over to answer it. It was Carl Langmead.

"Good morning, Winston, or I guess it's afternoon by now," said Langmead. "Are you still in town?"

"I was just on my way out," said Windflower. "But if you have time I'd love to get together."

"Great," said Langmead. "I'm picking up my son from hockey right now but I can meet you at the Tim Hortons near Fort Townsend," he said, "Half an hour from now?"

"Sounds good, Carl," said Windflower. "I'll see you then."

It only took Windflower about 20 minutes to reverse course and get back downtown.

Soon after he was sitting in the Tim Hortons, and looking out in the rain right into the St. John's Narrows, and further out into the Atlantic. Now isn't this grand, he thought. Where else but St. John's would you get a view like this from a coffee shop?

Detective Sergeant Langmead arrived a few minutes later, and after a few nods to fellow RNC officers, he purchased a coffee and joined Windflower in the window.

"At least you can see something today," said Langmead. "Most days it is too tick wit fog, as my Dad used to say, to see anything."

"It sure is a beautiful view," said Windflower. "I'm glad we had a chance to get together. There are a few things I wanted to check out with you. And we've had contact with Shawn Parsons, at least Tizzard did."

"We haven't been able to locate Parsons yet," said Langmead.

"This might help," said Windflower, and he handed Langmead the phone number he had just received from Tizzard.

"If you can track this down, you might be able to get closer. He's supposed to call me but I don't really want to talk to him. I thought you might want to have a chat with him."

"Thanks, we'll check that out," said Langmead. "No sign of your friend Yashin in St. John's yet, but a few of our guys recognized him from the photos."

"He was more than a regular at a strip club downtown, maybe a part owner or a representative of the owners, at least. He had a regular table and a backstage pass, if you know what I mean. And there's another interesting thing," said Langmead. "The late Mercedes Dowson was a one-time hostess at the same establishment."

"That is interesting," said Windflower. "My guys in Halifax tell me that Yashin was mixed up with a gang of Russians who were involved in a number of nefarious activities in that area," he said. "But they think that Yashin was just one of the crew. The real boss is a guy called Big Iggy Gregorinsky. Ever heard of him?"

"Doesn't ring a bell, but I'll check with my team. What are the Russians involved with in Halifax?" asked Langmead.

"Drugs, girls, and likely a number of murders involving the bikers," said Windflower, "Definitely not nice guys."

"One other piece that might fit in is that it looks like Yashin was also running a Chinese migrant scheme over here on the island. According to my guys in Nova Scotia, Big Iggy may or may not have known about it."

"This thing is getting more complicated all the time," said Langmead. "But it looks like Yashin knew both the murder victims, professionally as well as personally."

"If you can find Shawn Parsons he might be able to start connecting up some of the dots for us," said Windflower.

"There's another piece I haven't told you about yet," said Langmead. "But I don't want to talk about it here. Do you know where the Long Pond Trail is?"

"Is that the one up off the parkway, Prince Phillip Drive?" asked Windflower.

"Yeah, park your car at the Holiday Inn and I'll meet you there. We can walk and chat if you don't mind a little drop of rain."

"Rain, drizzle and fog are my life," said Windflower. 'I'll meet you there."

Windflower was stopped in the Holiday Inn parking lot when Langmead pulled up in a Ford pick-up. Both men got out and crossed the busy intersection at the lights.

"Have you ever been up here before?" asked Langmead as they started off on the trail that wound its way behind Confederation Building and Memorial University around the shores of Long Pond.

"I never have," said Windflower. "Although I've heard that it's a great walk on a nice day."

"That it is," said Langmead. "Here's what I wanted to tell you about."

He pulled a pink covered cell phone in a plastic bag out of his pocket.

"I'm taking a big chance in even showing you this, but I needed to talk to someone about it. I found it in Mercedes Dowson's purse. Nobody knows I have it."

"How did you get it?" asked Windflower.

"When I went through the evidence that your guys had collected in Meat Cove, I found it in a hidden compartment in her purse. All the rest of her things had been taken out and catalogued, but I guess they missed this."

"They weren't looking for it because they had already found what they thought was her phone. It must be my dumb good luck that when I picked up her bag I felt something inside of it. I found the compartment and it slid out into my hand. When I turned it on and had a look at the contacts here's what I saw," said Langmead, and he opened the phone to the contacts to show Windflower.

"What's the big deal?" he asked Langmead, without really looking at the names and numbers.

"I haven't yet confirmed all of the names and numbers, but I can tell you that there is at least one judge, one Member of the House of Assembly, and one high-ranking member of the Royal Newfoundland Constabulary in the late Ms. Dowson's phone contacts; and many more interesting names that caught my attention."

"Wow," said Windflower.

"Now you see why I am being so careful," said Langmead.

Windflower stared silently at his fellow police officer, dumfounded by the news he had just received.

"It's hard to know where to begin with this," he finally said. "I think you should hand it back in to the RCMP in Sydney."

"I don't think I can do that," said Langmead. "Even if I shouldn't have taken it, I can't ignore the fact that I have it now. And it is directly or indirectly tied to my murder investigation."

"Okay, why don't you simply report it now? You don't have to say where you found it. It might have been in Mercedes Dowson's apartment," suggested Windflower.

"I wish I could, but I'm not sure that would be a good idea either."

"I sounded my boss out on this without giving him many details. He said he would just bury it. He thought that if someone brought this information out into the open the powers that be would squash it and his career. It's happened to other guys," said Langmead. "These are some pretty powerful people we're dealing with."

Just then a gust of wind drove a heavy shower of rain down on their heads.

"Let's go over behind that building there," Langmead said pointing to one of the small buildings at the back of the university.

They ran across the back lawn and ducked under the overhang just as the sky decided to really cut loose with as much rain as they'd had all day. They were wet, but happy to avoid getting drenched.

"My plan right now is to try and find out exactly what this list means before I do anything with the phone," said Langmead.

"Why are you telling me all of this?" asked Windflower

"I'm asking for your help," said Langmead. "I need some time to find out more about Mercedes Dowson, and what type of activity she was engaged in before I do anything else."

"And what do you want from me?" asked Windflower.

"I would like you to keep quiet about this. And I want you to hold onto the phone until I can get that information."

"If my boss asked me directly for this I want to be able to say that I don't have it anymore. I'm not sure where this will all end up and I want to make certain that it doesn't somehow get 'lost'," he said, putting air quotations around the word, "between now and then."

Windflower paused again and looked at Langmead for a few moments.

Langmead could sense his apprehension and said, "If you don't want to do it, that's fine," and put the phone back into his jacket pocket.

"I'll take it, for one week," said Windflower. "After that I'm handing it back to you. And you keep me in the loop about whatever else comes up, Deal?"

"Deal," said Langmead as he handed the phone over.

The rain had let up a little and the men walked back up the trail to the Holiday Inn. They waved goodbye to each other as they drove off in separate directions.

Langmead was heading back to his home and family, and Windflower was cutting across the parkway to Kenmount Road, then out towards the Trans-Canada. The rain had slowed down a little but it had been replaced by some of the thickest fog that Windflower had seen in some time.

He was approaching Butterpot Provincial Park when he saw it starting to cross the highway. It was a fair-sized female moose, oblivious to the fog and rain and the steady traffic, trotting towards the median of the divided highway.

Windflower slowed down as quickly and as safely as he could, and parked on the side of the road. He turned on his full lights package to warn other motorists, but kept the siren off because he didn't want to startle the moose.

Despite his wall of flashing lights, not one driver slowed down until they saw he was a policeman. By now, the moose had successfully navigated the middle of the road, and was deciding whether to stop or go on.

An alert driver on the other side of the highway had seen Windflower's lights, and slowed down to see what the action was. This car was now parked parallel to Windflower's with its emergency lights flashing as well, but he or she had little more success than Windflower in getting people to slow down.

Somehow, the moose managed to cross all the way over without getting hit, but it was pure blind luck on the part of those crazy drivers, thought Windflower.

Until people learn to slow down so many more lives will be lost, was his other thought. Because the moose don't care, they're just big dumb animals. That would be unlike the smart ones, thought Windflower, who are hitting them with their cars on a far too frequent basis.

Chapter Thirty

Windflower turned off his lights and was settling back onto the highway when his cell phone rang again. He moved back onto the shoulder to take the call.

"Winston, it's Ron," Windflower heard when he answered the phone. "Are you still in St. John's?"

"Just barely," said Windflower. "But how can I help you today, Mr. Quigley?"

"I was hoping to grab a coffee with you. I'm at the wedding but it's between the church and the reception, and I don't want to be hanging around for three hours of pictures," said Quigley.

"I'm just at Butterpot right now," said Windflower. "But I'll come back a little ways for you. How about the Paddy's Pond Irving, just outside of town?"

"That works," said Quigley. "I'm in Mount Pearl. I can be there in about 20 minutes."

"Okay," said Windflower. "And watch out for the moose. They're maggoty out here."

Quigley laughed and hung up. Windflower got off on the Holyrood exit and turned around, heading back into St. John's.

This is getting to be a long, long day he thought.

He pulled into the gas station at Paddy's Pond and waited for Quigley to arrive. While he was sitting there his phone rang again. It was Sheila wondering where he was.

"I've been delayed a little," said Windflower. "Right now I'm waiting to see Ron Quigley just outside of St. John's.

"I thought you'd be back by now," said Sheila. "You know I worry about you when you're driving at dark on the highway."

"I'll be fine," said Windflower, deliberately neglecting to tell her about his moose encounter. "But I'm at least four hours away from home. I'll probably grab a sandwich for dinner at Goobies along the way."

"Well, drive carefully. I'm making some macaroni and cheese for supper. I'll leave some in the oven for you. Winston, please drive carefully," Sheila said. "You know what the moose are like and you can't see a thing in this weather."

"I'll be careful, promise," said Windflower. "I'll see you tonight."

After he had hung up with Sheila, he saw Ron Quigley going into the restaurant. Windflower caught up with him on the way, and they found an empty booth near the front door. They both ordered coffee and Quigley had a piece of lemon meringue pie. Windflower thought about it, but decided that he had better save himself for both his turkey sandwich at Goobies, and the supper that Sheila would have warming for him at home.

"I'm glad I caught up with you," said Quigley.

"Yeah, I almost escaped," said Windflower with a laugh. "So what's new with you?"

"There's not much new at my end," said Quigley. "I'm as busy as ever with work, and trying to stay out of trouble; you?"

"Kind of the same," said Windflower. "Sheila is back in Grand Bank and so am I, so that's good. It looks like she's going back to school after Christmas."

"In St. John's?" asked Quigley, scraping the last crumbs of pie off his nearly clean plate.

"Yeah, she's going back to MUN to finish her nursing degree," said Windflower.

"Good for her," said Quigley. "And you'll get more time in my favourite city. How do you feel about it?"

"I'm very happy for Sheila. She worked so hard to come back from her accident. She deserves good things to happen."

"But?" asked Quigley, sensing there was more that Windflower had to say about this subject.

"But I'm not sure I want another couple of years of a commuting relationship," said Windflower. "I think I'm ready to settle down into a nice domestic routine," he said.

"Oh, no," said Quigley. "I think I see another deserter from the lifelong bachelor's club. Soon I'll be the only member."

"It's not like I'm giving anything up," said Windflower. 'Sheila's a great woman and I'd be lost without her. But I'm not talking about marriage or anything," he said.

"That's what they all say," said Quigley with a sigh. "You know, maybe they would let you transfer into St. John's," he said.

"That's an option," said Windflower. "But you know, I think I'm a country boy at heart. I love being in Grand Bank and on the southeast coast. It feels like I belong there somehow."

"Oh my God," said Quigley throwing his hands up in the air. "They've turned you into a bayman."

Both men had a good laugh at that.

"By the way," said Quigley, "I did some checking into possible Chinese tours during the past summer. And some of the guys in Sydney reported that it seemed busier than usual in that regard."

"So I checked with the hotels in the area and we found a match with the dates that you gave me. A Chinese tour group was in the Cambridge Suites hotel in Sydney. The tour group was called," and Quigley pulled a note pad out of his pocket, "Gorky Park Tours."

"Did you get the tour guide's name?" asked Windflower.

"Yeah, but it wasn't your Yashin guy. It was another guy, Fetisov," said Quigley.

"Same guy," said Windflower. "That's just one of his aliases."

"Anyway, that's my intel," said Quigley. "Hope it helps."

"Thanks," said Windflower. "At least now we are getting a picture of how they're getting in and likely where they're headed." Quigley looked puzzled so Windflower added, "Toronto and north of Toronto, Markham and other suburbs with large Chinese populations."

"So, will you just turn this back over to Immigration now?" asked Quigley.

"Probably," said Windflower. 'But we're still looking for Yashin or Fetisov or whatever his name is for a few more things first," he said. "Have you talked to Simard yet?"

"Briefly," said Quigley. "We're getting together for breakfast on Monday morning."

"Tell him I was asking about him," said Windflower. "Anyway I gotta' run. I've got four hours on the road still ahead of me."

"By the way, thanks for the tip about the fish and chips place in St. Phillips it was fabulous. It's not as good as Leo's, but still great."

"Glad you enjoyed it," said Quigley. "But true, you can't beat Leo's fish and chips with dressing and gravy, Newfoundland poutine I calls it," he said with another laugh.

"You are a character, Quigley" said Windflower. "It's been good to catch up with you."

"Me, too," said Quigley. "See ya', and watch out for the moose."

Windflower waved goodbye to Quigley in the parking lot, and turned back onto the TCH to head west towards Goobies and home. The rain had slowed considerably, but the fog seemed more intense than ever.

At least I'm finally headed in the right direction, thought Windflower, as he cautiously navigated his way along the dark and desolate highway.

The ride to Goobies and the halfway point was slow but uneventful. No excitement and no moose made for a relaxing journey. He gassed up at Goobies, and got himself a turkey and dressing sandwich and a coffee for the trip down Route 210 to Grand Bank.

As an added bonus the fog lifted, the rain stopped, and the full moon lit up the highway as he passed through Swift Current, then through Marystown on the way home.

When the road was quiet and the weather was clear, Windflower really enjoyed the stretch of road past Swift Current. There were no houses, no people, and not even any communities for almost a hundred kilometres. That made for a lonely drive for some, but Windflower liked the chance to just be by himself and do some thinking. And he had lots to think about.

The cell phone that Langmead had given him was weighing down his pocket and his mind. The situation with Sheila had left him unsettled, and his dream adventures had opened up things that he hadn't thought about for years, if ever at all.

So, it was good to be alone and process all of these things so they didn't feel like a burden.

The easiest one to deal with might be the situation with Sheila. The more he thought about it, the more he realized that he would do whatever it took to keep this relationship alive and growing. It had become the most important part of his life, and he needed to make sure that his decisions reflected that.

He also needed to be honest with Sheila. He had some concerns about how they were going to maintain their relationship while she was either staying in St. John's, or travelling back and forth. They would both have to cooperate, but it was certainly doable, and Windflower had a few options of his own. He could stay in Grand Bank and hold the fort while Sheila was away, or he could apply for a transfer to St. John's while she was going to school. That would deal with the medium term. Now he only had to talk to Sheila about her thinking for the long term.

When it came to the future, the dreams that Windflower was having were making him think anew about his long term plans as well.

The dream about Anne-Marie was disturbing, and he knew that he had to phone her with the message that he had been given. He realized that the reason he had been hesitating was that he wasn't sure if he had wanted that part of his life, the possibility of a life with her, to be over. After the dream he was now sure, and would call her tomorrow. His future was with Sheila Hillier, whatever that future might hold.

The other dream involving the Beothuk lady was more difficult for Windflower to both internalize and accept. It was clearer that the gift of a doll had to relate in some way to children. Windflower also knew that he was having this particular dream in order to learn more about the earlier peoples who had lived on this land, and to find a way to acknowledge them, because they could not do so for themselves. But how did they fit together?

Then it came to him. He had never seriously thought about having children before. He hadn't ever thought about getting married, but now, recalling the discussion with Ron Quigley, he realized that might now be on the table as well. And he wasn't running away from it either.

So, if he was supposed to have children, then it made sense that he should have them with Sheila, and to have them here in Newfoundland.

What better way could he find to honour the First Peoples here than to do that, he thought.

Now, there were lots of holes in his theory, but at least his heart was open to the possibilities. He would have to do more about honouring the Beothuks in the community, but that would come in time. Hopefully, he wouldn't need another dream to get answers to how to deal with that.

That only left one question remaining, what to do, if anything, about the phone that Langmead had given him for temporary custody.

By the time Windflower got to this one, he was approaching the lights of Marystown. The shipyard was still busy, even this late on a Saturday. He'd heard that they were working around the clock, on a special project to build part of a new floating platform that would eventually be floated out to the Hibernia oil fields off the coast.

He thought about stopping at Tim Hortons to get another coffee, but he was only half an hour from Grand Bank so he kept on going.

It was only when the city lights had dimmed and Windflower was back on the highway that he started to fully comprehend what Langmead was asking him to do. He was now in possession of Crown evidence that was, at best, improperly obtained, but maybe even interfering in an on-going criminal investigation.

Maybe he should have refused Langmead's request to take the cell phone and hold it for him. But that was no longer an option, was it?

No, once Windflower agreed, it had become his problem, until he figured out what to do about it.

Windflower was still puzzling about this when he came to the Grand Bank exit. He drove up through town and he passed by the café and Stoodley's house.

That's it, he thought. I'll drop over to see Herb Stoodley tomorrow and talk to him about it. He's an old Crown Attorney and he won't steer me wrong.

Feeling at least that he had the makings of a plan was as far as a tired Windflower could get, and for tonight it would have to do.

Chapter Thirty-One

The lights were still on when he got to Sheila's house, and there was a note on the table and an inviting aroma emanating from the kitchen. The note read that she was too tired to wait up, but that his macaroni and cheese was warming in the oven. She said to wake her up when he came to bed.

Windflower took the hot Pyrex container out of the oven, and paused to breathe in the flavours. He loved Sheila's macaroni and cheese with sharp cheddar, mozzarella and parmesan cheeses. He also liked her secret ingredient, a large dollop of Keen's hot mustard spread over the noodles before the sauce went on, as well as the toasted bread crumbs on top sprinkled with paprika and spicy cayenne pepper.

It was hot on the inside and out, comfort food, thought Windflower as he devoured about half of the dish. He could have eaten it all but he wanted to save some for tomorrow. Nothing like warmed over mac and cheese!

In the morning he was up early, despite his long drive the night before. He slipped out quietly, without disturbing Sheila, and went to check out the morning's weather.

It was a full-time job trying to figure out the weather here. The proximity to the ocean meant that there was always a possibility of precipitation. The only question was how much and in what form. This Sunday morning it seemed that it would come as fog and drizzle. No rain yet, but it was still early.

Windflower put on his running gear and stepped out into the morning for his run.

I better get some exercise, he thought, if I'm going to continue to eat fish and chips, and macaroni and cheese.

He liked food too much to give up these favourites just yet, and was already thinking about supper although it was barely morning.

He had nearly completed his route and was going by the RCMP detachment when he saw Constable Evanchuk coming out, putting a handcuffed prisoner in the back of her car.

"Morning, Sergeant," she said when she saw Windflower.

"Good morning, Constable," said Windflower. "Where are you headed?"

"I'm on my way over to Marystown," said Evanchuk. "Fortier brought our friend in last night after a fight at Tuckers Lounge. He shouldn't have been doing almost any of the things he was engaged in. I'm taking him back for breach of conditions."

"Okay," said Windflower. "Watch out for the moose," he added, as he resumed his run.

Evanchuk waved and got back in her car.

Windflower returned home and put on the coffee. While he was waiting, he sliced up some potatoes and onions and put them on to fry. Then he scrambled four eggs with a little milk and salt and pepper. He was happily cooking breakfast and humming to himself when Sheila came up behind him and put her arms around him.

"Thank you for last night," she said.

"Thank you," said Windflower in response. "Coffee should be ready if you want a cup, and breakfast will be coming right up."

Sheila got a cup of coffee and sat at the kitchen table while Windflower cooked.

"You know, I've been thinking," said Sheila, "About us, you know, and I've realized that I may have been a little selfish when it comes to our future."

"I'm glad you said that," Windflower said. "I like the ring of that, 'our future', and I've been thinking too."

"Do you want to go first then?" asked Sheila

Windflower just smiled and said, "Ladies first."

"Okay," said Sheila. "I was thinking that I could take some of my courses electronically; they're all online now. I would only need to be there in person for my labs. That way, we could just stay here, in Grand Bank."

"Well, I was thinking, that it might be possible for me to transfer into St. John's while you were going to university," said Windflower. "I may or may not be able to transfer back here later, but at least we could be together for the next couple of years."

"It sounds like we have a few choices for the mid-term but have you thought further into the future, Winston?" asked Sheila. "Because, we have something special between us that I don't want to lose. I don't even want to think about that option."

"I have thought a little about it," said Windflower, "And you know what? I'm open to the possibilities that the universe may bring, as long as we're together."

"You are my crazy, beautiful man," said Sheila rising to give him another hug. "I love you, Sergeant Winston Windflower."

"I love you too, Sheila," said Windflower holding her tightly. "And I've also decided that I'd like to have children."

Sheila paused for a moment at this piece of news.

"That won't likely happen by yourself," she said with a laugh.

"No, I would need some cooperation in that regard," said Windflower, "Any suggestions?"

They both laughed and Sheila moved to set the table.

Soon, breakfast was ready, and Windflower piled their plates with scrambled eggs and the fried potatoes and onions. He added a few pieces of toast from the last of the Goobies bread that he'd taken out of the freezer for the occasion.

Sheila turned on the radio and they listened to Sunday Morning on the CBC while they enjoyed their mini-feast.

After breakfast, Windflower went home while Sheila got ready to go to an event that her friends from Fortune were organizing. They made plans to get together for dinner later at Windflower's. He suggested barbequing a couple of steaks that he had in the freezer, and Sheila happily agreed.

When he arrived home Windflower took the steaks out to thaw, and busily engaged himself in vacuuming and cleaning his house. He was humming to himself again, he realized.

That must mean I'm either going potty, or I'm one happy man, he thought. He chose the happiness option.

A few hours later he had a clean house, and was still singing to himself. He got out his secret supply of Cy's steak spice from his cupboard. Cy's was a famous steak and seafood restaurant in Moncton, New Brunswick that was long gone by now. But its steak spice lived on, thanks to people like Ron Quigley who bought cases of the stuff before it closed. He had gifted Windflower with two bottles of it, after Windflower had sung its praises following the first time Quigley gave him a taste a few years ago.

But now Windflower's supply was almost gone, and Quigley had already warned him not to ask for any more. When this bottle was gone, so was that taste that Windflower had grown to love on his grilled meats.

Still, if you are going to go, then go big, thought Windflower as he rubbed a generous portion of the spice into the thawing steaks.

Once completed, he returned the meat to the fridge to let the dry marinade work its magic.

That gave him plenty of time to hop over and see Herb Stoodley, if he was home. A quick phone call confirmed that fact. Stoodley had been given the day off from waitressing duties at the Mug-Up, and would love a chat with him.

Windflower thought about walking, but the rain that had held off earlier, was now back in the running with the drizzle and fog for weather-maker of the day. He felt a little guilty about taking his car that short distance, but not guilty enough to get soaked again.

Stoodley saw Windflower coming from his front window and opened the door to let him in.

"Get in out of the rain," said Stoodley.

"Thanks, Herb," said Windflower. "I keep hoping for an improvement in the weather, but that doesn't look like it's in the works."

"This damp weather doesn't do much for my arthritis, I can tell you that," said Stoodley, "But being more active does. I can't believe how much it helps my aches and pains to be over at the café with Moira. Would you like a cup of tea?"

"That would be great," said Windflower.

"Let's go in the kitchen then, and I'll put the kettle on," said Stoodley.

Windflower sat in a kitchen chair and told Stoodley about the murders and the cell phone that Langmead had given him.

"I'm more than a little uncomfortable about this," he said.

"I don't blame you," said Stoodley, pouring hot black tea into two mugs and getting a plate of assorted cookies from the fridge.

"Why do you think Langmead gave it to you?"

"Well, I do think he trusts me," said Windflower, "But, he must also think that someone might be looking for this, and he didn't want anyone else to find it."

Stoodley took a lemon square from the plate and passed it over to Windflower, who took a chocolate covered ball.

"Well, it sounds like an interesting list of names," said Stoodley as he bit into his square. "I am making an assumption that those people would not want to have this list made public."

"I'm not sure why the names are there, or what their connection may be to the late Mercedes Dowson," said Windflower. "But I am thinking that is a fair assumption to make. At least until we get some more information. If the RNC can find the Parsons brother, then we might find out a bit more."

"It looks like you're in a holding pattern, pardon the pun, for now," said Stoodley.

When Windflower gave him a wry smile he continued, "We had a case years ago, where the names of a number of high ranking officials were discovered during an investigation into an under-aged prostitution ring in Corner Brook. The person who found the information ended up getting kicked off the force, and it took years and a special commission to clear his name."

"Maybe that's why Langmead is being so careful?" asked Windflower.

"Sad to say, the system doesn't always reward whistleblowers," said Stoodley as he grabbed for another cookie.

"But you'll need to protect yourself as well, Winston. You are now creeping pretty close to the wrong side of the law. And just as possession is nine-tenths of the law, someone once said that the search for someone to blame is always successful."

"What the heck does that mean?" asked Windflower as he chose a date square from the plate.

"It means that in the eyes of the law, you are as guilty as Langmead, and maybe more so since you've got the goods in question. I'm assuming that you aren't likely just going to hand this evidence over to the appropriate authorities." said Stoodley.

When Windflower nodded, he went on, "In that case, you had better pray that this doesn't blow up before you can get rid of it."

"Thanks for the cheerful advice," said Windflower. "I hope you come and visit me in the hoosegow."

Stoodley laughed.

"There's another saying that goes, 'if you speak the truth, have a foot in the stirrups'," he said with another laugh. "In other words, get ready to run."

"Where do you get all this stuff?" asked Windflower. "Get me the name of a good lawyer, will you? The more you talk the more worried I'm getting," he said.

"Like most things, this'll likely look a lot better once you have some more information," said Stoodley. "It could all be some great misunderstanding, and those men were on that girl's contact list because she was taking orders for Girl Guide cookies."

"Thanks for the snacks and the tea," said Windflower as he stood to leave. "Maybe I shouldn't, but somehow I feel better about the whole thing. We'll see you at the Mug-Up later on in the week."

Windflower was still smiling to himself when he arrived home. Then he remembered the next part of his plan to deal with his dreams and uncertainties: call Anne-Marie. He rummaged through his pockets and found the number. He called and almost hoped, no, make that really hoped, that he would get her answering machine.

Chapter Thirty-Two

"Hello," came a confident voice from the end of the line.

"Anne-Marie, it's Winston," he said.

"Winston Windflower, well, this is a surprise," said Anne-Marie. "How are you, and where are you? Are you still in Newfoundland? I tried to call you last year. Did you get my message?"

"That's a lot of questions at once," said Windflower with a laugh. "But I'm fine and yes, I'm still in Newfoundland. I was moving around a bit last year and I did get your message, but I guess I must have lost your number. I just got It back again from my Auntie Marie."

"How is your Auntie?" asked Anne-Marie. "She is such a sweetie. I always like spending time with her when I'm back home."

"She's well too, thanks," said Windflower. "My Uncle Frank was here for a visit recently. Actually, that's why I was calling you, to talk about something he told me. Where are you by the way?"

"I'm in St. John's," said Anne-Marie. "I'm coming back from an indigenous healing conference in New York on my way back to Nunatsiavut for some more art therapy training. What were you saying about your Uncle Frank?"

"I had a dream," said Windflower. "And you were in it."

"That's a good thing isn't it, Winston? I think about you from time to time," said Anne-Marie.

"I'm not sure it's good news," said Windflower, and he told her about the dream of finding her dead in the bed beside him. "Uncle Frank says that you might be in great danger and that I should warn you."

To Windflower's surprise Anne-Marie simply laughed.

"I thank you and Uncle Frank for your concerns, but I can assure you that I am fine," said Anne-Marie. "In fact I have never felt better or healthier."

"I am glad to hear that," said Windflower. "The way Uncle Frank talked I was starting to wonder. I figured it would be better to be safe now than sorry later."

"That's very sweet of you, Winston. You know the reason I phoned you last year was because I had the feeling that something bad was happening to you or around you. I guess we must still have some form of connection," said Anne-Marie.

"You may be right," said Windflower. "So what else is new in your life?"

"Things are well, Winston," said Anne-Marie. "Like I said, my career is keeping me busy and grounded in the traditions. We should get together sometime, if we can figure out a way to have our paths cross."

"That'd be nice, Anne-Marie," said Windflower. "I'm in St. John's a fair bit and perhaps we could have lunch sometime."

"Well, you have my number," said Anne-Marie.

Windflower hesitated, and almost just hung up the phone, but he knew that he was supposed to do one more thing with Anne-Marie.

"I will call you," said Windflower. "Maybe you and I and Sheila could get together. I know that she would really like you."

"That would be good," said Anne-Marie. "Your Auntie keeps pretending that you and I will get back together, despite me telling her that was long ago," she said with a laugh. "Although she is right, Winston, we would have beautiful children."

Windflower laughed too at her last line.

"Just be careful, okay, Anne-Marie, I don't know what these dreams are really all about but I don't have a good feeling about them, and it scared me to think that you might be in danger."

"Well, thank you, Sergeant Windflower, you have done your duty and can stand down now. Call me and we'll have lunch, okay?" said Anne-Marie.

"I will," said Windflower.

As he hung up the phone he could hear Sheila coming in the back door.

"Hello Winston, I brought you a surprise," she called.

That got Windflower's attention and he went out to see what it was.

He saw the plastic wrapped cheesecake and reached for it but Sheila was too fast for him.

"This is your dessert," she said, pulling back the large piece of peanut butter cheesecake, and putting it in the fridge. "You owe me a steak dinner first," she said with a laugh.

"No problem, ma'am," said Windflower.

And deciding to come clean about his activities, he told Sheila about calling Anne-Marie, and of course about his dreams.

"Do you really think she was, or is, in danger?" asked Sheila.

"I don't know," said Windflower. "But Uncle Frank seemed convinced. If she's a little more careful, then I've done my job."

"Do you ever wonder what your life would have been like if you had stayed with Anne-Marie?" asked Sheila. "Maybe you'd have a whole brood of little ones running around by now."

Windflower looked at her for a few moments and said, "I thought at one time that was my path, but now I know that my journey is with you."

"Winston, you are a keeper," said Sheila. "So, will you ever get a chance to see Anne-Marie?"

"I told her that we would all have lunch together if we were in St. John's at the same time," said Windflower.

"That would be nice," said Sheila. "Thanks for telling me about all of this. You didn't have to, and I appreciate it. I think you earned a few points with me, Sergeant."

"I thought you told me that there weren't any points," said Windflower, with faux outrage.

"Of course there are points," said Sheila. "Only we girls get to decide when they're collected, and if and when they can be used."

"That's a rigged system," said Windflower, getting up to start cooking dinner. "But I think I'll try to redeem mine later tonight, before they run out."

Sheila laughed as Windflower started peeling potatoes and got up to give him another hug.

"Why don't you get us both a glass of wine and relax while I get supper ready?" he said.

After he peeled the potatoes and had them boiling, he cut up some broccoli pieces and put them in the steamer for later. Then he went outside, into the pouring rain, to light the barbeque. Luckily, he had a bit of an overhang, and that kept him mostly dry as he fired up the barbeque and left it to warm up. He went back inside to get the steaks and to turn down the potatoes, so that they wouldn't boil off and make a mess on the stove.

The steaks looked absolutely gorgeous with their speckled black and white spice covering. He put them directly onto the hot grill, charring the ribeyes on both sides, and then moving them to a cooler part of the grill to slow cook for about five minutes on each side. This would cook the steaks medium rare, which was just how he and Sheila liked them.

Windflower stood and took in the absolutely fabulous aroma of grilling meat and spices until they were done to his idea of perfection. Then he turned the barbeque off and put the steaks on the cool side of the grill while he got everything else ready.

Soon he and Sheila were sitting at the table enjoying their meal of garlicky mashed potatoes, steamed broccoli and steaks that were peppery and charred on the outside and tender pink in the middle.

"Perfect, as usual," said Sheila.

"Hmm," was the most that Windflower could mutter as he savoured each tender bite of steak. "I don't know what I'm going to do, though; I'm almost out of Cy's steak spice."

"Can't you just make some more?" asked Sheila as she popped a tender broccoli floret into her mouth.

"It's a secret recipe," said Windflower, "And I think Cy, if there was a Cy, is now dead, so we're just screwed."

"Another disaster," said Sheila. "But I'm sure that you'll come up with something equally as delicious."

"Thank you for the vote of confidence," said Windflower as he ate the last piece of his steak with great delight. "I am ready for my dessert now."

Sheila just laughed as she cleared the table and put the kettle on to boil. She got Windflower's cheesecake out of the fridge and slid it in front of him. Before she was back with tea, the dessert was long gone and he was trying to coax an extra taste out of the crumbs.

"I'm guessing you enjoyed it," said Sheila as Windflower just made his extremely satisfied smile. "You earned it. My dinner and my steak were so good."

"I'm glad you enjoyed it, m'dear," said Windflower. "Let's go in and watch a little TV. *Heartland* is on tonight. It reminds me a bit of home."

"I just like the horses," said Sheila. "I think they should call it 'Horseland', since most people are like me, just watching to see those magnificent animals running around."

Sheila and Windflower spent a very enjoyable evening just watching television and snuggling up on the couch. They were getting ready to go to bed when Windflower's cell phone rang.

"I wonder who that could be," said Windflower as he reached over to answer the phone.

"Winston, it's Carl," said the caller. "I thought you'd like to know we picked up Shawn Parsons this afternoon."

"That's good news," said Windflower.

"Yeah, we traced the phone number you gave us and found the person who it was registered to. When we paid him a visit, we found Parsons hiding in a closet," said Langmead.

"Have you had a chance to talk to him yet?" asked Windflower.

"Well, that's one of the reasons I'm calling," said Langmead. "He will only talk to you or Tizzard. He wants a deal."

"He says he's got evidence that he'll give us only if he gets witness protection. He said he's a dead man, inside or outside prison, if he doesn't get it. Can you come to St. John's to talk to him?"

"I guess so," said Windflower, "But I can't give him protection or immunity."

"He doesn't know that," said Langmead. "It's times like this I wish we could use the rack or something, but that's no longer an option."

Windflower laughed, but he wasn't sure that the other cop was being entirely facetious.

"I guess it's worth a shot. I can probably be there by lunch tomorrow."

"Thanks, Winston, really appreciate it," said Langmead as he hung up.

"Work?" asked Sheila, used to Windflower getting all manner of calls at all times of day and night.

"Yeah, I have to go to St. John's tomorrow," said Windflower.

"Hey, why don't I go too?" said Sheila. "I have to talk to the people at the university about my courses, and we could make it a little day trip."

"That might work," said Windflower. "I'll drop you off at MUN and then pick you up later. And I found another great place to get fish and chips. It's down in St. Phillips."

"Are you always thinking about food?" said Sheila with a chuckle. "After that dinner tonight I probably shouldn't eat again for a week."

"Well, you do have a point there," said Windflower. "I'll try and get a run in tomorrow morning before we go. Would around ten o'clock be good for you to head out?" he asked.

"That would be fine," said Sheila. "But we should also get some exercise tonight, don't you think?"

"I don't know how you do it, but you have read my mind again," said Windflower.

Chapter Thirty-Three

Windflower woke early and kissed Sheila gently on the cheek as he rose in the dark. He was planning on a run, but first he wanted to say his prayers.

He pulled his hoodie over his head and walked gingerly out onto his back porch. The fog, his constant companion, was back. But at least the rain had eased a little, and other than a steady drip above his head, it was actually quite pleasant for this early in the day.

Windflower smudged with his eagle feather, and as the smoke swirled around him he gave thanks to his ancestors for their guidance and wisdom. He said a special prayer for his Uncle Frank for his help with his dreams, and as he thought of Anne-Marie he said a prayer for her too. He hoped that she was truly out of danger and that her path would be smooth and peaceful.

When he had finished his prayers he pulled on his rain gear and started out for his morning run. It felt good to be out alone in the dark before the sun came up, and he loved seeing his adopted home of Grand Bank still sleeping through the night.

He made his circle around the beach and headed back downtown by the wharf for the final leg of his route. As he came down the driveway to the wharf he saw Constable Evanchuk in the distance. He slowed to say hello, but she just waved and kept on going. Windflower got a twinge that something was not quite right with her, but he too kept going until he arrived back home.

Sheila was up and dressed and after a quick hug, she was on her way home to get ready for the trip to St. John's.

Windflower put a banana, some yogurt and a few remaining strawberries in the blender and made himself a smoothie, which he drank standing up at the kitchen sink. He put on an egg to boil and then jumped into the shower. Afterwards he came back out and had his egg and a piece of toast for breakfast. He could get coffee at the office before he headed out for St. John's.

A few minutes later he was sitting at his desk enjoying his first cup of freshly brewed coffee, and reading the latest issue of the "Southern Gazette", the local weekly newspaper. He liked catching up on the community news and gossip. This week the highlight article was about the red fish controversy that had erupted in Grand Bank last week. Windflower read with interest Mayor Sinnott's suggestion that the problem would be resolved with a bit more cooperation from all concerned.

I like this guy, thought Windflower. I like him a lot.

Betsy was the first person to arrive, and Windflower was pleased to have a few moments to catch up with her before the day began. Betsy had an elderly mother she was looking after, and was now contemplating putting her in the Blue Horizon Seniors Home.

"It can't be easy, to make that decision," he said.

"I worry about the level of care that she'll get over there, but Mom is quite happy to go," said Betsy. "Every time we drive by, she wants to stop in and say hello to someone. Almost all her friends are there."

"It looks like a nice place," said Windflower. "They all look pretty happy, especially on Fridays when they have their little barbeque outside. It makes me want to stop in too."

"I guess it's time," said Betsy. "Anything new I should know about?" she asked.

"Tizzard is away for the week but the schedule looks good," said Windflower. "I have to go into St. John's later this morning, but I'll be back tonight. If anyone is looking for me, they can call my cell."

"Okay, sir, enjoy your day," said Betsy and she went back out to her desk in the front.

She called into Windflower on the intercom a few minutes later.

"It's Inspector Arsenault on line 1," she said.

Windflower picked up the phone. "Good morning, Inspector," he said.

"Good morning, Windflower," said Arsenault. "I wanted to check in with you about a couple of things. First of all what's going on with the human trafficking file?"

"Actually, sir, we're looking into a couple of incidents in our area over the past summer," said Windflower.

"In Grand Bank?" asked Arsenault.

"Yes, sir," said Windflower. "It looks like two groups of Chinese migrants came through here. They may have even landed by boat somewhere on the coast. We're still working on it, but it appears that they were on their way through Nova Scotia to the Toronto area."

"And nobody reported anything strange about this?" asked the Inspector.

"I guess people weren't looking for something like that to happen around here," said Windflower. "The community was happy to get the tourism business."

"This makes us all look pretty stupid," said Arsenault. "I expect you to get to the bottom of this, Windflower. Before you send off any reports I want to see them, okay?"

"Yes, sir," said Windflower. "Is there anything else?"

"Yes, there is," said Arsenault. "I saw Evanchuk yesterday in Marystown. She's a cute little thing, isn't she?"

Windflower did not know how to reply to this latest question, so he just remained silent.

"I need a personal assistant for a few weeks over here, and I am wondering if you could spare her?" asked Arsenault.

"We are a little short-staffed this week because Tizzard is away, and I have to go to St. John's, but I can get back to you on that sir." said Windflower.

"Sure," said Arsenault. "What are you doing in St. John's?" he asked.

Now Windflower was stuck. He didn't want to go too far into why he was going to St. John's or what he was doing there, so he had to scramble a little bit.

"I want to talk to the RNC," he said, thinking that much was true. "They might have some information that is connected to the Chinese migrants."

That was a stretch, but if Parsons had something to say about Yashin, aka Fetisov, it might be true.

"Okay, keep me informed. And let me know about Evanchuk," said Arsenault.

When the line went dead Windflower thought about that conversation including his part in it.

Why wouldn't he just tell his boss the full truth about what he was doing in St. John's? And why did he have another of those strange twinges when Arsenault talked about Evanchuk? More things to ponder on the highway, he thought, as he packed up his and left the office to pick up Sheila for their trip to the city.

But before he left for the day, he took the plastic bag with the cell phone that Langmead had given him and put it into a locked cabinet in his office.

Just to be on the safe side, he thought.

Sheila was just about ready when Windflower arrived. She was packing them a little lunch for the road; some apples, cut up carrots, red peppers, a couple of tea biscuits and a thermos of hot black tea.

Soon, they were on the highway wending their way through the Burin Peninsula, and up the road to the Trans-Canada.

They were both comfortable with being quiet while together and that was good, because Windflower needed to process his last interaction with Inspector Arsenault. They enjoyed the passing countryside and it wasn't until they were well past Marystown that Sheila spoke up.

"Penny for your thoughts," she said as she poured them both a cup of tea from the thermos, and handed Windflower a raisin tea biscuit.

"Thank you," he said as he took a bite of the tea biscuit, and then washed it down with a large gulp of tea. "I guess I've been thinking about a conversation I had earlier this morning with Inspector Arsenault."

He told Sheila about the chat and her response was, "It sounds like you don't trust the Inspector. I can't say that I blame you. I've always found him to be a little too greasy for me. Women have radar that tells them to stay away from guys like Arsenault. I can't really say why, but he makes me feel uncomfortable."

"Has he ever said or done anything to you?" asked Windflower, suddenly feeling a little protective about his girl.

"No. Maybe because he knows I'm with you, or maybe I'm not really his cup of tea," said Sheila. "But, I've heard stories about the Inspector. He fancies himself a bit of a ladies' man."

"Well, he's not married or anything," said Windflower.

"The story is that he likes very young women, Winston. I don't have any detailed information, just some rumours and my spidey sense," she said, "But I thought you got along well with the Inspector," she added.

"I do, mostly," said Windflower. "But I'm getting more and more uncomfortable with his attitude around women. I think that's affecting my overall judgement of him. And I don't know if I can trust him with some things."

"'It might not be as good as women's intuition, but I think you should go with your gut instincts, Sergeant," said Sheila.

"Thank you, Sheila. I think I'll do that. If there's no more of those buns, I can probably eat a few carrots or something now."

"Healthy eating, now that's a novel concept," said Sheila as she passed him the plastic baggie of vegetables.

"It'll fill the hole 'til I can get my fish and chips later," said Windflower.

The two ate their way through the remaining apples and red peppers as they passed through Swift Current and onto the TCH past Goobies. They were laughing and singing along to the oldies station on the radio all the way to St. John's.

Windflower came in Kenmount Road and dropped Sheila off at the university with a promise to pick her up in a few hours. He then crossed through town until he came to the RNC headquarters at Fort Townsend.

Fort Townsend was located in the centre of St. John's, at the top of one of the many hills that overlooked the harbour. It had been the site of the RNC headquarters since 1870, when the British military garrison was withdrawn. There was once a massive fort there, built to defend the old country's fishing interests, and home to a succession of Governors who ruled the colony in the early days.

But the old fort had been buried underground long ago and new buildings, like the massive RNC headquarters, along with the main St. John's Fire Department station, now occupied the site. Also on the same site nearby was 'The Rooms' building that everyone had been telling Windflower about. It was the new home of the Newfoundland and Labrador Provincial Archives, Art Gallery and Museum, and it was designed to mirror the 'fishing rooms' where families processed their fishing catches in years gone by. It soared above all the other buildings in the area, except for the Basilica of St. John the Baptist, and offered some of the most spectacular views of the city.

Windflower hoped to visit 'The Rooms' soon to check out the Beothuk exhibits, but today was a day for other business. He made his way to the reception desk and had Detective Sergeant Langmead paged.

Shortly afterwards, Langmead came out from behind the security glass to greet him and welcome him inside. The two men went up a floor to the Criminal Investigations section and Langmead led him to a small interviewing boardroom.

Chapter Thirty-Four

"I ordered us a pot of coffee," said Langmead. "Care for a cup?"

After both men had their coffees, Langmead said, "Thanks very much for coming, Winston. My colleague Charlie Halliday will bring up Parsons when we're ready for him, but I thought we should touch base first. Did you have a good trip up?"

"It was pleasant," said Windflower. "So, what kind of shape is Parsons in?"

"He's a little rough," said Langmead. "I think he's been drinking a lot and he's obviously scared. I get the feeling that he is less scared of us than someone else."

"Scared is good," said Windflower. "What do you want me to do?"

"I'm going to leave you here alone with him, if that's okay," said Langmead. "Let's see what he has to say for himself, and what he has to offer. Halliday and I will be behind the glass at the end," he said, pointing to the two-way mirror on one wall of the room. "Parsons will know we're there, but I don't think that'll matter much to him."

"I don't have any authority to offer him anything," said Windflower, "But I'm willing to listen to what he has to say."

"We've already checked in with the Crown Attorney," said Langmead. "We don't have any authority either. It's still worth a shot to see what we can find out. At this point Parsons is all we've got. If he offers up something worth considering, our C.A. said he'd take a look at it."

"Okay," said Windflower. "Let's see what Mr. Parsons has to say for himself."

"I'll have him brought up right away," said Langmead and he stepped out of the office.

A few minutes later another detective, whom Windflower assumed was Halliday, brought a dishevelled and obviously distraught Shawn Parsons into the interview room. Parsons was in his late twenties with long scraggly hair and a couple of days of unshaven growth. He had bags under his eyes and his hands were shaking. He looked hung over thought Windflower, from booze and maybe more.

"Coffee?" asked Windflower, pointing to the coffee pot on the side table.

"Yeah," mumbled the other man. "You Wingflower?" he asked.

"Windflower," came the reply. "That would be me. Do you have something to tell me, Shawn?"

"I want a deal," said Parsons. "I have a lot of information and I want a deal," he said, trying to sip his coffee but spilling most of it.

"As you can see from your surroundings, you haven't got much bargaining power in here," said Windflower. "As a matter of fact you're in pretty big trouble. Why were you on the run?"

Parsons started to wake up, recovering a little bit of the cockiness that Tizzard had told Windflower about, and started to laugh.

"I have information that you need," he said.

"So talk," said Windflower.

"Not until I get my deal," said Parsons.

"Listen, Parsons, I came here because I was told you have something to tell me. So either quit playing games and tell me or I'm gone," said Windflower.

When the other man gave him a scowl, Windflower picked up the pad on the table in the room and stood to leave.

"Okay, okay," said Parsons. "The information I've got is about prostitution and escort agencies, and women who're being brought into the country to do that work. And not all of them are as old as their passports say they are, either."

"I also know about a scheme to get illegal immigrants into Canada from Europe, and I was witness to a murder. Enough?"

"That's a good start," said Windflower as he sat down again. "What was your involvement in all this?"

"That's why I want a deal," said Parsons. "If I don't walk, then I don't talk. And I want the deal to be with you guys, the Mounties. I don't trust the locals."

"This deal you keep talking about," said Windflower. "What exactly are you hoping to get?"

"I want immunity from prosecution and I want protection. And I want some cash to start my life over, somewhere far from here."

"How about just helping to put your sister's murderer behind bars?" suggested Windflower. "Can you help us with that, assuming you had nothing to do with the murder?"

"I would never hurt Amy," said Parsons, rising unsteadily to his feet. "Can we deal or not?"

"First of all, I can't offer you anything now. But I can tell you that there is no money in this for you. Those days are long gone."

"Secondly, only the Crown Attorney can offer you any immunity from criminal prosecution. And thirdly, your information will have to be awfully good in order to get into the protection program."

"So what can you do, besides wasting my time?" asked Parsons.

"Listen up again, Mr. Parsons. I'm your only possible ticket out of here. I'm giving you the straight goods. I've done this before and I know how it works. If you don't want my help, I walk. And I'd be happy to do so," said Windflower.

"How do we start this thing?" asked Parsons.

"You give a statement to the RNC guys sitting behind the glass and we go from there," said Windflower. "If you screw around at any time in this process, they will shut it, and you, down. They probably have enough on you to prosecute right now."

"The way I see it, you don't want to have to spend any of your time on the range in the local pen if you can avoid it. I hear the residents don't like snitches much."

When Parsons didn't say anything else Windflower continued.

"The officers will then take your statement to the Crown Attorney to see what he thinks. If it's meaty enough, they'll see what they can do about limiting the charges against you. And if it's as substantial as you're making it out to be, I'll take it forward to the witness protection people."

"That doesn't sound like much of an offer," said Parsons, who was clearly disappointed and hoping for more.

"It's the only game in town," said Windflower. "You better make up your mind quick," he said and abruptly stood and left the room.

Langmead and Halliday came out to meet him.

"That was great, Winston," said Langmead.

"Good job," said the other man. "Charlie Halliday," he said holding out his hand.

"We'll let him stew for a little while, and then have a go at him. But it looks like you've softened him up considerably," said Langmead. "When we were questioning him last night he kept saying that we needed to talk to Mercedes, that she knew everything."

"So he doesn't know she's dead," said Windflower. "That's interesting. It certainly suggests he wasn't involved in killing her."

"Exactly," said Langmead. "We can take over from here. Thanks for all your help with this, Winston. I'll walk you out."

Windflower and Langmead went back towards the security desk at the front and Halliday stayed behind to keep an eye on the now highly agitated prisoner. Before he left Windflower, Langmead said quietly "I hope you still have our package."

"I do. It's in a safe place," said Windflower. "Although, the more I think about it, the less comfortable I am. Why exactly did you give it to me to hold on to?"

"Have you had a look at the contact list?" asked Langmead. "You might want to do that when you get home."

Windflower walked to the parking lot a bit more confused than ever, but relieved that the formal portion of his day was over. He opened his cell phone and called Sheila, but there was no answer so he left a message for her to call.

The sky had dried up a little, he noticed as he went to his car, but that might be a fleeting moment. If they were lucky, it might hold off long enough for him and Sheila to have lunch outside.

He walked down to the Tim Hortons just below police HQ, not so much because he wanted another coffee, but because he could sit in the window there, and take in that view all day. Half an hour later, his cell phone rang, and he was on his way back to MUN to pick up Sheila for their lunch date.

Windflower picked up Sheila at the Health Science Complex where the Nursing In-take Office was located, and zipped back onto the parkway for the short trip down to St. Phillips.

Sheila was very excited when she got into the car.

"I think I'm going to be able to work it all out," she said. "I met with my academic adviser, and she says that next term I can take all but one of my courses online. That means I only have to come in one day a week, and can still live in Grand Bank."

"That's great news," said Windflower. "I could move to St. John's if I had to, but I'd much rather stay with you in Grand Bank."

"It also seems that the following year I can do my first practicum at the Blue Horizon home in Grand Bank. I know the nursing supervisor there, and she told me she'd love to have me. That's perfect for me. It'll give me a first-hand opportunity to see if I like geriatric nursing or not."

"Betsy was talking this morning about putting her mother in there," said Windflower. 'It looks like a nice place."

"It is," said Sheila as they drove down the road to Portugal Cove. "How much farther is this fish and chip place? I'm starving."

"It's up ahead in St. Phillips," said Windflower. "We go past the Bell Island Ferry, and then it's not much farther."

They came over the top of a hill and they could see Bell Island a little ways off in the distance. The rain had stayed away, as Windflower had hoped, but he could see a large wall of fog just lingering out in Conception Bay.

A few minutes later, they arrived at the restaurant on the beach in St. Phillips, but so too did the fog. And even though people think that all fog is alike, Windflower could feel that this was one of those fogs that seeped right through your clothing, and left you feeling drenched on the inside. He suggested that they eat inside and Sheila readily agreed.

Windflower ordered his usual two-piece fish and chips and Sheila opted for the one-piece version. There were only a few other people in the restaurant this time of day, so they had the place almost entirely to themselves. That was good, because the small indoor seating area was poorly designed with tables crammed together and poor ventilation.

The food, when it came, was as great and as plentiful as before. But Windflower was glad to get back outside for a breath of fresh air once they had finished their meals.

That air came with thick, damp and sticky fog, now accompanied by a steadily increasing rain. Sheila tucked in close to Windflower as they made a run for the car.

"That was the second best fish and chips I've ever had in St. John's," said Sheila when they were sitting in the car.

"Another recommendation from Ron Quigley," said Windflower. "So far he hasn't steered me wrong in the food department. Some other time we're in St. John's we have to try out another of his suggestions," said Windflower. "It's an old inn a little ways up the Conception Bay Highway. It's somewhere around Topsail, I think. They specialize in traditional Newfoundland dishes."

"I've heard about that place," said Sheila. "I had friends who held their wedding reception there. It's supposed to be very nice. It would be great to go there sometime."

"If you play your cards right, that just may happen," said Windflower as he pointed the car back towards St. John's, and the Trans-Canada Highway.

He had just passed Paddy's Pond when he heard his cell phone ring.

Not again, he thought. The last time this happened I got stuck here for hours. He pulled the RCMP jeep over to the side of the road and answered the call.

Chapter Thirty-Five

"Winston, it's Guy. I wanted to let you know about some developments on our end."

"Hi Guy, what's up?" asked Windflower.

"It's about Gregorinsky," said Simard. "The deal he had moving is gone. I guess somebody higher up got wind of it, and didn't think deportation was a fitting punishment for murder; can't say that I disagree."

"So where does that leave your investigation?" asked Windflower.

"We're back to putting the case together, piece-by-piece," said Simard. "Iggy was released on bail, but I think that he and his outfit will be laying low for a while. The girls will still be working and the drugs flowing, but they likely won't be bringing in new shipments of either any time soon."

"Did you see Ron Quigley?" asked Windflower.

"Yeah, I had breakfast with Ronnie this morning," said Simard. "He talked about Yashin. I told him the word on the street is that Yashin's gone rogue, and my sources say that Iggy isn't pleased. And when Iggy isn't happy, nobody is happy; anything new on your end?"

"Just that we picked up the brother of the first murdered girl," said Windflower. "I talked to him today. He wants a deal too! What is it with these guys?"

"Watchin' too much TV," said Simard. "Anyway, I'm back to the grind. Now we've got to find willing participants to testify against Gregorinsky. Lowlifes, every one of them, and I bet they all want deals too," Simard said with a laugh.

Windflower laughed too. "Okay, Guy, let's stay in touch."

Windflower put his cell phone away and pulled back onto the highway. It was only late afternoon but the grey sky made it feel like almost dusk. The rain had eased, but the giant wall of fog was back for a return engagement.

Windflower smiled over at Sheila who had taken the opportunity of the pause in the action for a little snooze. He didn't bother to wake her until they arrived at Goobies.

"Do you want a coffee?" he asked as he turned off the car.

Sheila stirred and then woke quickly. "Goobies?" she asked, looking around. "You can't see a hand in front of you with this fog."

"I'm going to fill up. Why don't you go in and have a look around? I'll join you shortly," said Windflower.

When he went in to pay, he found Sheila standing inside the door with a smile on her face and two loaves of bread in her arms.

"Good job," said Windflower as he passed her on the way to the bathroom.

Sheila was in the line-up ahead of him when he came out, and soon they were back on the road with coffees in their cup holders, and steaming fresh bread in the backseat.

"I love the smell of fresh baked bread," said Sheila. "It reminds me of when my mother used to make it at home. Today hardly anybody would go through that much work. But it sure has a great aroma."

"Hmm," was Windflower's response.

In his mind, he had already sliced, toasted, buttered and slathered a slice of the bread with homemade jam. But he couldn't put all his attention to his next meal because he had to stay alert on the fog-shrouded highway.

It was slow going, but he and Sheila talked and listened to music, and generally spent a pleasant hour or so together on the drive.

They passed through Marystown at the five o'clock rush hour. That meant the line-up at the Tim Hortons drive-through stretched almost across the highway. Windflower saw a few familiar vehicles from the nearby RCMP detachment waiting for their after-work coffee. The traffic thinned again after they left town. That was a good thing since it seemed as if the fog had grown even thicker.

They were almost home, going past the Garnish turnoff, when Windflower spotted the moose on the side of the road and began to brake. Sheila had been dozing off but sat straight up when she saw the reason that Windflower was slowing down.

The car slipped a little on the wet pavement and started to slide into the moose who had decided that the safest place for her was to move into the middle of the road. At the last minute Windflower was able to swerve around the large animal, and only then did he realize that Sheila was crying, almost whimpering, huddled on her side of the car.

When he had brought his car to a safe stop, he parked on the side and turned on all of his lights. He flicked on his siren too, just to be safe, and hopefully to drive the moose back into the woods.

Windflower leaned over to Sheila and took her in his arms. She was still shaking and crying and wouldn't even look up. She stopped crying, eventually, but otherwise did not respond. He found her a blanket from the back and turned up the heat in the car.

Very slowly, he drove the last few kilometres home When they arrived at Sheila's house he brought her inside and ran her a hot bath. He went out to lock up his car and when he returned, Sheila was in the bathroom with the door closed.

Half an hour later he went in to see her. She didn't want to talk but she reached out her arms to be held. After she had drifted off to sleep, Windflower slipped out and made some toast and tea, but Sheila didn't stir for the rest of the night.

In the morning when Windflower woke, Sheila wasn't in the bed. He went out to the living room and found her writing in her journal. She smiled at him and said good morning, but went back to her writing.

Windflower continued into the kitchen and put on some coffee. Looking out of the window he could see that the fog was still a full-time resident of the Town of Grand Bank. When he went outside it was damp, but fairly warm. He did his rituals quickly, and at the end laid down a little tobacco for his lady friend.

Sheila was in the kitchen fixing a cup of coffee when he came back. Windflower went over and gave her a hug.

"The doctors told me that part of my recovery is emotional as well as physical," said Sheila. "I thought I was doing pretty well until last night when I saw the moose on the highway. I almost went out of my mind."

"It all came flooding back to me, the accident and hearing myself screaming, then the total blackness that seemed to last forever."

"It sounds like a flashback," said Windflower. "It may be related to post-traumatic stress from your accident. Some of the guys who have witnessed particularly difficult crime scenes or serious accidents have gone through it. It's just part of the process of recovery."

"I've had a few flashbacks before, but nothing compared to last night," said Sheila.

"Our spirits take time to heal as well," said Windflower. "In my non-medical opinion, I think you're doing great."

"Thank you, Doctor Windflower," said Sheila. "But I think I'll talk to my other doctor as well, just in case. And where's my breakfast? First there's no dinner and now no breakfast?"

Windflower smiled and pulled four eggs out of the fridge.

She's going to be just fine, he thought to himself.

After breakfast Windflower went home and had a quick shower and shave. He still made it to the office before Betsy. He had just put on the coffee when he heard her coming into the back room, singing.

"Good morning, Betsy," said Windflower. "You're in a good mood this morning."

"Yes, good morning, sir. I am in a good mood. I went off to see the manager at the Blue Horizon after work yesterday, and it looks like they might have a bed for my Mom after Christmas," said Betsy. "Mom is so excited and the people there seem really nice."

"Sheila may be working there for a while next year too," said Windflower. "She's going back to school to finish her nursing degree, and will likely do a placement at the home. She's pretty excited about it as well."

"Oh, that's wonderful," said Betsy. "I'll tell Mom. She really likes Sheila. That will be another reason for her to enjoy the place."

Betsy took her coffee and went to her receptionist desk at the front, probably to phone her mother, thought Windflower.

He didn't have much more time to reflect on Betsy's mom however because when he looked up from his paperwork, Constable Evanchuk was standing in the doorway.

"Do you have a minute, sir?" she asked.

"Sure," said Windflower, and he motioned her in to sit down.

"Do you mind if I close the door?" she asked.

When Windflower shook his head, she closed the door and sat down.

"I want to share something with you, Sergeant, but I need it to be confidential between you and me," said Evanchuk.

"Okay," said Windflower. "Please continue."

"It's about Inspector Arsenault," said Evanchuk.

"That's interesting," said Windflower. "The Inspector was asking about you. He wants you to come to Marystown for an assignment."

All of the colour seemed to drain from Constable Evanchuk's face at this news.

"Are you okay?"

Evanchuk gulped and started to speak.

"I saw Inspector Arsenault when I went to Marystown on Sunday. He must have seen me come in with the prisoner and followed me down to the underground garage. When I came out he was waiting for me, next to my car. He tried to grab me and kiss me, sir. I didn't know what to do. I guess I just froze."

Then she just stopped talking and hung her head.

"Go on, Constable," said Windflower.

"This isn't the first time he's tried something with me, sir," she continued. "When I first started working here the Inspector came over to Grand Bank for some event while you were still away."

"I was coming in from the first round of highway patrol. He was sitting in the back room and I think he was drunk, sir. He tried to grab me then too, but I managed to slip away. I didn't say anything because I was new, and I didn't want to cause any problems."

"You're not causing any problems," said Windflower quietly.

Evanchuk sighed and went on.

"I managed to get away from him again in Marystown, but he said something like, 'I always get what I want', as I was running away. I went back later and got my car. Sir, I can't go to Marystown with him."

"I know that, Constable. You won't have to," said Windflower and after a pause continued, "I think you should file a formal complaint."

"With respect, sir, I have seen what happens to people who file complaints against their superior officers, especially women. And I want to be a Member. I don't want to file charges, sir. Please don't send me to Marystown," she pleaded.

"Okay," said Windflower. "I'm prepared to respect your wishes, for now. But if anything else happens I will file the complaint myself, understood Constable?"

"Understood," said Evanchuk and she stood to leave.

"I'm sorry this happened to you, Constable," said Windflower. "If you need a few days off that will be fine, you know.

"Thank you, sir," said Evanchuk. "But in my family if you got bucked off, you got right back up on the horse. Thank you for your support, sir."

After Evanchuk left Windflower got up and closed the door after her. He needed a few minutes to process the news that the young Constable had just relayed to him.

That bastard, Windflower thought, that bastard.

Chapter Thirty-Six

Windflower was pretty much calmed down an hour later when Betsy chimed in on the intercom.

"It's Sergeant Quigley for you, sir, on line one."

"Good morning, Winston," came the cheery reply from the other person on the phone. Windflower had to smile despite himself. "How are ya, b'y?"

"Sergeant Quigley, I'm well, how are you?"

"Couldn't be better, Winston," said Quigley. "I have some good news, and some bad news. Which would you like first?"

"Give me the bad news and get it over with," said Windflower.

"The bad news is that he won't talk to us unless he gets a deal," said Quigley.

"Who wants a deal now?" asked Windflower.

"One Mr. Peter Yashin," said Quigley. "The good news of course is that we have found the elusive Mr. Yashin, dead drunk on the side of the road outside a bar in Cheticamp. They are transferring him over to Halifax today."

"That's in Cape Breton, isn't it?" asked Windflower.

"It is on the Cabot Trail," said Quigley. "And before you have to get your atlas out to look it up, it's not too far away from where Mercedes Dowson's body was discovered."

"I'm assuming that they've asked him about the late Ms. Dowson," said Windflower.

"Affirmative," said Quigley. "But he's not talking about that, or anything else, because he says he has information to offer. Trade was the term he used. And we have competition when it comes to talking to him. Major crimes, drugs, gangs, and of course our friend Guy Simard are all in the lineup to interview Mr. Yashin."

"This is the third deal I've heard about this week," said Windflower. "Did someone put out the word that we had a sale on deals or something?"

"It's the latest fashion," said Quigley. "Maybe we could have a new reality TV program, 'RCMP Informers'."

"Or maybe just 'Criminal Minds: Let's Make a Deal' version," said Windflower.

"I guess it's good news that we got Yashin. We've also got Shawn Parsons in St. John's. Actually the RNC have him in custody and he wants a deal too."

"Of course," said Quigley.

"What are the forensics like from Meat Cove?" asked Windflower. "Were Yashin's prints on the scene?"

"I haven't seen the evidence yet," said Quigley. "I think they're sending it over with Yashin later today. I'll see what they have and get back to you."

"Okay, Ron, that's great. Talk to you later," said Windflower.

Well, that's some more good news, thought Windflower. The more bad guys we have in custody, the closer we may get to the truth. Now it's a question of matching the evidence to the perpetrators. Evidence, he remembered, I have some evidence.

Windflower went to the locked cabinet and took out Mercedes Dowson's cell phone. He pushed the power button, and when it came on he looked for the contact list. He ran through the names and phone numbers quickly but didn't see anything that really interested him.

Then he scanned the names again, alphabetically. It didn't take him long this time around. Right there under the 'A's' was the name Arsenault. He had a look at the number next to the name, and then he pulled out his own cell phone and looked up Inspector Arsenault's private cell phone number that he had for emergencies. It was a match.

For the second time that morning Windflower was stunned. He sat at his desk for a few minutes, staring first at one phone, and then the other, thinking maybe he had made a mistake.

But, nope, no mistake. That was Arsenault's number in the late woman's cell phone. The question was, what was it doing there? And what the heck was this dead woman doing with all these people, including the Inspector, that she needed their personal phone numbers? What was the connection?

There was obviously a side to Inspector Arsenault that Windflower had not seen, or picked up on before. Or maybe he just hadn't been paying close attention. Somebody who would know about Arsenault's peccadilloes was Bill Ford, thought Windflower. He found Ford's number in his cell phone and dialed it.

"Hi Bill, how's it going?" he said when Ford answered the phone.

"Winston, nice to hear from you," said Ford. "I was thinking about you when I had a few of the boys over the other night. We had barbequed pork chops."

"Oh my god, I love those pork chops," said Windflower. "I hope you saved me some."

He could hear Ford laughing at the end of the line.

"How are you and Arsenault doing these days?" he asked.

"I think we've agreed to disagree," said Ford. "He's not too happy with me about the harassment issue, but so far he hasn't directly interfered. I hear he's up for a big promotion."

"Oh yeah, I didn't hear about that," said Windflower.

"Yeah, he wants to be a Deputy Superintendent for the province, at least the island part," said Ford.

"What do you think about that?" asked Windflower.

"It's not really up to me, is it?" asked Ford. "Arsenault's been around long enough; I guess he's paid his dues."

"You don't sound too enthusiastic," said Windflower.

"Well, he's not my favourite person right now, and we have a long history together," said Ford, "Some of it good and some not so good."

"He's been hitting on one of my Constables," said Windflower. "She doesn't want to file a complaint, but from what she told me it's certainly sexual harassment, if not more."

"Crap," said Ford. "I thought that stuff was over with him."

"There's been more?" asked Windflower. "Why didn't someone do anything about it?"

"Like I said, some of our history has been good and some not," said Ford. "Arsenault's had an issue with the ladies forever. Sometimes he went a bit too far, and I had to pull him out."

"What?" said Windflower, "You helped him get away with this stuff?"

"When I was drinking I got into a few jackpots of my own," said Ford. "Arsenault helped me get out of trouble on those and then held them over me a little. I guess I wasn't strong enough to push back. I'm not proud of it, but I tried to get him to change. He promised me after the last one that he was done with it."

"The last one?" asked Windflower.

"It was a girl in the office that Arsenault took a liking to, and wouldn't take no for an answer. It was all hushed up, and the girl accepted a buyout package to stay quiet. He swore that was the end," said Ford.

"Well, it wasn't," said Windflower. "And now I've got to deal with it. Anyway I gotta' go. Talk to you later, Bill," he said as he hung up brusquely.

Now Windflower's head was spinning. Fortunately for him there was a message on his cell phone from Sheila that included an invitation to lunch, something about soup and sandwiches.

Windflower grabbed his coat, and without checking the weather ran out of the office and up to Sheila's.

It was raining, but just drippin' as the locals would say, and the fog was hiding outside of Grand Bank, at least for the morning. It was a bit of a gloomy day, but nothing as dark as Windflower felt inside. He hoped that lunch and a good dose of Sheila would remedy that situation.

His instincts were right. The food and Sheila's company lifted his spirits considerably. He enjoyed every drop of his turkey soup and every last crumb of his ham and old cheddar sandwich on slices of the fresh Goobies whole wheat bread. He told Sheila about Betsy, and how happy she was that Sheila might be working at the retirement home with her mother.

"People just want to know that their folks are being looked after," said Sheila. "And the old ones don't want to cause their children any trouble. That's why having good seniors' homes is so important."

"And why they need kind and caring people like you," said Windflower.

"I have to go over to Marystown this afternoon to pick up a few things," said Sheila. "Do you want me to pick up anything for you?"

"If you can wait until tomorrow morning, I'll go over with you," said Windflower, "As long as you're not going to Walmart."

"No, I'm not going to Walmart," said Sheila, knowing how much Windflower disliked the giant retailer. "But they do have toothpaste on sale at 3 for $5 dollars."

Windflower laughed feebly when he realized that she was just egging him on.

"You can get it at the big Sobeys in Marystown for just as cheap," he said.

"Oh, Winston, it's so easy to get a rise out of you," said Sheila. "Tomorrow would be great. I'm going over to the church hall for the Ladies Auxiliary meeting tonight, but you can take the rest of that soup with you for your supper if you'd like."

'I would like that a lot," said Windflower.

Sheila sent him back to work with a plastic container of turkey soup and a chunk of fresh bread.

That will tide me over, thought Windflower, as he strolled back to work. When he arrived, Betsy told him that there was a visitor in his office, waiting to see him.

"Vijay, my old buddy, how's she goin' b'y?" said Windflower to the diminutive Dr. Vijay Sanjay who was occupying the visitor's seat of honour in his office.

"She's goin' good b'y," said Dr. Sanjay in return. "I had heard that you had returned, but I was away on a conference in St. John's. I am no longer the Chief Medical Officer for this community, but being Coroner has its perks."

"So I see," said Windflower. "Have you been keeping busy in your semi-retirement?"

"As busy as one can be with very few cadavers that aren't octogenarians or older," replied the doctor. "I manage to stay occupied with my writing and speaking at conferences when they remember to invite me. And your lady, Mrs. Hillier, she is well also?"

"Sheila is great, Doc," said Windflower. "I've been meaning to call on you, but I haven't stopped since I got back. We should play a game of chess sometime," he said.

"Absolutely, my dear friend," said the doctor. "My chess board has grown cold and lonely in your absence. How about this Friday evening? My fine wife will be away as of Thursday, and I have a bachelor's weekend that I would love to share a little with you."

"I would like that very much," said Windflower.

"Then it is settled," said the doctor. "And I have a special treat. I have just received a bottle of Talisker that I would love to try as well. It's a virgin bottle waiting for a couple of old fiends like us to open the cork, and let loose the demons."

"I have missed you, my friend," said Windflower. "I would be happy to join you in christening your latest acquisition."

Windflower had a smile on his face for most of the rest of the afternoon after his lunch with Sheila and the visit from his doctor friend. He had managed to put all of his problems and situations out of his mind until just before 4 o'clock when Betsy announced through the intercom with the news that Inspector Arsenault was on the phone for him.

Chapter Thirty-Seven

Windflower hesitated a moment, then punched the blinking light on his phone.

"Good Afternoon, Inspector," said Windflower, in his best imitation of a calm voice.

"Windflower, my sources tell me that you are somehow mixed up in murder investigations in two provinces," said Arsenault. "Do you mind telling me what the hell's going on?"

"Sorry, sir," said Windflower. "The investigations are turning up related events and it looks like some of the same people may be involved. The person I'm interested in connection with the Chinese migrants is also of interest in the murders in St. John's and Cape Breton. He may also be connected to a number of other criminal investigations dealing with a Russian gang operating in Halifax as well, sir."

"Chinese, Russians, who's next Windflower? Maybe you should stick a bit closer to home. I'm still waiting for my report on the Chinese people," said Arsenault.

"That might have to wait until after Tizzard gets back," said Windflower.

"Windflower, if you stayed focused on your own job, instead of everybody else's business you might get something done," said the Inspector. "What about my request for Evanchuk?"

"That might be a bit of a problem too," said Windflower. "I was planning to go over to Marystown tomorrow morning. Maybe I could drop in and talk to you about it, sir."

Windflower had already decided he was going to confront Arsenault in person on this issue. Even though Evanchuk had decided not to proceed with a formal complaint, he had to give the Inspector an answer to his request, didn't he?

"Okay, call Louise in the morning and get a time," said Arsenault, and he was gone.

Windflower wiped away the sweat that had been accumulating on his brow during this call with Arsenault. He tried out various and sundry names to call him in his mind, and finally settled on "scumbag". Tomorrow morning's conversation was going to be very interesting.

Windflower packed up his things and pointed his car for home. An hour, and half a hot rum toddy later, he was relaxed and soaking in his warm bath.

After his soak, he made himself a small green salad, threw a few baby carrots and some dried cranberries on top, along with a shake of parmesan cheese and the obligatory ground pepper. Then he heated up the soup in the microwave and buttered a sizeable chunk of bread to go along with his main course. Sitting at the kitchen table, he picked up his Joseph Boyden book and starting reading again about the woes of the Huron and Iroquois.

His phone rang just as he finished putting the dishes away from supper. It was his Auntie Marie.

"Winston, have you heard the news? There's been an accident and Anne-Marie is missing. The small plane she was travelling on in Labrador crashed and they are looking for survivors," said his aunt.

"Oh my goodness," said Windflower. "How did you find out about this?"

"Her sister called to tell me," said Auntie Marie. "Oh, Winston, this is terrible news."

"It surely is," said Windflower. "I talked with Anne-Marie last week. We were hoping to get together soon."

"She's such a lovely girl, everybody here is very shook up," said his aunt.

"Let me check with our guys in Labrador," said Windflower. "They may be able to provide some more information about what's going on."

"I think the family would appreciate that," said Auntie Marie. "Until we know for sure, we can hope for the best. Even if the news is bad, it is better than not knowing."

"That is true," said Windflower. "I'll see if I can find anything out and I'll let you know."

Windflower grabbed his coat and headed back over to the detachment. Lewis was there, making himself a cup of tea after finishing his first highway round.

"Anything happening on the roads tonight?" Windflower asked.

"Pretty slow, Sarge," said Lewis. "But that beats the alternative."

"I agree," said Windflower, thinking back to his highway patrol days in British Columbia, when pulling people and bodies out of wrecks happened far too often. "I hope it stays that way, at least until Thursday night," he said. And when Lewis did a double take, he added, "That's my night to do the evening highway shift."

Lewis just nodded, and went back to nursing his mug of tea.

"I'm going to check to see if there are any updates on a plane crash in Labrador. Did you see anything on it?" asked Windflower.

"I saw the initial report when I first came in," said Lewis. "They were reporting a small plane, a float plane I think, crashing between Nain and Hopedale. There weren't any casualty reports yet."

Windflower went into the small ops room at the detachment. It was little more than a converted closet with a dedicated emergency phone line and computer. He flicked the mouse to brighten the screen.

He first saw the report that Lewis talked about, and then a recent update that said there were four reported passengers on the plane along with the pilot. The report added that they were members of a fly-in mental health team. That might have been the crew that Anne-Marie was travelling with, thought Windflower.

He looked up the contact information for Nain, the place where the flight originated, as well as the headquarters for search and rescue in Labrador. He was looking for someone he knew that he could talk to, and found the name of Joe Benoit, an old buddy from his training days. He called the Nain detachment, and after a long wait, finally got through. He told the receptionist who he was, and asked if Corporal Benoit was on duty.

"They're all on duty tonight," responded the receptionist. That came as no surprise to Windflower. When there was a crisis or emergency, it was all hands on deck.

"Windflower, how the hell are you?" came the booming voice of Joe Benoit.

"I'm well, Joe. I guess you guys got your hands full over there," said Windflower.

"You know it," said Benoit. "Ever since we got the report it's been crazy. I've just finished the search and rescue briefing."

"What's going on with that?" asked Windflower.

"Well, they managed to get the 'copters up for a quick look a little while ago, but it's too dark to see anything. They'll be back in the air as soon as it gets light. That means that if there are survivors, they have to get through the night."

"The good news is it looks like the crash site is on land, and not in the water. The bad news is that we are having an early snowstorm. Not a lot of snow, but it's getting cold and windy, and hard to see anything. "

"Listen, Joe, a friend of mine, Anne-Marie Littlechild, may have been on that plane," said Windflower. "Do you have a passenger list yet?"

"Not yet, these little float planes are not required to post their list or manifest, and it's not like there's anybody here to check up on them." said Benoit.

"All we know was that it was a mobile mental health team, and that usually means some combination of nurses, psychologists and counsellors. But I think I know that girl you're talking about, good looking Aboriginal woman, teaches art classes or something. She seems nice."

"Yeah," said Windflower, "She is very nice. If you hear one way or the other if she was on that flight, can you let me know?"

"Sure, I can do that," said Benoit. "Listen I gotta' go, it's crazy here. Take care."

Windflower hung up and immediately called his Auntie Marie to give her the news he had learned, which wasn't much, he thought. But as his grandfather used to say, better to wait for the worst, than to plan for it. Not much consolation for the family, or for him, but it was the best he could come up with for now.

Windflower said good night to Lewis, and headed for home. When he passed by Sheila's house he saw her lights on and stopped in. He told Sheila the news about

Anne-Marie and they shared a pot of tea, and in near-silence they watched a little TV.

Realizing that he probably wasn't very good company for anybody but himself, Windflower decided to return to his own house for the night. They agreed to chat in the morning once Windflower knew what time he could leave for Marystown, and he kissed Sheila good night.

He had another warm bath, and went to bed to read more of his Joseph Boyden book. But that didn't last long, and before he knew it Windflower was fast asleep. Thankfully, that night he had a peaceful and dreamless slumber, until his alarm woke him in the morning.

Windflower walked out into the dim light of the early morning, and noticed right away that both the rain and the fog had vanished. They could return at any moment, but for now the clear skies called him to get his gear on and get out there. And this morning he really needed a run. He did a backwards loop this morning, heading down to the wharf first.

There were already a few members of the informal Parliament assembled there. They were mostly retired members of the community, who came each day to share a yarn and pronounce on the issues of the day. Windflower nodded his good mornings and thought that since no topic or person was ever off-limits he probably had more than a few judgements from the men on the wharf.

This was also the area where Uncle Frank hung out when he was around, and thinking of Uncle Frank got Windflower to thinking about dreams and Anne-Marie.

He was so deep in thought that he almost collided with Constable Evanchuk, who was coming down the little hill near the B & B, just as he was coming up the slope.

"Sorry, sir," said Evanchuk, a little out of breath.

"Probably more my fault," said Windflower. "I must have been blinded by the sun. I'm glad to see you though. I wanted to tell you that I am going to Marystown to see Inspector Arsenault this morning."

Evanchuk looked a little upset and said, "I thought we were keeping that matter confidential."

"I have to tell the Inspector why I will not release you to go to work with him in Marystown," said Windflower. "There are also other developments in this area that I need to discuss with the Inspector. I won't reveal the details you shared with me, but I do have concerns that I need to address."

Evanchuk looked puzzled and still a little upset, but she nodded and went to leave.

Windflower stopped her and said, "As much as possible I will keep you out of this, but it may be bigger than just a personal issue with you. I have your back on this, Constable," said Windflower.

"Thank you, sir," said Evanchuk, and she loped off to finish her run.

Windflower was soon back on his route again too, but when he got to the beach, he stopped for a few minutes to watch the sun rise over the Grand Bank Cape. It was magical and surreal, and a moment almost of second sight for Windflower as he felt the presence of other spirits in the morning light.

He prayed for his ancestors and his living family. He prayed for Sheila and his colleagues at work and he prayed a special prayer that Creator watch over Anne-Marie wherever she might be right now.

He went back home and had some yogurt and berries for breakfast, and after a very hot shower and shave he was dressed and ready for work.

Chapter Thirty-Eight

Windflower arrived at work and put the coffee on in the lunchroom. Then he called Arsenault's office and left a message for Louise to request for an appointment time. It was early, but Louise would call back as soon as she got in. Once he knew when he could see Arsenault, he could make his plans with Sheila.

As he was waiting for the coffee to brew, his cell phone rang. It was a 709 Newfoundland area code, but he didn't recognize the number. He did recognize the distinctive voice.

"Winston, it's Joe Benoit, I've got some good news. Your friend wasn't on the flight. She came in last night after I talked to you looking for information, and I recognized her right away. She said that she'd call you when she got a chance."

"Thank you, so much," said Windflower. "That is such good news."

"Yeah, I wish the rest of it was. It doesn't look good. The first reports from the crash site are in, and there's a lot of debris but no sign of life," said Benoit. "I have to get back to work but I wanted to share at least one piece of good news today."

"Thanks, Joe, I really appreciate it," said Windflower as he hung up the phone.

"And thank you, to Creator too," he said quietly to himself, "Thank you, so very much."

Betsy came in while he was on the phone and brought him a hot cup of coffee.

"Thank you, Betsy, and good morning," he said to her disappearing back.

Betsy called him a few minutes later to say his meeting with Inspector Arsenault had been confirmed for 11 that morning.

He called Sheila to tell her the good news about Anne-Marie and to make arrangements to pick her up around 10 a.m. She was happy about his news, and even happier to hear that his mood, like the Grand Bank skies, had lightened tremendously.

Windflower used most of the next couple of hours reviewing reports and trying to catch up on the backlog of journals and magazines that had accumulated during his assignment in Marystown. He worked at clearing his thoughts, and tried to get himself in the right frame of mind for what he felt certain would be a very difficult meeting with the Inspector.

About a quarter to 10, he drove over to pick up Sheila, and within minutes they were cruising past the Tidy Town sign, and up onto the highway for the trip to Marystown. This trip was both pleasant and uneventful, and Windflower dropped Sheila off at the Marystown mall before going over to the RCMP detachment for his 11 o'clock meeting.

It was a familiar walk up to Arsenault's office, but an uncomfortable feeling, as he prepared to confront his boss on his behaviour.

It felt like the student having to correct the teacher, Windflower thought, which likely was not going to make for a comfortable situation. But he'd come this far, so he stiffened his spine, and walked into Arsenault's office.

Someone was still with the Inspector, so Windflower spent a couple of tense and very long minutes waiting for his turn.

Finally, the inside door opened, and Louise motioned Windflower in. Arsenault was sitting behind his desk, making a note to himself. He acknowledged Windflower and nodded towards an empty chair in front of him. Windflower stepped forward, closed the door behind him and sat down.

"So, Sergeant, have you got better news for me about Evanchuk? I could order you to send her over, you know," said Arsenault.

"You could, sir," said Windflower. "But I don't think you really want to do that."

"No?" asked Arsenault, "And why not?"

""I do not believe that it is safe for Constable Evanchuk to work over here," said Windflower, "It's a health and safety issue."

"What are you talking about?" asked Arsenault, his voice rising and his face growing red.

"It's in the manual, sir," said Windflower. "Section 14 of the operational manual orders a commanding officer to prevent a subordinate officer from entering into a situation that might endanger his or her health and safety, or put them at unreasonable risk. I am invoking Section 14, sir," said Windflower.

"What did that girl say?" asked the Inspector. "I didn't lay a hand on her. You wouldn't take her word over mine, would you Sergeant?" asked Arsenault in a very hostile manner.

"It's not about what anybody said," Windflower replied calmly. "I am making my decision based on the best information available in order to protect my officers. You can overturn me, sir. But if you do, I will be filing a formal complaint on the matter with headquarters."

When Arsenault did not reply, Windflower stood and left the room. He didn't stop and almost didn't breathe until he got outside the building.

Well, now you've gone and done it, he thought.

Windflower needed a little air, so he walked over to Tim Hortons, but there were too many familiar faces. He decided instead to return to the mall to see how Sheila was making out. Along the way he remembered that he needed to call Auntie Marie to tell her the good news about Anne-Marie. It had been too early to call before, but she should be up by now.

"Hello, Auntie, it's Winston," he said when he heard his aunt answer the phone.

"Winston, have you heard the news? Anne-Marie is okay, she wasn't on the plane that crashed," said Auntie Marie.

"I did hear, but it was too early to call you," said Windflower. "It's a big relief. How did you find out?"

"She called her family very early this morning," said his aunt. "I am very sorry for the other poor people and their families, but we are all very happy here. And Winston, your Uncle Frank says to tell you that you must have done a good job."

"What do you mean? Oh yeah, the dreams," said Windflower. "Tell Uncle Frank thank you, for helping to guide me. He's the one who did a good job."

"I will tell him that," said Auntie Marie. "I knew that he went to visit you for a reason, but I didn't know what it was until now."

"Frank is still off the booze, and back practising his dream work again too. We never know why people are placed along our paths," said Auntie Marie. "But there is always a reason."

After he hung up with Auntie Marie, Windflower thought for a moment about what she had said.

If there's always a reason, then why is Inspector Arsenault in my life? Maybe to get me kicked off the force, thought Windflower, as he went into the mall to look for Sheila.

Sheila was coming out of the shopping centre as Windflower was walking in, and he strolled with her over to Sobeys where she could complete her shopping.

The day was still bright and precipitation-free, so Windflower walked back to get his car. As he approached the jeep, he saw Inspector Arsenault coming out the back door to the parking lot. At first he thought about ducking into his car and making a speedy getaway, but he realized that he couldn't run away from this.

When Arsenault saw Windflower, he too thought about avoiding the situation, but instead the Inspector walked over to Windflower and stood directly in front of him. Arsenault wasn't tall, Windflower had noticed that before, but what he hadn't seen was how stocky and muscular the Inspector was underneath his uniform. Although he was a little taller than Arsenault, Windflower figured the older man would put up a hell of a fight if it came to that.

But it didn't come to blows, as least not during this encounter. Instead Arsenault just stared at Windflower until the Sergeant finally turned away.

"You've picked the wrong man to piss off," Arsenault said as Windflower opened his car door. "You don't know who you're dealing with. I run this province."

Windflower did not respond, did not react. He simply got in his car, placed the key in the ignition and drove off.

His last thought, as he gazed back into his rear view mirror at Inspector Arsenault still standing in the same spot was, I think I've really stepped in it this time. He didn't have time to wallow in these thoughts though because as he drove up to the supermarket, he could see Sheila standing out in front with her cart. When she saw him she smiled and waved. He just had to smile too.

Windflower suggested going out for lunch, but as usual Sheila was ahead of the game. She had a fresh baguette among her purchases along with a bag of grapes, a chunk of pepper brie, a bag of salad, and several packages of cold cuts, including some Montreal-style smoked turkey that her friends in the church group had been raving about. Windflower smiled again, and went up to the drive-through at Tim Hortons to get them each a large tea to wash down their lunch.

Windflower was ravenously hungry, and readily agreed to Sheila's additional suggestion that they stop in Garnish for a picnic on the way home. Garnish was an old fishing community situated between Marystown and Grand Bank, and it had a beautiful walking trail right on the beach next to the ocean.

Nobody really knows how Garnish got its name, but some think it had something to do with the Grandys who were the first settlers in the place. Others thought that it might have been originally called Cornish because a lot of Newfoundlanders came from the Cornwall region in the west country of England. Somehow in true Newfoundland fashion this later warped into Garnish.

Windflower didn't really care where the name came from; he was more interested in the contents of Sheila's picnic bag. But Sheila was a bit of a local history buff, and she passed along her knowledge to Windflower with the baguette and cheese to cut up. According to Sheila, Garnish was well known in these parts for both fishermen and captains, once of the Grand Bank Schooners, and now of various sized boats, including the ferries around the island.

Sheila also noted that her father had told her of the old days in Grand Bank, when shipbuilding was still going strong. At that time, the wooded area around Garnish provided much of the timber required for the schooners. Although he was too young to remember it, her father said that they would cut it near Garnish Pond, and then float it down the Garnish River to get it to the sawmills, and ready for the shipyard.

Windflower listened carefully, but grew more attentive when Sheila handed over the smoked turkey and some baked ham for his baguette sandwich.

"Did you hear a word I said?" asked Sheila.

"Every word," mumbled Windflower, his mouth full of bread and meat and cheese. "I thought that the only thing Garnish was famous for was the bakeapple festival."

Sheila laughed and made herself a little sandwich as well.

After lunch they took their bag of grapes and walked along the beach. The time passed pleasantly, but quickly, and soon it was time to head back home. Windflower drove the short distance into Grand Bank and helped Sheila with her shopping bags. They made plans to get together later for dinner.

It was busy in the office when Windflower got back. Evanchuk was hanging around Betsy's desk, and it was clear she was waiting for him. Betsy handed him his messages and told him that he had a visitor. Meanwhile Fortier was guiding a woman and her teenage son into the back room as best he could, the woman seemingly content to continue to berate her child loudly at every possible occasion.

Windflower was happy to get away from this chaos and into his office.

Chapter Thirty-Nine

Sitting in a chair that was clearly two sizes too small for him was Mayor Bill Sinnott.

"Good afternoon, Sergeant. I hope you don't mind if I drop in for a minute," said the Mayor.

"No problem, Mr. Mayor. What can I do for you this fine day?" asked Windflower.

"Well, I wanted to thank you for your help the other day," said the Mayor, "And to let you know that I owe ya one."

"Thank you, Mayor Sinnott," said Windflower. "But it's not necessary…"

Sinnott cut him off with a wave.

"And I want to tell you to keep yer bobber up," he said.

"What do you mean?" asked Windflower.

"Your Inspector 'as it in for you," said the Mayor. "But you didn't need me to tell you that."

Wow, that was fast, thought Windflower.

He also thought about challenging the Mayor's statement, but kept his mouth shut in that regard and replied, "Thank you, Mr. Mayor."

"One good turn deserves anudder, that's what I always sez," said the Mayor.

"I guess I owe you one, now," said Windflower.

"Ah, that's my definition of community policin'," said Mayor Sinnott, as he struggled but managed to get up and out of Windflower's office.

Well, at least I've got one supporter, thought Windflower as he went through his messages. Three that caught his attention were from Bill Ford, Guy Simard and Carl Langmead. Before he had a chance to get to them, Evanchuk stuck her head in the door.

"Five minutes for me, sir?" she asked.

Windflower waved her in and she sat down, this time without bothering to close the door.

"I just wanted to say thank you," said Evanchuk. "I'm sorry if I was difficult about my situation earlier. I have trouble accepting help, and I really would like to make it on my own. But I do appreciate you sticking out your neck for me. And I want you to know that I am willing to do anything to support you in return."

"Thank you, Constable," said Windflower. "Now, get back to work," he said with a smile.

Evanchuk was smiling too as she left the office.

Make that two supporters, thought Windflower.

He picked up the phone and called Bill Ford.

"What the hell did you do to piss Arsenault off?" asked Ford.

When Windflower told him, he just whistled through his teeth.

 "You've taken a hard road on this one," said Ford. "Arsenault is not one to screw around with and I expect that you are not going to come away unscathed."

"He's already been onto the Mayor," said Windflower.

"He's just clearing the way for your execution," said Ford. "I've seen him do it before. He wanted me to go along with some cock and bull story when he called me too."

"He will try and set you up, Winston, and then he will shoot you down. I told him no, so I'm not exactly top of his list right now. But if there's any good news in this, it's for me and not you."

"Thanks for not throwing me under the bus," said Windflower. "But I've still got cards to play in this game."

"Just remember that Arsenault only knows one way to play, dirty. And he always plays to win," said Ford.

"If this thing breaks wide open, I'm going to need you to talk about your dealings with Arsenault and the harassment issues," said Windflower.

"My statements are already on the record," said Ford. "But you will need more than that, and more than me to beat Arsenault at this game."

"Okay, Bill, talk to you later," said Windflower, and he hung up the phone.

That would make it two and a half supporters.

Next on Windflower's list was Carl Langmead.

"Winston," said Langmead. "Thanks for calling me back. We've had a chance to talk to Shawn Parsons, and he has had some very interesting things to say."

"That's good," said Windflower. "I had a look at the list in Mercedes Dowson's phone since we last talked. That's very interesting, too. Now I know why you gave me the phone."

"You saw the good Inspector's name, I take it," said Langmead. "You can give it back if you want. I just thought you should know."

"Well, I actually might need it for a few more days the way things are looking over here," said Windflower. "We can talk about that later. Tell me what you got out of Parsons."

"Young Parsons is still squawking about a deal, but I convinced him to give us at least a taste of what he had, before he expected us to buy the whole cake," said Langmead.

"If we can believe him, he says that the Russians have been operating in St. John's for the last five years. That includes drugs, prostitution and escort agencies. At first they were running things remotely from Halifax, but then they sent over their own person," said the detective from St. John's.

"Yashin?" asked Windflower.

"Well, that's one of the most interesting parts," said Langmead. "The head of the Russian outfit in St. John's, according to Shawn Parsons, was Mercedes Dowson. Yashin was just a flunky to move the goods back and forth. Parsons says that Dowson recruited both him and Amy Parsons to work with her. He ran the drugs portion and Amy ran the escorts."

Windflower was silent as he processed this information.

"Parsons also said that his sister wanted to get out, but Mercedes Dowson wouldn't let her. He thinks that Dowson had her killed. He offered to testify against Dowson," continued Langmead.

"He still doesn't know Mercedes Dowson is dead," said Windflower.

"Nope," said Langmead. "If he's telling the truth, then I don't believe he's our killer. He did give me one more piece of news that I thought you'd appreciate though. He gave us the address of the safe house where the girls stayed, and where they entertained some of their clients. And he says that Dowson had security cameras installed in the place."

"That means that whoever came and went there was likely recorded," said Windflower. "If they were running an escort service, then the people who visited there would also be on tape. Have your guys checked the place out yet?"

"I have a forensics crew over there right now," said Langmead. "If there are tapes then it will be interesting to see if anyone on Mercedes Dowson's contact list might make an appearance."

"I've got a piece of news for you too," said Windflower. "Peter Yashin was picked up in Cape Breton and is now on his way to Halifax."

"That's good," said Langmead. "Any chance we can get in to see him?"

"I don't know," said Windflower. "They're talking to him about some big stuff over there, but I'll ask. It's starting to look like he might be your prime suspect for Amy Parsons, but I don't know how you're going to stick him with it."

"Well, he had means, opportunity and motive," said Langmead. "Of course, that's a long way from getting him charged, let alone convicted. I know that he might get caught up for the other things in Halifax, but we need justice for Amy Parsons as well. It looks like she got caught pretty far in over her head, and she may not be the only local girl involved."

"We've had two more girls from Regatta crews contact us. They were approached by Mercedes Dowson at parties and were asked if they wanted to make some extra money."

"At least you've shut down the business," said Windflower.

"I'm not even sure about that," said Langmead. "It feels like we've taken a bite out of the snake but the head remains intact. I guess that's why I hope we can also do something with that contact list," he said. "At minimum these guys were turning a blind eye to what was happening, and at worst may have been active participants."

"Let me know what comes out of the search of that house," said Windflower. "I'll check into what's happening in Halifax and let you know."

It was too late to call Guy Simard when Windflower finished up with Langmead, so Windflower made a mental note to call him in the morning, and started to close up shop for the night. He decided that he might as well make his way home and tell Sheila the news that he might be moving after all; just not likely to St. John's.

Sheila was reading a magazine on the couch when Windflower arrived and she moved over to let him slide in beside her.

"How was your day, Sergeant?" she asked.

"Do you want the good news or the bad news?" asked Windflower.

She listened to him relating his discussions with the Inspector and his two and a half supporters and said, "Mark me down as a supporter, too. I'm glad you're taking on that misogynist bastard."

Windflower was surprised. This was the strongest language he'd ever heard from Sheila.

"And if they kick you out we'll organize a protest," she continued. "There's too much of this going on and…"

"Whoa, slow down," said Windflower. "Thank you for your support. Right now you could really support me by giving me a hug."

"No problem, Sergeant," said Sheila, squeezing him tightly. "There's more where that came from. But I could make you dinner first if you want."

"That would be perfect," said Windflower, thinking it was a long time since his picnic lunch. "I could eat a horse."

"Sorry, "said Sheila. "We're fresh out of horse, but I picked up a couple of lovely pork chops at Warrens."

"Yum, sounds good," said Windflower.

"Okay, why don't you have a shower and relax, and I'll put supper together?" she said.

"That's why I love you so much," said Windflower. "You are always making me offers I can't refuse."

Chapter Forty

When Windflower came out from his shower, Sheila already had potatoes roasting in the oven, broccoli chopped up and ready for the steamer, and was seasoning the pork chops with salt and pepper. Windflower poured them each a glass of wine and sat at the kitchen table to observe the preparations. Sheila didn't mind and was quite happy to have both the company and the wine.

She put the pork chops in oil she had heating on the stove and while they browned on one side, she organized her ingredients for the salad dressing to go over the fresh spring mix she had picked up in Marystown. She turned the chops after a couple of minutes and mixed together some oil and cider vinegar, lemon juice, some hot mustard, and to Windflower's delight, a small bag of blueberries.

"Are those for the salad dressing?" asked Windflower.

"Very perceptive, Sergeant," said Sheila as she put all of the ingredients in the blender. "But that's the last of my stash. I was planning to go out tomorrow to get some more, but it looks like the good weather may not last."

"Too bad," said Windflower. "Maybe we can go together on the weekend and get the last few that aren't already picked."

Sheila poured the contents of the blender into a carafe and rinsed the blender clean. Then she took the pork chops out of the skillet and put on a sliced onion to fry up. In another bowl she whisked together up a concoction of apple juice, a little of the vinegar, a spoonful of sugar, and some chopped up and mashed apples and assorted spices. This mixture went into the frying pan and she brought it to a boil.

"Okay," she said. "Get the table ready."

While Windflower was putting the salad and dressing on the table, she dropped the pork chops back into the skillet and let them stew in the apple sauce for a few minutes. She turned on the broccoli to steam and took the golden brown roasted potatoes out of the oven.

Windflower eagerly passed her two plates, and she first put some potatoes and then a fat pork chop on each one, covering each with a thick ladle of sauce and drippings and fried onions from the pan. A couple of sprigs of parsley for decoration, and a side of steamed broccoli later, their feast was ready.

"Oh my god," said Windflower as he allowed his face and taste buds to linger a little over the steaming hot dinner in front of him. "Oh my god," he said again, when he tasted the first bite of pork chop in the hot apple sauce, a tinge of burnt-black on the outside and soft pink inside.

The roasted potatoes were perfectly done, and the salad with the tart blueberry dressing was a great match for the sweet apple taste from the chops and sauce.

As usual, Windflower said very little while he ate. Sheila was used to this by now and contented herself to witness his appetite and enjoyment.

When he was done Windflower said, "If that was my last meal as a Mountie, I can now retire in peace. Where did you learn to cook pork chops like that?"

"From 'Canadian Living', 2009," said Sheila. "What do you think I'm doing reading those magazines all the time?"

"That is a first place winner," said Windflower. "I would certainly give it Windflower's Seal of Good Housekeeping."

"I'm sure the millions of Canadian women who've tried this recipe would be pleased to know that," said Sheila. "I'd prefer it right now though, if you would give your approval and attention to this dish cloth."

"Yes, ma'am," said Windflower, as he rose to give her a salute, but changed his mind and gave her a large hug instead. Sheila returned the hug with equal fervour and the dishes had to wait; for a very long time afterwards.

Later, as they were curled up in their robes on the couch, Windflower told Sheila about his night shift for Thursday. Sheila shared her plans for dinner and a game of cards with her friends for Friday night. Windflower then remembered his commitment to Doctor Sanjay for chess on Friday as well.

"Look at us," said Sheila, "A pair of domesticated cats."

"A pair of happy, domesticated cats," said Windflower, feeling pretty content with his quiet little life in Grand Bank.

Now if only Inspector Arsenault would stop trying to interfere in it, he thought.

The night was peaceful with no phone calls and no dreams and Windflower woke up refreshed in the morning. Sheila was still slumbering softly beside him when he checked the clock and saw that it was a touch past 7 a.m.

There was no need to rush this morning, because when you worked the night shift you didn't have to go in until noon if you didn't want to. Windflower would go in long before 12, but right now he could let himself relax.

He got up and saw, as Sheila had predicted, that the weather had indeed returned back to normal. That meant rain, drizzle and fog with the only short-term changes being related to the thickness of the fog, or the intensity of the rain. The drizzle would remain constant for days and sometimes longer. In any case, Windflower had things to do inside, and after he put on his hoodie, he was protected as well as possible from the elements.

Windflower did his morning smudge, and offered up his prayers to the people in the spirit world, and on this earth, who were helping him on his journey. He made special thanks to Grandfather Sun and Grandmother Moon who were helping to guide him through the dream world, and for the messages that he had received from them. He gave thanks that Anne-Marie and her family been saved from tragedy, and that his Uncle and Auntie were still here to help him. He also gave thanks for Sheila, and for the love that was now lifting his heart.

Windflower's last set of prayers were for himself, not asking that his problems or troubles go away, although that would be nice, but that he receive the knowledge and wisdom to do the next right thing. And not to be afraid of what others thought, or what the consequences might be.

When he had finished his rituals he went back inside and put on the coffee. While he was waiting for the coffee, he decided to lie just a few more minutes in that nice warm bed with Sheila. When he woke up again it was 10:30 a.m.

Sheila was already up and about, and had made some scrambled eggs and toast. She was eating hers and pointed to the stove where his share was warming in the oven. He bolted down his food, kissed Sheila on the cheek, and jumped in the shower.

Just after 11 a.m. he walked in the door of the RCMP detachment. Betsy was sitting there looking like she was going to cry, and she simply pointed towards his office.

When Windflower walked in he saw a smug looking Inspector Arsenault sitting at his desk.

"Good morning, Sergeant, glad to see you decided to finally come to work today."

Windflower stood in the doorway, watching Arsenault.

"But you needn't have bothered, because you are suspended from duty, effective immediately. Ms. Molloy is typing up the letter right now. I'll have your badge and your weapon," said Arsenault.

"What is the charge against me?" asked Windflower.

"Insubordination, to start with," said Arsenault. "And there's surely more to come after the investigation."

"I will appeal any action you take against me," said Windflower, who was trying his level best to maintain his cool.

"You do whatever you want," said Arsenault. "But I would recommend that you seek a transfer out of this province as soon as possible, if you don't want to face further sanctions."

Windflower handed over his service weapon and his RCMP identification badge. Inspector Arsenault smiled, put them in his pocket, and walked out of the office. He paused at the front to sign the letter that Betsy had prepared, and a memorandum which ordered the staff in Grand Bank to report directly to him until further notice.

"And Ms. Molloy, I want you to inform all of the other officers that Sergeant Windflower is not allowed access to these premises or any of the files and materials here. Is that clear?" asked the Inspector.

"Yes, sir," said Betsy.

As Arsenault drove away Windflower heard Betsy murmur under her breath something about that "mean old bastard".

He pretended not to hear that, and simply told Betsy not to worry, and that things would work out. If she needed him for anything, he would still be around. As she handed him his copy of the suspension letter, he also told her to get somebody to pick up his overnight shift.

At least I have a night off, he thought.

Windflower left the detachment and walked down to the Mug-Up to get a cup of coffee. It was quiet at the café since it was between the 10 o'clock crew and the lunchtime rush. As luck would have it, Herb Stoodley was finishing up his morning shift, and had time to join Windflower at his usual corner table.

"That's disappointing news," said Stoodley. "But I've been looking for another waitress to open up in the morning."

Windflower laughed despite himself.

"Thanks for the offer, Herb. If it comes with free food, I'll take it."

This time Stoodley laughed.

"You might as well laugh. You know you haven't done anything wrong and if your suspicions are right, Arsenault may well have opened the door for your counter-attack."

"What do you mean?" asked Windflower.

"I'm guessing that this is not Arsenault's first time feeling a little heat for his unwanted amorous intentions. And need I remind you that his name is on the dead girl's phone. Can you find out a bit more about his past and connect it up with the present?" asked Stoodley.

"You don't know how things work in the RCMP," said Windflower, a little glumly.

"Really?" said Stoodley. "I've dealt with crooked cabinet ministers, malicious mayors, and cops who stank so much that they still smelled rotten after you hung them on the clothes line for a week."

"Justice isn't easy, but honesty and courage will always win out in the end. Sometimes it takes a little longer, but eventually the bad guys fall."

Windflower simply nodded and said, "Thank you Herb, I appreciate your support and encouragement. I may need you to run interference on a few things. Do you think you could help?"

He told Stoodley about his latest conversation with Langmead, and outlined the activities that Mercedes Dowson was engaged in.

"Sure thing, Winston, you can count on me," said Stoodley. "Anything that can get me out of this apron for a while is a welcome blessing. Let me go tell Moira that I'm off on a special assignment."

While Stoodley went into the back to talk to his wife, Windflower's cell phone went off. It was Guy Simard from Halifax.

"Winston, it's me, Guy, and I've got Ron Quigley on the line with me," said Simard. Windflower cut him off in mid-sentence.

"I'm under suspension, Guy. Arsenault has suspended me indefinitely pending some sort of investigation," said Windflower.

"For what?" asked Simard.

"I think I rubbed him the wrong way," said Windflower.

He could hear the two voices on the other end of the phone talking together but couldn't hear what they were saying. Finally, he heard Quigley's voice on the line.

"Even a suspended Member can talk to a few old friends, can't he?" asked Quigley.

"I guess so," said Windflower.

"Then we'd like to tell you some news we heard about a Mr. Peter Yashin whom we believe you are acquainted with," said Quigley, "Unless you'd prefer not to hear."

Chapter Forty-One

"I'd love to learn the latest news about Mr. Yashin," said Windflower.

Guy Simard came back on the phone. "According to the officers downtown, Yashin started out as a man of steel, but he has proved to be more a man of rubber, if you know what I mean."

"Flexible," said Quigley, "Especially since we hit him over the head a few times with the evidence from the Mercedes Dowson murder. His fingerprints are all over the car, and he was even seen in a bar around Ingonish, arguing with her. Once he realized how much we have on him he started to be more cooperative."

"That's when they brought us in," said Simard. "We've got him on tape at the airport with several groups of ladies, from Romania, Estonia, Belarus and other places. Yashin started the ball rolling against Iggy, providing names, dates, people, and places."

"He's given us the people who pulled the triggers, and the people who called the shots," said Quigley. "It was as if after the Dowson murder he had nothing left."

"In any case our guys are beginning the intake process for protection, and talking to the Crown Attorney about a plea bargain."

"What kind of a deal can a guy like that get?" asked Windflower.

"Probably 15-20 in segregation, and then relocation," said Simard. "It's not a pretty world, Winston, but you know that already. If he's lucky he survives the pen, and maybe gets a second chance while always looking over his shoulder. We get to solve a few outstanding murders, and shut down a growing criminal empire."

"It sounds like you've got plenty of your own troubles," said Quigley. "If there's anything I can do, just call."

Simard shouted, "Me too!" from his side of the speaker.

"Thanks guys, I appreciate it. You can also do me a small favour. Is there any way we can get Langmead from the RNC in to talk to Yashin? It seems a shame to have the first murder in this chain of events go unresolved," said Windflower.

"That's a tough one," said Simard, "But if we can't get him in, I can ask the investigator to put it on the list of cases that they're reviewing with Yashin."

"Okay, thanks again," said Windflower. "Talk soon," he said, just as Stoodley was coming back from the kitchen, apron-less and wearing a wide smile.

"So who have you got on your side in this situation?" asked Stoodley when they were out of the café and in Stoodley's car.

First they drove to Sheila's to give her an update, and then home for a change of clothes.

If he was going to be suspended, he might as well change into civvies, thought Windflower.

"Well, there's Langmead in St. John's," said Windflower. "We should talk to him first to see if he's got any update on the security cameras."

When he saw Stoodley's puzzled face he added, "I guess I didn't tell you, but they had surveillance cameras, at the front entrance from one of the business locations of the 'girls'."

"That would be helpful," said Stoodley. "As a CA, we used to always say that pictures don't lie. That isn't true by the way, but video evidence has a lot of uses."

"And there's Bill Ford, but he's a bit shaky on the Arsenault front," said Windflower. "It appears that they share the same closet, if not the same skeletons."

"I can talk to Bill. I'm assuming he knows about previous incidents involving the Inspector," said Stoodley.

"One particular one got hushed up, and the woman was paid off," added Windflower. "I don't know if Ford will talk, but give him a call anyway."

"And then there's Constable Evanchuk. She's the last one I want to bring into my pickle, but we may have to," said Windflower, frowning at this option.

"As your representative, I strongly suggest that we get an affidavit from her about her 'experiences'," said Stoodley. "We can hold it for now, but we'll need to have it in our pocket for later; especially she was persuaded to change her story."

"She wouldn't do that," said Windflower.

"We don't understand the pressure that can be brought to bear on a young female officer when it comes to protecting a senior member of the force," said Stoodley. "I've seen cases like this where a woman's own family urged her to drop a complaint. Let's nail that down right away."

Windflower wanted to say more, but knew that Stoodley was right.

"Here's your first stop," said Stoodley.

Windflower went into Sheila's and while she was a little surprised, she was happy to see him.

"That was a short day," she said with a smile.

"My hours have been cut dramatically," said Windflower.

He went on to tell Sheila about his encounter with Inspector Arsenault and showed her the letter he had received.

"Is he crazy?" asked Sheila. "Why would he suspend his best cop?"

"Thanks for the vote of support," said Windflower. "Crazy may be too strong a word, but stubborn and mule-headed and very, very angry might fit the bill. Herb Stoodley has volunteered to be my chauffeur this morning, he's waiting outside."

"Take Herb's advice, whatever it is," said Sheila. "He's been around the pond a few times himself. He can help you."

"I've already recruited him, ma'am," said Windflower. "He's my most trusted adviser."

"Don't let that awful man get to you," said Sheila. "You could have this whole town in an open revolt if you told them what was going on."

"My plan is to win," said Windflower. "Right now I don't want, or need, any public displays on my behalf. Let me and Herb see what we can do."

"Sometimes you have to nudge justice along the right path," said Sheila.

Then coming close so she could hold him tightly said, "I just want you and me to be happy and together, Winston. Nothing else is really that important."

Windflower hugged her back, kissed her and waved goodbye.

"I'll check in later," he said on the way out.

He was smiling when he jumped back into the car with Herb Stoodley.

"It's great to have a good woman by your side, isn't it?" asked Stoodley.

"It is great," said Windflower. "Now, Jeeves, take me home, please."

Stoodley dropped Windflower in his driveway and headed off. They had agreed to meet up again around 1 o'clock to go for lunch.

Windflower was going to the bedroom to get changed when he saw the message light blinking on his phone. He picked it up and dialed into his messages.

There were several on the machine, including one offering him a free trip to the Bahamas. That could come in handy if things didn't go as planned here, he thought. Another was trying to sell him a new credit card, and then there were two real messages.

One was from Auntie Marie giving him the latest gossip from home, and the other from Anne-Marie, thanking him for giving her the dream message, and asking him to call.

He wrote down the number and thought about calling her later. Then he thought again, and dialed her number.

'Hello," came a quiet, soft voice over the phone.

"Anne-Marie, it's Winston," he said.

"Winston, it's so good to hear from you," said Anne-Marie. "I'm glad that you called so I can thank you in person, at least over the phone. I know I might have laughed off the dream message at the time we talked, but it kept coming back to me. Even though I practice many of the sacred teachings in my work, sometimes I'm not as vigilant in my personal life."

"I know that experience," said Windflower. "Especially for me when I'm so far away from my home and my family. I'm just grateful you're safe."

"I'd been thinking about what you told me, and I realized I hadn't been paying attention to many other messages that were being sent to me through other messengers," said Anne-Marie.

"That night when all of the other people were getting on the plane I could hear your voice, but also the wind was singing to me too. I decided that it must not be the right thing to do. At the last minute I chose not to board the plane."

"Wow, that was close," said Windflower. "I'm very sorry for the loss of your friends and colleagues on that plane, but I'm glad you made that decision."

"It was not my time," said Anne-Marie. "I still have unfinished work to do, I know that now. Some of that finishing has to be done on my inside world."

"So, I'm taking a break from my art therapy programs. I have trained many helpers who can carry on the work and I need to go home and spend some time with the people I love. That's the most important thing I can do right now."

"So, if you and your lady friend and your eventual little papooses are ever out this way please come and see me. Meegwich, Winston."

"We will, Anne-Marie. Be safe," said Windflower as he hung up the phone.

Chapter Forty-Two

When he went into his bedroom to change into his jeans, Windflower saw a small wooden chest on the top shelf of his closet. It was his special chest, what his Auntie Marie called a memory chest, when she gave it to him many years ago.

The most important things in the world to him, except for one, were in that little cedar chest. There were pictures of his mother and father on their wedding day.

His parents had actually married twice; once at the church because the local missionaries insisted on it, or they would have their rations cut off for the winter. The second occasion took place on the land, with their family and friends joining in a celebration that featured dancing, singing and a community feast.

Windflower also had a small picture of his mother in a locket that was given to him by his father just before he died. His mother had long dark hair, bright eyes and a welcoming smile. Inside the box were a number of mementos, like a lock of hair from the very first time he had his hair cut when he was a child. His Auntie told him to guard it safely, because his enemies could control his mind if they got their hands on it. I'm glad Arsenault can't get it, he thought.

As he was putting away the pictures and treasures he noticed something sparkling in the light. It was his mother's engagement ring that had been passed down to him after she had died. It wasn't typical for a Cree woman to have an engagement ring but his father had won it in a poker game in the logging camps, and gave it to her to seal their commitment. It was old silver and a little tarnished, but it also had what looked to be a full carat diamond in an exquisite antique setting.

Windflower put everything else away except for the ring. That, he put in his coin tray on top of his dresser. Then he heard a car pull up and went out to meet Herb Stoodley.

"Lunch?" asked Stoodley.

"Another offer I can't refuse," said Windflower.

The two men pulled up at the Mug-Up just as the lunch crowd was leaving, but there were enough luncheon diners remaining to make it difficult to find a seat. Stoodley and Windflower were waved over to a near-empty table by the Mayor who was saying goodbye to some of his other constituents.

"Come in and sit yerself down," said Mayor Bill Sinnott. "I was hoping to run into you, b'y. I've been talkin to a few of my fellow elected officials up and down the coast and we figure that the devil ye knows is better than the one ya don't."

Windflower looked puzzled at the Mayor's comments but Stoodley translated for him.

"I think the Mayor is offering you his support, and that he can probably get the other local Mayors on board too, if you'd like," said Stoodley.

When Windflower still looked confused he added, "You can say thank you now."

"Thank you, very much," said Windflower, and the Mayor made a big show of standing up and offering his hand to Windflower.

"Listen to your adviser," said the Mayor. "I gotta' run but we'll be in touch. I still want to talk to you more 'bout that community policin' stuff," said the Mayor as he ambled slowly out of the café.

Moira Stoodley came out of the kitchen with two bowls of turkey soup and two grilled cheese sandwiches.

"I thought you might need a bite," said Moira. "We all support you, Winston," she said as she returned to the kitchen.

"All we need now is some support from the RCMP," said Windflower. "Have you talked to Bill Ford?" he asked Herb Stoodley as he blew on the soup in his spoon to cool it.

"Not yet, but I've got a message in to him, and I'm seeing Constable Evanchuk after her shift, around 4:30," said Stoodley.

"This soup is so good," said Windflower, as he managed to snag a piece of turkey from the hot broth. "What makes it so tasty?"

"Now that I've been let into the inner sanctum of the kitchen, I can tell you that the secret is fresh turkey, of course, along with a healthy sprinkling of Newfoundland savoury," said Stoodley.

"What is Newfoundland savoury anyway?" asked Windflower.

"I'm not sure exactly," said Stoodley. "I just know that it is grown on a farm at Mt. Scio in St. John's, and that it is sum good b'y," he said with a laugh.

"It is sum good," said Windflower, as he devoted his full attention to emptying every bite and sip from his soup bowl.

After lunch, Stoodley had some errands to run for Moira, so he dropped Windflower back at Sheila's. But when Windflower got there, he found the door locked and Sheila gone.

She probably went to get her hair done, thought Windflower.

In any case he had a key, and was quite comfortable to sit and wait for her. He remembered that he'd left his book, *The Orenda*, there, and went into the bedroom to find it.

He started to read again about the story that Joseph Boyden was weaving through history. It was following the lives of a Huron warrior, a wild Iroquois girl who had been taken prisoner after her family was killed, and a young Jesuit priest on his first voyage to the New World to save the souls of the heathens.

Windflower had gotten over the vivid descriptions of primitive savagery that were sprinkled throughout the book. That was part of a violent culture in a violent past. Now, he could just enjoy the descriptions of the culture and traditions of the Huron and their allies.

He became very absorbed in reading about a special ceremony that this group of Huron undertook whenever they moved their village in a search for better soil for their crops of corn and beans. It was an elaborate rite that took place over several days to honour their dead family members, and to bring both their bones and their spirits with them to their new location.

Windflower's reading was interrupted by the ringing of his cell phone.

"Windflower here," he answered.

"Winston, it's Carl Langmead. How are you?" asked the RNC detective.

"I'm okay," said Windflower, for some reason hesitating to tell Langmead right away about his situation.

"Good," said Langmead. "I wanted to give you an update on Shawn Parsons, and to see if you heard anything from Halifax yet."

"I've asked Halifax to let you in, but it doesn't look good," said Windflower. "They're moving towards putting Yashin into a witness program. He's confessed to the Dowson murder and he's spilling the beans on the gang's activities in Nova Scotia."

"I did ask them to put the Amy Parsons case on the list, though. I'll let you know if and when I hear anything. So what's new with Shawn Parsons?"

"Parsons is singing like a canary, but most of what he has to tell us we already knew. He's given us a few leads on the drug operations in St. John's, but not a whole lot more. He did tell us that Dowson and Yashin were more than friends, and that Yashin wanted it to be exclusive, but Dowson wasn't so sure. When we finally told him that she was dead, he wasn't in the least surprised," said Langmead.

"Any word on the security tapes?" asked Windflower.

"No, it seems that there was a camera but no tapes to back it up," said Langmead. "I guess they didn't bother with that."

"By the way, it looks like we're getting ready to wrap this stuff up down here, so would it be possible to get the cell phone back?"

"I guess so," said Windflower. "But you'll have to come and get it. I've been grounded by the Inspector."

"What?" asked Langmead with surprise in his voice, "You're suspended? What did you do?"

"I'm really not sure yet," said Windflower. "But it appears that I have stepped directly on Inspector Arsenault's corns."

"Well, good luck with that," said Langmead. "I'll be over tomorrow to get the cell phone."

That was weird, thought Windflower. He called me to tell me about Shawn Parsons but didn't have anything to say. And then he just about admits that they're not going to do anything about the names in the cell phone. It's starting to feel very lonely out here on this limb all by myself, he thought.

Before Windflower could dive back into his book, he heard Sheila's car pull up in the driveway.

"Hi, Sheila," he called as she came in the door.

"If this is what suspension looks like, I'll take some too," said Sheila, surveying Windflower's relaxed manner and his open book on the coffee table.

"Cuppa' tea?" she asked.

"That would be nice," said Windflower as he followed her to the kitchen.

"Did you have lunch?" Sheila asked. "I could make you a sandwich if you're hungry."

"No thanks, we ate at the Mug-Up," said Windflower. "We had sandwiches and turkey soup. I'm stuffed."

"Anything new?" Sheila asked, as she poured hot water onto the tea bag in the teapot.

"Well, the Mayor is drumming up support for me," said Windflower.

"You know, I like that guy," said Sheila. "He's straightforward and seems very connected to both the people and the issues. And I like him even more now," she said, handing Windflower a cup of tea.

Just then Herb Stoodley's car pulled up behind Sheila's in the driveway.

"Hello, Sheila, m'dear, how are you?" said Stoodley as he gave her a hug. "Your hair looks great."

"I'm grand," said Sheila. "Thank you for noticing," she said, while giving Windflower a soft version of the evil eye.

"Would you like a cup of tea, maybe some dessert?"

"I was just about to say how beautiful you look with your new 'do'," said Windflower. "But my so-called friend beat me to it. What was that you were saying about dessert?"

Sheila went to the fridge and found the remains of a cherry pie, which she cut into two pieces and placed on the table along with Stoodley's tea.

"I was telling Sheila about the Mayor," said Windflower, as Stoodley nodded with a mouth full of pie. "It's good to have friends. On the other hand it looks like St. John's is shutting down their investigation," he said and he told Sheila and Stoodley about his conversation with Langmead.

Chapter Forty-Three

"That is not good," said Stoodley. "It may mean that we have to act sooner than planned."

"What do you mean?" asked Windflower.

"We're going to have to find a way to shake the temple until the walls start falling down," said Stoodley.

"Like Joshua knocked down the walls of Jericho," added Sheila.

"Enough of the Biblical references," said Windflower. "What are you talking about, Herb?"

"First of all let me tell you some good news," said Stoodley. "I talked to Bill Ford, and he is completely onboard. He's pretty upset about your suspension and knows a hatchet job's on the way. He told me he turned down Arsenault's request to lead the investigation into your actions. He's getting me the contact information for the woman who lost her job."

"Great," said Windflower and Sheila together, "But what about this idea of knocking down walls? What's going on with that?" asked Windflower.

"All in good time my friend," said Stoodley, "All in good time. Now if you'll excuse us, ma'am, we have an interview to carry out."

"Bye, Sheila," said Windflower as he kissed her on the forehead. "Wish me luck with this crazy man."

"Good luck to both of you," she called out as they were leaving.

"I asked Evanchuk to meet me at my house," said Stoodley. "I've also asked my neighbour, George Grandy, to come by and witness, if that's okay with you."

"Sounds good to me," said Windflower. "Should I be there when this interview is going on?"

"No, we'll stick you on the back porch in the studio while we're doing it," said Stoodley. "It's better for you and her if you make yourself scarce."

When they arrived at Stoodley's house he led Windflower to the back while he tidied up the living room and set up his tape recorder.

Windflower could hear Stoodley's neighbour arrive by the sound of the friendly voices. He also heard another car drive up that he assumed was Constable Evanchuk's. He didn't hear much more except for muffled voices over the next half hour, until he heard doors closing and a car drive way.

Stoodley came in to tell him that the coast was clear. "How'd it go?" asked Windflower.

"She was solid," said Stoodley. "If we need her, she'll be like a rock. Now if you'll excuse me, I have a few phone calls to make."

Windflower relaxed in the gallery out back as he looked out over the ocean. It was a rough day on the water and the seas were dotted with whitecaps. The rain had lessened as the day went on, but the fog had moved closer than ever, and now threatened to swallow up Grand Bank whole.

There's always something happening with the weather here, thought Windflower. He remembered the old Newfoundland saying: 'If you don't like the weather, don't worry, it'll change any minute now.'

Stoodley called Windflower out to the kitchen.

"I guess it's you and me for supper," he said. "Moira called to say she's working late. So what do you fancy? I've got a few sea trout that George Grandy dropped off if you'd like to try them out?"

"That sounds great," said Windflower. "Anything I can do to help?"

"You can peel us a few potatoes and carrots, and this half of a turnip," said Stoodley. "I'll get the trout ready for the broiling pan."

"It looks to me like Langmead is under pressure to shut up about the names on the cell phone," said Stoodley. "It's starting to smell like a cover-up to me."

"I thought it was kind of strange," said Windflower. "He was the guy who was so gung-ho about this earlier."

"He's not so gung-ho that he would stick his neck out," said Stoodley. "One of my calls was into the RNC. I want to know if an order came from higher-up to shut this thing down. I should have an answer by tomorrow morning, one way or another."

"I guess if they shut it down there, we can't really do much about it at our end, can we?" asked Windflower.

"That depends," said Stoodley.

"On what?" asked Windflower.

"On whether we want to play defence or offence," said Stoodley.

Seeing that puzzled look come over Windflower's face again he added, "Just leave it to Uncle Herb for now, okay?"

"Okay," said Windflower, not feeling like he had a whole lot of choice in the matter.

Just keep rowing the boat, he thought; sooner or later we'll reach dry land.

Windflower chopped up his vegetables and put them in a pot to boil, while Stoodley deboned his four medium-sized trout on a cutting board. Then he added a dash of salt, a heavy couple of sprinkles of black pepper and the same of cayenne. His final flourish was a pinch of chili powder for each piece of fish. Then he put them in the pan to broil. By the time the vegetables were done, so were the trout.

Stoodley had turned them just once during this period, and the fish were gleaming brown and pink on top and crunchy black on the bottom. He whipped the potatoes and carrots and turnip with some butter and a splash of milk and several more shots of black pepper. Then he plopped a large ladle of each on both men's plates along with one of the trout.

Windflower took one small bite of his fish and murmured to himself. About halfway through his first trout, he paused for air, and complimented Stoodley on his meal.

"They're gorgeous, aren't they," said Stoodley. "Grandy gets a few here and there from his son-in-law, and every so often he passes some along to me. They're called sea trout but actually they're brown trout that run the river mouths as they empty out into the ocean. The British brought them here, maybe a hundred years ago, and they're still going strong."

"It tastes a little fishier than other trout I've had," said Windflower, "If that makes any sense."

"It does to me," said Stoodley. "All I know is that they taste fresh, right out of the water, which of course they are. I can eat those farmed rainbow trout from the supermarket in the middle of winter, but they taste like cardboard compared to these."

"Agreed," said Windflower, as he held his plate up for round two of the sea trout and another ladleful of hash.

After they had finished their supper, they cleared up their mess and went into the living room to watch the news. Stoodley had put some coffee on and they were waiting for their stomachs to subside a little before they contemplated dessert.

Stoodley got up to answer the phone and Windflower could overhear some of the conversation, at least Stoodley's portion of it.

"Yes, Ms. Buckingham, thank you for calling me back," Windflower heard before Stoodley closed the door to the parlour where the phone was located.

Before long, Stoodley was back in the living room carrying two cups of coffee and another package of those deadly cookies from the café. He was also wearing a smile from ear to ear.

"Windflower, my boy," said Stoodley. "You will be filing a formal complaint against one Inspector Kevin David Arsenault for harassment, defamation of character, and wrongful demotion. Plus sexual harassment of subordinate staff and conduct unbecoming a Member of the RCMP, and whatever else we can come up with."

"I am?" asked Windflower, as he grabbed the first of what would be several cookies from the tray.

"You are," said Stoodley. "The ball is now in our hands, and we are going on the offence."

He then explained to Windflower that he had just talked to the woman who had been forced out by Arsenault, and that she would be happy to file a formal complaint. So too would Constable Evanchuk. When they added his complaint to the pile, along with Ford's cooperation, the higher-ups in the RCMP would have to pay attention.

"I am going to get Ms. Buckingham to swear out a statement tomorrow, at the Crown Attorney's office in Stephenville, where she's living now. Once we have that, we'll ask your lawyer to send off your complaint at the same time. If it all works out, we'll have this whole pile of animal excrement hit the fan before close of business tomorrow. I have a friend at RCMP HQ who will make sure that the complaints get into the right hands, and Inspector Arsenault won't know what hit him," said Stoodley.

Windflower took another cookie from the dwindling supply and asked, "Won't that make Arsenault even angrier?"

"Maybe," said Stoodley, reaching into the cookie tray for a lemon square. "But what's he going to do, suspend you?"

"True," said Windflower, taking the last snowball.

"And besides, that's just our ground game. Wait until he sees our air attack, said Stoodley."

The two men heard a car pull up in the driveway outside.

"Who could that be?" asked Stoodley. "It can't be Moira; she won't be home until after 9 o'clock."

In through the living room door came Corporal Eddie Tizzard.

"Tizzard," said both Windflower and Stoodley together.

"I didn't think you were back until the weekend," said Windflower.

"I didn't think that you were going to go and get suspended," said Tizzard. "What's a fella got to do to get a cup of coffee around here?"

"Come out and I'll get you a cup, Eddie," said Stoodley. "I'm glad you're back. Let's get another tray of cookies out. I think we're going to need them."

I'm glad he's back too, thought Windflower.

Chapter Forty-Four

Stoodley and Tizzard remained a long time in the kitchen. When Windflower came out of the living room he could hear them talking in hushed voices.

"What's the big secret?" asked Windflower.

Tizzard, with his hand in a cookie tray, and his face looking like he had been caught in a cookie jar, quickly said, "Nothing, Boss."

But Stoodley just smiled and said, "We're planning our comeback. Have a cookie, Sergeant?"

Windflower had to laugh at the pair of them conspiring with him against the world, or at least against the Inspector.

"What's so funny, Sarge?" asked Tizzard.

"Be careful where that grey wolf leads you, little cub, is what my grandfather used to tell me. It might be good advice to follow," said Windflower. "I'm the one that's suspended right now, and you have to be careful that you're not next on Arsenault's hit list."

"You won't be suspended long," said Tizzard. "Not if me and Herb have anything to do with it."

"Oh my god, the Caped Crusader and the Boy Wonder," said Windflower. "Can one of you superheroes give me a ride home?"

Tizzard jumped up before Stoodley had a chance to say a word and was outside before Windflower had his boots on.

"Thanks for everything, Herb," said Windflower. "I appreciate the company most of all. This would have been a very long day without you, and the trout were fabulous. If you ever get a few more and want help to finish them off, just let me know."

"I think I know where to find you. Talk to you tomorrow, Winston," said Stoodley as he led them out the door.

"So how was your trip to Ramea?" asked Windflower when he got into Tizzard's vehicle, the RCMP jeep.

"It was good to visit, but there's less and less there for either me or my dad now," said Tizzard. Then seeing Windflower looking around the vehicle in feigned surprise, he said "Yes, this is the RCMP jeep. I picked it up when I went by the detachment earlier. You weren't using it, so…."

"So you took it back as fast as you could. You don't miss a trick, do you Tizzard?" asked Windflower playfully.

"Not if I can help it, sir," said Tizzard. "This is your stop, I believe."

Tizzard had pulled up in front of Windflower's house where the lights were on and Sheila's car was parked in the driveway.

"I just wanted to say that I believe everything will come out okay. My dad always says that it's sometimes darkest just before the dawn."

"Thank you, Corporal, but as you can see it is pretty dark out now," said Windflower.

"It'll look brighter in the morning," said Tizzard.

"Goodnight, Pollyanna," said Windflower, and he got out of the car to go inside his house.

He didn't have to look to know what would happen next. A short flash of light and a loud squeal of tires marked Tizzard's departure.

Just like the good old days, thought Windflower.

Sheila had already had her bath, and Windflower went in to have his while she sat on the couch and watched one of her favourite programs, *What Not to Wear*.

When he got to the bathroom, there was his Boyden book sitting on top of the clothes hamper. Sheila had remembered to bring it over with her from her house. Several pages into his book and several minutes into his bath, a wave of exhaustion came over Windflower.

He got out of the bath and dried off. Sheila had already turned everything off and was sitting up in bed with her magazine. Windflower hoped it was "Canadian Living" so he could take a peek at the recipes, but before he got a chance Sheila had inched her way close to him.

 Soon Windflower was fast asleep, and when he woke up the only dream he could remember was one where he was picking blueberries.

Now, that was a message he could really appreciate.

The weather outside was not exactly conducive to him realizing that dream, at least not today. It was damp and rainy and that giant fog bank had eaten up most of the Grand Bank Cape and was coming back in for a second meal.

This was a morning for a lie-in, thought Windflower.

Without wasting any more thoughts, he crawled back into the warm and cozy warren that Sheila had created. She mumbled a bit at him about being cold or something, but Windflower assured her that she'd warm him up soon enough. Seconds later they were fast into their morning sleep-in.

It was after 10 a.m. when Windflower stirred again, and he noticed Sheila was sitting up and reading in the bed beside him. He rudely interrupted her reading time by pulling her under the covers with him, and after nearly smothering her with kisses he released her, laughing and gasping for air.

"I could use my coffee, now," she said, trying to resume some semblance of order out of the chaos that Windflower had created.

"Yes, Your Majesty," said Windflower, "Your wish is my command."

Sheila threw a pillow at him as he attempted to accompany this with a low bow.

Windflower laughed and went to put the coffee on. The weather situation hadn't improved much since earlier in the morning, so Windflower turned on the radio to see if the weekend held out any better hopes.

While the coffee was brewing Windflower went outside and did his morning rituals. When he came back in, Sheila was sitting in the kitchen drinking her coffee. His cup was sitting right next to her.

"What's the weather forecast?" asked Windflower.

"More of the same today," said Sheila. "But they said it should be clearing late tonight and sunny and cool tomorrow."

"Let's go get the last of our blueberries then," said Windflower. "We can go up the trail to the tower tomorrow afternoon and get a few gallons."

"We might get a few cupfuls," said Sheila. "But let's do it."

"So, is there any breakfast in this café, or what?"

"Coming right up, ma'am," said Windflower, as he took eggs and milk and cheese out of the fridge.

He still had a little smoked salmon left and some hot pepper cream cheese that would go well with a couple of those Montreal-style bagels that he took out of the freezer to thaw. With a still-fresh cantaloupe to go along with his cooked food, he figured that he was all set.

Half an hour later, breakfast was ready. He placed half an omelet, along with some of the cantaloupe and a toasted bagel with cream cheese and smoked salmon on Sheila's plate as she sat in the living room watching TV. He grabbed the coffee pot and re-filled their cups before sitting down beside her with his identical plate of food.

"Like I said before, if this is suspension, bring it on," said Sheila.

"As long as it doesn't turn into retirement, I'm happy with that too," said Windflower.

Their morning reverie was broken as Tizzard motored his jeep into their driveway. Windflower could tell by the howling tires and the barking dogs that it was Tizzard, long before he arrived.

"Good morning, missus," said Tizzard. "Is the Boss around?"

"He's loafing in the living room," said Sheila with a wink to Tizzard.

"Morning, Sarge," said Tizzard.

"Good morning Corporal, what can I do for you today, in my unofficial capacity?" asked Windflower.

"Well, sir, Herb asked me to confirm when Langmead would be coming today. And also if you heard anything else from Halifax?" said Tizzard.

"I haven't heard anything yet, but I'll call Langmead and Guy Simard to find out what's going on," said

Windflower, "Any other orders from Commandante Stoodley?"

"Yes, there is one, actually," said Tizzard. "Since Herb has domestic duties today, he can't drive you around. He did say that you can borrow his station wagon if you needed wheels. Here are the keys."

"Thank you, Corporal," said Windflower. "What's the mood like at work?"

"People are pretty upset, especially Betsy," said Tizzard. "Arsenault has phoned several times already today to pump her for information. I told her to take the rest of the day off."

"That's a good idea," said Windflower. "I feel badly about dragging everybody into this with me."

"Don't feel bad, sir. I don't think anybody blames you for anything. There's not much love for the Inspector, though," said Tizzard.

"Just be careful, Eddie," said Windflower. "Don't let any of them do anything stupid either, okay?"

"Would it be stupid to offer you a ride to pick up your car?" asked Tizzard.

"No, I think that would be okay," said Windflower.

Tizzard very quickly drove him to Herb Stoodley's where the old Ford station wagon was sitting in front of the house.

Windflower got into the station wagon and waved goodbye to Tizzard. Despite the miserable weather he decided to take a drive out to the L'Anse au Loup T. It was a perfect place to think, and, on a day like this, to be alone.

Windflower drove down the bumpy road trying to avoid the numerous potholes, and almost succeeded in that from time to time. He arrived at the T and sat in the parked car for a moment watching the ocean crash into the shore, thinking that this same scene had been going on here uninterrupted for thousands of years.

He got out of the car and pulled his RCMP hoodie up over his head. The rain and wind still got in underneath, but he wasn't planning on staying there long. He just wanted enough time and space to clear his head and his heart.

He said a silent prayer to the wind to send him courage, and to the ocean to give him some of its deep strength. He breathed out all of his fears and breathed in the fresh, salty air. He felt totally refreshed and renewed by his short stint by the water.

Why don't I do this more often, he thought, as he drove the station wagon back up the highway.

On his way back home he stopped by the Mug-Up for a coffee to take out when his cell phone rang.

"Hi, Winston, it's Langmead, I'm just at Goobies. Can you meet me when I get in, probably about two hours from now, maybe at that cafe?"

"I'll pick you up there," said Windflower. "I'd rather talk to you somewhere more private than the Mug-Up. I'll see you when you get here."

Windflower went inside just as Herb Stoodley was leaving.

"Langmead called, he's on his way," he told Stoodley. "He's at Goobies right now."

"Good," said Stoodley. "Bring him over to my house when he gets here. By the way, I need the cell phone for about an hour before he gets here. Have you got it?"

"Yes, I mean not with me," said Windflower. "It's in my office. Is it okay for me to go and get it?"

"Get Tizzard to get it for you, and tell him to bring it over to me. I'll be at the house," said Stoodley.

Before Windflower could ask what he wanted with the phone, Stoodley was gone, leaving Windflower standing a little stupidly by himself in the doorway of the café.

Two of the older ladies were smiling at him when he looked up. He thought that one of them even gave him a thumbs-up sign, but maybe that was his imagination. He smiled back at the ladies and proceeded to order his coffee. While he was waiting, he phoned Tizzard and asked him to join him at the Mug-Up, sooner rather than later.

He shouldn't have added that condition because it seemed that Tizzard was there before Windflower sat down with his coffee.

"Cuppa coffee for me too, please, Marie," Tizzard shouted to the waitress as he sat down beside his Sergeant.

Chapter Forty-Five

"I need you to go into my office and look inside the metal cabinet. Here's the key. There's a plastic bag with a pink cell phone in it. Take the bag and its contents to Herb Stoodley. Got it?" asked Windflower.

"Got it," said Tizzard, as he sipped his steaming mug of coffee that had just arrived.

"What, no tea biscuits? That doesn't seem right," he added indignantly, and went back to the counter to place an order for two raisin tea biscuits.

"I think you eat more than me, which must be quite a lot," said Windflower.

"I'm still a growing boy," said Tizzard, spreading a thick layer of butter over his hot biscuit when it arrived.

"Well if you're not careful, you'll end up growing the other way too," said Windflower as he bit into his still-steaming snack.

As fast as the treats had arrived they were gone, and so too was Tizzard, on his mission to retrieve the cell phone and to get it to Stoodley. That left Windflower a little time to enjoy the rest of his coffee and to make his call to Guy Simard.

"Guy, it's Winston," he said when the other man answered the phone.

"Winston, how's it goin'? I'm glad you called," said Simard. "The Yashin situation is going crazy over here."

"Based on what he's told us, we've got a dozen guys locked up, including Iggy who tried to make a break for it. We had some people watching and when he ran, we just picked him up again."

"You'll also be happy to know that Quigley got in to ask Yashin about the human trafficking because he's on that task force with you. He said to tell you that Yashin confirms that Mercedes Dowson was running the St. John's operation, and one of their specialities was under-age girls."

"The Russians would bring them in through Halifax or Montreal and then send them to Newfoundland for what Yashin called training exercises. Dowson looked after that, and that was what Amy Parsons was upset about, according to Yashin. She didn't want any part of it, and that's why Dowson wanted to get rid of her."

"Yashin didn't confess to doing anything, but it's starting to look pretty clear what unfolded," said Simard.

"That would seem to jibe with what Shawn Parsons told the RNC," said Windflower. "Quigley didn't ask him about the Chinese, did he?"

"No," said Simard with a hearty laugh. "But I have a feeling that Yashin will have a story to tell about that one too. He's got so many stories going all at once that it's hard to keep up."

"One line that we're following up on is that they paid off the local cops, and maybe more, to turn a blind eye to their operations."

"That's interesting," said Windflower. "There's some suspicion that more than a few people, who should definitely know better, are mixed up with the escort side of the business in St. John's."

"That wouldn't surprise me, as sad as it is to say," replied Simard. "I'll put that in the hopper over here, and let you know if anything pops out."

"Thanks, Guy, that would be great," said Windflower.

"How are you holding up, Winston?" asked Simard.

"Surprisingly, I'm pretty calm. I've got a great woman and wonderful friends to support me; that's as much as any man can hope for," said Windflower.

"You're right about that," said Simard. "Good luck, Winston."

That's another good friend that I can call on if I have to get out of here, thought Windflower. Although he never thought he'd need a get out of jail free card while working for the RCMP.

Windflower was waiting outside the café when Langmead showed up. He waved to him, indicating that he should follow him. Langmead went close behind Windflower for the short trip to the Stoodley house.

Windflower went around to the back door near the gallery and Langmead followed him in.

"How were the roads?" asked Windflower.

"They're a bit slick, but the fog is more worrisome," said Langmead. "The shadows make it look like there's a moose around every corner."

"There just might be, down this way," said Windflower.

"Is that you, Windflower?" called out Herb Stoodley. "Come on in."

Windflower led Langmead into the parlour where Stoodley had an inviting fire going in the hearth.

"Carl, this is Herb Stoodley. Herb, this is Detective-Sergeant Carl Langmead from the Royal Newfoundland Constabulary."

The men shook hands and Langmead said to Windflower, "Do you have the cell phone?"

"I do," said Stoodley.

"And why would he have it, Windflower?" asked Langmead, his voice rising a little.

"Well," said Windflower. "He's my er..."

"I'm his adviser," said Herb Stoodley. "I'm a former Crown Attorney with the Province of Newfoundland and Labrador, and I'm here to make sure that Windflower's interests are protected."

"I just want the cell phone, and I would suggest that you turn it over immediately," said Langmead. "As a former Crown Attorney you should know better than to get in the middle of an active police investigation."

"That's just it," said Stoodley. "There is no longer any active investigation going on here, Detective. I've got my contacts inside the RNC, and they tell me there's a cover-up going on that might reach the very top levels of the Constabulary. I know that they're squeezing you, Langmead. But this stuff is going to get out, and when it does I want both Windflower here, and you, protected."

"What do you want from me?" asked Langmead. "If you've checked, then you must already know that I tried to get this opened up, and all it got me so far was a threat of suspension unless I shut my gob."

"All we want from you is the truth," said Stoodley. "I need you to read and sign this statement. It says that you found the cell phone noted in the statement in the personal effects of the late Mercedes Dowson, and that you took it for investigative purposes. Finally, that you gave it to Sgt. Winston Windflower of the RCMP for safekeeping, and that he returned it to you on the date noted below."

"That's it?" asked Langmead.

"That's it," said Stoodley.

"I'm not going to testify about what was on the phone or say anything else about it," said Langmead. "Once you give me the phone, we're done."

"Once you sign the paper, we're done," said Stoodley.

"Okay," said Langmead and he took the pen that Stoodley offered him to sign the statement.

When he handed the paper back with his signature on it, Stoodley took the cell phone out of his pocket and gave it to Langmead.

"I don't know what you're going to do with this, but I sincerely wish you better luck than me," said Langmead.

"Stay tuned," was all Herb Stoodley said, as Windflower walked Langmead back out to his car.

"Be careful on the highway," said Windflower as Langmead got into his car.

"You're the one that needs to be careful," said Langmead. "Some powerful people are looking to bury this stuff deeper than the mines on Bell Island. Make sure they don't bury you with it."

"I'm guessing that you're probably not going to tell me what all this is about, are you?" Windflower asked Stoodley when he went back inside.

"All will be revealed, in due course," said Stoodley.

"I'm taking that as a no," said Windflower. "Okay then, one question? If the phone with the names and contact numbers is so important, then why did we give it back so that they can bury it like Langmead says?"

"They might have the phone, but we have all the information we need to reconstruct the evidence."

"I needed the hour to get my techie friend to download the contents onto this portable disk drive, and to take screen shots of the applicable names and numbers."

"Now we have written confirmation from an official of the RNC about where the phone was found, and in whose possession it has been since. It's easy to trace the number back to the original owner, and we have an unbroken chain of evidence chain that nobody, not even the biggies at the RNC, can challenge," said Stoodley.

"But what are we, or you, going to do with this evidence?" asked Windflower.

"You've had your one question. Now don't you have some weird Scotch-tasting ritual to attend with your doctor friend?"

Seeing that resistance really was futile when it came to Herb Stoodley, Windflower decided to accept his fate, and for now at least, to trust his friend.

Windflower wished him a good evening, and drove home for a relaxing bath and a few minutes with Joseph Boyden, before his evening with Doctor Sanjay.

Soaking in the tub can do wonders for an aching body, and the time relaxing was rejuvenating for Windflower. He treated himself to a few bubbles from Sheila's stash, and settled in with his book for a good soak.

The story was riveting as Boyden's characters ended up in Champlain's fortress in New France. Allegiances were formed and strengthened between the French and the Huron, who were their allies. Plans were made to attack or repel the British, Spanish and Dutch, who continued to crave a bigger share of the new world. At the same time, their mutual enemy, the Iroquois, seemed to be waiting around every bend in the river, ready to pounce on the unsuspecting enemy.

Windflower became so engrossed that he lost track of time, and in the end had to hurry to get over to Doctor Sanjay's on time. He walked despite the still trickling rain, because he would be drinking later. Though he wouldn't be drinking a lot, he didn't want to be a hypocrite. He couldn't warn others about the dangers of drinking and driving, and not follow his own advice.

Doctor Sanjay lived with his wife in a beautifully restored salt-box house just across the brook. At one time it had been on the wrong side of town, but over the years these class distinctions had evaporated. The house had been freshly painted this summer, one of the old deep green colours that were so popular years ago, now making a retro comeback.

Windflower went in the back door, which was actually the front door for most of the people in this community. Someone once told Windflower that the front door was only used to let the preacher in, and to carry the body out.

"Hello, Doc," called Windflower as he took his shoes off in the porch.

He could feel the heat as soon as he opened the door. Sanjay liked it hot, but Windflower had worn only a light shirt on under his coat. He could also smell that delicious combination of spices that signalled that Sanjay had prepared his special curry for them.

"Welcome, welcome, to my humble abode," said the doctor. "I am sad that my good wife, Repa, is not at home to greet you, but she is away again in St. John's. She asked me to extend her best wishes."

"It's nice to be here again," said Windflower. "I like your choice in colours for your house."

"Yes, that is something called 'Nature's Passion'," said Sanjay. "It looks like forest green to me," he said with a laugh.

"Come in, come in. I have a few papadams for us and the chessboard is waiting, but first, the magnificent Talisker. Are you ready for your initial taste, Winston?"

Chapter Forty-Six

"I am," said Windflower and Sanjay led him to the sideboard where there was a water jug, tasting glasses and three bottles of scotch. Sanjay made a great flourish of opening the bottle of Talisker and pouring a little into each man's glass. They sniffed first, then sipped and swallowed, as Windflower had been taught.

"Um, that is good," said Windflower. "It tastes a little bit like the sea somehow."

"Yes indeed," said Doctor Sanjay. "Oh, I almost forgot," and he turned and rushed into the kitchen.

He returned moments later with two side plates. On each were three opened oysters.

"They're from PEI," said the doctor. "I was reading about Talisker on the Internet and someone commented that it had a taste like fresh oysters."

The men slurped an oyster, and tried another sip of the scotch.

"What a perfect combination," said Windflower, as Sanjay sighed contentedly.

They moved over to the waiting chessboard, finishing off the oysters and the stack of homemade papadams in no time. The doctor handily beat Windflower in the first two games, but the third was at least competitive.

Or perhaps he was just stringing me along, thought Windflower.

After the third game, which Windflower inevitably lost as well, they returned to their Scotch tasting. This time it was a Glenrothe that Windflower had so enjoyed on his last visit to the Sanjay house. It was a beautifully smooth Scotch but it also reminded him that the last time he had tasted it was also the night of Sheila's car accident. He had a moment of panic he hoped that Sanjay didn't notice, and decided that he would call Sheila as soon as he could when the evening with his friend was over.

More chess followed, and finally, on game five, Windflower broke through the winless column, and excitedly proclaimed, "Checkmate."

Even Doctor Sanjay seemed pleased that his friend had won a game at last. The doctor put the chessboard away and led Windflower to the kitchen, where the aromatic curry had been making Windflower salivate since entering the house.

"I hope you enjoy," said Sanjay, as he scooped generous portions of steamed rice onto Windflower's plate, and covered it in a thick chicken curry that smelled of chili and ginger and cardamom and cloves.

Windflower did enjoy his curry, a lot. And the second plate just as much. However even he had to refuse the third offering. He and the doctor had a great chat afterwards over coffee, and Windflower was quite mellowed out as he put on his coat and boots in the hallway.

"Thank you Vijay, for an outstanding evening," said Windflower as he shook his friend's hand goodnight.

"You are always welcome in my house," said Vijay. "Come back soon, my friend."

Windflower walked back over the bridge and noticed that while the evening had cooled, the rain had dissipated as Sheila's forecast had predicted.

Sheila, he thought, with that edge of panic returning. All that eased when he called and heard her voice.

"Hello, Winston, how was your evening?" she asked.

"It was grand," said Windflower. "But now that I'm talking to you, it's even better."

"Oh, Winston, ever the charmer," said Sheila with a little laugh. "Are you coming over?"

"I am on my way, ma'am," said Windflower.

In the morning, the sun streaming in through the open bedroom curtains woke Windflower before he was ready to get up. Once his eyes became accustomed to the light he realized what a joyous moment this really was. It was finally sunny again in Grand Bank.

Windflower slid out of bed and crept out of Sheila's house as quickly and as quietly as possible. He walked over to his own house, almost whistling in the sunlight.

The weather not only meant that his blueberry picking date was on with Sheila for the afternoon, but that if he was quick enough he could also get his clothes washed at the laundry, and have them hung up on his clothesline to dry before breakfast. Windflower was not a softie by any stretch of the imagination, but he loved that fresh crinkly-clean smell that only came from laundry that had dried in the wind and the sunshine.

It was only half-past 7 but Windflower knew that by 8 o'clock the washers at the laundromat would be full, and he would have to wait until later to do his wash. By then the sun might be gone, so timing was essential to his plan.

He moved through his little house with precision, throwing clothes and towels and sheets ripped from the bed into his laundry basket. Then, grabbing the detergent and a roll of quarters, he jumped in the car and drove à la Tizzard to the laundromat.

To his surprise, he wasn't the first customer of the morning, and half of the washers were already spinning. He only needed two, for a white and a dark wash.

He loaded up the washers, and took a stroll down by the water while his clothes were being washed, and rinsed, and spun clean.

This was another thing that he loved about living here. Where else in the world could you walk two minutes from the laundromat to the ocean?

The water had calmed considerably from the past few days, but there was still a stiff breeze blowing in from the southeast. At least it was blowing the fog further along the coast. It might change its mind at any moment, but for now it was paradise again in Grand Bank. There was nothing but blue skies and an even bluer ocean, as far as Windflower could see. It reminded him to be grateful for the many blessings in his life, and he took a few moments on the beach to sit and pray quietly.

After a short walk along the beach, Windflower went back to get his laundry and was very pleased with himself. All of the washers were full, and two women were sitting and chatting while they waited their turn.

Windflower smiled and wished everyone a good morning as he piled his wet laundry back into his basket for the return trip. He almost didn't even need the car to get home. He could have made his way there on the energy from his smile and his smugness, at having once again cheated the laundry gods.

Windflower found a bag of clothespins and went out to the back to raise his clothesline. Usually Mondays were laundry day, but for Windflower any day it didn't rain was a good day for laundry.

Today was perfect, he thought, as he pinned up his wet clothes and went back inside for his first coffee of the morning. He had that coffee and a boiled egg with some toast, and minutes later he was sitting on his back porch. His fresh laundry was snapping in the breeze and he happily settled back into the story of *The Orenda*.

Sheila called a bit after 11 a.m. to say that she would be ready to go berry picking around 1 p.m., if Windflower wanted to come by then. She also reminded him that they were scheduled to go to the ladies auxiliary dinner and dance later on at the Lions Club.

Windflower was hoping that she would in fact forget that, but repeated the two words that have saved many a man, and many a marriage, "Yes, dear."

Windflower barely had enough time to take his laundry in, fold it and put it away before it was time to go. He grabbed an apple out of the fridge to tide him over and he encouraged himself with the hopes that Sheila would pack them a little picnic to get them through the afternoon.

He knew he was in luck when he saw Sheila come out of the house with her wicker picnic basket. He gave her a peck on the cheek and asked, "What was in that basket you put in the back seat?"

"No lunch until we get our berries," said Sheila. "I know you; berries first, and then we'll have our lunch."

Then, seeing Windflower's fake puppy dog eyes, she said, "And a special treat if we can finish early."

"You are the best, Sheila," said Windflower.

"I know," said Sheila.

Windflower drove over to the Health Centre, and both of them were surprised at how many cars were in the parking lot at the base of the walking trail.

"A lot of other people had the same idea," said Windflower, pointing at the cars.

"People want to try and capture the last few good days of summer," said Sheila.

They unloaded the car and Windflower carried the picnic basket while Sheila had their picking containers, a blanket that she hung like a shawl around her neck, and a large bottle of water. They walked all along the trail on the way to the turnoff to the transmission tower. There were a few berry pickers on the route, but most of the low area had been picked clean by now.

Windflower and Sheila went all the way to the top of the trail that led to the base of the tower. The air was thinner here and so too were the pickers. They found a spot just a few yards from the path that looked promising and started picking.

An hour later they had filled their small containers, and as Windflower's grumbling tummy announced, they were getting a little peckish too. Sheila spread out the blanket on the ground and laid out their lunch.

The remaining cold cuts from the trip earlier in the week had been augmented with generous portions of chicken that Sheila has roasted that morning, along with a mixed green salad with cranberries and walnuts. She also brought the last third of the Goobies bread, already sliced and buttered, a chilled half-bottle of sparkling white wine, and a small white cardboard box.

"That's for last," she said as she saw Windflower eyeing up the box.

It was a little coolish, but the sun warmed their luncheon and they both ate their fill from Sheila's lunchbox of delights. When the main courses were done, Sheila opened the white box and watched as Windflower peeked inside. His eyes grew wide and a smile came across his face. Just like a child at Christmas, thought Sheila, as he realized that his dessert was his absolute favourite cheesecake.

He reached over and gave Sheila a thank you kiss, and then completely devoted himself to his peanut butter cheesecake.

Afterwards, they could have picked a few more blueberries, but they just lay around enjoying each other's company and the beautiful sunshine. They might have stayed a little longer, but a few more aggressive berry pickers came along and disturbed their reverie.

They packed up their stuff and walked together, holding hands, all the way back to the car.

Chapter Forty-Seven

The fundraising event started early, so Windflower dropped Sheila off to get ready, and went home to do the same. He had a quick shower and put on his second-best suit for the 'do' at the Lions Club.

An hour later, Sheila and he were sitting at a table eating their cold plate of sliced turkey, ham, and several salads along with homemade rolls and fresh butter. The highlight of the meal for Windflower was the dessert table. It was laden down with every type of pie and tart imaginable. He started with a piece of lemon meringue and finished with a blueberry crumble.

"Good, but not as good as yours," he whispered to Sheila, who immediately shushed him for fear of offending one of the other women.

When supper was over, there were speeches by the minister, and the head of the women's auxiliary, but Windflower didn't hear much and was actually dozing off a little, when Sheila gave him more than a gentle nudge.

He straightened up, at least momentarily, when the head of the women's group challenged the men in attendance to double their existing donations to help out the cause. Windflower didn't think that applied to him since he had not made a previous donation, but another nudge from Sheila convinced him to raise his hand when the hostess was looking for $100 contributions.

"Now I know why you brought me," he mumbled to Sheila, half under his breath.

This brought another 'shush', and an even sharper dig into his ribs.

Soon after, the formal activities were over and the DJ began the evening's musical entertainment. Most of the music was the Newfoundland style country music that Windflower didn't really care for. But there were a few old Irish songs that prompted him to take Sheila out on the dance floor.

They didn't stay late at the dance though, and were back home by 10:30 p.m. That was late enough for both of them. It had been a long day and a long week, and they were happy to have a few moments to share some quiet time together.

As they were falling asleep, Windflower could hear the little pitter-patter of rain beginning to fall. That was the end of the good weather, thought Windflower, but he didn't remember thinking or dreaming anything else until he woke in the morning. He glanced at the clock and saw it was early, so he rolled over and snuggled back into Sheila.

When he woke again it was just before 9 a.m., so Windflower got up and went out to the kitchen to make some coffee. He usually listened to CBC on Sunday morning and he hoped to catch the news headlines at the top of the hour.

He was pouring water into the coffee maker when he heard the announcer say…

"This just in... The CBC has learned that a recent murder in the province may be linked to a Russian sex trafficking gang who were operating an escort service in St. John's. Here is reporter James Fogwill with the latest details."

'The body of Amy Parsons, a champion rower from this year's Annual Regatta was found dumped in an alleyway in St. John's less than three weeks ago. The Royal Newfoundland Constabulary has been investigating this case with little success until recently. Now, sources close to the investigation say that it appears that the murdered woman might have somehow got on the wrong side of a gang of Russian mobsters who have been seeking to expand their territory into Newfoundland and Labrador.'

'CBC News has been investigating the rise in street prostitution and escort services linked to the expansion of the offshore oil development, and some of the negative effects of the booming economy in the city. This has been borne out by several studies done by the City and Memorial University. But this is the first time that organized crime has been rumoured to be a player in the City. Experts, like criminologist Mark Gushue from MUN's social science department, have been warning about this happening for the past two years. Here's Dr. Gushue from earlier in the week.'

'If this is true, and we now have organized crime operating in our city, then we had better brace ourselves for a lot worse to come,' said Dr. Gushue. 'They follow the money, and violence follows them. It is inevitable. They are rough, violent and dangerous men.'

'Dr. Gushue went on to say that with organized crime always comes corruption, and if they are here, some people on the public payroll are almost certainly benefitting from these illegal activities."

"There are also unconfirmed reports that a number of prominent public officials including a judge and a Member of the House of Assembly, and senior police officers from both the RCMP and the Royal Newfoundland Constabulary may have ties to this gang and the escort service. There has been no comment yet from the RNC on these reports, but we are expecting to hear more from RNC officials when they give a press conference at noon today.'

'James Fogwill, reporting for CBC News, in St. John's.'

Windflower was standing still and holding the coffee pot when Sheila came out of the bedroom.

"What's going on, Winston. Are you okay?" she asked.

"I'm okay," said Windflower. "But I have to talk to Herb Stoodley. I think the air attack has begun."

Windflower was a little excited when he finally got Stoodley on the phone.

"Herb, what the heck is going on? I didn't sign up for this. The story is all over the news. Did you give them this information?"

"Slow down, Winston; come over and I'll give you all the details," said Stoodley, sounding much calmer than Windflower would have preferred. "And if you and Sheila aren't busy why don't you both have brunch with us? Moira did the morning shift but she'll be off at 11. Ask Sheila if she'll join us, will you?"

With that, Stoodley was gone, leaving Windflower to try to explain what was happening, and oh yeah, to invite Sheila for brunch with the Stoodleys.

Sheila was as calm as Stoodley. An excited Windflower threw some clothes on and raced over to the ex-Crown Attorney's house.

Herb Stoodley was sitting out in his gallery, putting the finishing touches on another of his seascapes when Windflower arrived.

"Grab yourself a coffee and come on back in here," said Stoodley.

Windflower did as he was told and came and sat beside Stoodley.

"I know I'm supposed to trust you, Herb, and I do, a lot. But you better walk me through this slowly, because I'm really not comfortable," said Windflower.

"Fair enough," said Stoodley. "I knew you might have difficulty with some of the things I'd do, which is frankly why I didn't tell you. But I have more than just a crazy-looking plan. I have some inside information."

"Go on," said Windflower. "So far I agree only that the plan looks crazy, but I'm listening."

"What I didn't tell you before and what Langmead knew, was that there actually are security tapes from that house in St. John's. My source in St. John's confirmed it, and said that the Deputy Chief of the RNC approved the shutdown of the investigation."

"That was because he was trying to protect the Superintendent who heads up the C.I.D. The same Superintendent who's on the phone contact list, and who shows up on the security tapes too," said Stoodley.

"And that would be Langmead's boss," said Windflower.

"Exactly," said Stoodley. "Langmead and the other guys on the investigation were told that the case was closed, and there was no point in bringing embarrassment onto the RNC by making any of this other mess public. Langmead was supposed to get the cell phone back and everybody else was told to dummy up. The Deputy Chief told them that they would look after it internally from there on."

"So, there are more than a few disgruntled RNC officers, besides Langmead?" said Windflower.

"Oh yeah, and more than one approached my source to look for a way to get this information out to the public."

"They also tipped off my source that the CBC was already investigating escort services and organized crime in St. John's. We just fed this information in to the CBC anonymously, and that led to the story today," said Stoodley.

"So what happens now?" asked Windflower.

"Now we wait," said Stoodley. "Did you hear on the news that the RNC has a press conference for noon? I'll be very interested to hear what they have to say. Then we'll know whether the Chief is ready to take some action, or if they'll try and ride this one out."

"How do you think that will go?" asked Windflower.

"I think this Chief is a straight arrow," said Stoodley. "But there'll be a lot of pressure to hunker down and see if the storm blows over. In any case we've done what we can."

"I guess it's the right thing," said Windflower. "But they don't teach us in training to go running off to the media to fix our problems."

"Desperate times call for desperate measures," said Stoodley. "The die has been cast and the game's afoot."

"Okay, okay, enough with the quotes and the Shakespeare," said Windflower. "Do you have to be so dramatic?"

"How about helping me get brunch going?" said Stoodley.

"Now, that I can handle," said Windflower.

The two men went out to the kitchen and Windflower got the job of making the fruit salad. Soon he was scooping out a melon and slicing and dicing apples, while Stoodley was making the sauce for his Eggs Herbilicious. He also had rounds of pea meal bacon frying in a pan and a package of frozen English muffins thawing on the counter.

Herb melted some butter and whisked together the egg yolks and lemon juice and added cayenne pepper and dried mustard. Then he popped the sauce mixture into the microwave to thicken up. When everything else was ready he started making the poached eggs.

By the time Sheila arrived and Moira came home from work, Windflower had set the table and put out the fresh fruit salad, while Stoodley was just spooning the warm sauce on top of the steaming poached eggs.

Windflower guided the ladies to their seats, and Stoodley poured everyone a hot cup of coffee. The women looked very pleased and the men were grateful to sit down and eat.

It was a very pleasant brunch and the women offered to clean up while the men went out to catch the 12 o'clock news on the radio.

Chapter Forty-Eight

The CBC newsreader gave the highlights of the previous story that the men had already heard and then went live to their reporter at RNC Headquarters in St. John's.

'We're still waiting for the Chief of the Royal Newfoundland Constabulary to make his arrival and answer questions, but we do have a copy of the press release issued at 11:30 this morning. Here is part of the text:

The Royal Newfoundland Constabulary has been conducting an on-going investigation into the murder of Amy Parsons of St. John's. While that investigation is on-going and no suspects have yet been identified, we have discovered some connections between that murder and an organized gang of criminals operating in the Atlantic Region. We have been cooperating with the RCMP on a number of other investigations in this regard and we can inform you that they involve prostitution, drug, and sex trafficking activities. Some of these operations have been identified as occurring in and around the St. John's area.

In addition, officers of the RNC Criminal Investigations Division have discovered a property in St. John's that they believe was being used for illegal sexual activities and may have involved under-aged girls. Surveillance tapes have been discovered at that scene, and a number of individuals have been identified on tape as having visited this location over a period of time. Officers from the RNC Criminal Investigations Division are in the process of attempting to positively identify these individuals, and will be questioning them in regard to their presence at this location.

"No further arrests have been made as of yet by the RNC in connection with this investigation, but the authorities are continuing to interview witnesses in the St. John's area. In addition, the RCMP has a person of interest in custody in Halifax that we believe has information that will assist our investigation. We will be interviewing this person in the next few days. The RNC will continue to inform the public and the media of any developments in this situation, and we ask for everyone's cooperation in ensuring that all innocent parties are protected and that the on-going investigation is not compromised.

'The Chief will be soon making his way to the podium here at RNC Headquarters and we will have continuing coverage throughout the day.'

As the news resumed, Stoodley turned down the radio.

"So what happened?" asked Sheila as she came into the room.

"Don't ask me," said Windflower. "I'm just the running back. I put my head down and look for the opening to run through."

"I think we just scored a touchdown," said Stoodley with a broad smile on his face.

"The RNC has decided to get out in front of this instead of hoping it will go away," said Stoodley. "That's good news."

"They are going to belatedly try to take credit here, which means they believe the C.I.D. guys and Langmead. It's unclear yet what they're going to do with their Superintendent. It actually looks like they're stalling a bit on that. But that may just mean that they've asked him to resign as part of some package deal."

"Of course they are pretty peeved at the CBC for breaking this story, but it looks like, at least for now, they aren't going to get too whacked out about the leak," said Stoodley.

"Does that mean they're not too mad with us either?" asked Windflower.

"Oh, they're pretty mad at us, all right," said Stoodley. "They're just not likely to do anything about it. As long as we stay quiet from here on, I think we'll be okay. I'll make some calls later to get the inside scoop."

"Thank you for doing this, Herb," said Sheila. "This was a big risk for you to put your name and experience on the line for Winston."

"I really appreciate it - *we* really appreciate it, Herb," said Windflower. "So, what's next?"

"Now we wait and see what the great and famous Royal Canadian Mounted Police are going to do," said Stoodley.

"They have been in touch with the RNC or else the Chief wouldn't have put their name in the press release. And they have the complaints that we sent them on Friday afternoon. So I would say enjoy the rest of the day. Even though the sun is gone, it is still a beautiful Sunday in paradise."

Windflower and Sheila thanked Herb and Moira Stoodley for their hospitality, and Sheila gave Herb an especially long hug on the way out the door.

The day was dark and wet and dull outside, but Windflower felt good on the inside. They drove back to Sheila's, and at her suggestion, found an old movie on the television and settled in for a quiet afternoon.

Might even be time for a nap, thought Windflower. It doesn't get much better than this.

The movie was a real classic and one of Windflower's favourites, Bette Davis in *What Ever Happened to Baby Jane?* It was about a former child star who torments her wheelchair-bound sister in an old mansion.

Sheila got a blanket to cover them both, and despite Windflower's interest in the movie and his best intentions, he was soon fast asleep on the couch, his head resting on Sheila's shoulder. He didn't know how long he was out, but when he awoke Sheila was shaking him, and telling him that his cell phone was ringing.

"It's Carl Langmead," the voice said after Windflower answered the phone. "I just wanted to touch base. After all that's happened I figured I owed you a call."

"Okay," said Windflower, trying to shake the nappy cobwebs out of his brain.

"It looks like things are going to work out on our end, and I know that we have you and your adviser, Stoodley, to thank for most of that," said Langmead.

"Well, that was almost all Herb Stoodley," said Windflower. "But I'll pass along your good wishes."

"I also know that you may think that I ditched you on the road during this process, but I had a lot of pressure on me," said Langmead. "I was pretty much on my own for a little while here, and a lot of people wanted me to just shut up. Anyway I want to say I'm sorry if you think I screwed you around."

"We're all on the same side," said Windflower. "You did what you had to do and I understand. No hard feelings on my end."

"Thanks, Winston. So what's happening with you and the suspension?"

"It's not clear yet," said Windflower. "I've got a complaint in and we'll see what the brass has to say about it all. I'm okay with whatever happens. Like you, I did what I had to do."

"Well, good luck Winston. I hope it works out for you," said Langmead as he hung up.

Yeah, me too, thought Windflower, as he snuggled back into the warm bundle under the blanket.

"I guess we should start thinking about dinner," said Sheila. "What do you feel like?"

"Why don't we pick up some fish and chips at the takeout?" asked Windflower. "That will save us the trouble of cooking and cleaning up afterwards."

"Why not?" said Sheila. "We might as well make it a full day of rest."

"That's why we have Sundays, m'dear," said Windflower, as he went to call in their order.

Fifteen minutes later they both had heaping piles of fresh fish and chips, and were happily engaged in devouring them when Windflower's cell phone rang again.

"Don't you wish we could go back to the good old days and unplug the phone for the night?" asked Windflower, before reaching over to answer the phone.

"Windflower," he said.

"Sarge, it's Tizzard, you'll never guess what's happened."

"If you are going to make me guess, I will hang up right now," said Windflower.

"Arsenault is gone," said Tizzard. "He's left Marystown and is on his way to St. John's. I got a call from my buddy over there who says the whole place is buzzing after the news on the radio. Even though I didn't say anything, they all think that Arsenault is the RCMP guy that the CBC is talking about."

"Slow down, Corporal," said Windflower. "What exactly is going on?"

"Okay," said Tizzard, taking a deep breath. "Here's what I know: The guys in Marystown say that Inspector Arsenault has been called to a meeting in St. John's. Some of them think that it's connected to the story on the news, and that Arsenault is in deep doo-doo."

"Thank you, Tizzard," said Windflower. "So apart from the speculation of your friends in Marystown, all we know is that Inspector Arsenault has gone out of town, maybe to St. John's."

"Yes, sir," said Tizzard. "But don't you think it's good news?"

"It'll be good news when I can go back to work," said Windflower. "I'll pass this information onto my special adviser, who seems to know everything. Thanks for calling, Eddie."

Windflower finished his fish and chips with Sheila and put the kettle on to make some tea. Sheila offered him dessert, but he was stuffed. He phoned Herb Stoodley while he waited for the kettle to boil.

"Evening, Winston," said Stoodley when he realized it was Windflower. "I'm glad you called. I have some information to pass along. My contact at RCMP HQ said that our complaints caused quite a stir, although not as much as the story that was on the news."

"Arsenault may have been able to generate some support and sympathy against a rank and file complaint, but people at the top were hopping mad when they learned that he was on that contact list."

"That might explain what Tizzard was talking about," said Windflower.

"You lost me there. What was Tizzard talking about?" asked Stoodley.

"That was the reason I called you," said Windflower, and he told Stoodley what Tizzard had said about Arsenault.

"That might be," said Stoodley. "I'll try and check to confirm, but we might not hear anymore until tomorrow morning. I think we should take it as a positive development."

"If you say so; I guess I have to trust you now," said Windflower.

"So far, so good," said Stoodley. "Get some sleep, and we'll check in again in the morning."

"Good night, Herb," said Windflower, not at all confident that a good night's sleep was on the agenda.

He spent a couple of hours with Sheila trying to relax and not succeeding, when she offered to make him a bath.

"It might help you to get rid of some of that stress you're carrying around like a sack of potatoes on your shoulders," she said.

He smiled weakly, but agreed with her suggestion, and was about to step into the hot bath when he could hear his cell phone ringing. He thought about not answering it, but could not resist the pull of the phone.

Damn you, he thought, I'm addicted to my cell phone. He picked up the phone and answered, "Windflower."

"Sergeant Windflower, this is Corporal Mario Leclerc. I am calling you from the office of Deputy Commissioner Karl Hendrickson. The Deputy Commissioner will be calling you at 10:00 Newfoundland Standard Time. Will you be available to take his call?"

"Sure, I mean yes," said Windflower.

"Then it is confirmed. Deputy Commissioner Hendrickson will call you at the RCMP Detachment in Grand Bank at 10 o'clock tomorrow morning. Good night Sergeant."

"Good night," said Windflower, but the line was already dead.

"Did I hear you talking on the phone in the bathroom?" asked Sheila. "Do you have a secret girlfriend or something?"

"No, but I have a call with the Deputy Commissioner tomorrow morning," said Windflower.

"Is that good or bad news?" asked Sheila.

"I've given up trying to figure that out," said Windflower and he lowered himself into the bathtub.

Somehow, Windflower did get to sleep that night, and he even slept all the way through. The light was shining in through Sheila's bedroom window so brightly that Windflower blinked several times before he could see.

Sunshine? I'm taking that as a good omen, he thought.

Windflower snuck out of bed while Sheila was still solidly asleep. He left the bedroom and blew her a kiss before walking over to his own house. It was brilliantly sunny, but the wind was blowing sharply in off the water, making it seem more like early winter than late summer.

Windflower didn't really mind. He was grateful to the wind for making him feel alive and awake.

At his house Windflower made some coffee and sat quietly drinking it when he heard a car in his driveway. He looked out to see that it was Tizzard.

"I was just driving by when I saw the light on in the kitchen," said Tizzard. "Wanna' go for breakfast?"

Windflower didn't want to go for breakfast, but Tizzard was almost begging him, like a puppy wagging its tail, so he said yes. He told Tizzard that he'd meet him over at the Mug-Up.

After the corporal left Windflower did his morning smudge and prayers. This morning he was especially thankful for all the friends and supporters he had in his life. He acknowledged and prayed for each of them, especially for Tizzard, so that his heart would stay as pure as it was today. Then he got cleaned up, changed into his red serge and walked over to the Mug-Up.

Herb Stoodley was on the cash again this morning, and Windflower spent a few minutes talking to him to tell him about his phone call later in the morning.

He got himself a cup of coffee and went over to sit with Tizzard who had secured their usual corner location.

Chapter Forty-Nine

Eggs, bologna and homemade toast was the consensus decision for breakfast, and Windflower and Tizzard made the most of their time at the café by greeting all the early morning locals who popped in for coffee or breakfast.

Their food arrived and was rapidly dispatched. Tizzard hung around a little longer, then headed up to the office. Windflower stayed a few minutes after Tizzard, and since it was a little before 9 a.m., he walked back up to Sheila's to say good morning before his 10 a.m. meeting.

Sheila was awake and watching the morning news when Windflower came in. He arrived just in time to see the TV cameras following the RNC Superintendent of Criminal Investigations out of RNC headquarters. The caption on the bottom of the screen read *"Senior Constabulary Officer Resigns"*.

"Well, that's one down," said Windflower as he watched the screen without really hearing any of the words.

"I'm glad they're getting rid of some of these morons," said Sheila. "They've betrayed us and the public trust. They don't deserve to be police officers."

Windflower didn't say anything. He just put his arms around Sheila and gave her a tight squeeze.

"You know part of me, a bigger part than I thought, would be just as happy to stay here with you today, than go to work," he finally said.

"I know what you mean," said Sheila. "I'm not sure that I would want you underfoot 24 hours a day, but it is really nice having you around a bit more. I'm kinda' getting used to that, Sergeant."

Windflower smiled and squeezed her tighter, releasing her with a kiss on the forehead.

"Well, you may have more of me than you planned. I'm off to my meeting."

"Good luck, Winston, let me know how it goes," said Sheila, as she returned the squeeze.

Windflower walked over to the RCMP detachment and went inside. Betsy was talking to Lewis and Fortier, who said a quick good morning, and vanished just as fast. Betsy gave him a smile, although Windflower could see that she, once again, was close to tears. He walked to the back, nodded again to the other officers, poured a cup of coffee, then went to his office to await the call.

At 10 a.m. exactly, according the clock on the wall in Windflower's office, the phone rang.

"Sergeant Windflower," he answered.

"Please hold for Deputy Commissioner Hendrickson," a voice answered.

Windflower waited another minute and Hendrickson came on the line.

"Good morning, Sergeant," said the Deputy Commissioner.

"Good morning sir," said Windflower.

"I've had a chance to look at your record, Sergeant, as well as your complaint. You are not really one to rock the boat are you?"

"No sir," said Windflower.

"Until now," added the Deputy Commissioner. "Why is this issue so important to you, Sergeant?"

"I guess it just goes against my basic sense of fairness," said Windflower. "I was brought up to treat women with respect, sir. If we are going to have women on the Force then they have to be treated as full Members, with all the respect that every other Member should receive."

"What do you want to see happen out of this complaint?" asked Hendrickson.

"I just want to go back to work, and I think that the two women involved should get an apology, sir," said Windflower.

"Thank you Sergeant, you can return to work, effective immediately. I will send you a letter formally removing the suspension and all documentation from your files."

"I will take your suggestion about an apology back to my team for their advice on how to proceed. Everything we do today has to be looked over by our lawyers first," said the Deputy Commissioner.

"Thank you, sir," said Windflower.

"We are going through a few growing pains," said the Deputy Commissioner. "But hang in there; we're going to make it."

"Thank you, sir, I think so, too," said Windflower.

"Good day, Sergeant," said the Deputy Commissioner, and the call was over.

Almost as soon as Windflower put the receiver down, Tizzard bounded into Windflower's office.

"So, how did it go?" he asked Windflower.

"I think I just got my job back," said Windflower.

"Wahoo!" yelled Tizzard so loudly that everybody in the office came running.

Betsy came in first and didn't wait for Windflower, but just rushed up and hugged him. Lewis and Fortier were next, and they too offered their congratulations.

After the initial celebration had died down, Tizzard winked at Betsy and said, "I guess we can show him his surprise now."

"C'mon," he said to Windflower, and he and Betsy led the happy party out into the front area, where Betsy went to her desk and handed Tizzard a set of car keys.

Windflower still had no idea what was going on until Tizzard pointed the key fob out the window, and a set of car lights blinked in the parking lot. When they went outside Tizzard handed the keys to Windflower and said, "This would be yours, Sergeant Windflower. It just arrived this morning."

It was a 2014 fully loaded Jeep Liberty, Windflower's new vehicle.

"I hope that you'll let me drive it sometime," said Tizzard. But when he saw the pained look on Windflower's face he added, "Just to test it out."

"Stay out of my car, Tizzard," said Windflower, and everyone laughed because they could feel their old boss, and their old friendly rhythm, coming back after a few tense days.

"Okay," said Windflower, "Everybody back to work."

Windflower returned to his office to share the good news with Sheila, who was as happy and relieved as he was.

"Let's go out to dinner tonight to celebrate," she said. "We can go back to the B&B. I hear they have a great stuffed sole."

"That sounds like a plan," said Windflower. He was hoping to get out to see Herb Stoodley at the Mug-Up to give him the good news too, but Betsy interrupted him with a buzz on the intercom.

"It's Staff Sergeant Ford on line two," said Betsy.

"Congratulations," said Bill Ford when Windflower punched on the number two button. "You fought the law and you won."

"I think the law won, too," said Windflower.

"I think you're right," said Ford. "You've probably heard, but Inspector Arsenault is gone. He was called to St. John's and they're working out what happens to him next."

"Whatever that is, he won't be going back to Marystown. In fact they have offered me his job, at least on a temporary basis."

"Congratulations to you, too, then," said Windflower.

"I haven't decided whether or not I'll take it yet," said Ford. "I just put my house on the market in Marystown. I also wanted to talk to you first. If I take it, then I want you to be on my team."

"I am honoured that you would think of me, Bill, but I'm not sure that I want to leave Grand Bank," said Windflower.

"You don't have to," said Ford. "I think that if you are willing to pass a bit more of the day-to-day onto your young Corporal, you could still oversee the Grand Bank area, and work with me on projects as they arise. What do you think?"

"I think I would like that, Bill, or maybe I should say, Inspector Ford."

"Acting Inspector," said Ford with a laugh.

"Thank you Winston, I really appreciate it. One of my first actions as Acting Inspector will be to recommend that you be promoted to Acting Staff Sergeant, so you should get used to a new title too."

After Ford had gone Windflower tried out his new title, out loud. Tizzard who was passing by heard him and popped his head in.

"Are you okay, Boss?" he asked.

"Couldn't be better," said Windflower. "Come in Corporal, I want to talk to you about something."

"First of all, I want to tell you that I'm very pleased with the way you handled everything while I was in Marystown, with two notable exceptions that we'll talk about later. Would you be interested in continuing taking on a few additional duties?"

"Sure, Boss," said Tizzard, "But you're not going back to Marystown are you?" he asked, sounding a little worried.

"No, I'm staying here," said Windflower. "But we're going to have a new Inspector, and he's asked me to help him out from time to time."

"So, I was right," said Tizzard. "Inspector Arsenault is gone. Who's the new Inspector?"

"Acting Inspector Bill Ford will be taking over," said Windflower, ignoring Tizzard's claim of predicting Arsenault's demise.

"Fordy?" said Tizzard. "That's great." Then remembering Windflower's earlier comments he asked,

"What were the two areas we were going to discuss further?"

"The first is paperwork," said Windflower. "This may be a police operation, but everything still runs through channels. And you need to stay on top of the paperwork and the electronic files, to make sure that the system doesn't get clogged up."

"I try to keep up but…," started Tizzard but Windflower cut him off mid-sentence.

"Everything after but is B.S.," said Windflower.

"Listen, when I first started out I didn't have a clue, but then I realized that we have an expert right on-site."

"Betsy," said Tizzard.

"Exactly," said Windflower. "You just have to let her lead you on the paperwork. But don't screw her around. Hell hath no fury like a woman scorned, especially at work. Follow her directions and you'll be fine."

Tizzard nodded and Windflower noticed that his Corporal had a slight grin.

"What's so funny Tizzard?" asked Windflower.

"I can always tell when you've been around Mr. Stoodley for a while," said Tizzard. "You suddenly start quoting Shakespeare."

"Let's go see the man himself and get a cup of coffee. We can talk about your other deficiency along the way. It is better to know your faults so that you can correct them, Tizzard. 'Ignorance is the curse of God; knowledge is the wing wherewith we fly to heaven'."

"Oh my God, spare me," said Tizzard with a laugh.

"Let's take my new wheels," said Windflower. "But you're definitely not driving," he quickly added.

To really test out his new vehicle, Windflower took the long route to the café, first down by the wharf where Parliament was still in session, and then down the highway to Fortune.

"What I wanted to talk to you about was the Chinese," said Windflower.

"That's a big subject," said Tizzard. "There must be at least a billion of them."

"I don't find it particularly funny that 60 or so of them could have passed through here as illegal immigrants, twice this summer, do you Corporal?" asked Windflower a little sharply.

"No sir," said Tizzard, sensing correctly that the time for joking was over.

"I want you to do a full and complete report on both incidents as it relates to Grand Bank, and why we didn't notice so many strangers in our midst. Or why nobody bothered to ask any questions about it either."

"I want dates, times, places and at the end I want some recommendations about how to make sure it never happens again," said Windflower.

"I've actually been thinking about that sir," said Tizzard. "Not about doing the report which I will certainly do, but why we didn't notice anything strange was happening around us? And why nobody on the coast reported anything about these people being dropped off and picked up, and then ferried all over the province."

"Go on," said Windflower, sensing that his young Corporal had something more to say.

"I think it's because they don't trust us," said Tizzard.

"When you think about it, the RCMP has not traditionally been their friends. We may be guarding the locals from danger, but they may not always see it that way. They're more likely to see us as watching or spying on them, since the only things we have to do with them is to arrest them for smuggling liquor or cigarettes, or catching them speeding, or driving impaired."

"I think you're onto something there, Tizzard."

"There's somebody I want you talk to about this, how we can improve the relationship between the Mounties and the communities. He might even be in here this morning," said Windflower as he pulled his sparkling new vehicle up in front of the café.

Chapter Fifty

Herb Stoodley was putting his apron away when Windflower and Tizzard came into the Mug-Up.

"I hear you're back on the job," said Stoodley.

"I am," said Windflower. "Why don't you come over and I'll tell you all about it?"

"I will," said Stoodley. "Do you want a sandwich or just coffee?"

"A turkey sandwich, with dressing on whole wheat would be great," said Windflower.

"I'll have one too," said Tizzard.

"You have someone to talk to first," said Windflower, and he gently nudged Tizzard towards a table in the window where Mayor Sinnott was holding court.

"Good morning, Mr. Mayor, sorry to interrupt," said Windflower, "I was wondering if you could spare a few moments with Corporal Tizzard. He's been tasked with improving relations between the local communities and the RCMP. I was hoping you could give him some suggestions."

"You mean like community policin'?" asked the Mayor.

"That's it exactly," said Windflower.

"Yes, b'y. I'd be happy to do that," said the Mayor. "Sit right down Tizzard, and we'll have a little chat."

Leaving Tizzard firmly in the grip of Mayor Sinnott, Windflower went over to his usual table where Herb Stoodley was laying down their sandwiches and coffee.

Stoodley laughed when Windflower pointed out his young associate and the significantly older Mayor.

"That looks interesting," he said.

Windflower laughed too, watching Tizzard trying to get a word in on the Mayor.

"At the very least it'll help Tizzard to learn how to listen," said Windflower.

"And to be patient," said Stoodley.

"How poor are they that have not patience," said Windflower.

"Not bad, Winston," said Stoodley. "I hear that Arsenault has been placed on special assignment."

"Bill Ford told me the higher-ups are still trying to make up their minds what to do with him," said Windflower. "Ford's coming back, by the way. He'll be replacing Arsenault."

"That's a good choice," said Stoodley. "I told you that everything would work out, Winston. Arsenault is gone, you're getting a great new boss, and the world is a safer and happier place."

Windflower laughed and said, "You were right, Herb. I should have had more faith in you and the process."

"Well, we did nudge the process along a bit," said Stoodley. "But all's well that ends well."

Both men laughed again and finished off their lunch.

Afterwards, Windflower took his jeep up by Sheila's to show her his new wheels. She was suitably impressed, but really just happy to see him.

When Windflower got back to the office Betsy handed him a stack of paperwork, and he simply handed it back to her. Betsy looked shocked when he told her that Tizzard would be the first contact for all correspondence from now on.

"Don't worry, Betsy. You and I are going to train him. I told Corporal Tizzard that you would give him direction, and I want you to report him to me if he doesn't cooperate. Is that clear, Betsy?"

"Yes sir," said Betsy and she went away with a very big smile.

That must have lasted for a long time because when Tizzard came in he asked "What's Betsy so happy about? You think she'd won the lottery."

Windflower didn't tell Tizzard the reason for the admin's pleasure. He'd find out soon enough, he thought.

"How did it go with the Mayor?"

"You know, I was very surprised but that old coot, I mean, gentleman, actually has a lot of good ideas. He suggested putting together a committee of local elected officials in the area to get their suggestions about how to improve policing," said Tizzard.

"We're also going to do up some notes for a program called Coastal Watch, like Neighbourhood Watch, and to come up with a mascot to promote the program to kids in school. Mayor Bill is going to talk to some local businesses about donating a few prizes so that we can get it going right here in Grand Bank, maybe early in the New Year. What do you think?" asked Tizzard.

"I think that's a great way to go," said Windflower. "You have my green light to get things going, and when Bill Ford gets here we'll see if we can't make it a regional or even provincial initiative. Good job, Corporal."

"Thank you, sir," said Tizzard. "By the way sir, it's good to have you back."

"Couldn't be better than to be here," said Windflower.

An hour or so later, as the sun was starting to fade from the sky, Windflower closed up his office and turned out the lights.

He drove back to his little house and sat silently in his kitchen drinking a cup of tea and being grateful. He offered a few special prayers for all the help he had received from the living, and those who had passed on, and then he went to get dressed for dinner.

Tonight was a celebration night and Windflower chose his best suit, one that he had purchased at Benjamin's, a high end men's store in St. John's.

It was a chalk-striped dark blue suit that Windflower wore with a crisp white shirt and a deep purple tie, along with a matching handkerchief in his pocket.

Not too bad, thought Windflower, as he surveyed himself in the mirror, even if I do say so myself.

Sheila looked stunning. When he entered her home she was just putting her shawl over her shoulders. Sheila was wearing her short black dress and high heels, the look that drove Windflower crazy every single time he saw her in it. She had her hair up, with ringlets dancing down both sides, and a single strand of large white pearls to complete her look.

Windflower almost said, "Let's just stay home tonight", because he didn't want to share her with the rest of the world. Instead he offered her his arm and they headed off to dinner.

Windflower was surprised when they arrived at the restaurant at the B&B and saw Doctor Sanjay and his wife, Repa, sitting in the small lounge awaiting their dinner reservation.

He was even more surprised when he saw Herb and Moira Stoodley come in through the door shortly after them. He was not surprised at all when Tizzard and his new girlfriend, a real stunner from Marystown, showed up.

Windflower smiled at Sheila and whispered, "Thank you".

The eight of them were invited to sit at a large round table in the middle of the old-fashioned house, a place where the master of old would have presided over the nightly dinner ritual as well as any important family or business gatherings.

Sheila had ordered champagne and the cork was popped and glasses were passed around. She looked to Windflower to propose a toast but he deferred to Herb Stoodley, the bard of the group.

Stoodley stood, raised his glass and said "I count myself in nothing else so happy, as in a soul remembering my good friends; to good friends."

"To good friends," said the octet in unison, clinking their glasses.

They sat sipping their wine and talking quietly amongst themselves until their salad arrived. When it came, Tizzard exclaimed in mock horror, "It's broccoli, it's a broccoli salad."

"Relax, Eddie," said Sheila. "That looks like bacon in the salad dressing. I think you'll survive."

Everyone laughed and dug into their salad, which was tart and tasty. There were small broccoli florets in a sauce featuring plenty of cooked bacon pieces, red onions and raisins, combined together in a kind of sweet and sour creamy vinaigrette with a sharp flavour of balsamic vinegar.

"That was much better than I thought it would be," said Tizzard.

"Keep an open mind," said Windflower. "You never know what the main course will be."

"It's not vegan or anything, is it?" asked Tizzard, sounding really worried.

Tizzard didn't have anything to fear, because even though the entrée was meatless it was definitely not in the vegan strain.

It was sole stuffed with fresh and rich-tasting crab meat that had been mixed with mayonnaise, bell pepper and parsley and then covered with bread crumbs and fried in garlic oil and a combination of salt, pepper and other spices. It was a little crispy brown on the outside and creamy smooth on the inside. It came with a rice pilaf and steamed green and waxed beans.

There was not much talking while everyone enjoyed their feast and even Tizzard was gushing over the meal and the presentation.

"It looked so good I almost didn't eat it," said Tizzard.

"Then why is your plate so empty?" asked Doctor Sanjay.

But so, too, was everyone else's plate. It was a fabulous dinner but there was still dessert to look forward too, thought Windflower, as he gazed around the table at his new Grand Bank family.

The dessert, Baked Alaska with a Newfoundland twist, was a fitting touch to end their meal. There were the usual bananas and ice cream in the rich meringue that had been baked hard, and the chef wheeled their dessert out into the dining room on a cart and turned out the lights. Then he warmed up a little Newfoundland Screech, poured it over the meringue, and set it on fire.

The dessert and the entire meal was a tremendous success, and after bidding their friends good night, Sheila and Windflower sat with the owners of the B&B to share a coffee and thank them for their meal.

Soon after they were on their way home to Sheila's, relaxed and satisfied with their evening.

"Thank you, Sheila. That was such a nice thing to do tonight," said Windflower.

"I'd been thinking about how to get everyone together in the one place to celebrate both of us being back, and it finally worked out," said Sheila. "I'm going to start my bath. Why don't you come to bed when you're ready?"

Windflower channel-surfed for a few minutes, but couldn't really find anything that interested him. He switched off the TV, turned out the lights and went to the bedroom where Sheila was waiting for him.

He looked at her lying in bed with her beautiful dark red hair lying over her shoulders and simply said, "I love you Sheila, thank you for being in my life."

"I love you too Winston. Now turn off the lights and come to bed. It's a little lonely in here without you," said Sheila.

Windflower didn't need any more encouragement than that, and was soon snuggled in tightly. The rest of his evening was as special as the first part, and afterwards he didn't remember a thing, until he realized that he was dreaming again.

It must be a dream, he thought, because he was back in the forest with the Beothuk lady, running after her as she headed toward the river. When she got there she smiled at him, and walked into the river. He followed suit and was soon falling further and further into the deep and cold water.

He felt his feet hit bottom, and from experience he knew to reach down into the sandy soil to see if there was anything there.

He found something that was small and hard and round, and he forced himself back to the surface. When he got back into the sunlight the object gleamed at him, and he saw that it was a ring.

But this was not just any ring; it was his mother's engagement ring that he remembered was now sitting on top of the dresser in his bedroom.

Then he woke up.

The End

The Walker on the Cape

A Sgt. Windflower Mystery

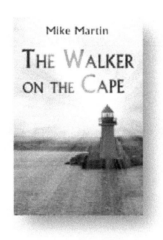

A man's body is found on the Cape overlooking Grand Bank, Newfoundland. At first everyone thinks it's a heart attack or stroke. But then it is discovered that he was poisoned. Who would do this and why? Finding that out falls to Sergeant Winston Windflower of the RCMP along with his trusted side-kick Eddie Tizzard. Along the way they discover that there are many more secrets hidden in this small community and powerful people who want to keep it that way.

Windflower also discovers two more things; a love of living in a small Newfoundland community that is completely different from his up-bringing in a Northern Alberta reserve and maybe the love of his life. He gets a taste of Newfoundland food and hospitality as well as a sense of how crime and corruption can linger beneath the surface or hide in the thick blanket of fog that sometimes creeps in from the nearby Atlantic Ocean.

www.walkeronthecape.com

The Body on the T

A Sgt. Windflower Mystery

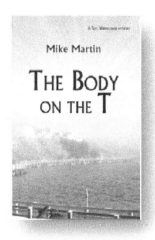

Sgt. Winston Windflower is enjoying an idyllic life in the small town of Grand Bank, Newfoundland when a mysterious and very dead body washes up on a nearby beach. Follow along with Windflower and his team as he tries to solve this mystery and uncovers a whole lot more lurking under the fog on the southeast coast off Atlantic Canada.

Windflower is the ultimate outsider, an RCMP officer and a Cree from northern Alberta, yet he feels right at home with the rich culture, food and history of this part of the world. But his world is shaken by a series of events that threaten his new-found happiness. And it all starts with the discovery of The Body on the T.

www.bodyonthet.com

About the Author

Mike Martin was born in Newfoundland on the East Coast of Canada and now lives and works in Ottawa, Ontario. He is a long-time freelance writer and his articles and essays have appeared in newspapers, magazines and online across Canada as well as in the United States and New Zealand. He is the author of "Change the Things You Can: Dealing with Difficult People and has written a number of short stories that have published in various publications including Canadian Stories and Downhome magazine.

The Walker on the Cape was his first full fiction book and the premiere of the Sgt. Windflower mystery series. The Body on the T was the second book, and Beneath the Surface is the third installment in this series.

He is a member of Ottawa Independent Writers, Capital Crime Writers, the Crime Writers of Canada and the Newfoundland Writers' Guild.

For more information or to comment on this book, please visit:

www.beneaththesurface.co

Milton Keynes UK
Ingram Content Group UK Ltd.
UKHW021314141223
434366UK00029B/1343